EXPLORER

Part I of *The Anthanian Imperative* Trilogy

Roger Floyd

EXPLORER — Part I of *The Anthanian Imperative*, by Roger Floyd

A science fiction novel of 139,000 words, set in *Book Antigua*

Cover illustration and landing site map prepared by Kathy Schuit

Also by Roger Floyd:

TRAVELER — Part II of *The Anthanian Imperative*

WARRIOR — Part III of *The Anthanian Imperative*

To Marilyn

With the deep love, respect, and admiration due such a wonderful woman.

If ever two were one, then surely we.
If ever man were loved by wife, then thee;
If ever wife was happy in a man,
Compare with me ye women if you can.

— *Anne Bradstreet (ca. 1612 - 1672)*

Come, my friends,
'Tis not too late to seek a newer world.

—*Alfred, Lord Tennyson* (1809-1892)

CONTENTS

SUMMARY OF ANTHANIAN MEASURING SYSTEMS

Science is the refuge of the enlightened and the tool of the prudent.

> —From comments made by the Anthanian
> Emperor Samaros IV at the Council of
> Lemtos immediately prior to the beginning
> of the year 001.

Originally spread around the planet, independent and sovereign, the city-states of Anthanos were consolidated by Emperor Samaros IV into one planetary nation as much by force of personality as by force of arms. At the Council of Lemtos, he instituted by decree, to take effect planet-wide immediately, several new systems of measurements, eliminating the hodge-podge of systems used by the different cities. Included within this new plan was a carefully designed method of recording the passage of time, and the year 001 began at the end of the Council's deliberations. The summary below gives the major Anthanian systems of measurement and the closest *approximate* value in Earth-based systems.

Anthanian   **Earth-based**

Time

On a planet tidally locked to its sun and which rotates only once on its axis in its yearly trip around the sun, no convenient shorter period is available to use as a basis for marking the passage of time. The Anthanians divided their planet's year into 1000 *Time Sectors* (usually shortened to *T-sector*), and each T-sector was further divided by elements of 10.

Anthanian	Earth-based
Year	400 days
T-sector (on Anthanos)	9.6 hours (10 subsectors/T-sector)
T-sector (on the blue planet)	12 hours (12 subsectors/T-sector)
[*Note*: On the blue planet, the lighttimes were the odd-numbered T sectors, the darktimes were even-numbered.]	
Subsector (10 or 12 per T-sector)	1 hour
Millisector (10 per subsector)	5 min 45 sec
Microsector (10 per millisector)	35 seconds
Nanosector (10 per microsector)	3.5 seconds

Instantaneous time values were grouped as a *Time Element*, containing in order, *year.T-sector.subsector.millisector*, for example, 461.184.9.5. If the year is known or otherwise understood, it may be omitted.

Distance

Link	10 inches
Decilink	1 inch
Anthan	1.57 miles

    [*Note*: One anthan is 10,000 links.]

Astronomical Distances

    Light-year (distance light travels in one year): 4.15 trillion anthans

    Light-sector (distance light travels in one T-sector): 4.15 billion anthans

Weight

Krill	3 lbs, 3 oz
Dekakrill	30 lbs
Kilokrill	3000 lbs
Millikrill	5 oz

Temperature

1 Tal	1° Centigrade

    [*Note*: Water freezes at 0 Tal and boils at 100 Tal.]

Angles

100 degrees	90°

Volume

Trilink	985 cubic inches, or 16,000 cubic centimeters
Eighth-trilink	2 quarts or 2 liters

CHARACTERS

The Blue Planet Landing Team and Each Member's Area of Specialization:

Case Sabentos – *Commander of Landing Team, Pilot of* Explorer

Jer ("Jair") Ventenian – *Vice-Commander of Landing Team, Co-pilot of* Explorer

Dell Sentelvos – *Physician and Space Surgeon*

Mina Sen-Darsen – *Microbiology and Molecular Biology*

Jad Til-Lentos – *Astrophysics and Astronomy*

Wila Casparian – *Astronomy, Planetary Science, and Meteorology*

Col Montolenian – *Botany and Plant Cultivation*

Trea ("Trāy") Tuvalos – *Zoology and Animal Husbandry*

Bent Donsento – *Geology and Mineralogy*

Lilea ("Lī-*lay*-a") Kalatarian – *Anthropology*

Notable Others:

Nuri Kendavos – *Director-General of Anthanos's Spaceflight Command*

Kal Mada – *Overall Commander of Planetary Landing Expedition I, and Commander of the Interstellar Spaceship* Star Voyager

Tam Kos – *Chief Engineer of* Star Voyager *and Vice-Commander of the Expedition*

Lan Porsento – *Chief Navigator of* Star Voyager

Tac Dinroc – *Medical Director and Chief Space Surgeon for* Star Voyager

Jasi ("*Jazz*-ē") Donasto – *Chief of Records for* Star Voyager *for Planetary Landing Expedition I*

Taeni ('*Tāy*-knee') – *Jad's first girl friend*

A PROCLAMATION

FROM THE PEOPLE OF ANTHANOS

TO ALL CONCERNED IN THIS SECTOR OF THE GALAXY

A Declaration of **The Anthanian Imperative**

For over four hundred years, we the people of Anthanos have known that our sun, the embodiment of the Great God Arteamos, has entered the early stages of increasing in size to become a red giant star. It will eventually expand sufficiently to engulf our planet and absorb it into its substance, as it has already engulfed the planet Altamnos, which for most of its eight-billion-year lifetime had been the planet nearest the sun. Anthanos now possesses that dubious distinction and, like Altamnos, will suffer the same fate.

But many thousands of years before that happens, the encroaching sun's surface will heat our planet to temperatures that will certainly make life here impossible. Our scientists estimate that we will reach the minimum of those temperatures within the next one to two hundred years. This increase in heat will cause the breeze that comes out of the cold side of our planet to increase in intensity and eventually reach violent and unlivable proportions. Well after those events happen, a nova explosion will occur as the sun depletes its hydrogen fuel and begins to use helium as a source of fuel for its thermonuclear reactions. As a result of that blast, all planets and moons in our solar system will be rendered uninhabitable, if not destroyed completely. Additionally, no other planets or moons in our solar system are habitable, or can be made habitable for the entire Anthanian population.

Therefore, the continued existence of the Anthanian race

requires that we find, investigate, and colonize another planet outside our solar system.

This we assert is our ***Anthanian Imperative.***

Our scientists have searched for more than one hundred years to find a planet with the appropriate factors that would render it colonizable. Under the leadership of the astrophysicist Jad Til-Lentos, a suitable candidate planet has been found. Preliminary investigations using a robotic satellite probe in orbit around that planet have determined that it possesses the necessary octet of conditions to nurture an enduring civilization: a stable sun, breathable atmosphere, appropriate temperature, suitable gravity, strong magnetic field, low eccentricity orbit (with an average distance to the sun of fifty-nine million anthans), abundant water, and sufficient land area to provide living space. In addition, the presence of large areas of plant life on the surface, and of large animals (and presumably of smaller animals as well) indicates an evolving ecosystem similar to that which existed on Anthanos millions of years ago. The presence of highly "intelligent," or "sophisticated" beings which might present a difficulty to colonizers cannot be ascertained from the probe information. The Anthanian Legislative Assembly has approved sending a team of ten scientists to explore the planet's surface and report back its findings. The future of our civilization demands it.

Because of its intense blue color as seen through our telescopes, the planet has been given the provisional name the "Blue Planet," pending adoption of a formal name.

Upon the return of the team, the Assembly, with guidance and recommendations from Spaceflight Command and the Anthanian Science Council, and using the objective data and conclusions generated by the team, will make the final decision whether to accept this planet for colonization. The subjective impressions and perceptions of the members of the team about the planet, as well as their thoughts and opinions, even their doubts and fears, will also be essential in reaching a decision.

We the people of Anthanos wish the team well in its endeavor. Let us begin and not waste time.

Approved this T-Sector In Legislature Assembled: 459.500.

Han Zelin

President of the Anthanian Legislative Assembly

Lill Panatos

Vice-President of the Anthanian Legislative Assembly

Nuri Kendavos

Director-General, Spaceflight Command

Tanita Verner

Chair, The Science Council of Anthanos

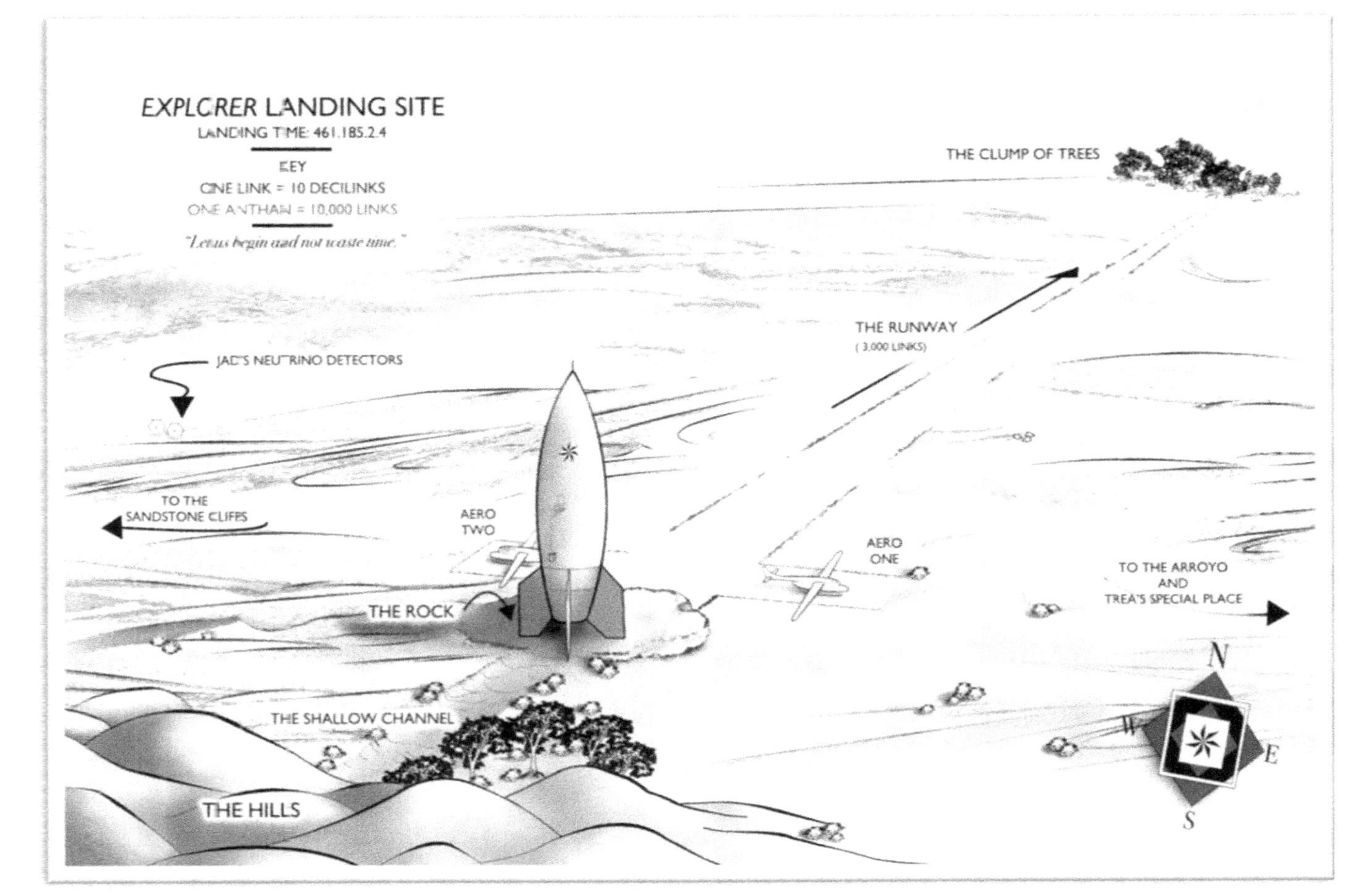

EXPLORER LANDING SITE
LANDING TIME: 461.185.2.4
KEY
ONE LINK = 10 DECILINKS
ONE ANTHAM = 10,000 LINKS
"Let us begin and not waste time."
THE CLUMP OF TREES
THE RUNWAY
(3,000 LINKS)
JAC'S NEUTRINO DETECTORS
TO THE
SANDSTONE CLIFFS
AERO
TWO
AERO
ONE
THE ROCK
TO THE ARROYO
AND
TREA'S SPECIAL PLACE
THE SHALLOW CHANNEL
THE HILLS
N
E
S
W

CHAPTER 1

LANDING

Time Element 461.185.2.4.

Down—finally—solid ground. The spaceship *Explorer* has landed on the Blue Planet.

Lilea stood in *Explorer'*s main airlock amid the murmurings and quiet dialogue of the others on the team. The tedium of spaceflight was over and the eagerness to get outside and explore this planet had been building ever since the ship entered orbit ten T-sectors ago. Now, only one subsector after landing, everyone had gathered in the main airlock, waiting for team leader Case to open the exterior door and give them their first close-up look at the surface.

In the excitement and anticipation, Lilea took in a deep breath. "I can't wait to get outside."

Lilea's husband, Bent, stood beside her. Her dark green cloth sampling kit hung from her left shoulder, and she'd strapped an electronic hand weapon in its holster to her right thigh. A canteen of water dangled from her belt.

Case was the last to enter. He latched the inner door and edged his way past the others to stand next to the outer door. "Has everybody got everything? Personal Communicators? Weapons? Water? Sun protection cream?"

He turned around and touched a red marker on a small com screen beside the door. The airlock turned quiet as a faint hissing indicated the air pressure in the airlock had been equalized with the outside.

Then Case pressed two yellow markers—**CATWALK** and **DOOR OPEN**. With a slight *pssst*, the door's airtight seal deactivated and the door popped inward and rolled fully to the left. Beyond the door extended a twelve-link-long catwalk with handrails.

Conversations of hurried whispers and expressions of wonder and amazement began again as the team stepped out onto the catwalk and glanced around at the landing site. Though they'd landed on a blue planet, the landing site was the mottled tan of a desert. Spaceflight Command had selected this little patch of desert as their prime landing site because it resembled as nearly as any place on the planet the terrain on their home planet Anthanos. They'd become familiar with the larger details of the site because they studied it closely during the ten T-sectors they were in orbit before landing.

The door faced southwest. A dry westerly breeze swirled over the team, rustling Lilea's light blonde curls the way the breeze on Anthanos did. She inhaled deeply and let the warm air hit her full in the face.

Quite a contrast to the cool, moist breeze at home, she thought. *There's even a faint scent in the air. It's like nothing I've ever smelled before. I wonder where it's coming from.*

Barely two hundred links south of the landing site stood the hills. They rose precipitously from the desert floor, shooting almost vertically to eight hundred links, towering over the ship. An opening in the wall of sandstone led into a shallow channel which ran north toward the exposed area of the huge rock on which the ship stood. Almost obscured by the hills, the sun welcomed the visitors to this planet with a warm glow through thin streaky clouds high in the southern sky.

But as the team gathered on that walkway, the foremost thought that went through Lilea's mind—even more so than the astonishment that gripped her as she took in all around—was the unknown. The possibility of a serious emergency on this mission had been drilled into every member of the team since the beginning of training back on Anthanos, 700 T-sectors before they left. They'd been warned repeatedly—almost anything could happen. A threat they might not recognize could materialize and strike them down within a nanosector. Those hills in particular, so close by, felt so ominous as Lilea scanned their imposing height. She eyed them with suspicion, even a little trepidation. She didn't like them, they were too close and dominating, though everyone else seemed to pay little attention to them. They could be protective and sheltering, yes, possibly shielding their ship from some unknown hazard. But they could also be dangerous, even menacing, especially so near.

An elevator, controlled through cables that ran back into the body of *Explorer* just above the door, hung at the far end of the catwalk. Case entered the elevator and descended the one hundred links from the catwalk to ground level. With his weapon in his hand, he scrutinized the area at the base of the ship, stepped out, and shouted back to the others.

"Everything's clear."

The rest of the team made its way to the surface. The little elevator would hold only four people at a time so Lilea, with excitement pounding in her chest and the smile of great good fortune mingled with a little melodrama on her face, took the second group with Bent.

The rock that formed the touchdown point for *Explorer* lay mostly buried in the sandy soil of the landing site. Only the flattened peak protruded a few links above ground level, and that made it a firm, solid, and relatively level base for the ship. Case had chosen this landing point in spite of its closeness to the hills because it was the only area free of the drifting sand that covered the surrounding desert.

As soon as everyone was down, they congregated at the base of the elevator until Jer, second-in-command and environmental officer arrived, the last to descend. She'd already noted the exact time Case's foot hit the ground, 461.185.2.8.7, and the time she stepped out, 461.185.2.9.2. Case finally broke the silence.

"All right, people. Let's get started."

Now everyone walked away, each in his or her own direction, each looking for all the things for which they'd been trained. Lilea assumed Case would say a few words about the importance of the landing to Anthanos, and she was surprised when he abruptly turned around and trotted off to examine the base of the ship. But that was Case, the consummate technician and pilot. He'd never been one to deliver speeches, he just did his job and did it well. It was as though he and the rest of the team were little more than a few explorers stepping onto another planet to look around. After all, that's what the Proclamation said, "Let us begin and not waste time." Case took the admonition literally.

Lilea and Bent followed Case down the slight rise off the rock that formed the actual touchdown point where the ship rested onto the sandy desert that made up the greatest part of the landing site.

Time Element 461.185.2.9.

Lilea and Bent stood at the base of *Explorer* facing north. "It's actually quite beautiful," she said. "The wide, flat landscape reminds me of home."

"Home doesn't have the vegetation." Bent reached down and plucked a tannish-white pebble from the dusty soil at his feet. He studied it briefly and dropped it in his pocket.

Lilea remained quiet for a couple of nanosections while she surveyed the terrain around the landing site. "That's true. But it's a shame."

Except toward the hills south of the ship, the tan soil of the landing site—now officially termed 'Site One'—swept outward from the ship in all directions. Smooth for the most part, but blemished here and there by a slight mound or depression, though none so great it disrupted the image of a broad, flat plain. Overlying the sandy plain was the vegetation, as though the soil formed a sweeping canvas on which were sprinkled accent colors of red, yellow, brown, and green. Occasional small trees, bushes, and flowers of several colors grew nearby, and larger trees dotted the landscape farther out. Ground cover by grasses of different varieties grew in patches over the plain, though it'd been burned out completely around the landing area by the blast of the ship's engine. Farther north, well beyond the forest that encircled the entire site, several dark rock-like structures, some flat on top, others markedly rugged, projected above the trees.

To the southwest, a row of vertical, jagged, sienna-colored cliffs began about an anthan away, gradually gaining height and blending into the more rounded hills directly south of the ship. Horizontal streaks of brownish-black permeated the sandstone forming an irregular ladder-like effect along the cliff face.

Lilea pulled her camera from her sampling kit and took several images of the desert. Enchanted by the landscape, she lost track of time until Bent broke the spell.

"I'm going to look around and collect some specimens," he said as he walked off to his left.

Lilea remained quiet, barely acknowledging his leaving. "I'm going to stay here a few microsectors. My legs are still weak."

"I told you to use the exercycles and treadmills more often, Lanie," he said over his shoulder, a smart-alecky smile on his lips. "You can't just take the microgravity pills."

"Oh, be quiet. You know I hate those damn machines." She flexed her legs and did a couple of deep knee bends, trying to work out the stiffness that had settled into her muscles and joints since they left the artificial gravity of the Personnel Module of the huge interstellar spaceship *Star Voyager* fifty T-sectors ago.

Lilea liked Bent's pet name for her. Lanie meant 'white flower,' an allusion to her alabaster skin and blonde hair, which contrasted so unmistakably with Bent's umber skin and dark hair. She'd been acutely aware of the distinction when they first started dating, but now she rarely gave it a second thought. She was proud of the step they took: they were the first interracial couple to take spaceflight training in Anthanos's Spaceflight Command.

She took several more images of the desert, finishing a full sweep, east to west. She understood why SpaceComm had chosen this little patch of desert as their landing site. It bore a striking resemblance to the mostly flat Lifezone which encircled Anthanos at the terminator. On a planet such as Anthanos, tidally locked to its central star, the terminator — the dividing line between the light and dark sides — was the only place on the planet comfortable enough to nurture biological forms. Strung through the Lifezone like beads on an endless string were the cities, the urban areas large and small, oases of life in a vast sterile desert. The golden brown sands which covered so much of Anthanos gave it the nickname "The Golden Planet," though in a somewhat ironic twist of fate no elemental gold existed in those sands at all.

As Lilea scanned the landing site, she brought out of her long-term memory some of the probe images, especially those taken in the vicinity of the landing site. On 455.802, SpaceComm dispatched *Star Voyager* on an expedition to the Blue Planet to place a spherical robotic probe in orbit around it. The probe beamed back more than fifty thousand images before the ship returned on 457.620. Ten T-sectors later, SpaceComm released the images to its scientific employees, especially to those with a real need to see them, like Bent the geologist and Lilea the anthropologist.

Lilea pored over the images in excruciating detail, but found almost nothing that would indicate an intelligent, reasoning civilization. She found large swaths of plant life — that wasn't too surprising in her mind — but the presence of so many animals startled her. Large and small, singly, in groups of two or three, or in groups of thousands, they seemed to be everywhere. In her mind that suggested hunting by intelligent people — *are the largest of those animals at the top of the food chain, or are they prey for more sophisticated hunters?* — but she found no evidence for it, so she looked for cultivation or farming. Again she found nothing, though she did find a few tantalizing examples — an opening in a forest that looked too nearly circular to be natural, an area near a large river that appeared as though it could have been cultivated at one time, a tributary of a small stream that might have been used for diverting water for cultivation. Nowhere, though, was there any solid evidence of intelligent peoples, and she wondered if they existed at all.

Still, nothing I've found rules out intelligent life. On a planet teeming with this much plant and animal life, there's got to be intelligent life, too. There's just got to be.

CHAPTER 2

DESERT

Time Element 461.185.3.0.

The most valuable and unmistakable message Lilea got from the probe images was that finding artifacts of intelligent species on a planet so vastly different from her own would be problematic. On Anthanos, she knew where to look and what to look for, and she was proud of her sixth sense that told her where the remnants of civilizations long past might lie. But as she stood near the base of *Explorer* and stared at the terrain around the landing site, she wondered if her knowledge and training would work here.

To supplement the probe images, she made several high definition sweeps of the landing site from orbit just before landing, to far more detail than those the probe had taken. None showed any sign of intelligent creatures. No evidence of houses or huts, or trails or roads, nothing that looked as though it could have been made by a reasoning civilization. No straight lines, no vehicles, no indigenous people, no electronic commun-ications. She scanned large areas of the planet during light and darkness, but saw no fires or lights, other than flashes of lightning. That didn't bode well for finding any real samples on the surface. But small signs — a frag-ment of bone used as a tool, a stone chipped in a certain way to fashion an arrowhead or spearhead, a piece of wood whittled in a distinctive manner or burned in a fire — might still be present in the area, an indication of intelligent natives, if not living here, then perhaps passing through.

Early Anthanians made many small symbols to their sun god, The Great God Arteamos, easy to find if one knew where to look. Some were buried only a few decilinks under the sand, and Lilea knew how to rec-ognize the surface signs that told her where these artifacts might lie. Would she be able to apply the same logic to her search on this planet? She vowed to find out.

On the images taken from orbit, she'd seen a dry stream bed east of the landing site about 1500 links away. It probably carried water in the past and natives might've used it. Artifacts could be plentiful there, so she made it her first priority after landing. She'd told Case about it, but Space-Comm regulations required team members to sign out on the Local Exploration Sign-in/Sign-out List when they left the immediate vicinity of the ship. She pulled out her Personal Communicator and logged onto the list, and then ambled easterly, away from the slight hillock that defined the rock on which the ship stood onto a sandy area dotted with small flowers and brush. Oddly-shaped plants with sharp spines that pricked her finger when she stooped to examine them dotted the desert floor, and grayish-green bushes with ivory-yellow blooms were plentiful farther out. But the one plant that most intrigued her had a tall central stalk—many of the stalks taller than she—shooting up from a tight growth of sharp, spiny, sword-like leaves. From that central shoot hung forty to fifty delicate creamy-white blossoms.

As she walked, she thought about the work she had to do. This would be her chance to prove she was worthy of being the anthropologist SpaceComm had selected for this team. It was quite an honor to be picked as the one to find out if intelligent life existed on this planet. She was good at her job and this was her chance to prove it.

Yet, though she had the highest degree possible and six years of field experience in anthropology, she understood there must have been a lot of discussion about her by the Crew Selection Committee at SpaceComm. At thirty-five, she was the youngest on the team and had the least experience in deep-space flight. They probably wondered if she could handle the task. She had all the essential knowledge and expertise of course, but in her short career had she developed the insight, the instincts, and the intuition to face an unknown civilization? Would she even recognize highly intel-ligent individuals if she came across them? Did she have the innate judg-ment, the understanding, yes, even the *wisdom* to handle the complicated task of making first contact? After all, when SpaceComm picked Bent as the geologist for the team, they got her too, since they were setting up the team as all married couples. That *did* fit their needs well—they wanted an anthropologist to look for intelligent life. But she was the only anthro-pologist who applied, and SpaceComm certainly would have preferred someone with more experience. That may have been why they encouraged her to only observe and not approach any intelligent natives. Perhaps they thought she wasn't experienced enough to take that step.

But by far the one concept that gave her the most pleasure, and the one she kept securely hidden from everyone except Bent, was the un-deniable fact that this expedition would give her the chance to practice her skills in a totally new and exciting world. She longed to be known for her scientific acumen as much as Bent or Jad, or the others on the team. Well, perhaps not Jad, after all, he's a top-tier astrophysicist and the one who discovered the Blue Planet in the first place. It would be her world, her niche, and she secretly hoped she would become known all over Anthanos as the person who found and studied intelligent life on the Blue Planet.

Now she was in her element and ready to show SpaceComm she could do the job. But a tightness in the pit of her stomach belied her confidence.

As she walked toward the stream bed, she stopped every ten to twenty links to examine the soil, looking for the same signs of Anthanian habitation she knew from home: a small eruption of sand under which artifacts could be found. She either swept the sand away with a small brush or let it trickle from a hand spade, watching for anything that might appear.

Nothing.

After about three millisectors, she stopped and took a long drink from her water bottle. The sun behind her, slightly past its midpoint in its travel across the sky, felt blazing hot on the bare skin of her face and neck, and she rolled up the sleeves of her jumpsuit. She pulled out the bottle of sun protection cream made especially for a sun that put out more UV light than her own, and spread a dab of the lotion on her exposed skin.

She turned around and checked her position. *Explorer* wasn't difficult to spot—that 204 link-tall rocket ship with its dark blue landing fins and silvery main section polished to a mirror finish standing vertically in the desert could be seen least an anthan away. The laser range finder in her vision aid—variable-power, gyroscopically-stabilized, microprocessor-controlled binoculars—told her she was 824 links from the ship. Bent, Case, and some of the others still wandered around the base of the ship. Reassured, she started out again, heading east.

CHAPTER 3

WALK

Time Element 461.185.3.4.0.

As Lilea made her way across the desert, she soon became aware of a sensation rare for someone from Anthanos: silence. She stopped and listened carefully. The ship itself was quiet, the venting of excess gasses that took place immediately after landing had ceased and she was far enough away from the others she could no longer hear their jabbering. The westerly breeze had died down and the totality of silence pleased her. This wasn't like Anthanos where the breeze that whirled out of the cold, dark side of the planet constantly hissed and whispered in your ears, your eternal companion wherever you went. On the Blue Planet this was pure silence, the total absence of sound, the noise of nothingness.

But as she stood there, she became aware of a peculiar sound that came from ahead and slightly to her left. A rapid clicking or buzzing, or, no, a rattling. She scanned the area, but couldn't tell what was making the noise. Then it stopped.

She took a few hesitant steps in the direction she last heard it, carefully watching where she stepped. She hadn't heard the sound for almost a microsector and was about to give up and continue on when she saw the reason for it, a long, slender animal without any feet or legs coiled up in the shadow of a large rock to her left.

She crept around to the front of the rock that shaded the animal. Its dart-like head followed her as she moved, and a black forked appendage which she took to be a tongue constantly flipped in and out. The tail twitched and rattled furiously and a malignant fire simmered in its gray-green eyes.

A cold, unpleasant quality hovered about the animal and she was repulsed by it, yet it fascinated her too, in a grisly sort of way. No creature like this ever prowled the sands of Anthanos. She certainly wasn't going to reach out and try to pick it up—she'd been warned by Trea, the team's zoologist, before they left: "Don't touch or attempt to handle any animal until you know it's safe."

She stood in front of the animal for a few microsectors, carefully distinguishing the tan to rusty-brown colors that made up the distinctive pattern of diamonds along its back. Her eyes traced the deep S-curve in the neck directly behind the head. She understood intuitively, if not overtly, that that curve would allow it to thrust its head forward rapidly and easily. She snapped several images with her camera, but decided to leave this animal alone. She retreated a few steps.

As she turned to walk away, a quick flash of movement caught the corner of her eye. A small furry animal hopped nimbly, almost playfully, along the ground, coming from her right. A reddish-buff little fur ball about four decilinks long, it had short front legs and long rear legs, and a slender tufted tail longer than its body. It bore a vague resemblance to a pet she had as a child, but she didn't have time to admire it. It hopped past her, landing squarely in front of the coiled animal, no more than a link away. The furry animal may have been oblivious to the presence of the other — then again, maybe it wasn't — but it hesitated before jumping again.

The head shot forward — the mouth opened —

"Oh, my gosh!" Lilea gasped and took several steps back, stunned, her eyes wide open. The furry animal staggered off, hopping erratically along the sand, bleeding from two marks on its side. The predator uncoiled and slithered out from behind the rock, following the faltering animal. She took several more images as it twitched along the sand.

How does it move? My gosh, that thing must be six links long.

The furry animal collapsed several hundred links away. When the predator reached the lifeless body it opened its jaws and began to devour it, starting at the head. It took several millisectors to engulf the entire carcass, and when it finished it slithered away, the tufted tail dangling contemptuously from its mouth.

She took several more images and then turned and headed toward the stream bed, her heart still pounding in her chest. She played the incident over in her mind as she walked.

I should have called Trea to come see this but everything happened so fast —

Lilea had expected predation on the Blue Planet — that was never in doubt. With all the animals Trea had imaged from orbit before landing, predation would certainly be a normal part of life here. But she hadn't expected to see so vicious an example of it so soon after arriving. Things like that existed on her planet, but only in the distant past. Hundreds of thousands of years ago large carnivorous animals preyed on smaller ones.

To see it actually happen in person it's chilling, even a little frightening, but it's exciting too. Like going back to prehistoric times on our planet.

One point she didn't understand. *How did the predatory animal kill the furry one? It made one bite . . . was there a toxin or a poison or a venom?* She walked on with her head down, replaying the attack in her mind until she looked up. The stream bed lay a few links beyond.

"Time to get back to work," she told herself and pushed the attack into the long-term memory sector of her brain where it would be retained until she wanted to review it in complete detail.

Time Element 461.185.4.3.

Lilea turned around to check her position again — 1454 links from the ship. The sun hung deep in the western sky and a clump of dark gray clouds approached from the west. She watched the clouds for a few nano-sectors, but figured they weren't dangerous and assumed they would pass by overhead. She hiked over a slight rise and took a few steps down into the vicinity of the stream bed, stopping first to stack several rocks together in a small cairn to mark the point where she entered. Then she dropped into the dry channel. The eight-link deep western sidewall of the stream shaded the bottom almost completely, the first shade she'd encountered since leaving *Explorer*.

She walked slowly south along the bottom for almost two hundred links, most of the time with her head down. Every few steps she stopped to check the soil for artifacts and examine the dirt as it trickled from her spade. She filtered some of the sand through a sieve and inspected the residue for anything suspicious, often with a magnifying glass. She pulled up rocks and studied them, and on some chipped off a piece to check its composition. Other rocks she cleaned with a small brush to look for signs of use.

She spent by far the greatest amount of her time, though, scrutinizing the sidewall of the bed, delving into the history of the terrain revealed by the exposing action of water over many years. But she concentrated so heavily on her search she paid little attention to the clouds as they drifted in from the west, darkening the sky overhead. She finally gave up looking and decided to return to the ship. *There's nothing here.* Then her Personal Communicator beeped. It was the double beep of a minor emergency.

Jer's voice crackled through the PersComm's small speaker. "Lilea. There are some scary-looking clouds overhead. You should come back right away."

"Okay." Lilea terminated comm and tucked the PersComm back into the left thigh pocket of her jumpsuit. She cut footholds in the side of the channel with her spade and climbed over the top. As she emerged she felt the brisk, cool breeze that accompanied the clouds, and it alarmed her. This wasn't the gentle, warm breeze that'd been around during the earlier part of this lightime. The sight of *Explorer* in the distance lessened the tightness in her chest, but a grayish haze extended upward toward the clouds overhead and enveloped the ship. She looked up at the clouds and a drop of some liquid hit her — *splat* — right in the eye.

"What was that?" As she lowered her head to wipe the liquid away, she could see the miniature craters formed by more drops as they hit the sandy ground at her feet. Several drops splashed her bright blue-green jumpsuit, several hit her bare forearms and the top of her head.

"Oh, my god!" Instantly she understood what was happening. *Seth, you magnificent bastard, you were right! Water* does *fall from the sky.*

Seth's report had been right. Seth, the astronomer, had predicted that water could fall from the sky on the Blue Planet, but few on Anthanos believed him. All his computer models and cloud-chamber experiments said it would happen, but most ignored him. "Water isn't going to fall from the sky," they said. Water never fell from the Anthanian sky. And water never fell from the sky on any of the moons of the outer planets in their solar system, so why would it on the Blue Planet? His idea was so novel and unorthodox SpaceComm even relieved him of his spaceflight credentials. He never flew in space again. Yet, here they were — large drops of water pelting her jumpsuit in dark spots all over.

She grabbed her sampling kit and bolted for the ship. The faster she ran, the faster the water came as the wind whipped it directly into her face. After a few hundred links she was soaked, but she continued to run.

When she reached the ship, she ran to the elevator, but it was at the top and no one else was around. She hit the 'Down' button on the elevator's call box and dashed under *Explorer* to stand in a small dry area beneath the 8-link diameter rocket exhaust bell — an extremely serious violation of SpaceComm safety regulations. If Case ever found out . . . *Yeah, but SpaceComm regs weren't written for a planet where water falls from the sky.* After a few nanosectors, the elevator arrived, but she hesitated.

How long does this go on? For millisectors, or even subsectors? Should I try to get back into the ship, or wait out the storm?

As she lingered there trying to make up her mind, a stream of water trickled through the channel from the opening in the hills. A dark grayish-brown stream, it split around the lower medial fin — one of the four landing fins that held the ship upright — that had settled on the rock at the end of that channel. The water swirled down to where she stood and splashed against her already muddy boots. After a few nanosectors the flow became heavier, strong enough she could feel it on her feet, and she finally decided to take the elevator to the top rather than remain underneath and possibly get swept away. She sprinted to the elevator and pressed the 'Up' button. When the elevator reached the top, she bolted down the catwalk and through the open door of the airlock. Jer waited for her.

"My gosh, you're soaked. This is astonishing. We had no idea —"

Lilea stood in the center of the airlock soaked to the skin. Her hair was plastered against her face and the water spilling off her jumpsuit formed a puddle on the floor. "Well, now we know, water *can* fall from the sky. And it comes down in big drops, too. I'm going up and change." She climbed the ladder beside the airlock that led to the Personnel Deck one level above.

"Am I glad to see you," Bent said as she entered the living area of their compartment. "Good god, you're soaking wet — what happened? Are you okay?"

"Yeah, I'm okay, just wet." She dropped her equipment on the floor.

"Everyone else came back on board when we saw those black clouds come overhead. We wondered where you were. We thought you saw them, too."

"No, I didn't see the clouds until Jer notified me. I was busy in a ditch out there looking for artifacts, but I didn't find any. I need to get out of these clothes."

She entered the bedroom and crossed to the wardrobe on the other side where she pulled out a dry jumpsuit. As she passed the bed she glanced through the porthole-like window above the bed. The bright sunlight and blue sky told her that water had stopped falling from the sky

CHAPTER 4

MEETING

Time Element 461.186.9.7. (461.2.0.0 Blue Planet Time)

"All right, people. Let's get this meeting started. We've got several things to talk about."

Case dropped in one smooth glide down the interdeck ladder from *Explorer's* Command Deck to the Life Sciences Deck one level below, and strode over to a circular table in the center of the room. After the team had consumed their second meal of this T-sector, and as the orange-yellow sun hung elegantly in the southwestern sky, they assembled around the table to listen as Case described the state of affairs at the end of their first lightime on the Blue Planet. They sat in a semicircle around one side of the table, from Jad and Wila at the far left, to Col and Trea at the right. Lilea and Bent sat near the middle of the group, Jer beside them.

This wasn't the first time they'd met. Case started these little gatherings when training first began on 459.701. They continued throughout the tedious 700 T-sector trip to this planet in *Star Voyager*, and even during the 40 T-sector flight to the Blue Planet, and the 10 T-sectors they were in orbit before landing. Now, less than two T-sectors after landing, they met for the first time as visitors to this new world. Case stood opposite the others at the table, his electronic notebook open in front of him.

The pose he took at these meetings was so typical of Case—tall, proud and erect, his arms folded across his chest, his feet shoulder-width apart. Years of weight lifting and body-sculpting had produced in Case an angular, muscular physique, and his jet-black hair peppered with tiny flecks of gray gave him the appearance of youth well below his sixty-three years. Occasionally, he'd glance at his notebook, but mostly he fixed his gaze one-by-one on each team member as he talked. "While the rest of you were beginning your explorations, I made a detailed inspection of the lower part of the ship, particularly the radiators in the fins. I didn't find any obvious damage, and most importantly, I didn't find any sand in the shutter mechanism. That means we can seal the radiators before we take off."

"Excellent." Col tapped the table with an index finger.

"But as far as the leveling system is concerned, we may have a problem." Case brought up on the four com screens at the table several images he'd taken of the landing fins at the bottom of the ship. He pointed to them as he spoke. "The lower medial and the right and left lateral fins are okay—they're sitting on solid rock. But the leveling pad on the upper medial fin—that's the one that points north—is extended almost eight links. The rock we landed on dips at the north end. That's okay, it'll hold at that extension. What bothers me is that the landing pad itself overlaps a groove about one link deep in the surface of the rock. We just missed putting down in that groove. The leveling system could have handled that depth, though. What concerns me is that the edge of that groove is supporting one-quarter of the weight of the ship, and if that edge shatters or fragments, the ship will tilt slightly for a few nanosectors until the leveling system can correct. The leveling system can correct up to ten links. But the rock edge seems to be holding, and this ship is stable now. I don't think there'll be a problem. Nothing is going to move this ship."

"That's good to know," Lilea said, but quietly, more to herself than to anyone else.

"Jad has reset the time-recorder calibration factor and entered it in the ship's computer so each of you can reprogram your chronometers. Remember, this is the first of the longer T-sectors. For your information, we landed at 461.1.6.3 by the new system."

Lilea glanced at the digital chronometer on her left wrist. At 461.187.0.2, this would normally be waking-up time. On Anthanos, she routinely slept during the even-numbered T-sectors, as did most in Space-Comm.

"Also, now that we know that water can really fall from clouds, Mina collected a sample and analyzed it. It's really very pure water. Pure enough to drink. So, if you get caught out in it like Lilea did, it just gets you wet. If you're out using one of the runabouts or aerodynes, that should be a good place to get away from the water. Any questions?"

Case paused and glanced up from his notebook. Lilea was never sure whether he really expected questions at these meetings, or whether he was just pausing to refresh his memory about the next topic. But no one spoke, so he went on.

"Okay, now, about the runabouts and aerodynes. We'll begin to assemble the runabouts next lightime. I expect we can assemble runabout 1 next lightime, and runabout 2 the time after that. Then we'll tackle the aerodynes. We've scheduled two lightimes to get each one assembled. We did those in the simulators back home, and we can do it here. Then Wila and I will begin the test flights. Once those are code blue, we can begin our regular explorations. That means"—his eyes danced as he glanced toward Bent—"you guys get to examine the gorge. Any questions?"

"Case," Col asked, "what happens to a runabout if it gets wet? It wasn't designed to get wet like that. I'm concerned the water may short out the electric motors in the wheels."

"I don't think so. The motors are inside the wheels. They were put there to keep them away from the dust and sand, and there's plenty of dust around here. They should be well protected. Besides, the motors have to be cleaned periodically, and they can be removed and disassembled, so if they get wet, I don't see a problem. Any more questions?"

The room stayed quiet for a few nanosectors, and Case went on.

"It's getting dark outside right now, and we've been awake since 183 or 184, so we need to get some sleep. We'll have to adjust our sleep cycles until we can sleep during the darktimes and work when it's light outside. We did it in the simulators, so we can do it here. Be sure and send out your reports. Kal and Jasi will want to see them as soon as possible. It's now 461.2.1.2. All right, people, let's get going. We need to get some sleep."

CHAPTER 5

INTERLOPER

Time Element 459.685.7.2.

It was the sun, Anthanos's expanding orange-red sun that slowed the rotation of the planet, tidally locking it into one rotation per revolution. The intense heat baked the side of the planet that faced it and drove the evaporated water to condense on the dark side in massive plates of ice, several anthans thick in some places. That side became one of the coldest places in the solar system. But the sun did something else, too.

Out of that cold, dark side came the breeze. Not really a wind, the breeze swept over the Lifezone like a cool, moist zephyr, set up by the difference in temperature between the hot and cold sides. It brought a touch of moisture to the Lifezone, enough to cool the skin and make breathing pleasant, though certainly not enough to be considered "humid" by any stretch of imagination. The breeze was as much an unvarying factor of life on the planet as the constant air temperature, or the brick-red sun sitting perpetually on the horizon, or the cloudless blue sky overhead.

Case and Jer lived in a modest single-family, one-story house on the far outskirts of Sabean, the capital city of the nation-planet, not far from the city limits on the side of the Lifezone that faced the cold side. Like most homes on Anthanos, it'd been built on a thick slab of concrete, securely anchored in the sand beneath to prevent shifting.

But as Lilea and Bent sat in their runabout during the four millisector autodrive from their apartment to Case and Jer's house, she didn't dwell on the house or on the trip through the city. Her mind was much farther away. She was still dizzy from the meeting they'd attended earlier this T-sector, and the details of that meeting kept spinning around in her brain.

They'd gone to a special meeting at SpaceComm headquarters on the Sabean Spaceport around 685.2.0, and were the last to arrive at the conference room on the second floor of the Main Administration Building. Eight other people, four couples, all spaceflight veterans, sat around the table in the center of the room. Six of them she recognized immediately — she knew them from SpaceComm. One couple she didn't know, but the number of gold seven-pointed stars arranged vertically on the upper sleeves of their flight suits — the four of a Senior Command Pilot on his, the three of a Command Pilot on hers — told her they were highly experienced spaceflight veterans. After she and Bent took their assigned seats, Space-Comm's Director-General Nuri Kendavos arrived to chair the meeting. As he sat down at the head of the table, he pressed a red button on a control panel to his right, and a single word in bright blue letters appeared on a silver screen behind him.

CONGRATULATIONS!

What's this? Lilea opened her eyes a little wider. Nuri began to speak.

"You've all known for some time that we're putting together two teams to train for the landing on the blue planet . . . we're calling this Planetary Landing Expedition I . . . the prime team we're calling the Gold Team . . . and the backup team, the Blue Team. The ten of you have been selected as the Gold Team."

What? I'm on the Gold Team for the blue planet? No way. Oh, my god!

When Lilea joined SpaceComm in 458 to take her basic spaceflight training, she thought she might be selected for a blue planet team, but figured her chances of making the prime team were less than about one in several hundred — at best. She was so new to spaceflight they wouldn't pick her. Bent had already joined in 453, doing geology for SpaceComm on some of the moons of the outer planets looking for the rare metals that were so vitally important in the building of ultrahigh performance spacecraft, but which were so profoundly lacking in the sands of Anthanos.

But she remained puzzled. A voyage to the blue planet was the ultimate, the apex, the zenith, for an Anthanian space traveler. Its value to the future of Anthanos was so obvious — *We could be exploring our new home.* How much more important could a mission be?

And this idea of using married couples. It wasn't unheard of. Space-Comm had sent married couples into deep space a few times, but now the entire landing team would be couples. *An unusual development.*

Lilea had finished her basic spaceflight training only 185 T-sectors earlier, on 459.500, and earned the single star of a Subpilot to wear on her upper sleeve. That made her eligible for real missions, including the advanced training necessary for those missions. But as important as it was, she assumed only veteran space travelers would be picked for this mission. And as she scanned the room, she noticed that, yes, everyone else did have at least two stars on their uniforms, which meant they all had a minimum of five hundred T-sectors of deep space experience on their flight records.

Still, she wasn't a world-renowned anthropologist. She had the highest degree in her field and six years as a field operative for the Sabean Museum of Natural Science. Could that be why they picked her? After all, she *was* the only anthropologist to undergo spaceflight training. And she *was* married to the only geologist in the room. But SpaceComm needed other specialties too — zoology, botany, medicine, molecular biology, astronomy — and they got that by picking all couples. *How interesting.*

So the giddiness of her sudden promotion from lowly spaceflight trainee to exalted Gold Team member had barely worn off later that same T-sector as Bent set their runabout's autodrive to take them to Case and Jer's house for a quiet get-acquainted dinner party. The party could be quiet for a short time. Their names wouldn't be released to the public for another two T-sectors.

Time Element 459.685.7.5.

Case and Jer's house had a quiet dignity about it: simple construction using a rectangular design, a rough stucco-like exterior, a golden bronze color — darker than the sand around it, but not so dark as to stand out harshly. The cobalt blue front door had been chosen, as many on Anthanos had, to signify, "This is where the omnipresent red light from the sun ends." A short walkway from the street led to a small stoop at the door.

Bent parked the runabout manually on the street, and as they walked along the sidewalk toward the house, Lilea noticed an elderly gentleman approaching. She estimated he was eight links tall, taller than Jad by almost a link, and slender, approaching gaunt. Clean-shaven and dressed in an immaculate white shirt and pants, his straight white hair would have fallen past his shoulders had it not been rustling in the breeze. His fair, almost pale skin led Lilea to assume he was of the same racial group as she, that he was Tarkuu, but unlike Tarkuu, he had dark brown eyes, much like Bent's. *How could that be? Tarkuu always have pale to medium blue eyes. Like mine. But he can't be Morokuu, like Bent. He's got pale skin. Must be mixed race.*

The man seemed of little threat, merely someone walking along the street, and Lilea paid no more attention to him as they turned up the walk to the front door.

Just as they made the turn the man spoke in a lyrical bass voice. "Is there anything I can say to persuade you to not make this trip?"

The unexpectedness of his speaking interrupted the quiet of the suburban neighborhood and it startled Lilea, but she and Bent continued up the walk to the front door where Bent pressed the door-announce button. The man came up the walk and stopped about ten paces behind them.

"I strongly urge you not to make this trip." He enunciated his words independently and forcibly. "It will be dangerous. Very dangerous."

Lilea glanced briefly at the man, but Bent ignored him.

"There will be danger on this trip." The man's face remained blank, devoid of emotion. "Much danger. Be warned. You don't know what you're getting into. There is a lot about the blue planet you don't know. There is danger in ways you cannot even imagine. In ways you will never know about. You are putting your lives in great peril on this journey. I cannot emphasize too strongly—"

Jer opened the front door and yelled at the man. "Go away. Get out of here. Stop bothering my guests."

"Who was that guy?" Lilea asked after the door was closed.

"I don't know," Jer said, her face contorted by frustration. "I've never seen him before. He comes up and lectures each couple as they arrive. He says the same thing to everybody. About the danger on the trip. I can't get rid of him. Case has already notified Public Safety."

Jer led them through the living room toward the dining area where several others waited, snacking on appetizers and talking with Case. Dell, space surgeon for the team, and his wife Mina, a molecular biologist, had already arrived, as had Col the botanist and Trea the zoologist.

"Let's go out onto the patio." Jer rolled open the glass patio door. "The breeze is nice out there." The group turned silent for a few nano-sectors as they crowded onto the patio, savoring the breeze.

But the land over which the breeze passed was not as accommodating. Stretching outward from the house lay a barren, desolate expanse of golden-brown sand. It was as though a hand had reached down and plucked all life from the sand, leaving a sterile wilderness that seemed exaggerated by its starkness. A few houses and other small buildings stood on the sand a short distance away, and a few low hills rose randomly farther out, but none were large enough to block the view of the interminably featureless desert that made up the Lifezone of the planet.

"Those houses are outside city limits," Case told the group. "You can tell by the water tank on the roof."

Almost as soon as the conversation got going, Jad and Wila arrived.

Jer brought them out to the patio to join the others. They too had been approached by the elderly man, though Public Safety Officers were nowhere in sight.

"I certainly hope we don't encounter him or people like him after our names are announced to the public," Col said. "That could negatively affect our training."

"How did he know we had been selected to make this trip?" Trea asked. "Our names haven't been announced. How did he know who we were?"

"Several people at SpaceComm know by now," Lilea said. "Nuri, the Crew Selection Committee . . ."

"The Committee's been debating who to put on the Gold and Blue Teams for several hundred T-sectors," Bent said. "It might've leaked out."

"That's right," Mina said. "H-He might be somebody's g-grandfather. Somebody who works at C-Command Administration. Maybe he l-lives around here."

"Well, he can go away and stay away for all I care," Wila said. She threw out an arm in a dismissive motion and stuffed another finger sandwich in her mouth.

Lilea agreed with Wila, but only to a point. She never held any animosity toward the old man and never wished him any ill will. To her, the man was merely quaint, an oddball with a dubious sense of foreboding, though she wasn't terribly keen to meet him again either. She had more important things to think about and dismissed him from her mind as quickly as he arrived.

CHAPTER 6

THE GORGE – FLIGHT

Time Element 461.18.11.0 (Surface Time).

As Jad finished loading his duffel and started cramming a few items into the smaller daypack, he glanced through the window above the bed. Each of the five living compartments set around the outside wall of the Personnel Deck on *Explorer* had two circular windows, one over a small table in the food preparation area, the other over the bed. The windows in Jad and Wila's compartment faced south and slightly east, and from the bedroom, looking obliquely through the window, he could see the light from the rising sun bathing the hills south of the ship, though the sun itself had not yet appeared.

This lightime Jad and Wila had risen several millisectors before the sun. *Explorer* was quiet as they packed a few personal items, preparing for the trip to the gorge about seventy anthans west of Site One. Wila stepped into the living area and called up the meteorological data on the compartment's com screen, checking especially the outside air temperature. "Seven Tal. It gets cool here when the planet rotates away from the sun."

"What was the high temperature last lightime?"

"Twenty-two Tal. Much warmer."

As Jad watched, a faint band of crimson poked a sleepy eye above the hills. The color grew in intensity and pushed upward, slowly changing hue, first to a reddish pink, then to an orange-red. The billowy clouds above the hills caught the color and it spread from cloud to cloud. It ran horizontally along the hills and pushed vertically into the sky. Even before the sun itself could be seen, the color had spread over thirty degrees of horizon.

Jad tried to continue to pack, but he spent more and more time watching the sunrise. Finally, he stopped and knelt on the bed at the window.

Wila joined him. "What are you looking at?"

"The colors of the sunrise. They're amazing. I would never have predicted anything like this. Look how the color spreads all over. I thought the sun would just appear at the horizon. I didn't realize the color display would be so spectacular. I can get a better look outside."

Jad walked the few short steps around the circular walkway from his compartment door to the interdeck ladder, and descended to the Entry Deck, one level below. Using his personal access code, he entered the air-lock and opened the exterior door and stepped onto the catwalk. The ship's air pressure had been equalized with the outside, so both doors could be open at the same time. He walked to the end of the catwalk and gazed left toward the eastern end of the hills, several hundred links lower than those near the ship. The reddish-orange orb of the sun, now fully exposed, sat directly atop the hills.

Then the yellows appeared. Horizontal bands of lemon and ochre shot through the reds and pinks, above, below and within. Several trees on top of the hills stood stark against the brightening sky, and the clouds were a medley of warm colors. As the sun pushed upward over the low hills in the east, it threw a blood-red tint on the sandstone cliffs to the west.

Captivated by the way the colors kept changing, Jad compared it to the Anthanian sun. From the Lifezone of Anthanos, the red sun sits direct-ly on the horizon, it neither rises nor sets, nor does the light spread over wide areas of the sky. As he wondered if the greater amount of dust in the Blue Planet's atmosphere could have something to do with the spreading light, Wila joined him on the catwalk.

They wore only their regular jumpsuits, long-sleeved, but not meant for warmth against the cool morning air. Jad was comfortable, but Wila pulled the sleeves of her jumpsuit down to her wrists and jammed her hands in her pockets. Jad stood behind her and put his arms around her, but she shivered too much for comfort and after a millisector went back inside.

"I'm going in and prepare lumyon," she said as she entered the air-lock. Anthanians usually ate only two meals per waking T-sector, and lum-yon was their first. But on the Blue Planet, with its longer T-sectors, they'd begun taking three meals per T-sector.

Jad stayed on the catwalk another millisector and was about go in-side when a Level 1 alarm — a single repeated *bong* marking a predeter-mined value — sounded in the airlock. He checked the com screen just inside the door. The temperature had dropped to the preset alarm limit of 15 Tal.

Well, that'll wake Case. He locked the exterior door and scrambled up the interdeck ladder. *I'll have to check the dust in the atmosphere. It may have something to do with the scattering.*

Time Element 461.19.3.4.

"All right everyone, seat belts." Wila climbed into the front left-hand seat of the larger of the two aerodynes, Aero Two. "Chest restraints, too."

Jad, sitting to the right of the pilot's position and the central joystick, latched his belt and chest straps as Wila finished her preflight inspection. Behind them, Bent and Lilea occupied the center pair of the ship's six seats. A framework of metal racks holding two food coolers had been installed over the two rear seats.

They'd nicknamed themselves the 'Gorge Team.'

The runway stretched ahead of the aerodyne, three thousand links due north from the edge of the rock on which *Explorer* stood — plenty of room for either aerodyne to take off or land. Over the six lightimes immediately after landing, the team had assembled the runabouts, the four-wheeled vehicles that gave them mobility around the landing site, and the aerodynes, the rocket-powered aircraft that would take them to different places over the continent to conduct their detailed exploration. After assembly, Jad and Bent had helped Case put the dozer blade on one of the runabouts which he used to scrape and smooth a runway out of the desert, and Jad glanced briefly down the runway, admiring Case's work.

But Jad's real focus was the gorge, not the runway or the desert. He'd flown with Wila many times before. She loved to fly and had been flying since she was old enough to see over the cramped control panel in front of the pilot's seat. She owned a special one-seat aerodyne with an enlarged fuel tank and a wing and fuselage-mounted reaction control system that allowed her to take it to the edge of space where the air was too thin for aerodynamic control. She used it as a platform to make the planetary observations she enjoyed without interference by the planet's atmosphere. As an astronomer, Jad appreciated her use of the aerodyne that way, but he never liked letting her fly that high alone. He was always irritated when she dismissed his concerns with a curt, "Don't worry, I'll be all right."

Next Wila activated the fission reactor that was the heart of the rocket engine, and when she was ready she pointed to Case, standing with the others to the side of the runway. He held one hand up, palm toward her in a "hold" signal. He made one last check to be sure no one stood near the rocket exhaust, then with his right hand he pointed directly to her — the "go" signal.

"*Explorer*, this is Aero Two, do you confirm reception?" Wila asked Jer in the Communications Station on Deck 2 near the top of *Explorer*.

"Confirmed, Aero Two, reception good, carrier signal optimum."

"Affirmative, *Explorer*. All codes are blue. Starting engine."

Wila engaged the fuel pump and a muffled whine came from below the passenger compartment. She paused a nanosector for the pump to stabilize, and then touched the marker **ENGINE START** on the central com screen. Instantly from the rocket exhaust bell at the lower rear of the ship came an earsplitting scream of squealing treble and thundering bass as the ultracold liquid hydrogen fuel hit the hot reactor and expanded violently rearward. Even inside the aerodyne and insulated from the greatest part of the noise, Jad winced at the deafening blast.

"I hate that noise," Lilea muttered. Jad glanced over his shoulder to see her cup her hands over her ears.

I don't blame you.

"Okay," Wila said. "All codes are blue. Here we go."

She reached forward and moved the throttle bar on the Engine Power Dynamics screen to **CLIMB 1**. The engine roar intensified and the aerodyne began a cautious slide down the runway. The ship's titanium landing skids grated and squealed as the ship slid over the rock that made up the southern-most end of the runway, but when it hit the dirt part of the runway it picked up speed, zipping smoothly north. Wila pulled back slightly on the joystick at her right hand and the ship left the ground. She hit **CLIMB 2**, and the ship jerked forward and shot upward at a 50-degree angle. At two hundred links she retracted the skids.

She put the ship on a southwest heading and reduced the throttle by two set points to the **CRUISE** setting. The noise level inside the aerodyne dropped to a mild hum.

Much better.

"Okay, everyone," Wila said. "You can relax the chest restraints if you want, but keep the seat belts. And break out the jell juice. It's in the right cooler in back."

Time Element 461.19.3.8.

Wila held the flight to one anthan. "I want to take a look at the terrain between here and the gorge," she said as she looked out the window to her left.

Jad, like Bent and Lilea behind him, also scanned the surface. Below Aero Two stretched the forest, a heavy, closed forest, the same forest that encircled Site One. It ran unabated under the ship, a smooth carpet of dark green. Here and there a dusty tan area, devoid of larger vegetation would occasionally appear, and Jad mentally evaluated each space as a potential emergency landing site. SpaceComm required everyone during all flights to keep a close watch on the ground for possible emergency landing sites, but the only areas Jad saw were invariably either too small or too rocky and rugged for an aerodyne to make a forced landing. Occasionally, a larger space would emerge, long enough for an urgent landing, but so rocky or hilly as to make a safe touchdown dangerous, if not impossible.

The probability of an emergency occurring in one of these newly assembled and checked-out aerodynes was small, of course, but it wasn't zero, and the lack of a suitable space troubled Jad as he scanned the ground below. To take his mind away from the disturbing terrain, he decided to change the subject.

"I went out and watched the sun come up," Jad said, still gazing out the window. "It can be as spectacular as the sunset."

"The sunrise?" Lilea leaned forward in her seat.

"Yeah. The colors. You should see it once."

Lilea didn't respond and Jad said nothing further. He continued to stare out the window, admiring the terrain below, yet still troubled by the lack of emergency sites.

After about a half-subsector, the green forest gave way to an artist's palette of warm color. Vibrant reds, brilliant whites, vivid tans, and rusty browns danced in the sun's radiance. Behind Jad, the faint *bzzzt*-click of Lilea's camera as she took image after image of the striking terrain was the only sound to keep him grounded in his Anthanian world. He wasn't conscious of the noise of the engine, ensconced as he was in otherworldly hues. Within another millisector the ship was above a river, nestled in a small canyon where it entered from the southeast the larger river that ran through the gorge. Wila brought the ship to five thousand links and began to cruise parallel to the south rim of the gorge.

"Oh, my god, will you look at that!" Wila said, as the gorge opened up beside the ship.

"Look at those colors," Jad said. "The images from the probe didn't show anything like this at all."

The gorge was spread before them in all its magnificence. They could see clearly the cliffs, temples, terraces, and stepped canyon walls that gave it its unique appearance. Prominences and promontories reared their rocky heads above the surrounding terrain. Deep in the canyon the river, a pale bronze ribbon, curved restlessly through the bottom, erupting into white here and there for almost no reason at all. The sun, near the midpoint of the lightime, illuminated the canyon walls with a brilliance that seemed to pull color from the interior, silencing everyone in the ship. But no one could stay quiet for long.

"All those reds and browns," Bent said. "I had no idea from the simulations that the gorge would have such intense color. There's so many different shades of red I can't even count them. There's a lot of green down there too, that must be vegetation. We never saw anything like that in the simulations. And huge . . ."

Wila circled the gorge a second time and the ship turned quiet, the only sound the dull roar of the rocket exhaust and the click of Lilea's camera as she took more images out her window. Jad watched the passing landscape, fascinated by the variety of terrain, by the colors, and by the immensity of the opening, almost not hearing when Wila announced she was ready to land.

"Chest restraints." Wila'd returned to the eastern end of the gorge and throttled back. She extended the skids, and after a smooth approach from the east, gently set the aerodyne down in a dusty open area about one by three anthans near the southern edge. Much more small vegetation than Jad would have liked dotted the area, and the site was rockier than he anticipated, but the aerodyne slid effortlessly for almost a thousand links, drifting to a stop near the center of the opening, several hundred links from the rim.

"We're here," Wila said, and three doors opened.

Time Element 461.19.5.6.

Lilea opened the door to her right and dropped to the ground. Warm air washed over her. *My gosh, it must be 30 Tal.* On the left side of the ship, Bent didn't stop to consider the temperature. He grabbed his daypack and took off at a brisk walk around the front of the aerodyne toward the canyon edge. Lilea watched, annoyed that he would walk away without waiting for the others. Then she heard Wila contact Jer to inform her they'd landed.

Wila finished engine shutdown and joined Jad and Lilea as they started out for the southern edge, following Bent. They found him standing at the edge of a precipice of more than a thousand links.

"It just begins without any warning," Lilea said as she approached the edge. "This is so much steeper than the Taksumos Gorge back home."

They stood at the edge for several microsectors before anyone spoke further. Lilea studied briefly the distant northern edge with her camera, and then dipped the view below the rim to scan the bottom. She swept the camera right and left, up and down, taking in large panoramic views. She imaged several animals inside the gorge, all well below the rim. She also captured one large, deep golden-brown flying creature, circling below the rim. After a few microsectors, she lowered the camera.

She stared out over the canyon toward the northern edge, more than an anthan away, visible in the haze of the distance. She looked into the bright blue sky and then swept her gaze fully around the point where she and the others stood at the edge of the chasm. She felt like a stranger in this magnificent land — plucked from her safe homeland to travel to this planet and explore its commanding elegance. Standing at the edge of this vast canyon brought a detachment, a reclusiveness. She wasn't here as an explorer, she was here as a visitor, merely to record and describe what she saw and heard and felt and did. The act of visiting brought with it a sense of isolation, of remoteness. She turned and looked south. There was the aerodyne, the shiny silver bird parked on the plain several hundred links from the edge. It was a reassuring sight, though in this desert region it seemed somewhat out of place. With its long, straight, glider-like wings and upswept tail, and the rounded nose that contained so many instruments and control electronics, it was a symbol of presence — it marked her place in the schedule of events. She was here — she was really here. She turned back and looked north.

As she stood on the rim, she made a mental comparison of Anthanos with this planet. Her home failed in the contrast. *Compared to this planet, ours is so empty and barren. It's just one big desert, except for the ice on the dark side.*

She went over in her mind what she'd learned about the Blue Planet — the zillions of facts and figures that were thrown at her during training, the thousands of probe images she'd had to examine.

Nothing like this existed on Anthanos. The Taksumos Gorge of which she spoke earlier was little more than a rift in the sand on the hot side of her planet, several hundred anthans long but only a few hundred links deep. What did her planet have that rivaled this? This gorge was so spectacular, the view from the rim so breathtaking, the expanse in which it lay so magnificent it defied imagination. As she looked out over the abyss, sending as much as she could to long-term memory, one mundane facet of her presence here intruded into her mind and the feeling of isolation dissipated.

She and the others had been asked by SpaceComm to give a simple recommendation in their final report after their return home. Would they suggest that a second expedition be sent to continue the evaluation of this planet? Or did they feel the planet wasn't suitable for colonization and that exploration should end with this trip? They weren't required to say anything, but SpaceComm would pass their opinion on to The Assembly who would make the final decision. If asked now, she'd give a resounding "Yes," but 480 T-sectors remained before they were scheduled to leave and things could change. As she thought about that for a few nanosectors she became aware of Jad and Bent jabbering about the formation of the gorge.

"I'm not so sure," Bent said. "That doesn't quite fit. There must have been something else going on. Water isn't going to be able to wear down rock like that by itself. It must have had help somehow."

"That's true, but I suspect that the river—"

Wila intervened, cutting off Jad. "I hate to break up this interesting discussion but we need to set up camp. You know the rules: set up camp and secure the area."

As pilot of the transport that brought them to the gorge, Wila had the right to claim the position as leader of this little expedition. But as Bent conceived and planned the expedition in the first place, that made him the nominal leader. Under Wila's prodding, Lilea reluctantly followed the others to the aerodyne, though Bent lingered at the rim another microsector.

They erected the inflatable hemispherical shelter on the south side of the aerodyne just behind the left wingtip. The entrance faced south, and a power cable ran from an outlet on the side of the aerodyne. A small monitoring computer sat on the floor at the rear of the shelter between the vents from the inflating fans. Bent and Jad set up the tall whip-like omni-directional emergency antenna behind the shelter, and placed the four substations of the intruder alert system to surround the ship and shelter in a rectangle of security. Articles of scientific equipment were brought from the ship and the camp was complete.

"We're going to take a walk around to scout the site," Wila told Lilea and Bent. "We'll start south and work our way all around the area."

SpaceComm was adamant: a full sweep of every campsite before any real exploration could begin—security was essential. As the sun—just past the midpoint in its daily travel—sizzled in the sky, Jad and Wila headed south from the shelter.

"I'm going back up to the rim and look for a way down into the gorge," Bent said.

"All right." Lilea grabbed her camera and caught up with him. Bent's fascination with the gorge had become almost legendary among the members of the team. Ever since he first saw it on the probe images he wanted to get down into it, and he argued fervently to place this expedition on the Expedition Planning Calendar when it was drawn up on Anthanos. Of all the sites on the planet, he explained, this is the most significant. If we can get down into it, it will give us a vast amount of information about the planet's early history, a history we would have trouble getting otherwise. It would be like, as he put it, taking an elevator downward into the past history of the planet. SpaceComm understood his enthusiasm and placed it first on the Calendar. Now he had to find a way down.

CHAPTER 7

THE GORGE – VISITORS

Time Element 461.19.9.7.

Lilea took more images as she stood on the rim of the gorge, but spent most of her time scanning the canyon with her vision aid, trying to imagine intelligent beings living in this rugged wilderness. She'd begun to think of the gorge more as a geological curiosity rather than a dwelling place for intelligent life—not so much an apartment building as a tourist attraction. Life would be too rugged around here, the terrain too rocky, the atmosphere too intense. The relative lack of water would make habitation here difficult, except perhaps at the bottom of the canyon. But the infrared thermal imager on her vision aid told her the air temperature near the river was well over 35 Tal, and that seemed to rule out anyone residing at the bottom. But as for living near the edge, in or within the nearby forest, well, that was a different matter. Intelligent species might live here.

She and Bent stayed at the edge for a subsector, scouting the western end of the landing site.

When Jad and Wila returned, Lilea and Bent had the third meal of the lightime ready—prepared in the open air on a small portable stove. They brought out several small stools and sat in a semicircle outside the shelter entrance, enjoying this, their first hot meal away from Site One. The cool southwesterly breeze made for a delightful ambience.

As they ate, a small cloud of dust appeared on the horizon, southeast of the camp site, near the edge of the forest. It grew larger and seemed to be approaching. Lilea poked Bent.

"What's that?"

"I don't know."

They watched as the cloud grew, drawing nearer. From within the cloud came a low throbbing or drumming. At the front of the cloud, five or six four-legged animals with dark, prominent horns galloped across the plain. Their brown and white coloration blended closely with the tan of the ground, and they were almost invisible until they got closer to camp.

Unusual projections on the tops of their heads . . . back-curved at the tip . . .

pointed at front . . . I wonder what they're used for? Bent and Jad drew their weapons as the animals passed within three hundred links of the camp, but Lilea dashed inside the shelter to grab her camera. She arrived outside just in time to record the animals as they sprinted away. Wila edged closer to Jad.

"What's making them run?" Jad said as the animals entered the forest.

"They may have been chased by a predator," Lilea said. "Did anyone see anything following them?"

Bent holstered his weapon, though Jad kept his in his hand. Jad's face seemed paler than usual, and he couldn't keep his hand still, fidgeting constantly with his weapon.

Lilea's first thought was about hunters — intelligent beings that might inhabit the area, and she entertained a fleeting idea she might have a chance to meet them. *So soon after arriving. Wouldn't that be something?* Her heart pitter-patted at the prospect.

"I didn't see anything," Jad said. "But with all the dust, maybe that's one of their evasion strategies — kick up so much dust that a predator can't see them, and they can . . ." He paused, squinting at the cloud of dust still hanging in the air.

Lilea turned toward him. "Can what?"

". . . get away."

She turned back toward the dust cloud. Out of the dust came a different kind of four-legged animal, trotting directly toward the camp. Much shorter than the others, only about two links tall at the shoulder, with sandy-gray fur and a bushy tail that hung almost to the ground. Its head was down, and with a face that ended in a long snout tipped by what Lilea took to be a nose, it seemed to be sniffing the ground as it trotted. When it raised its head and saw the camp, its ears flicked up and it stopped immediately. It whiffed the air as though to find out who these visitors to its home turf were. It reminded Lilea of an extinct predatory animal from Anthanian prehistory. But it was almost certainly the reason the other animals had galloped past the camp.

The animal stood still about two hundred links away, staring at the team, and the team stared back. It seemed curious about them, yet a little wary, as they grew more curious about it.

"Everyone stay quiet," Lilea whispered. "Don't startle it. I want to get an image." As soon as she raised her camera to begin recording, she heard Bent say, "No! Don't shoot," and immediately came the unmistakable pop and hiss of an electronic weapon discharge.

"No, don't," Bent said again, a little louder.

"What?" Lilea jerked the camera down. "Jad, what did you do?" She spoke in a coarse whisper, hoping to avoid scaring the animal.

Jad's weapon, as required by SpaceComm, was set on level 1, the lowest setting, and he'd deliberately fired slightly to one side. The electron beam splattered harmlessly in the dust beside the animal, but it seemed to know it was being shot at. It tensed its body, lurching to its right, splaying its feet farther apart, and it whipped its head around to the left to check where the beam hit. But it didn't run. It held its body rigid, next glancing quickly to the right as if to gauge the distance to the safety of the forest.

"Don't shoot anymore." Lilea raised her voice slightly this time. She wasn't angry at Jad, she only wanted to make sure he heard her. "He doesn't look like a danger to us. I just want to get a recording."

"Shoot, Jad," Wila said. "Shoot at him again. He could be dangerous. We have to be careful."

The animal held its ground.

"No—don't." Bent and Lilea spoke almost in unison. Lilea took several steps from behind Jad and crept over to Bent, keeping him between her and the animal. "Let me get an image of him." She raised her camera again, and then walked out from behind Bent toward the animal.

"Lanie—wait. Where are you going?"

"I want to get a close-up." Her voice was cool and matter-of-fact, her eagerness overwhelming any sense of danger. She crept closer, step by step, crouched somewhat to reduce her overall profile. The animal glanced again toward the forest, but didn't move.

"Use the telephoto. Don't go any farther. Lanie—watch out. He could be—"

"Lilea, come back," Wila yelled after her. "This is dangerous. Case will be upset."

The animal held its ground, ears still perked up, staring at Lilea as she approached. She crept to within about a hundred links, and then slowly dropped to a squat to bring the camera to its level. Through the telephoto lens at 25X magnification, the animal's grayish-brown eyes stared directly at her. They flipped now and then to the right or left, apparently checking everything going on around it.

Hmm, binocular vision – he's probably a predator.

Lilea didn't detect any fear in those eyes, they seemed to reflect only curiosity or wariness. But the animal watched her carefully, occasionally sniffing the air or the ground. Now and then it would emit a low growl or bare its teeth.

After a few nanosectors, Lilea cautiously stood, aware for the first time of Bent standing behind her, his weapon ready. But even though she tried to stand slowly and quietly to avoid startling the animal, it turned and scampered back toward the forest, its tail tucked between its legs. After it disappeared, she lowered the camera.

"Why did you shoot at him?" she asked Jad as they returned. "He wasn't any danger to us."

"I wasn't trying to kill him, I just wanted to scare him." Jad holstered his weapon, then returned to his seat and picked up his plate of food.

I hope Jad isn't going to shoot at every animal we encounter. Lilea understood Jad's concern about the danger the animal could present, but she was a little peeved that he might have scared it away before she could finish studying it. She wanted to try and get more close-up shots before leaving it alone. That animal certainly could have been the most intelligent creature on the planet, and she didn't want Jad's careless shooting to ruin her attempts to communicate with it. Especially not in the future.

"Jad, you know the regs," Bent said, his voice quiet, not demanding. "No excessive use of force."

"That wasn't excessive. I just wanted to scare him. I didn't want him coming any closer." Jad didn't look at Bent. He continued to eat.

"I think he did the right thing," Wila said, nodding her head. "It could have been a dangerous animal. Better safe than sorry." Then her eyes narrowed and her face turned to a scowl as she glared at Lilea, perhaps ready to shake a finger at her. "Lilea, you took an awful risk. He could have attacked. When Case finds out, he's —"

"I still had my weapon," Lilea replied, and Wila said nothing else. Lilea turned back to Bent. "Trea is going to be excited to see these images," she said, then lowered her voice. "But she's going to be pissed to hear that Jad shot at it." She too sat down and finished her meal.

They were treated to a spectacular sunset this lightime.

CHAPTER 8

JAD

Time Element 461.20.11.5.

The mellow aroma of zlotcake simmering in a pan, the pungent scent of warm jell-kell juice, both part of the traditional Anthanian lumyon, drifted through the shelter, swirling its way to Lilea's side over and around the curtains that separated the sleeping areas. Lilea sat up in her sleeping bag, rubbed her eyes, yawned, and stretched. Bent lay asleep beside her in their section of the shelter. A small red lamp near her sleeping bag gave just enough illumination that when her eyes adjusted to the dimness she could see general shapes and discern broad movements in their sleeping area, though it wasn't bright enough to see detail. The faint red light kept away "the demons of the dark," her description of her fear of total darkness, her fear of being isolated in a confined, darkened space.

Lilea's fear of the dark wasn't a disabling fear, not enough to keep her off the Gold Team. Rather, it was like a subtle terror that invaded her mind and clutched at her chest if she ever encountered a darkened place. Many on Anthanos had a similar fear. Light was so much a constant factor of life on their planet that many Anthanians, accustomed to the permanence of the sunlight, became wary of the dark, especially the deep darkness of a room without any light at all. In Lilea's bedroom in their house on Anthanos, the windows were covered with vertical shutters which blocked most of the light, though some still leaked around the edges. That gave enough illumination she could still make out objects as dark masses in the room. That was enough to let her sleep comfortably.

"I'm going outside and watch the sunrise," she heard Jad say. A nanosector later came the *whiiisssp* of the zipper as Jad opened the shelter's front door and stepped into the clear plastic airlock that surrounded the front door. Then he re-zipped the door and she heard the muffled sound of the zipper around the outer door as Jad stepped outside.

Normally a late riser, even on Anthanos where she could program light, easy music to awaken herself near the beginning of an odd-numbered T-sector, Lilea decided she had to see this new phenomenon. Like most on the team, she assumed the sun just made its appearance in the sky and that was that—no color, no display, nothing unusual. But Jad's comments during the flight to the gorge and his decision to rise early and go out in the cool morning air to watch the sunrise had so aroused her curiosity that she forced herself out of her sleeping bag. She switched the lamp from red to white light and slipped into her jumpsuit, jacket and boots, and joined Jad outside the shelter looking east. Bent continued to breathe heavily in his sleeping bag, a good indication he remained asleep.

She checked the temperature recorder at the shelter's entrance. "Eight Tal,"

Jad stood away from the shelter, just inside the intruder alert field near the tail of the aerodyne. "The colors aren't as good this sunrise." His voice was calm and monotonous. "No clouds in the sky to reflect the light."

Lilea didn't respond. She fastened her jacket tightly against the cool air and plunged her hands into her pockets. She watched the red sun make its way over the forest in the east, turning orange, then yellow as it rose further. She tried to concentrate on the developing sunrise, but she found it so less enthralling than Jad that her mind drifted to other things. She went over the schedule of exploration for this lightime. They'd decided to hike the trail they'd found the lightime before. Several secondary trails split off the main trail, but the primary route seemed to lead to a plateau below, several thousand links below the edge. Jad and Bent decided to rappel down the edge of the plateau to whatever lay below. It wasn't the trail to the bottom Bent was looking for, but it would allow them to enter the gorge and give them a chance to see into the geological past, and, she hoped, find clues to previous civilizations. The next lightime they would return to Site One.

But as she lingered outside the shelter's airlock trying to contemplate the rising sun, her attention was drawn more and more to Jad. He stood quietly about twenty links away, staring directly into the sun through dark glasses, his arms folded across his chest, his feet spread about a link apart.

He looks a lot like Case, standing like that. Though at almost seven links tall, Jad's lanky profile was so much leaner than the muscular Case.

Of all the others on the landing team, Jad had always been the most difficult to read. By that very fact she found him intriguing, yet was so often stymied trying to learn more about him. She knew only a few odd facts about his public life. He was the Anthanian who—at age twenty-two, no less—made the seminal observation that led to the identification of the graviton particle. That, in turn, led to the antigraviton drive of the Command Ship, *Star Voyager*, the ship that brought them here from their home, thirty-five light-years distant. He also spent several years in SpaceComm's Planetary Visualization Division where he was the first to view the Blue Planet.

More than anyone else on the team, Jad kept his personal life secure. He spoke to Lilea only when she tried to engage him in conversation, and seldom made eye contact even when he did. One of the few things she knew for certain about him was that he loved to run. She'd seen him from one of the windows in her compartment as he jogged up and down the runway at Site One. Over three thousand links, out and back, several times. Athletically, he was in top shape, but he rarely ran with a partner other than Wila, and since Wila ran only infrequently, Jad usually jogged alone.

As she stood watching him, she wondered what he was thinking. About the sun, certainly, but she didn't understand how anyone could find the sun that interesting.

Enough already. The chill in the air and the grumbling in her tummy finally persuaded her to return to her section of the shelter and fix lumyon. Jad's fascination with the sunrise was another manifestation of his inscrutable personality, and she gave up trying to understand him.

Time Element 461.21.5.1.

"Jad! Oh, my god, Jad! What's the matter?" Wila screamed as Jad sank to his knees.

Jad and Wila had gone no more than twenty paces from the trailhead on their way back to the shelter, but Jad was breathing rapidly and sweating profusely. His head swum, his heart pounded, and his legs wouldn't hold him up. An overwhelming thirst parched his throat and he wanted to take a drink from the water bottle in his daypack, but he couldn't make his arms reach around to slip the pack off. He grew weaker and weaker.

"Jad! Can you hear me? Are you all right?"

"Can you get my water bottle?" Squatting on his hands and knees, Jad's voice had turned quivery and shaky.

"Oh, my god, yes!" Wila pulled out the water bottle and handed it to him. "Can you drink? Are you going to be okay?"

Jad turned over and sat on the ground. He faced into the sun to keep the heat off the back of his neck. He took a small drink of water. "Get my towel, too."

Wila pulled his towel from the pack and draped it over his head and neck, shielding them from the hot sun.

"Drink some more water. I'm going to get Bent and Lilea."

"Don't bother them. I'll be all right."

"'Don't bother them?' Are you crazy? You may need help. I'm going to get them. Stay here." Wila took off for the trail at a dead run.

Stay here? Tell me, where am I going?

Jad was in trouble—this was heat exhaustion. He knew the signs and symptoms. He'd just taken his first drink of water since the lumyon almost four subsectors earlier. All that rappelling he'd done, down the side of the plateau almost one thousand links into the heat of the lower gorge without staying properly hydrated. There wasn't any shade down there, and he didn't take a drink of water the whole time he was down. Bent drank from his water bottle every now and then, but Jad didn't. He didn't feel thirsty, and with the warm weather, much like Anthanos, he was sure he didn't need a drink.

Hell, I don't drink that much at home. Why should I here? Except after jogging. Well, yeah.

Images of the rappel flashed through his mind. *At least Bent and I got a lot of good specimens. I remember how heavy the bag was. Lilea told me some of them had fossils in them. I thought they might be interesting.*

He stayed quiet in the sun, continuing to sip water from his bottle. His thoughts turned to how this incident will be received at Site One. *Dell won't say much.* Dell, the team's space surgeon, wasn't the type to yell. His calm, professional demeanor always impressed Jad. *But Case is going to be pissed.*

With his head bowed and the towel covering his head and neck, he felt better. At least he wasn't so dizzy and nauseated anymore. He drank some more water, a mouthful at a time, and it seemed to help settle his stomach. Wila would take several microsectors to find Lilea and Bent on the trail, and they would take several more to get back to him—but he was suddenly aware of Bent's voice. It seemed far away, and in his dizziness he could barely make out what Bent was saying.

"Are you okay?" Bent knelt beside Jad and put a hand on his back.

"Yes, yes. I'll be okay. I was just a little exhausted." Even Jad could hear the trembling in his voice.

"Exhausted, I'll bet. Heat exhaustion. I've seen this on the hot side at home. People don't realize how much water they lose out in the hot sun."

"Can you walk back to the shelter?" Wila knelt in front of him, her arms on his shoulders, and Jad felt her shadow covering the towel shading his head. He heard Lilea join them.

"In a little bit." His voice was still quivering and shaky.

"We need to get you back to the shelter," Bent said. "We can't do much more this T-sector — it's too hot. Do you have any water left?"

"Yeah, some. I'm okay. I'll be all right." Jad took another drink of water. He showed them his water bottle, half empty.

"The shelter's a half-anthan away," Wila said. "Can you walk back?"

Jad paused, nausea rising and subsiding in his throat. "Yes, I think I can."

"Drink some more water."

"I . . . I don't need any more."

Jad's hands shook noticeably and he still felt faint and shaky as Bent helped him slowly regain his feet. But the nausea had not completely subsided, and as he stood the water tumbled out of his stomach in a sudden, gurgling rush.

"Uh-oh," Bent said. "He's gonna get even more dehydrated. Let's get back to the shelter. He needs to lie down."

They started for the campsite and the coolness of the shelter. Jad kept the towel over his head and neck, walking slowly with his head down, almost shuffling. Wila stayed to Jad's left holding his hand, and Lilea walked on the other side, carrying Jad's and her own daypack.

"I'm going back and put the cover back on the rappelling motor and power supply," Bent said. "I'll be right back."

"Okay. Hurry back."

Jad had to stop and rest twice during the walk back to the shelter — once dropping to his knees — but the cool air was a welcome relief. It felt almost frigid. He collapsed on his sleeping bag and fell asleep, but before he drifted off, he heard Wila say she was going out to the aerodyne and contact Jer

Uh-oh. Cuse is gonna be pissed.

CHAPTER 9

CLOUD MASS

Time Element 461.23.4.0.

Aero Two jumped easily into the air and Wila banked 180 degrees right, out over the gorge. She leveled off at two anthans.

"Okay, you can relax the chest restraints," she said, "but keep the seat belts." She contacted Jer at Site One. "*Explorer*, this is Aero Two. We've just lifted off the surface at the gorge and we're on our way home. Estimate six millisectors flying time."

"Understood, Aero Two," Jer replied. "Do you need a vector?"

"Negative, *Explorer*. We'll fly by heading from here."

"Okay, Aero Two, we'll be waiting for you. We're not going any-where."

Lilea unhooked her chest restraint and relaxed for the trip home. She leaned forward in her seat and gazed through the window to her right. They were above the brilliantly colored terrain again, and the reds seemed particularly intense in the mid-lightime sun. Even the whites reflected the sunlight more brilliantly. She found particularly compelling the way the various shades of red were layered through the terrain, laid down by some unknown mechanism.

Bent might have an idea how that came to be. I'll let him explain it.

Beneath the sands on Anthanos, she'd seen similar layering, but on a much reduced scale because Anthanos didn't have the wind and water-weathered terrain of this planet. Artifacts of early Anthanians could some-times be found in these layers, and the same might be true here. She also wondered if the colors indicated specific compounds that intelligent natives might use as pigments, perhaps in their pottery. As she briefly considered asking Case to allow her to schedule a trip to the area to look for signs of intelligent life, she became aware that Wila was jabbering about something.

"What's that?" Wila pointed to a line of dark clouds about forty degrees left of the ship. "Is that what the water coming from the clouds looks like from a distance?"

"It might be," Jad said.

"That does look like what I saw," Lilea said, a hesitation in her voice. "I remember the gray haze like that."

"Let's take a look at it." Wila turned and looked at Jad.

The cabin stayed quiet for about a nanosector, when Jad turned to Bent and Lilea in the middle seats. "What do you think? Want to take a look?"

"Okay," Bent said, but there was an uncertainty in his voice, too. "But be careful."

Lilea continued to stare at the clouds and pulled out of memory images of the water drops pelting her in the face as she ran toward *Explorer*. The cold, clammy feeling of her soaked jumpsuit had sent her body into shivers, and she struggled to maintain her composure as she ran. But more importantly, and perhaps more than the others who'd remained high and dry inside *Explorer*, she understood the potential in that little shower. The wind had blown the water directly into her face as she ran, and she wondered as she stared at the clouds out the window of the aerodyne how much more powerful a larger storm could be. But what scared her even more was not that this was simply a larger version of that little storm, this was broad band of ominous dark gray clouds that stretched most of the way across the horizon and jutted god-knows-how far into the sky, and it frightened her.

"I'm not sure I like that idea," she said. "It could be dangerous." But Wila either didn't hear or chose to ignore her, and the other two seemed ready to jump right in.

"*Explorer*, this is Aero Two," Wila said on comm. "We're going to investigate some dark clouds several anthans to our left. This should divert us for three or four millisectors. I'll notify you when we're back on course for landing. We may need a vector."

"Okay, Aero Two," Jer said. "Let me know when you're ready to return. Be careful."

Time Element 461.23.4.1.

"I've set the ITS." Wila touched the marker **INERTIAL TRACKING SYSTEM** on the main com screen. She banked left and headed directly for the clouds. Nothing seemed to be out of the ordinary until the aerodyne got within one anthan of the main storm front when drops of water began splattering the windshield.

"That's just what it looked like before," Lilea exclaimed. "Just like that—" From below something threw the ship upward.

"What was that?" Wila lowered the nose of the ship.

"Probably a strong air movement," Jad said.

More gusts buffeted the aerodyne and the splattering from the water increased, pelting the ship in a metallic rat-a-tat.

"I can't see anything," Wila said. "Maybe we should divert—" But before she could finish, a large gust of wind hit the ship from below and lifted it upward again. "My god! What the hell is going on?" Another gust hit the ship on the right side and swung the right wing upward.

"Wila—turn around and get outta here," Lilea said. Her hands were cold and clammy and drops of perspiration had begun to form on her forehead.

Wila corrected the roll, but the wind continued to buffet the ship, knocking it from side to side, up and down. The ship yawed and rolled in large swinging arcs, and Wila struggled against the heavy gusts to maintain control. The ship hurtled closer to the clouds.

"Let's get out of here," Jad said.

"I can't control it!" Wila yelled back. "Every time I try to turn the ship gets caught—"

The ship was now totally engulfed by darkness and visibility outside was zero. Torrents of water splashed over the ship, and Lilea's chest tightened and her heart rate shot up. "What the hell." She looked all around but saw nothing but the gray of the cloud interior. "Wila—where are we?"

Heavy bursts of wind slapped the ship around too much for Wila to control, and backpacks and any other equipment not held down bounced around inside the cabin. Lilea placed one foot on the tripod attached to her tricolor theodolite, holding it securely to the floor. At 5000 monetary units, it was the most expensive piece of equipment she owned, and even though it was issued to her by SpaceComm and the only one in existence, she participated in its design, and that made it, in her eyes at least, worth far more.

"Watch the attitude indicator," Jad said. "Keep the nose up."

"I can't! It keeps getting knocked around."

Red codes began to appear on the main com screen—first one, then several at once—and a double-bong alarm reverberated through the cabin. Without warning, the altimeter reading on the screen dropped to all zeros and went flashing yellow. Lilea gasped. The double alarm became a triple.

"Pull up! Pull up!" Jad yelled.

Wila pulled back on the joystick at her right hand and the nose of the ship shot upward almost vertically. As she pushed forward on the stick, a high-pitched tremulous squeal, like a siren, pierced the cabin above the alarm.

"The wings are stalling!" Jad yelled. "We need to get outta here."

"Com control is out," Wila yelled back. She flipped a small switch on the panel in front of her seat, and a blue light marked **HYDRAULICS** came on. She pushed forward on the control stick, but the nose dropped only slightly. "I can't get the nose down."

With both hands, Jad grabbed the stick around Wila's hand and helped her push it as far forward as it would go, forcing the ship into a steep right bank. The squeal stopped but the bongs continued.

Jad continued to hold the control stick with both hands clamped over Wila's right hand—now as much in control of the ship as she. The attitude indicator above the com screen spun like a toy top in its housing, and the magnetic compass readings on the screen changed so rapidly they too became useless. That caused them to turn yellow and the alarm just got louder.

"We've lost compass headings!" Jad yelled. "We've gotta get out of here." He pushed the throttle forward to **CLIMB 2**, pushing the engine almost to maximum, but kept one hand tightly secured over Wila's, holding the ship upright and level against the winds.

As abruptly as it had come on, the shower slackened and the ship slipped out of the clouds. The turbulence was gone. The craft flew fast and straight, and Lilea glanced at the ground below and estimated they were flying at about five thousand links. Visibility was good, but now, to visitors from another planet and unfamiliar with the terrain, a big problem glared back at them. A vast, rugged desert spread in all directions, and no landmarks existed they could identify. Jad removed his hands from Wila's and she throttled back to **CRUISE**. He tapped **ALARM SILENCE** on the main screen, and then tried voice communications.

Time Element 461.23.4.5.

"*Explorer*, this is Aero Two. Jer, can you give us a vector?" Jad paused for several nanosectors, but Jer didn't reply.

Lilea released her chest straps and leaned forward. She stuck her head between the two front seats and listened carefully to comm.

"Jer, do you read us?" Jad said again, but received nothing but silence.

He tried again. "*Explorer*, this is Aero Two. Do you receive our transmission?"

Still no response. Jad checked the computer screen for comm parameters, but most markers were flashing yellow. He shook his head. "Voice comm isn't working. I bet it was damaged in all that water. Everybody look around and see if you see anything you recognize."

"Jad—"

Lilea raised her head, startled by Wila's shaky voice. She'd been so engrossed in the com screen she hadn't looked through the forward window for almost a microsector.

"What?" Jad looked up. A curtain of deep gray clouds stretched fully across the horizon directly ahead. "Oh, crap."

"All these clouds." Wila pointed ahead. "We're headed into more of the storms. I'm going to have to go right."

"Right, right—go right—go right." Wila put Aero Two into a tight bank, coming around almost 150 degrees. Directly ahead of them lay a narrow strip of sunlit desert, but the ship itself remained in shade, and dark shadows obscured the ground below. The storm extended almost all around them, threatening to engulf them in a dark, monstrous hand. An unnerving flickering of light came from within the clouds.

They flew in the same direction for several microsectors, but the terrain remained unfamiliar. The sinuous channel of an unknown river passed below. Even after three more microsectors nothing recognizable appeared.

Where are we?

Lilea's heart beat faster as she scanned the terrain below, looking desperately for something she recognized. But all she saw was a montage of unfamiliar forest, desert, rivers, canyons, cliffs, and elevated plateaus. It looked so strange, though if she could only look at the probe atlas she might recognize the area, and plot a route out of here. Bent had stashed a probe atlas, made from images from the probe, in his duffel in the cargo hold, but out of reach from the aerodyne's cabin. *Little good that'll do us now.* Then she had an idea.

"What about PersComm?" She pulled hers from its pocket.

"It probably won't work," Jad replied. "PersComm transmissions have to go through the aerodyne's comm system, and that's out. Besides, if Jer gave us a vector, I don't think the computer could display it. The ITS is dead. We'll have to get back on our own."

Get back on our own? How? Comm's out, ITS is gone, flight parameters dead. What can we do ourselves? A trace of panic pushed into Lilea's mind and tightened her chest, but she resisted and forced herself to look out the window. She jammed her PersComm back in her left thigh pocket and joined the others in scanning the terrain below. The cabin remained quiet, the only sound the muffled roar of the engine.

CHAPTER 10

BEACON

Time Element 461.23.4.9.

"We got so turned around in that storm we could be flying north, for all I know," Jad said. "Magnetic compass readings are zero. I can't see anything I recognize at all."

"We're going to have to go higher and circle," Wila said, "and find something we recognize."

Jad shook his head. "That won't work. We're trapped between storms. If we go higher, all we'll see are clouds."

"I'm looking for shadows," Bent said, "but I can't get any feel for where the sun is. I can't tell which direction we're flying."

Large beads of sweat had formed on Lilea's forehead and were beginning to drop onto her nose and cheeks. She kept going over in her mind their situation—no compass headings, no comm, neither transmission nor reception—trying to come up with a solution. *Wait a microsector.* "Jad. What part of comm is out? Reception, transmission, or both?"

Jad pulled up communications parameters on the main computer screen. "Both—wait, no, the carrier signal is still good. How could—? We're still transmitting. But just the carrier. Signal integration is out."

"How is that possible?" Lilea asked.

"The carrier signal is generated in the transmission module," Wila said. "It's in the roof, under the antenna. It may not have been damaged by the water."

"That means they're still receiving us," Bent said. "Maybe if you—"

"Right—let's shut down the comm system," Jad said. "That'll turn the carrier signal off and they'll send out Aero One."

"No, don't!" Lilea blurted out. Jad's comment scared her. The first thing that crossed into her mind was the effect a carrier signal termination would have at Site One. Jad ignored her, reaching forward as though he intended to turn comm off. "No, Jad, no! Don't!" She jerked forward from her seat and grabbed his sleeve, pulling his hand away from the screen.

"Hey!" Jad threw up his arm, almost striking Wila. "What're you doing?!" He pushed Lilea's hand away, but she grabbed back.

"No, Jad, don't do it!"

"Lilea!" Wila yelled. "Stop that! I'm trying to fly this damn—"

"No—Jad, don't—please, don't." Lilea kept one hand on Jad's arm. "If you do that, they'll assume we've crashed. Think about what'll happen at the ship when that alarm goes off. It'll scare them to death. They won't know where to send Aero One."

"There is the emergency beacon . . ." Jad's voice trailed off. He paused, but he did take his hand away from the com screen. He glanced at Wila.

"Lilea, we've got to do something," Wila said, her voice rising and cracking. "We can't keep flying forever. We can't receive a vector, and we can't tell where we are." Her face had turned pale, almost ashen, and the taut look of fear morphed around her eyes.

"We've got to get away from these storms," Bent said. "They're all around us."

Lilea looked left and right. Dark, ominous clouds swirled around them. Only directly ahead was sunlight, but the aerodyne still flew in shadow, and shadows covered the terrain below. The narrow opening of light directly ahead was beginning to close and engulf the ship in a shrinking pocket of calm air. "We're going to have to land. And ride it out."

Time Element 461.23.5.3.

"Land?" Wila said, her voice still agitated. "Lilea, are you out of your mind? If we land, the storms will engulf us and we may never get off the ground."

"The clouds have dropped water on the aerodynes at Site One before, and nothing happened. We can do this. We'll be okay on the ground."

"Lilea, the only time clouds dropped water at Site One were small storms. Nothing like this. And only once since we assembled the aerodynes."

"Where will we put down?" Bent asked. "We're over forest now."

"Back there—behind us. I saw a long area—good enough to land. Then we can activate the emergency homing beacon. It's in the tail. It should be okay. They'll know where to find us from that."

"That beacon has a limited range. How do we know they'll get it?"

"The beacon's okay," Jad said. "I saw that on the screen."

"But how do we know they'll hear it?"

"It's worth a try," Lilea said.

"But we don't know where we are." Anger had pushed Wila's voice louder. She looked over at Jad. "How do we know—we may be too far away."

The cabin turned quiet for a couple of nanosectors before Jad spoke. "Let's try it. Better than flying around using fuel." Wila put Aero Two into a steep left bank, headed back toward the darkest part of the storm.

"There it is." Lilea pointed to an elevated plateau as it came into view a few microsectors later. But at the far end of that plateau, less than an anthan from the area where Wila pointed Aero Two was the storm, and as the ship slid along the dusty surface, a deep thundering blast rippled through the cabin and a heavy splash of water washed over it. Everyone winced.

"Okay," Jad said as the ship drifted to a stop. "I've activated the beacon. Com says it's working. But it'll be a while before they can get to us."

Now the wait began—two, three, four millisectors, while the water and wind buffeted the ship. They heard the thunderous noise again, but muffled. Lightning flashes lit up the sky.

"It's all right," Jad said after a particularly brilliant flash and a loud crash of noise. "Lightning is strictly within clouds. It shouldn't be a threat to us."

"What's causing that noise?" Lilea asked. "It's scary."

"It's related to the lightning," Jad said in a low voice. "Computer simulations of the lightning on the outer planets in our solar system have suggested there should be a loud audio-range blast after each lightning strike, but nobody's ever heard it."

When the downpour tapered and the clouds parted, Jad, Bent and Lilea jumped out of the ship into the chilly, muddy terrain. Puddles of water lay everywhere around the aerodyne, and Lilea estimated the air temperature at around 10 Tal. She'd stuffed a jacket in her duffel in the aerodyne's cargo compartment, but figured Aero One would be here soon enough and decided it wasn't worth the trouble to get it out. The three met near the front.

Aero Two stood headed almost directly into the sun. "We landed west," Jad said. "We were flying east when we turned around."

The group turned quiet, the only sound the gentle whish of a cool breeze from the west. Lilea faced into the wind and inhaled deeply of the chilly air. It relaxed her and dried her forehead.

She scanned the plateau. The landing site was clear, nothing ahead of the ship would interfere with takeoff. They spent most of their time searching the sky, listening for the characteristic sound of an aerodyne engine. But Bent started nosing around, picking up rocks. A few he dropped into his pocket.

"We could pull out the omnidirectional unit," Jad said, still staring at the sky, his voice low and hushed.

"Shouldn't be necessary," Lilea said. "They should be here soon." But a grain of doubt stuck within her mind. She still had no answer to Wila's question about the range of the emergency beacon and it bothered her. She rubbed her hands together in the cool air, trying to take her mind off the situation. Eventually Wila joined them at the front of Aero Two, her face still pale, her eyes congested with fear. They continued to scan the sky, listening in the stillness for Aero One to make its appearance.

Time Element 461.23.6.2.

Most of the puddles had disappeared, evaporated or percolated into the soil, and the surface was nearly dry when, from the left of the ship, came a high, thin, piercing sound mixed with a deep, rumbling bass. Aero One flashed by at about two thousand links and began to circle.

"Thank god," Lilea whispered to Bent.

"Let's go," Jad yelled. "Get in and get off the ground."

They scrambled into the ship, and before Aero One could complete a low pass to scout a landing approach, Wila had energized the fuel pump and the ship jerked forward. Aero One led the way home, but Aero Two landed first on the runway at Site One. Four doors opened almost simultaneously and four weary — and still a little scared — explorers dropped to the ground. Col and Trea waited with one of the runabouts, ready to pull Aero Two into its parking space off the west side of the runway. Aero One dropped onto the runway a microsector later, and Case and Dell jumped out.

"What happened to you guys?" Case said as they walked up the runway. He had a funny look on his face, anger, certainly, but mixed with curiosity and concern. "We got an emergency beacon signal and homed in on that. We thought you'd crashed. Scared the crap out of us."

"No," Jad said, "comm was out, but the carrier signal —" and that's as far as he got. Wila's eyes closed, her face turned pale, and she let out a small whimper. Her knees buckled and she tugged on Jad's arm. Jad caught her on the way down. "What —"

"She's fainted," Case said. He grabbed Wila's arm and gathered her into his arms. "Let's get her into the runabout." He set her on the rear seat of the runabout and put her feet up on the back of the front seat.

"Somebody get some water," Dell said. He grabbed Wila's wrist and felt for a pulse.

Lilea pulled a water bottle from her daypack and splashed a handful of water on Wila's face. She came out of the faint almost immediately, but her eyes stayed glassy and unfocused. "What happened?" she asked and put an embarrassed hand over her face.

"Take it easy," Dell said. "We'll get you back to the ship."

As the others drove Wila up the slight rise to the elevator, Case turned to Bent and Lilea. His usual hard expression had disappeared, replaced by a look of concern bordering on anxiety. He put his hands on his hips, and bore down directly onto Bent and Lilea. "What could have happened that would make Wila faint? I've never heard of her fainting after a flight. She loves to fly. Tell me what happened out there."

Bent shook his head. "It was the flight back."

"What do you mean?"

Bent began. He recounted the return flight, the violent updrafts and downdrafts in the storm, about almost getting enclosed by the line of storms as they flew, about Wila's going to hydraulic control of the flight surfaces, then he and Lilea defended their decision to use the emergency beacon.

"Good god," Case said, several times.

"I was terrified myself," Lilea said. "With all that, is it any wonder she fainted? I'm sure she was scared out of her mind."

"Let's take a look at the ship." Case led them over to Aero Two. He jumped into the left seat and checked the com screen. Wila had shut the engine down, but the reactor remained active, and all systems had power. Most entries on the computer screen were flashing red or yellow.

"The ship is facing west, so the compass heading should be 300. But it's all zeros. The only code I can find that's still blue is cabin temperature." Case ran through several of the system maintenance screens, all indicating short circuits in many of the flight performance sensors.

"I can't believe it," Case said as he jumped down. "We had no idea this'd happened. Was there any damage?" He circled the aerodyne, checking carefully. He seemed satisfied the ship hadn't suffered any damage, but near the end of his inspection, when he squatted to peer up into one of the skid retraction wells, he pointed to several drops of water at the seam where the nose cone joined the passenger compartment. "Water got into the nose." He pointed to a drop of water, about to fall from the seam. "It may have damaged the flight performance and navigational sensors. I'll take a look later. Right now I want to talk to Wila. We'll have to have a meeting to talk this over."

Case shut down the aerodyne's reactor and Bent and Lilea stashed the coolers on Deck 11, the Food Storage deck.

Then he scheduled a team meeting for the next lightime at 3.0.

CHAPTER 11

GRASSLANDS

Time Element 461.25.3.0.

"All right, people. Let's get this meeting started. We've got several things to discuss." Case scurried down the interdeck ladder from *Explorer's* Command Deck to the Life Sciences Deck and strode over to the table in the center of the room. Lilea and Bent had just taken their regular seats as Jad and Wila, the last to arrive, stepped off the interdeck elevator next to the ladder. Wila still seemed shaken from her ordeal in the storm, her eyes downcast, her face still pale and shocky, and Lilea leaned over and gave her a brief hug as she sat down.

"The first thing we need to discuss is the matter of drinking enough water while we're out on exploration runs. Four T-sectors ago we had an incident at the gorge where one person didn't drink enough water"—he stared directly at Jad—"and almost passed out from dehydration and heat exhaustion. This isn't an acceptable way to do our jobs here, people." His voice rose. "We need to maintain adequate water intake if we want to explore this planet. SpaceComm regs require everyone to drink an eighth-trilink of water every lightime, more when you're out in the hot sun. This isn't the comfortable climate of our own planet. Everyone has been issued two water bottles, and there are extra bottles on the Storage Deck, so keep your bottles filled and keep them in your backpack when you go out. Clear?" He paused, probably not expecting an answer.

"Second, Wila and I did a complete examination of all systems on Aero Two last lightime. The water got into the nose through the forward cooling vents. It saturated the air filters and blew them out of position. We dried everything out, but we had to replace a few circuit boards and some other components. Aero Two is now code blue."

Case paused again, probably to let the information sink in. "Next, and most important, people, we need to discuss the flight into the storm the gorge team took last lightime. We almost lost an aerodyne and a lot of equipment during that flight, not to mention four people, and we should set some rules about how to fly when storms like this are around."

"'When storms like this are around?'" Col said. "Are you suggesting that more of these storms are possible? How do we know—this might have been the odd happenstance. It may never occur again."

"That may be so," Case replied. "But I think we have to assume that if there was one, there will be others. We've had storms here at Site One. That may have been one of those storms."

"That's only partly true," Wila said. "The storm we flew into was a lot bigger and stronger than any we've had around here. It stretched a long way. We almost couldn't outfly it. The wind in that storm was a lot scarier, too."

"So, people, just avoid the storms altogether. Wila tells me the storm was well defined and easy to see, so it should be easy to avoid. Anyone have a problem with that?"

A few people said, "No." The rest shook their heads.

"Before we left Anthanos we were told not to fly into the clouds," Wila said. "I think we should stay grounded when clouds are around at all. I don't want to go back up into something like that."

"Wila, SpaceComm didn't say we *couldn't* fly into clouds," Lilea said. "They just recommended we—"

"I don't know about you, but I sure as hell don't want to go through that again." Wila spat her words out and the flush of color enveloped her face. She seemed agitated.

"But you were the one who suggested flying into the storm in the first place—"

"No, I didn't! I didn't want to fly into it. I just wanted to examine it close up. There's a difference."

"Lilea's right," Case said. "We can't stay grounded just because clouds are around. Clouds are around a lot. If we stay grounded when clouds are around, we'll be on the ground half the time—"

"But do you want to take the chance that if you fly somewhere you'll run into a storm like that? I don't."

"But, Wila," Trea said. "We've got to be able to fly."

Wila leaned forward, putting both elbows on the table. She stared directly at Trea, well around the table to her right. "Okay, maybe you can fly, but stay out of the clouds. I wouldn't take off if there were any clouds around. Once you get into the clouds, there's no way to see the ground, and you can't tell where you are. It's damn scary."

"All right, people," Case interrupted. "Just stay away from the clouds." He turned to his left. "Col, your group is scheduled to take Aero

One east this lightime. Have you checked the probe images? Have any storms shown up?"

"Negative," Col said. "The images show clear air from here to the projected landing point. We should have superior flying weather for our trip."

"Okay, you should get going. Aero Two is code blue for backup. Before we terminate this meeting, I want to remind the members of the gorge team to write up and send out a complete report on your explorations sometime during this lightime. Kal and Jasi will want to see the details of everything that happened. All right, people, let's get back to work."

Time Element 461.25.3.6.

As the meeting ended, the Grassland Team—Col, Trea, Dell and Mina—began loading the four-seat aerodyne, Aero One. Using one of the runabouts, Bent and Jad pulled it out of its parking space off the east side of the runway, and set it facing north. Col took the pilot's seat.

Lilea and everyone else stood to the side of the runway. As Case gave Col the "go" signal, she donned her ear protectors, the large, bulky, headphone-like sound balancers which were supposed to eliminate the noise from an aerodyne engine by providing a counter-signal at exactly the same frequencies, but 200 degrees out of phase. They worked well enough when she tested them on Anthanos, but some sound still leaked through.

She gritted her teeth, waiting for the roar from the engine. When it started, a blue-white flame shot from the coal-black engine bell, and the bell itself turned red, then orange, and finally stabilized at a dusky yellow under the intense heat of the exhaust. The ship began a cautious slide down the runway, rapidly picked up speed and jumped into the air a few hundred links short of the runway's end. It passed over a clump of dark green bush-like trees, and when it reached one thousand links Col banked right and turned to a heading of 100 degrees—due east.

Lilea stayed beside the runway for a few microsectors to watch as Aero One headed east. Everyone else walked up the slight rise toward *Explorer*, but she kept an eye on the aerodyne as it dwindled to a tiny dot in the sky, and continued to watch as the sound faded. The dot grew smaller and smaller as it headed east for an area Col deduced from the probe images to be a small patch of low rolling hills clothed with an abundant green covering.

A twinge tightened Lilea's chest and rose into her throat. At first she couldn't explain her feelings, and she kept her eyes on the ship until it disappeared from view. She thought it might be a spasm of concern for the four team members, not scheduled to return until next lightime.

"I hope Col doesn't run into any storms," she muttered to herself as she hiked up toward the elevator, and it finally dawned on her why she held such a deep concern for the Grassland Team. It was the aerodyne flight back from the gorge. Those aerodynes are so vulnerable. *If flying through water would damage it to that extent, what else could happen?* But Col was a good pilot. Like Wila, he enjoyed flying, and he certainly wouldn't do anything to jeopardize the ship or the team.

But there was more to her concern. Something else might come up, something worse. Compared to the placid environment of Anthanos, this planet was wild and unpredictable, even turbulent, and almost anything could happen. She hadn't felt concern like this before because she was on the first team to leave on a full expedition, and it didn't occur to her that the team members left behind would feel a sense of apprehension, even foreboding, for the travelers. She'd been grumbling too much about the engine noise during takeoff to be concerned with what others might be thinking. As she boarded the elevator she wished the Grassland Team a silent *good luck* on their journey, then pressed the **UP** button.

Time Element 461.26.7.0.

    BONG—BONG—BONG

"What the hell is that?"

Bent threw back the bed covers and ran barefoot into the compartment's front room. The triplet-bonging signal was blaring from computer terminals all over the ship.

"Holy crap!" he yelled when he saw the computer screen.

Lilea jerked herself upright in bed, dreading to know what the emergency was. The high, piercing noise had jolted her from a deep sleep and she screamed "Oh, no!" as a deluge of reasons for the alarm flooded into her still-groggy mind. She ran after Bent into the front room, struggling to put a robe on over her nightgown.

"Oh, my god!" Lilea said. Right there on the screen was the bright flashing-yellow message no one ever wanted to see:

AERO ONE CARRIER SIGNAL TERMINATED

A scream came from Jad and Wila's compartment.

Bent and Lilea ran back into the bedroom and changed into jumpsuits. Bent jammed his feet into his boots, but Lilea stayed barefoot. They ran into the circular walkway outside the ring of compartments, headed toward Case's compartment, passing Jer fastening her jumpsuit as she sprinted through the center of the deck instead of around the blue carpet that circled the deck. She passed the central exercise equipment and jumped onto the interdeck elevator next to the ladder. Jad and Wila came around the hallway from the other side. In her haste, Jer had left the door open.

"D'you know what happened?" Bent asked as they entered the compartment.

Case stood in the center of the dark room staring at the computer screen, his hands on his hips. The only light in the room came through the open door. "No, I don't," he replied, shaking his head. His face was tense and taut, his voice low and quiet. "All I know is their comm system has shut down." He touched the marker **ALARM SILENCE** at the bottom of the screen and the bonging stopped, but the flashing message remained, casting sharp, flickering shadows of everyone on the opposite wall. He reached over and turned up the room lights.

"Where was Jer going?" Wila asked.

"She went to Comm. The first thing to check is reception. This could be caused by a malfunction of our system. She's going to switch to the backup system."

"But doesn't that happen automatically if there's a malfunction?" Bent asked.

"It should," Case replied, "but she's going to check."

"If the loss of signal is real, what do we do now?" Jad asked.

"There isn't much we can do. According to regs we have to send out Aero Two to check on them and see what happened. But we can't do that until lightime arrives. That won't be for a few more subsectors."

"At least we got Aero Two cleaned up and repaired," Wila said. "But I never imagined we'd need it."

"What about the emergency omni unit?" Lilea asked. "Can you contact them through that?"

"Jer will try."

"How are you going to handle this?" Jad asked. "Who do you want to go out and check on them?"

Case stared at the screen and said nothing. A few nanosectors later, the ship's comm beeped, the single high-pitched beep of an incoming call. Even though Lilea had heard that single beep many times, she still let out a sudden gasp. Jer was online.

"I can't get any indication of a carrier signal with the backup system. It doesn't appear to be a malfunction of the primary. I also don't get any response with the emergency system. All the diagnostics I ran indicate intact systems. As much as I hate to say it, I think the loss of signal is real."

"Oh, crap." The lack of a response with the emergency comm system scared Lilea the most. It had its own isolated power source, independent of the aerodyne's computer or comm, and it had been programmed to send out a signal automatically when the main system carrier signal was cut off for any reason.

"All right," Case said. "I'm going out as soon as the sky is light enough. There can't be more than two of us because if the carrier signal is off that could mean the ship is destroyed, and we may have to bring all four of them back in Aero Two. We'll assume the worst. In the meantime, all we can do is wait. Who wants to go with me?"

"I'll go," Lilea blurted out. Just like her to be impulsive and spontaneous, not stopping to think about what she said. Bent frowned at her, but didn't say anything.

"It should be light in about four subsectors. We'll leave then."

"Okay. I'll be ready."

"Oh, that's great," Wila said. "We've got four of our best friends in trouble on a strange planet, and all we can do is wait. I don't know about you, but I can't go back to sleep now." She turned and left the compartment. Jad followed.

"I keep wondering why the signal stopped," Bent said. "Obviously something happened to the comm system. But what? Is it just a small malfunction, or did something larger happen?"

"I hope it's just a small malfunction," Lilea said. "I hope they didn't crash or something."

"I can't believe they crashed." Case turned away from the screen but stared at the floor, his hands still on his hips. "Col knows better than to go flying around in the dark. That's against all flight regs. Even if they did go up in the dark, like there was an emergency, Col would have notified us before they left." He looked at the others and shook his head. "No."

"Besides," Jer said as she walked in the door, "we got a report from Col earlier last lightime that they'd landed about 25.6.3, but they never said anything about going back up. All Col said was they were going to explore the area. Everything was fine—no problems. I can't imagine they went anywhere and crashed. That's too . . . no, that's impossible." Jer entered the bedroom shaking her head.

"Was the emergency transponder activated?" Case asked.

"No," Jer replied from the bedroom. "But they may be too far away."

"Maybe a storm came up and damaged the ship, like it did ours," Lilea said. "They could have been sitting on the ground and a storm might have dumped so much water on it that it shorted out the comm system."

"That's a possibility," Case said. "We won't know until we get there."

CHAPTER 12

WINDSHIELD

Time Element 461.27.0.0.

Wila made the preflight inspection of Aero Two, and at 27.0.0, initiated the reactor. Lilea loaded supplies for a one lightime trip and met Bent at the side of the runway. He had an anxious look on his face and he stared right at her, gazing into her eyes with an almost pleading look she'd rarely seen from him. "Are you sure you want to do this?" he asked. His emphasis hit the word "sure." She'd been so concerned about getting ready for this flight she'd put aside his worries about her flying off into a potentially dangerous situation. She put her arms around him. He hugged her back.

"Yes, I do," she whispered. "It'll be okay. I'm sure. I love you." They shared a brief kiss—perhaps a little too brief for her in this anxious moment, but she heard Case call her name and she had to board the aerodyne.

Everyone gathered at the side of the runway to watch as the aerodyne lifted off and passed over the same clump of trees and took the same heading Aero One had taken the lightime before. They'd been flying for six millisectors when a message came in from Jer. The upbeat, almost cheerful tone in her voice sent Lilea's heart into a flutter.

"Case, I just heard from Col. They're okay. Everyone's okay. They had a storm during the darktime and it damaged the antenna on the top of Aero One. That's why the signal was cut off. The cable that runs from the transmission unit to the antenna was jerked out of position, but they finally got it repaired. It also knocked out the emergency system. That's why we didn't hear from it. I told them you were on your way, but they still want you to come because the storm did some other damage to the ship. It may not be flyable."

"Not flyable? What happened?"

Jer's voice turned tentative, as though searching for the right word. "The way Col tells it, the storm was, well, this is a little unusual, um, the way he tells it, um, a bunch of ice balls came down from the sky and damaged the ship."

"Did you say 'ice balls'?"

"Ice balls?" Lilea mouthed silently. That sounded faintly humorous and she screwed up her face, though she tried not to smile, afraid Case might think she was taking a serious matter too lightly. But still, that's just ridiculous.

"Yes, millions of balls of ice came down from the sky during the darktime and damaged the aerodyne. He says they really did a number on the windshield."

"They *what?*"

"They smashed the windshield."

Case's face turned puzzled. He and Lilea looked at each other. "Yes, I guess they would. Did they do any other damage?"

"He says they dented the upper surfaces all over. No severe damage, but lots of dents. He says you can see them when you get there."

"Oh, this is too bizarre for words." Case released an angry sigh. "All right, tell him we'll be there in about a subsector. Tell him to activate Aero One's homing signal."

"Okay."

That's curious. Seth did predict that ice could fall from the sky too, not just water. But balls of ice? How could that be? It is bizarre. But more than that, it's . . . it's ludicrous and almost unbelievable. It's not like Col to toy with us like that.

About two microsectors later a vector heading appeared on Aero Two's com screen. Case banked two degrees left, set the ITS, and they reached Aero One twelve millisectors later.

Time Element 461.27.2.4.

"Like landing on ball bearings," Case said as Aero Two came to rest on the ice-laden grass several hundred links southeast of Aero One. Lilea opened the door and jumped out. The grayish-green grass would normally have come to her waist, but the ice had flattened much of it, and it lay in irregular whorls and eddies over the earth. Many of the flowery blooms had begun to rise after their pounding, and they swirled about her in the cool morning breeze. At her feet lay several lumpy, white, round objects. She reached down and picked one up.

About three decilinks in diameter and ice cold, it began to melt in her hand as she and Case made their way through the grass toward Aero One.

How did something this heavy come down from the sky? Were they formed in the sky or were they picked up from somewhere else?

As they passed the shelter, she noticed an accumulation of similar ice spheres around the base of the shelter in a miniature moat of ice. At the top, several of the seams in the dark green fabric had been ripped, and she stopped to stare at them.

The shelter must have taken a terrific beating. And everyone inside — my gosh.

They ducked under the left wing of Aero One, headed for the front of the ship where the Grassland Team had gathered. But as she and Case approached, the others weren't watching her or Case — they seemed fixed on the ship's windshield.

"L-Lilea. Wh-what are you d-doing here?" Mina's stutter sometimes got worse during times of stress.

"I couldn't stay away."

In spite of her frail attempt at humor, an uncomfortable stillness held the group. No one talked or greeted her. Dell did glance in her direction, nodding as she approached, but that was oddly quiet for him, he usually said, "Hi." Even the ordinarily spirited Trea remained quiet, staring at Aero One. Lilea turned around and saw the reason for everyone's unease. She dropped the stone.

A web-like smash covered Aero One's windshield on the right side. Serrated white cracks radiated in all directions from the center of the smash like the spokes of a wheel, and a series of irregular concentric circles spread outward from the heavily damaged center. The left side of the windshield remained untouched.

"Good god," Case said. "That's one hell of a whack. How's the windshield from the inside? Is it stable?"

"Not entirely," Col replied. "It crackles to a slight degree if you press on it. It's been shattered all the way through. I'm afraid it could implode if we try to fly."

"How about the engine and reactor?"

"The engine wasn't damaged. We still have full power."

Case examined the windshield from several angles, then climbed into the ship and pressed gently on the inside. He stood in the ship's doorway and reached around as far as he could, pushing inward with his fingertips on the outer surface of the windshield.

"Probable," he mumbled, and then paused, apparently lost in thought. "What concerns me more is the damage to the upper surfaces. There could be some real damage. Let's take a look."

From the doorway, Case crawled up onto the right wing. He ran his fingers over many of the shallow dents, probing the extent of the damage. He crawled to the end of the wing, checking flaps and ailerons as he went, asking Col in the pilot's seat to actuate the joystick so he could check their movement. He tapped the wing with his fist several times, listening for structural damage, and crawled across the fuselage and performed the same inspection on the left wing.

He jumped down and circled the ship several times. He opened inspection ports on the wings and probed the internal darkness with a fiber optic light. He checked the ship's computer for red or yellow codes but found none. After five millisectors he finished and met with everyone near the front of the aerodyne.

"Well, I'm satisfied. I think it's flyable—"

"Flyable?" Trea said, raising her eyebrows. "In that condition? Who's going to fly it? I certainly wouldn't fly it like that. That windshield looks like it'll collapse if you —"

"I'm not so sure." Case shook his head. "That glass is high temper. It's made to hold itself together even when smashed. I'll bet if we fly that thing back to Site One, it would hold the whole way."

"Perhaps," Col said. "But I have my doubts . . ."

"Still, who's going to fly it?" Trea asked.

"I'll fly it," Case said. "Col, you take Aero Two—"

"Is that wise?" Col said. "After all, SpaceComm advised you, and Dell too, I might add, not to take any undue risks. You two especially are to be more circumspect and prudent than the rest of us."

"Oh, well, I don't think it's that much of a risk. It's—"

"I think it is. Kal would be infinitely displeased if he found out. I'll fly Aero One, you take Aero Two."

"Col," Trea said, jerking his arm. Her eyes narrowed and her face tightened. "You're not flying that thing. It could be dangerous."

Col looked at Trea. "Someone has to fly it back. Would you?"

"Not me. And you're not either."

Col started to say something, but a pained look crossed Trea's face and he hesitated.

"Well, then, who's going to fly it back?" Case crossed his arms over his chest. "I'll open it to volunteers. If no one wants to try it, I'll pick someone. Anyone?"

The group turned quiet as the request sank in. Lilea pondered the evidence Case presented, and he sounded convinced of the windshield's stability. She knew of the charge to Case and Dell—really, almost a direct order—to be more cautious in their explorations to minimize risk to the team leader and physician, and she agreed that was a wise precaution.

That leaves the five of us. Col's out—Trea doesn't want him to fly it, and Trea won't volunteer. Dell's out too, and Mina's out—she's too short. Didn't meet the height requirements to fly.

Case's face hardened. He took in and let out a deep breath. "One of you will have to take it back." He paused slightly. "You'll be flying low and slow to minimize airflow stress on the windshield. It shouldn't be difficult. Shall I pick someone?"

"If you really think it's flyable, I'll try it," Lilea said. Everyone turned and looked at her.

"Lilea," Mina hissed. "What d-do you think you're d-doing?"

Lilea stared at Mina, but she saw little of her best friend's face. The realization of what she'd volunteered for was gelling in her brain. Her palms and forehead turned sweaty and her chest tightened. *My god, what have I gotten myself into?*

CHAPTER 13

FLIGHT – I

Time Element 461.27.3.5.

"Good," Case said. "We'll leave as soon as we can."

"We hadn't planned to leave until after the second meal," Col said. "We're still collecting specimens. Can you wait for us?"

Case hesitated. "All right." A trace of annoyance infiltrated his voice and his forehead furrowed a definite frown. "But don't take too long. We need to get started in a few subs. While we're waiting, Lilea and I will check the nose of the ship for water."

"Eminent thinking," Col said, and the Grassland Team went back to work.

Case and Lilea removed the maintenance access panels on the nose of Aero One but everything inside was dry—no water had been blown in during the storm. Apart from the damage to the windshield and the upper surfaces, they found nothing that would prevent the ship from flying. Lilea even made her own brief inspection of the outside of the ship, concentrating on the ailerons and elevators, concerned, like Case, that the dents might have altered their function. But when she operated the joystick in the cabin, and carefully watched how they moved in the little representation of the ship in the display on the central com screen, they operated well enough, and she felt marginally better.

As she sat in the pilot's seat after the inspection she punched her name into the computer. The seat rose slightly to her usual flying height and moved forward almost a link to allow her to reach the instruments directly in front. The joystick moved forward a few decilinks and down about one decilink to adjust for her smaller hand, and slid infinitesimally left to her favorite position. She turned on the air cooler to counter the warm interior, and checked the ship's functions—reactor, propulsion, electrical, navigation, hydraulics, communications—everything was normal. Aero One was ready. She was ready. So why weren't Col and the rest of them?

Time Element 461.27.5.1.

Soon Lilea's mind turned to a different aspect of this flight. She was just now beginning to realize how surprising it was she would volunteer to fly this damaged ship back home. She took Case's word that the windshield would hold together, but piloting was not her forté. She'd flown Aero One several times on Anthanos before leaving, but only twice here on the Blue Planet, both times shortly after it had been assembled. She enjoyed flying, though certainly not with the same relish as Wila, but piloting a ship with a damaged windshield and dents all over the aerodynamic surfaces was not her idea of an enjoyable flight.

I guess if no one else volunteered, I should do it. But Bent is going to be upset. I hope he doesn't get too angry. Maybe Wila can give me some help. She raised *Explorer* on comm and asked to speak to Wila.

"I can't really tell you anything that would help you too much," Wila said. "Fly low and slow. Keep the skids down. That way if anything happens, you'll be ready to land. That's one less thing you'll have to worry about in an emergency. We'll keep our fingers crossed."

"Thanks. That's reassuring."

She terminated comm and dropped to the ground. Her nervousness was increasing and she wanted to stay busy to take her mind off the impending flight. She decided to walk forward of Aero One to scout the area of the takeoff run through the long grass.

Most of the grass had recovered from its pounding in the storm, and the flowers quivered in the gentle westerly breeze. As she walked, she became aware of a scurrying noise ahead, as though something scampered through the grass nearby. The noise came from ahead and both sides. She stopped and drew her weapon. The scurrying seemed to dart father ahead, and after a few microsectors, was gone. She made a mental note to tell Trea, and cautiously walked on.

As she walked, her mind dwelt more on the flight itself than the takeoff, but she was drawn to her surroundings more and more. Most of the ice balls had melted by the time she set out, though a few residuals remained. Only a few wispy clouds in the west spoiled the enchantment of an Anthanos-like clear blue sky. She estimated the air temperature was near 22 Tal and she rolled up the sleeves of her jumpsuit. She turned and looked back in the direction she'd come, and realized she'd walked more than a thousand links from Aero One.

Even from this distance she could see the smash on Aero One's windshield. It stood out as an indistinct white splotch on the right side. She turned and started to walk again, an occasional ice ball crunching under her boot. She picked up one of the melting stones, a fragment of its original size, then turned around again and gazed upward at the blue sky overhead and the aerodyne in the distance. The incongruity of the powerful storm with the clear sunny sky confused her at first, but slowly she understood — somewhat hesitantly, then more deeply and intently — how the storm fit into the life of the planet. Like the slithering creature that attacked and devoured the furry animal, the storm was real, as real as the chunk of melting ice she held in her hand. In its reality it belonged here, it was as much a part of this planet as the grassland on which she stood. The storm attacked then left, devouring the windshield almost as surely as the slithering creature devoured the furry one. It was the nature of this planet, a nature they would have to put up with, like it or not, were they to live here. They would find a way to shield the aerodynes against the ice and water storms of the future. They would have to — no other choice existed.

Lilea stood in the tall grass for several microsectors, staring up at the sky, at Aero One on the ground, and the others packing the shelter and loading supplies into Aero Two. She'd found nothing to prevent Aero One from making an easy takeoff. But deep down inside she wished she had. She dropped the stone and strode back to the ship, the scurrying sound behind her.

Time Element 461.27.6.1.

Four subsectors after Lilea and Case arrived, both aerodynes were ready to leave. All supplies had been loaded into Aero Two's cargo hold, and everyone boarded. Case decided that he and the rest of the Grassland Team would fly slightly ahead of and to the right of Lilea so he could maintain a visual check on Aero One's windshield.

"That way, if anything happens, we'll be nearby and available to help," he told Lilea as she sat in Aero One's left-hand seat. He stood on the ground outside her open door. "I'll set my comm system to yours so we can talk to each other, and *Explorer* can hear us too. Leave comm open all the time. Don't make any sharp turns. That might put too much stress on the windshield."

"Okay. I contacted Wila and she suggested I not raise the skids. It might help if I have to land suddenly."

"That's okay, but you'll get an alarm. The computer will want to know why you're flying with the skids down. Just hit 'alarm silence' on the screen. You'll have to fly by manual control all the way. The computer won't let you activate autocontrol with the skids down. It thinks you're getting ready to land. Come to think of it, you may be flying too low and too slow to activate autocontrol anyway. When we get to Site One, you land first. We'll circle and wait for you to stop."

"Okay," Lilea said, and Case left. She closed the door and fastened her seat belt and chest restraints. But the metallic "click" of the belt fastener only magnified her sense of isolation, sitting alone in the pilot's seat. She stared at the complex cluster of dials, gauges and com screens in the instrument panel in front of her. "Why do I get myself into these situations," she muttered as she energized the fuel pump. "They should give me a damn medal for making this flight."

She donned her dark glasses, put on the comm headset, and opened comm.

Aero Two took off first, and after it was airborne, she started Aero One's engine and winced as the noise jolted her eardrums. She hit **CLIMB ONE** and the aerodyne began to move. It slid easily through the grass and jumped into the air, surprising her at how effortlessly it left the ground.

"Okay, I'm airborne," she said into the microphone. "The windshield's holding."

"Good," Case said.

Case had taped one of the curtains from the interior of the shelter to the ceiling inside Aero One's cabin to Lilea's right to cushion any pieces of glass that might come off during flight. She didn't think it was necessary, but he insisted. If the windshield collapsed, the entire windshield would hurtle inward, and the cloth would be useless. It also limited visibility to her right. She had to pull it back to see Aero Two.

My pressure suit helmet would have been better.

"I'm level at five thousand," she reported. "Airspeed one hundred. Everything's okay so far. The windshield's crackling a little, but it's holding. It's flying easy, but there's more turbulence than usual."

"That's because the skids are down."

As she terminated comm, she heard a noise over the roar of the engine, like a pop or a crack. She didn't pay much attention at first, the windshield had been creaking and groaning since takeoff, but then she heard another pop. It sounded like something hit the seat beside her.

"What was that? I thought I heard something."

"What's going on?"

"The window is cracking more. It's louder now." She pulled the cloth back slightly and looked at the smash, but couldn't see anything obvious. As she watched, a piece of glass snapped off the center of the web and landed in the seat.

"Parts of the window are popping off! There's a hole in the windshield!"

"Do you want to land?"

Lilea briefly considered landing, but they'd left airspace over the grassland and she couldn't see any landing site within the blanketing forest below. "No, it seems okay, just little pieces are coming off. But the window is vibrating even more now. I think it's flexing a little bit."

Without warning, a large crack shot through the windshield from the center of the smash to the lower left-hand corner — right across Lilea's field of view — and the windshield flexed inward slightly. Only the seat belt and shoulder restraints kept her in her seat. She threw up her left arm in front of her face as though to protect herself, and her right hand jerked involuntarily on the joystick. The ship rose slightly.

"Oh, shit!" Her heart pounded in her temples.

"What? What?"

"The windshield is cracked all the way across! It's getting weaker. It's crackling a lot now." Even Lilea could hear the quivering in her voice.

"Land. Put it down — now!"

"I can't. There's no place to land." Below the ship was forest, stretching as far as she could see, with no open areas that could contain an aerodyne.

"Reduce speed. Get down lower. That ship will fly down to thirty anthans per sub."

Lilea reached forward and reduced the throttle setting. She let the aerodyne drop to 2000 links by the reflection altimeter where she trimmed the controls until it flew level at fifty anthans per sub.

"It's still cracking and flexing some. Not as much. But I can still hear it."

Pieces of glass kept popping off the largest part of the smash, and the hole in the center continued to grow. Another crack shot through the windshield to the upper left.

"It's still cracking!" Her heart pounded in her chest, and her right hand was getting sweaty on the joystick. Perspiration trickled down her face and neck, and had an annoying tendency to drop off her brows onto her dark glasses. She took deep, heavy breaths to try to relax.

"I can see the cracks from here. If we come to an open area, land."

"There's still too much vegetation." Lilea yelled into the microphone far louder than necessary to convey the information. She wiped the perspiration from her face with her left sleeve and turned the louvers of the ventilating system to blow directly on her face. More pieces of glass popped off the window, landing in the right-hand seat. She released her shoulder restraints and reached forward and touched the windshield. It seemed solid and didn't flex, but she could still hear the creaking and crackling.

"I think it's okay," she said. "Let it go for a while." Her voice still quivered and her heart still throbbed. "So far, so good," she muttered to herself, trying to control the panic that was poised to seize her brain. She released her grip on the joystick and wiped her palm on her pant leg. A bead of sweat dribbled into her left eye.

"Are you sure?" Case seemed unusually demanding.

"Yes, yes." She started one of the breathing exercises she'd been taught to relieve tension during the heavy acceleration of *Star Voyager*. "In through the nostrils . . . *deeply, deeply* . . . out through the mouth . . . in through the nostrils . . ." Over and over she tried it, and her heart rate dropped slightly, but she was still faced with a disintegrating windshield and many anthans to go. She did a rough mental calculation . . . *fifty anthans per sub . . . still several hundred anthans from the landing site . . . it'll take several more subsectors to get there . . . still several subsectors of lightime remaining . . . going to be close . . . may have to land early.*

She took a deep breath and wiggled her butt to get comfortable in the seat.

Several more pieces of glass popped from the window. The hole had grown to about three decilinks in diameter, and the wind whistled through the hole, rustling the cloth beside her. The noise of the engine came through louder, too.

She looked closely at the windshield, but she couldn't tell if it was flexing or not.

Is it really not flexing, or is it that I just don't want to see it? As long as all that happens is that little chips come off, I'm okay.

She settled back in the seat. Her arm ached from her tense grip on the joystick, and she took another deep breath and tried to relax her hand. But her heart still palpitated in her chest.

CHAPTER 14

FLIGHT – II

Time Element 461.27.11.3.

The sun hung about 20 degrees above the horizon, glaring through the cracked front window as Lilea approached Site One. The flight had taken almost five subsectors, but the windshield held. A few more chips broke off, but they landed in the right-hand seat, and the three large pieces, defined by the two cracks, remained in place. The forest below had begun to thin out, too. She was relieved to find more tan, dusty areas that pockmarked the terrain.

I've made it this far, I can make it the rest of the way.

Aero Two hovered nearby, like a mother guarding its young. Lilea's heart rate had dropped and she relaxed her grip on the joystick. With the lateness of the lightime came cooler temperature and she turned the digital display of the air temperature controller slightly upward.

As she sat in the pilot's seat, trying to look past the two ominous cracks, a dark but familiar-looking obelisk appeared on the horizon in the distance. She shielded her eyes from the sun to get a better view. It looked so small from this distance, but it could be nothing other than home. She breathed a heavy sigh of relief and almost yelled into the microphone.

"*Explorer*, I can see you."

"Great," Jer said. "We've been following everything that's happened. Welcome back. The runway is yours."

Lilea flew directly over *Explorer*, and looked down to get her bearings. Still at 2000 links, she'd have to take an easy bank to the right to get aligned with the runway. *Don't put too much strain on the windshield.* She wiped her right hand on her pant leg for what seemed the hundredth time, and then eased the joystick slightly right.

Reduce speed. Get the ship lower and slower. Keep the nose up.

She touched the marker **ALTERNATE LANDING SERIES** on the central com screen, and a new set of five throttle positions appeared on the Engine Power Dynamics screen. She touched **3** in the middle of the new series, and she could feel the engine throttle back.

Trim. Keep the nose up. Stay out of the red zone. Don't stall the wings.

She reached forward and edged the little marker **ELEVATOR TRIM** upward, and the nose of the craft rose almost imperceptibly. As she trimmed the ship, she watched the ship's attitude on the central com screen and stopped when the nose reached normal landing position. Now the skids were in their proper relation to the ground, and she let out a big sigh.

Airspeed had dropped to forty anthans per sub, close to minimum for this ship without flaps. She was still in the turn, swinging around to face the runway. She retracted the cloth beside her to watch as *Explorer* swung slowly toward the center of her field of view. Now Aero One was aligned with the runway, directly ahead. She reached forward to lower the wing flaps when the horrible realization struck her — something is wrong — the ship is still too high!

Reduce speed — I'll overshoot the runway —

Jer's voice startled her. "Lilea — you're too high. You're too high!"

"I can't land. I have to go around."

"Okay," Case said. "Take your time. Take your time." His voice sounded so reassuring.

Lilea reached forward to advance the throttle slightly, but *Explorer* was dead ahead and coming *fast*. "Holy shit!" She started to pull back on the joystick, but no — not enough room — bank right!

"Lilea, what are you doing? Look out!" Jer didn't sound as calm as Case.

Lilea jerked the joystick right, and Aero One lifted its left wing and banked into a tight turn. The computer, sensing a potential stall, increased fuel flow to the engine and the ship shot forward. The windshield crackled and groaned as the three large pieces shifted independently within the framework that held them in place, and two more large fractures shot across the windshield with a simultaneous loud *wham*, and she threw up her left arm to protect her face. A cluster of small pieces disgorged from the bull's-eye, spewing over the inside of the cabin. Several pieces hit her right hand and others fell into the back seats. But the windshield held as Aero One roared past *Explorer*, the skids passing only about twenty links from the entryway catwalk. Lilea lowered her arm — the hills! She screamed and jammed the joystick far right. The ship swung tightly west and when blue sky filled her view, she let out a big sigh of relief.

"Oh, my god!" she yelled between breaths.

She wiped her right hand on her pant leg again, and mopped her forehead with her left sleeve. Sweat dribbled off her nose into her lap and ran down her neck onto the already saturated collar of her jumpsuit. Her forearm ached from her crushing grip on the joystick. Her mouth was painfully dry and she desperately wanted a drink of water. And she had to pee—bad. She leveled the ship, reduced the throttle slightly, wiped her hand on her pant leg, and began another broad right-hand turn.

She took a wider turn this time—with four large cracks in the windshield every little vibration seemed to cause the five big pieces of glass to shift in place with a sharp grinding *screech* that sent a chill down her spine. She swallowed hard and wiped her hand on her pant leg again. Blood covered the back of her hand.

Halfway through the second turn, she returned the throttle to position **3**, and the nose of the ship dropped back to landing position.

Just get this damn thing on the ground. Then it'll be over.

Aero One swung slowly around again, and she aligned it with the runway. She checked the computer screen: attitude's good—nose up—rate of descent good—trim good—skids already down. Everything looks good. She focused on the clump of trees at the end of the runway.

"Here we go!"

She lowered the flaps to 40 degrees and the airspeed dropped. As the ship settled onto the dusty runway a loud *grrraaack* came from the windshield as the five large pieces shifted position, grinding against each other, compressing the middle piece so tightly it shattered into thousands of tiny white bits that exploded in a cloud of glass fragments right back into the ship's interior, right into her face, pelting her cheeks and forehead, though her dark glasses protected her eyes. She screamed and threw up her arm. The high-temper glass had disintegrated into thousands of small, chunky pieces, none with seriously sharp edges, but one piece managed to thwack her lower lip. That stung and she tasted blood, but she retained enough presence of mind to release the joystick and grab the mechanical fuel interlock behind the joystick that shut down the engine. Even in her day of full electronic control of almost everything, the most reliable way to shut down an aerodyne was to cut fuel to the engine. Case will be pissed because it takes a subsector to get inside the engine to reset the interlock.

Hell, he would've done the same thing.

The sudden quietness inside the cabin startled her momentarily and she closed her eyes as Aero One slid up the runway. When it hit the rocky portion of the runway, it came to a grinding halt, jerking her forward against the chest restraints. Jad and Bent sat in one of the runabouts at the head of the runway, ready to pull Aero One into its parking space. Aero

Two landed a few microsectors later.

"My god, what a flight!" Lilea said as she opened the door. The muscles in her legs and back were stiff and sore from sitting in the same position for almost five subsectors, so when she jumped from the seat she collapsed to the ground. Her right hand and arm throbbed from the crushing grip she'd held on the joystick. Bent came running over.

"Are you okay?" He squatted and put an arm around her. "I heard everything."

"Yes, yes, I'm okay." She put one arm around his waist as he helped her stand. "I need to go up and lie down." She shook her right arm and flexed her right hand, trying to work out the tension and stiffness. "I'm exhausted."

Bent kept his arm around her. "I can't believe you volunteered to make that flight. What were you thinking?" He pulled out a handkerchief to hold to her lip. "I've got a good mind to . . ."

"Please, I don't want to talk about it now. I'll explain later. I just want to lie down." She walked haltingly to the elevator, but by the time she got to her compartment she was running toward the bathroom. She collapsed on the bed and fell asleep.

CHAPTER 15

AFTER THE MEETING

Time Element 461.28.3.0.

The meeting Case called to discuss the flight back from the grasslands lasted about a half-subsector, and most returned to their compartments afterward. But Lilea, Wila and Mina lingered, forming a small conversation group to one side of the interdeck ladder.

"This is the first chance I've had to talk to you since you got back," Wila said. "That was some flight you made. You must have been terrified. I know I would have been."

"It wasn't all that bad," Lilea said, but with a tiny twinge of guilt for misleading her friends about the flight. She still felt weak and washed out from fighting the tension of the flight, but she wasn't about to admit how scared she really was. Tiny red welts covered her face and the back of her right hand, and her lip still burned. "After the first subsector or so, things settled down. I got to relax a little."

"But you could have been killed. That was a dangerous flight."

Lilea shrugged her shoulders. "I didn't think too much about it after I left the ground. I just wanted to get back."

"Oh, wow, yes," Trea said as she approached the group. "Congratulations." She leaned over and gave Lilea a brief hug. "I sat behind Case and I could see you out the window, and every time I looked out, I mean—wow—I got so scared. My heart was pounding the whole way. I said a prayer for you. You seemed so calm. Weren't you afraid the windshield would blow in? That's what I would've been afraid of. I could just see that entire windshield coming at me."

Lilea smiled. Trea had always been so exuberant, always so much into anything she did. Tall and svelte, almost as tall as Jad, and nimble though not particularly graceful, Trea never seemed to settle down. She was without a doubt the most colorful person on the expedition. With her short reddish-brown hair and slender, muscular physique, she stood out in any crowd. She threw herself into her work with a gusto that outperformed everyone else on the team. She enjoyed not only the work she did, but she took great delight in the simple fact that she was the one chosen to study the animal life on this planet. To the others, Lilea sometimes felt, being on this planet was merely a job, not a delightful holiday of fun and fancy as Trea did so unmistakably.

"No, I wasn't afraid of that at first," Lilea said, her smile fading. "A few pieces of glass kept popping off, but the windshield held up okay. It was those big cracks that scared me the most. Every time I looked at them—I just hoped it would stay like it was with just the smashed area, like Case said. But when those large cracks shot all the way across, I did get scared the whole thing might come in. But by then, there was nothing I could do."

"Except land," Wila said. She leaned back against the benchwork that encircled the deck.

Lilea shook her head. "But there wasn't any place to land until we got most of the way home. I was afraid if I landed, it might not get off the ground again, and we'd lose one whole aerodyne, and exploration might be over. I wanted to preserve the ship if I could."

"I know what you're saying," Wila said. "We have to keep these ships working. If anything happens to them we might as well pack it all in. I keep thinking of what's happened over the twenty-eight T-sectors we've been on this planet. It's almost as though every time we try to do something, a disaster happens. First, a storm, then balls of ice. Now both aerodynes are damaged, and we haven't been on this planet for more than about twenty-eight T-sectors. I can't help thinking it's trying to tell us something."

"What do you mean, 'tell us something'?" Trea asked. She held her notebook against her chest, her long arms crossed over it and a quizzical look on her face.

"Sort of, like, 'If you're going to live on my surface, I'm going to make life as difficult as I can.'"

"Gee, sure," Trea said, hesitating. "We knew that before we came here. Sure, it's going to be difficult, but . . ."

"I realize that," Wila said, "but I'm just so puzzled about why both aerodynes were damaged so soon after we landed. Is this an omen of things to come? Or just coincidence?"

"I think it's just coincidence. We've just started. We've got a long way to go and a lot of exploring to do."

"Sure. That's okay as long as the aerodynes hold up."

Time Element 461.28.3.3.

"Boy, you're quite the hero now," Bent said as soon as the door to their compartment was closed. An element of sarcasm pervaded his voice.

"What do you mean?" Lilea entered the food preparation area of their compartment to fix her portion of the third meal, but the tone of his voice stopped her. He rarely made disparaging comments like that and she turned and looked at him, wondering. He stayed in the living area and didn't follow her into the food prep area to prepare what he wanted for the meal. That was unusual—they usually fixed and ate a meal together.

"You should've let Case pick someone. You could've been killed."

"I explained that to you. Nobody else volunteered."

"Yeah, well, you could've let him decide. He might've picked someone else. I bet he would've picked Col."

Lilea hesitated, unsure of where this conversation was going. Was he trying to second-guess her decision? That was so unlike him. He'd never done that before. He'd always accepted her lifestyle choices. "Maybe, but someone had to fly it back. I'm just as likely as Col." She pulled a frozen entrée from the small freezer underneath the countertop and placed it on the counter. "I bet he would have picked me anyway. I'm sure he wouldn't have picked Trea, maybe not Col. Dell or Mina either." She slipped the dinner into the microwave oven. "I'll bet he didn't *want* to pick anyone. I'm sure he wanted someone to volunteer."

Bent stayed still, watching her, anger still set deeply into his face. He seemed stymied by her reply. "Well, I don't like it. I don't like it at all. Next time, call me first." He turned and left the compartment, closing the door heavily. Not really slamming it, but she understood his intent.

"Bent—" she called after him. "Do you want to heat anything . . . ?" But he couldn't hear her anymore.

CHAPTER 16

QUAKING

Time Element 461.55.8.9.

Wila brought the newly repaired Aero One down smoothly onto the runway at Site One. All four of Bent's seismic recorders had been installed, and Jad's arms ached, and the painful stiffness of overuse cramped his shoulders. He'd never done so much physical labor in his life, lugging that heavy drilling motor around and pulling the bulky drill bit and drill extensions out of the ground. He and Bent had installed the fourth and final recorder on a broad plain several hundred anthans east of Site One, finishing a rough diamond pattern around the site, and now Jad was looking forward to activating them and investigating the upper layers of the crust of this planet.

"I'll meet you on Geo," Bent said as everyone jumped down from the aerodyne.

"Okay," Jad replied. Bent took off at a brisk trot for the elevator.

All three met on the Geological Sciences Deck, two decks above Personnel, around 55.9.2, and Lilea joined them. Bent sat in front of a 3 X 5 link high-def computer graphics screen displaying the readings of all four recorders simultaneously, one above the other. He activated each recorder individually through *Explorer*'s com, and four flat, black lines began to inch their way across the screen. As he worked, he kept up a quiet but rapid patter, explaining each step, throwing out comment after comment as the activation proceeded.

Hey, they're working. That makes all the hard work we did installing the recorders worthwhile.

As they watched the screens, Case and Jer arrived and stood quietly with the others.

"Okay," Bent said, turning to address everyone. "As you can see, nothing's happening right now at any of the sites   huh? What's that?"

The line representing the activity of recorder No. 1 abruptly developed several low, serrated peaks.

"Which is recorder one?" Lilea asked.

"It's west of here," Jad said, "not far from where the river that runs through the gorge turns south." He turned to Bent. "Do you have any idea what that means?"

"Not yet," Bent replied. He stared at the screen, absorbed in the deep black lines. The peaks got higher and higher, slashing from top to bottom as though someone was haphazardly running a marker over the screen. "Something big is definitely stimulating the recorder's probe unit. Let's watch and see what else occurs." A few nanosectors passed and the peaks continued. "Yes—look here—see?" His voice rose and a smile curled up the corners of his mouth. "Wow," he said quietly. "It even affected recorders 2 and 3. Especially 2. That recorder is north of here. Number 3 is south."

"What does all that mean?" Case asked.

"It means the event was strong enough to be transmitted all the way from its epicenter to these recorders. This is a big event. I've never seen anything like this on Anthanos. Some of those peaks are off scale . . ." By this time, the screen was almost black all over. Irregular peaks and troughs intersecting with each other dominated all four tracings. Tracing 1 stayed the most dramatic, its peaks rising so high they ran off the screen. "The magnitude of this event will be—it's moving the surface, I'm sure of it, it's got to—it's that big."

"Moving the surface?" Wila said. "That *is* big. That's never happened on Anthanos."

Moving the surface? Jad'd heard of this being possible on some of the moons of the giant outer planets in his home solar system, particularly the third moon of Tekaa, but no one had ever seen or recorded any surface movement. On one other moon, the quaking of the surface was simply the movement of chunks of solid methane ice on the surface of a liquid methane sea, and Jad once stood on one of those floes and felt its quivering, but that movement was a gentle rocking, not the sudden activity this planet had produced.

"Let's see if I can . . ." Bent mumbled as he typed a few commands on the geocom keyboard. His voice faded, and a few nanosectors later an image of the prime continent appeared on the screen. A bright red circle covered the extreme southwestern region and a big red "**25**" stood beside it. "There," he said, tapping the screen with self-congratulatory confidence. "I've located it. The computer calculates the events are located within this circle with an error of plus-or-minus 25 percent."

"That's a pretty high error," Wila said.

"Right. But the chance of the computer being correct is still seventy-five percent. I could enlarge the circle — the bigger the circle, the smaller the error — but it would cover so much area, it would trivialize the data. This is a reasonable compromise." He turned to face Case. "I need to install a recorder in the center of that circle."

Case didn't say anything for several nanosectors. Typical of Case, he crossed his arms over his chest and stared at the screen. "How many recorders did you bring with you?"

"Eight. The first four are installed. The other four are for extra sites — and this certainly qualifies as an extra site. But I also brought — "

"They only gave you eight? How come?"

"Space. Limited space on the Equipment Deck. But — "

"Won't that be kind of limiting, I mean, in what you can do?"

"Well, yeah, but I also brought twelve of the smaller less sensitive recorders. I'll use them closer to the landing site to map its subsurface structure more closely."

Case paused. "How soon do you want to install this fifth recorder?"

"As soon as possible. And, we can do a little hiking around to pick up samples while we're out there."

"Okay. I'll work something out. I'll have to integrate it into the Expedition Calendar. There are some empty spaces coming up in a few T-sectors when the aerodynes aren't being used. When do you plan to install the smaller recorders?"

"As soon as I can. I'll put them in a circular pattern around the landing site so I can map the rock this ship is sitting on. That'll finish that part of the Complete Survey Project."

"All right," Case said, scratching his head. "I'll let you know what I decide."

Wonderful, Jad thought, massaging his biceps. *Installing more recorders.*

Time Element 461.70.3.0.

"I keep thinking of the number of disasters we've had in the short time we've been on this planet." Wila had just finished reviewing the latest weather data at Site One on the com screen that faced the couch in their compartment, and she curled up beside Jad. Two cups of warm jell-kell sat on the low table in front of them. Jad put his arm around her and she nestled into the crook of his elbow. As she spoke, she ticked the disasters off on her fingers one by one. "Look, some of us are almost killed in a storm, there's another storm of ice balls that almost destroys an aerodyne, now a quaking of the ground out there. Who's to say there won't be a quaking of the ground here? It could knock this ship over. I wonder if there's more to these than just random events. Something more than we see on the surface."

Jad was puzzled by Wila's comments. He'd never thought of the incidents as anything other than random occurrences, and he didn't really understand what she was trying to say. "What do you mean?"

"I don't know exactly, but I know what I feel. With all these disasters—or near disasters, if you want—and we've only been on this planet for seventy T-sectors. That's only thirty-five revolutions of the planet on its axis. I can't help but think there's more to this than we can see or detect by instruments or sensors or whatever. Who's going to want to colonize a planet like that?"

"They're probably random. Don't you think they could be random?"

"Well, logically, I suppose they could. But I still have this feeling . . ."

"Do you think something will happen on this coming trip? Out west?"

"I don't know." Wila shrugged her shoulders. "It might. Tremors can occur long after the initial shock. I've seen it. It's happened on the moons of the outer planets. You remember? I showed you the seismic recordings. On the third moon of Tekaa. Why couldn't it happen here?"

"Nobody's ever seen surface movement on the third moon."

"That's right, but there have been aftershocks. And if there've been aftershocks there, why not here?"

"I don't know." Jad couldn't answer Wila's question, but it stuck in his mind until they went to bed and fell asleep later this darktime.

CHAPTER 17

EXPEDITION – ARRIVAL

Time Element 461.73.0.0.

During the darktime water had fallen steadily for several millisectors just before dawn, dampening the ground and producing a chilly, clammy fog that greeted the team when they rose. Everyone was up by sunrise, and the drizzle moistened his jumpsuit when Jad emerged from the shelter.

The Mountain Team had flown in the lightime before in Aero Two, setting up camp on a sandy surface amid a mélange of trees, shrubs, flowers, and grasses. All around them lay a flat, almost featureless desert. A few stands of grass poked up here and there, and a pile of driftwood lay in tangles on the bank of a narrow creek a few hundred links south of the camp site. Trees and bushes hugged the creek, and other vegetation sprouted nearby. Farther out a few flowers grew in small clumps, but beyond was only the scrub and low grass of the open desert. The crisp white peaks of a mountain range jutted up on the horizon to the north and west, and a small lake lay about a half-anthan north of the ship's position. It all looked so pleasant and peaceful to Jad, especially when he viewed it in the delicate pinks and oranges of the previous lightime's sunset. Yet, far below the sands on which he stood lurked an anomaly, a sort of ground-shaking peculiarity, almost a monster, waiting to strike a second time. Could it? Would it?

Bent had brought Aero Two down in a northwesterly direction, and Bent and Jad immediately installed the collapsible drilling tower on a flat, sandy area about two hundred links north of the right wing tip, in an area free of the larger vegetation of trees and shrubs. A cable from the aerodyne supplied power, and while they attended the drilling, Case and Jer made the obligatory security sweep, set up the shelter in the standard position just outboard of and slightly behind the left wing tip, and installed the intruder perimeter.

They used the second half of the lightime to gather specimens from the desert around the landing site. The drilling had produced a good core specimen, but Bent wanted rocks and soil samples, too. Mina had asked for water specimens, and Col wanted plant life, so Case and Jer, by default, were assigned to collect these.

Bent and Jad headed south, and Case and Jer took off north toward the lake. Almost as soon as they left the campsite, Bent began picking up rocks and soil. For each sample he followed a strict protocol. He imaged it in its natural state, then carefully removed it using a spatula or forceps, and placed it in a small numbered polyethylene box. He painstakingly entered data about the sample — time, weather conditions, its overall condition — into his electronic notebook. After he collected about thirty specimens and exhausted his supply of boxes, he and Jad started back.

Time Element 461.73.11.9.

To Jad, geology was something of a novelty. He was an astrophysicist, not a geologist, and though he knew a little about geological sciences from his studies in planetary science, learning the details of geological exploration was a new experience. To him, being the astrophysicist on the landing team was a badge of honor. He'd always had a vast interest in the stars and planets, how they worked and moved, and the forces that played on them. He knew of quantum dynamics and the field theories that described the subatomic interactions inside stars. In fact, he published the first scientific report on his special research project he called *quantum plasma hyperdynamics*. He was immensely proud of his knowledge and he liked to consider himself a little more scientifically sophisticated than anyone else on the team. More so than anyone except Wila — his wife, his love, his eternal companion — who shared his fascination with all things astronomical. She took astronomy to a more practical end, though, limiting her interest to planets, especially their composition.

But seated deeply within Jad's eager attraction to astrophysics lay a measured streak of self-importance. He sometimes looked down on some of the other team members, especially Bent and Lilea. To him, they were "digger scientists" because their professions required a lot of digging in the sands of Anthanos or the moons of other planets. That was beneath him, he felt, though he kept his opinion tight to his chest because he knew SpaceComm would jerk anyone from the team if they detected even a hint of vanity or conceit.

So it came as a rude shock to Jad when SpaceComm informed him that one of his duties would be to assist Bent during the geological exploration of the Blue Planet, and that meant he had to learn — dare he even think the word? — geology. He had to learn to get his hands dirty, in the literal sense of the word. He had to look for the different types and compositions of rocks Bent expected to find on the planet. He had to learn to operate the portable drilling rig Bent intended to use to install the seismic recorders that would monitor the interior of the planet. He'd been assigned the task of carrying the portable drill and drill bit that would be used to place the seismic charges Bent would set off to begin the process of mapping selected areas of the planet's crust.

None of this brought anything really new to Jad. His studies in astrophysics had exposed him to enough chemistry that he felt comfortable learning about the compositions of the various rocks he had to collect. His only problem now was he actually had to collect them.

Follow around some digger geologist and pick up rocks?

He took some comfort in the fact that SpaceComm, in addition to his geologic duties, wanted him to do some real astronomy during the exploration. They asked him to study the sun close up—they wanted real details about that star. But they also wanted planetary studies. Several large planets existed in this solar system, one remarkably similar to the large gas giants he was so familiar with at home. And there were other smaller, rocky planets closer to the sun. What do they look like? What are they composed of? Do they have an atmosphere? What is their mean surface temperature? That was so much more interesting than geology.

But as Jad accompanied Bent on his little rock-and-specimen gathering expedition, he was well aware that his first perceptions of Bent had been, perhaps, somewhat flawed, now that he saw Bent in his element. As they walked, Jad became more and more impressed with how easily Bent could explain the most complicated matter. Bent went out of his way to impart a tidbit of knowledge about each specimen as he plucked it from the ground. He made some of the more complicated points of geology understandable, and he obviously enjoyed explaining a few elementary details about each specimen as he collected it. To Jad, it even became, well, interesting. Other than the brief instruction in basic geology Jad received from Bent during Gold Team training, he'd only occasionally seen this side of Bent. After all, training was more about spaceflight than geology.

Bent and Jad arrived back at the campsite around 461.73.11.9, with plenty of light in the sky. Several millisectors later Case and Jer walked into camp carrying a sample bag bulging with specimens, and they too sat down in the warm atmosphere of the shelter for a rest. Bent checked the activity from the new seismic recorder, watching the results on his electronic notebook, but everything was quiet. No disturbances had rocked the sensor two hundred fifty links below the surface.

That made Jad feel marginally better about this trip, but he still had reservations in coming out here so soon after the ground had shaken, though he wasn't ready to challenge Case or Bent openly. He hadn't re-solved his own hesitation, and Wila's words that something "might" happen still stuck in his mind.

But Bent and Case were looking forward to this trip, especially the hike this coming lightime. Bent wanted to get into the mountains and take readings and collect specimens, and Case, from what Jad could gather, wanted to hike, to stretch his legs and get some exercise.

Oh, what the hell, Jad thought as he stood outside the shelter scanning the drizzly skies. *Let's go for a walk. If the mountains fall, they fall.*

Time Element 461.75.0.0.

The team prepared lumyon in the comfort of indoors, and then wandered outside into the morning's approaching warmth to pack their backpacks for the trip. Everyone took at least four eighth-trilinks of water and food for several days. Cold-weather gear and some scientific instru-ments made it into the packs. Jad and Bent took the precaution of packing only those supplies they decided they'd need, preferring to leave behind items of low utility, such as an extra jumpsuit. But they watched with some consternation as Case jammed his pack so full it almost overflowed and he had trouble fastening the upper flap.

"Do you think you should take so much?" Jer asked.

"Why not? The gravity on this planet is only 90 percent of that on Anthanos. I ought to be able to carry 10 percent more, right? It should be easy."

Jer stared at Case, concerned, certainly, but she said nothing further.

"All right, people," Case announced as soon as all backpacks were loaded. "Let's go." The time was 75.1.0.

Jad pulled his PersComm from one of the pockets of his pack and made a few entries on its miniature keyboard. "I've set my PersComm to continuously monitor the weather, including barometric pressure. It'll give us altitude readings as we hike. I've set it to zero now."

They swung their packs and started out, marching around the front of the aerodyne. The sun poked through the clouds in shafts of intense sunlight that burned away much of the haze, and the western sky had almost cleared. The outside air temperature was 18 Tal.

"If it's this hot this early," Jad said, "it's gonna be real hot later."

CHAPTER 18

EXPEDITION – TREK

Time Element 461.75.1.1.

Case set a generous pace, but remained careful not to travel too fast for the others. Jer trailed Case, Jad behind her, and Bent brought up the rear.

Jad enjoyed the hike. For him, carrying a large pack was somewhat akin to jogging — it forced him to exert himself. It got his heart beating faster and he was breathing heavily and regularly. For Jad, a good workout.

As they approached the mountains, the terrain changed. Hiking easily on what appeared to be animal trails through the desert, their route had been effortless and rock free, but their pace slowed as more rocks appeared on the trail. The Anthanian flat-soled boots they wore — made particularly for the smooth, regular sands of Anthanos — provided almost no traction on the trail, but being tightly bound to the lower leg there was little chance of anyone turning an ankle. They took their time, working their way carefully through and around the rocks, eventually reaching the other side of a narrow valley where the trail started upward more steeply. Here, one subsector after starting out, Case called a halt and everyone took a short break. Jad pulled out his notebook. "Twenty-eight Tal," he said.

They got underway again around 75.2.0.

Now they were in the mountains proper. They'd left the desert behind and the air temperature had dropped. Taller plants predominated here — erect, towering giants eighty to a hundred links tall, but several types of lower, more rounded plants also dotted the terrain at this level. The rocky trail turned steeper and the going got slower, but a nippy refreshing breeze whistled along the trail directly at them as they hiked, cooling their sweaty faces. Case's precise, deliberate pace kept the team together even when the trail petered out.

"Up ahead," Case said. "Looks like a trail." He walked on and found a narrow trail that led through and around the rocks. After several anthans, the trail turned north and worked its way several hundred links up the face of a cliff, then switched back and headed for a visible rock outcropping not far ahead. "We'll stop there for a subsector and get something to eat."

Several types of large trees shaded this rocky area and formed a natural campsite. The air was cooler, not as humid. Jad pulled out his Pers-Comm and worked his way through the readings. "Twenty-two Tal," he said. "We're about two thousand links above the area where the aerodyne is parked."

"I'm going to take a walk around," Jer said. "I need to collect some specimens for Col. There's an interesting scent in the air. I wonder where it's coming from."

Time Element 461.75.4.7.

A subsector later they swung their packs and took out over the trail. Bent led, with Jad behind him. The rocky trail became smoother as it led slightly downhill from their rest site, but soon the trail rose again and the rocks returned. Many areas of the trail were muddy, and Bent picked his way carefully, trying to avoid the wet areas.

The trail led out onto a ledge with a steep drop-off of more than a thousand links to their left, and a sheer wall of solid rock to their right. As they hiked, the ledge got steeper and narrower, but several hundred links ahead stood a small, wooded peak. Between them and the peak the trail narrowed considerably.

"This is becoming more and more interesting," Bent said. He stopped briefly and tapped the wall to his right with his hammer. A small flake chipped off and he caught it. He held it for a few nanosectors, turning it over in his hand, absorbed in examining it closely. Then he put the hammer away and set out again, slowly forward, uphill.

Areas of mud and clay still dotted the trail amidst the rocks. The hikers made their way slowly and carefully, dodging the hazards as best they could. Jad had become concerned by the narrowness and steepness of the trail, and of being confined to a slender ledge between the cliff and the rock.

With all the mud and clay on the trail, it was inevitable that someone would step into the wet spots. No one could avoid every hazard, and their boots gave them little or no traction in the slick mud. Jad found he could plant his foot against a rock on the trail to get a secure foothold, but he slipped several times on the muddy trail, sometimes only momentarily losing his balance without falling, but twice he fell forward and had to catch himself on one hand. The presence of a heavy pack didn't help him maintain his balance either.

These boots don't give us much traction. Jad's left foot slipped again — for the fourth or fifth time. He fell forward, catching himself on both hands, forcing himself to resist the turning force of his pack.

You sure don't have much room to catch yourself if you slip. Someone might slip and — what was that? It was like a bump, or a thump, or . . . a moan.

"Case!"

Time Element 461.75.4.9.

"What was that?" Jad stopped walking and slowly turned around. His pack brushed against the stone wall, and he had to avoid being pushed toward the edge by the heavy pack. Jer lay flat on her belly leaning over the edge of the trail only a few links away, reaching for something. *My god, she's slipping — do something. Hurry!*

Jad took a quick three or four steps and leaned down and grabbed Jer's backpack just before she slipped over the edge. But as he grabbed her, the force of her falling pulled him down flat onto his stomach. He held tightly onto Jer's pack, trying to keep her from slipping completely over the edge. A rock jutted painfully into his left side. "Jer! Grab my arm!" he yelled. Finally she swung completely around facing him, her legs hanging precariously over the edge. She grabbed at his arm, and as he helped her climb back onto the trail he felt another force pulling on him, pulling him back, too.

Jer didn't appear to be injured, but as she scrambled back onto the trail she jumped up and threw off her pack and ran down the trail yelling. "Case! Case!"

Panicky thoughts ran through Jad's mind. He looked down the trail, beyond where Jer was running but he didn't see Case. *Where is Case? I don't see him. He's nowhere around. Why didn't he come over and help Jer get back on the trail — uh, no!* Jad cautiously glanced over the trail's edge. Something familiar lay sprawled on the rocks below. The unmistakable blue-green color of a jumpsuit. "Oh, crap! That's Case! He's fallen over the edge!"

Jad picked up Jer's backpack and took out after her, watching carefully as she ran ahead. She ran too fast for the trail and slipped or tripped and fell several times, once cutting her face. But she ran and ran, screaming and screaming. "Case! Case!"

Jad ran more slowly than Jer, taking his time to avoid falling on the rocky trail. With two backpacks he didn't want to fall and compound the tragedy. Jer must be looking for a place to get off the trail onto the rocks below, but she'd have to run a long way to get that far. She passed the site where they rested, but the drop-off was still too high, and she ran on down the trail, taking the switchback to turn back toward the grassy area below. Finally, she jumped off the trail at the base of the rock where she could run back toward Case. Jad stayed right behind her.

Now the running was easier and Jad could run faster. Even carrying two packs, he caught up with Jer, though he remained behind her.

Jer ran more easily, too, still yelling. "Oh, no! Please, no! Oh god! No!" She came to the rocky area below the trail where Case lay, but he was absolutely still. He lay on his back spread-eagle on the rocks, his head thrown back at a funny angle. His backpack had come off and had been tossed several links away. Much of the contents of that overstuffed pack had spilled into the area around him. Jer knelt over him.

"Case! Can you hear me? Can you hear me?"

Case didn't move or respond. Jer threw herself onto his body and locked her arms around his neck, enclosing his face and upper body with hers. She continued to yell. "Case! Can you hear me? Oh, god no! Case! Please tell me you can hear me!"

Bent arrived. Jad dropped Jer's backpack and removed his own. Bent pulled a first-aid kit from his pack while Jad grabbed Case's left arm and felt desperately for a pulse, but he couldn't find one. He couldn't use the pulse in Case's neck because Jer held on to him so tightly he couldn't get to it.

"Jer," Jad said. "Let us try to help him." But Jer refused to move. "Jer," Jad said again, a little louder and more firmly. "Let us try to help him."

Jer hesitantly relaxed, and the first thing Jad saw were the blood-red stains on Case's salt-and-pepper hair. Blood covered Jer's arms, too. Jad took Case's head in his hand, but the head moved too easily and he became suspicious. Something wet smeared his hands at the back of the head. He let go and his hands were spotted with blood.

"The back of his head is injured," Jad said. "I think his neck is broken." Jer let out a sound Jad had never heard coming from another Anthanian—part gurgle, part moan, part cry—and she collapsed on the rocks.

Bent grabbed the portable intubator from his first-aid kit and inserted it through Case's mouth into his throat. He attached the chest inflator to the tube and tried to expand the lungs. Jad attached the small electrocardiomonitor to Case's left arm and began CPR.

"The cardiomonitor should beep with every heart beat," Jad said as he thumped Case's chest. "Keep inflating the lungs!" he yelled. He pumped and pumped, and Bent inflated and inflated, but the cardiomonitor never uttered a beep.

"Get the solution!" Jad yelled, and Bent grabbed the injectable cardiostimulator solution from the first-aid kit. He unsheathed the six-decilink long needle and plunged the entire needle into Case's chest, through his jumpsuit and between the ribs directly into the silent heart. He injected the solution, but the cardiomonitor never beeped. Jad kept pumping.

Microsectors passed. Millisectors. Three, four, five millisectors. Both worked frantically. Jad wasn't thinking—he worked only on the epinephrine his adrenal glands were pouring out. Six millisectors passed. Seven.

"Quit, Jad," Bent finally said, dropping the inflator. "Quit. That's enough. We've done all we can."

"We can't quit now. Keep inflating!"

"It's no use. We've done all we can. I never heard one heartbeat." Bent placed a hand on Jad's arm.

Jad quit in exhaustion and stood up beside the body. Nothing he or Bent did had any effect. Nothing made any difference. The result was now clear—Case was dead.

Jer still lay on the rocks, sobbing uncontrollably.

CHAPTER 19

STRETCHER

Time Element 461.75.5.8.

No one moved for several microsectors after Jad quit CPR. He just stood there, trying to think of something else he could do to revive the lifeless body at his feet. He didn't know what to say, he didn't know what to do. He wasn't sure he even knew what to think.

Questions flooded his mind. *What happens next? Who's landing team commander now? Jer is — obviously Jer. But can she accept command now? We had all those lectures and discussions with the psychiatry and mental health people about how to handle death and injury, even if the Commander of the Landing Team is killed . . . and we had first aid and CPR . . . but I never really thought anything like this would happen. This changes things.*

As he stood beside the body, he became conscious of Jer, sobbing on the rocks behind him. He turned to speak to her, and Bent came around from the other side.

"Jer," Bent said. "I'm so sorry. I don't know what to say."

Jad couldn't think of words that would express his sorrow either. He was a scientist—his training had taught him to be objective and dispassionate. He knew nothing of how to deal with death, especially how to talk to someone who'd just lost her husband. He sat down on a rock near Jer and placed a hand on her shoulder. But the thought that came most prominently into his mind was the conversation he'd had with Wila before they left on this trip. She was right, something *did* happen, and he wondered what she was thinking right now. "I'll call *Explorer* and let them know what happened." He pulled his PersComm from his pack. Mina, on duty on the Communications Deck, answered.

"Mina, this is Jad. We've had an accident." He walked several steps farther down the rocks so Jer couldn't hear as he spoke into the tiny microphone on the PersComm. "Case is dead."

Mina seemed hesitant to answer. "J-J-Jad, what did you say? Is-is this some sort of joke?"

"No, this is real. I'm not joking. Case is dead. He fell off a cliff. The cliff we were hiking on. His neck is broken."

"Oh, m-my god." Mina spoke slowly and quietly. There was a pause. "Is everyone else okay? J-Jer. How's Jer?"

"Yes, everyone's okay. Jer's hysterical, but she's not injured. Can you tell Dell? We'll need the stretcher to carry the body out with."

"Yes, yes. I-I'll tell him. I'll get back to you. Or D-Dell will."

Jad deactivated the PersComm and went back to Jer and Bent. No one spoke. Jad wanted to sit down beside Jer and try to comfort her, but he couldn't think of anything to say, and besides, sitting down in this situation seemed the wrong thing to do. It might look like he was giving up. He should *do* something. Something to make everything better, to make everything all right again. To bring Case back. After about a microsector, his PersComm beeped. Dell was on the other end.

"What the hell happened?"

"Case is dead. He slipped off a cliff and fell several hundred links to some rocks below. We think his neck is broken. We tried to resuscitate him, but we can't. We'll need the stretcher to carry the body out. Can you or Wila bring the other aerodyne?"

"Oh, god, no." A long pause. Dell seemed to be trying to catch his breath. He spoke slowly and carefully, but his voice shook. "Yes, yes, of course we can."

"I'll activate Aero Two's homing signal, then I'll meet you at the ship and take you back where the body is."

"All right. I'll meet you there in about two subsectors."

Jad terminated comm and returned to Bent sitting with Jer. "I'm going back to the aerodyne. Dell's coming with the stretcher. We'll take Case's body back when they arrive." Bent nodded okay.

Jad found Case's PersComm on the ground several links from the pack. It was scratched and dirty and dented in one place, but it still worked, and he used it to activate the aerodyne's homing signal. Then, before he left, he removed his shelter half from his pack and placed it over Case's body. Jer turned from where she sat, watching. She drew closer to the body and lifted the side of the sheet and took hold of Case's right hand. She sobbed quietly, her eyes closed, murmuring to herself.

"No, no, no. Please, no, no. Oh, god, no." Her tears dropped onto the shelter half and rolled softly onto the rocky ground.

Time Element 461.75.6.1.
"Wh-Where have you been?" Mina asked.

"Over near the hills." Lilea stepped out of Runabout 2 near the base of the elevator. She'd been in the dry stream bed near where it emerged from the hills, and drove back along a narrow strip of flat land at the foot of the hills. "Dell said there was a Level Two Emergency and I should come back right away. What's going on? Why would Dell call an emergency?" Lilea glanced down toward the runway where Col and Dell were loading a shelter package into the cargo hold of Aero One. That was odd because with one aerodyne away on an expedition, the other one was always held as a backup, and getting it ready for a flight could mean only — *oh, my god* — something serious had happened. "Why are they getting Aero One ready for a flight?" Mina didn't say anything right away and that just exaggerated Lilea's bewilderment. "Mina? What's going on?"

Mina turned slightly away from Lilea. "C-Case has been killed. He f-fell off a cliff."

"Oh, my god. No!" Lilea jumped at Mina's statement, but she had something else on her mind. "Bent?" she mumbled.

"Bent's okay." Mina turned and looked at her. "Jad's okay too. H-He was the one who told me about it. They're going to take the stretcher to the mountains and bring C-Case's body out."

"I . . . I don't believe it. Are you sure? Jer? How's Jer?"

"Jer's okay too. But I gather she's devastated."

"Oh, my — I guess so . . ." Lilea's mind spun, her heart raced. She tried to speak, but words came with difficulty. She thought of Bent. *He must be beside himself.* She should go and be with him. "Who's going on the flight?"

"I-I don't know. I'll ask Dell." They walked down the slope to the aerodyne. "Dell, who are you planning on taking with you?"

"Wila will fly, and Col and I will go. Mina, you and Trea and Lilea stay here. We'll need you on comm."

"There's room for one more," Lilea said. "How about letting me go, too?"

Dell paused for about a nanosector, but he continued to stare at Lilea. "Okay, get your sleeping bag and grab some food. We're going to have to spend the darktime there before we come back."

Aero One lifted off at 461.75.7.0.

Time Element 461.75.9.1.

By walking fast and jogging wherever the terrain would allow, Jad reached Aero Two about a subsector and a half after he started out. Very little other than the death of the landing team leader and its consequences ran through his mind as he made his way back through the desert. Just as he reached the landing site, he heard the unmistakable sound of Aero One beginning its landing approach.

Wila put Aero One down several thousand links from Aero Two and allowed it to slide up behind the first ship when she cut the engine. They pulled the stretcher from the cargo hold and Jad, Col, Dell and Lilea began the long hike back. Wila stayed behind to set up the shelter.

They reached the accident site two subsectors later. Lilea ran over to Jer and gave her a big hug, part of the traditional Anthanian greeting, and Jer hugged her back.

"Why don't we go over there?" Lilea motioned to a smoother site among the rocks near Jer's pack. Jer had stopped crying, but her face was still streaked with tears. Lilea wet a cloth with water from her bottle and wiped the tears and blood from Jer's face, especially below her right eye where she'd cut herself falling on the trail. Then Jer closed her eyes and placed her head in her hands and sat absolutely still.

Dell pulled the shelter half back and examined Case's head and neck. "You're right, his neck is broken. He died as soon as he hit the ground." He replaced the shelter half and walked over to where Jer and Lilea sat.

"Jer, can you hear me?"

Jer nodded. She stared off into the distance, but spoke slowly and softly. "He's dead. He's dead." Several more tears rolled down her cheeks.

They placed Case's body on the stretcher, strapped it down, and replaced the shelter half. Before they left, Jad watched as Dell examined the area. He seemed to be most interested in the cliff and the position of Case's body on the ground. Several times he looked up at the trail above, and once he paced off—as well as he could among the rocks—the distance from the base of the cliff to where the body lay.

When he finished, he picked up Case's backpack. "It was damaged in the fall. Look how the back is smashed in. The top flap is torn. A lot of stuff came out." He and Jad gathered as much as they could—mostly clothing and food—and crammed it back into the pack.

Jad glanced at his time recorder as Dell and Col picked up the stretcher—75.11.0.

"I'm hoping we can get the body back to the shelter before darktime," Dell said. "But we'll have to leave soon. Right away, in fact."

The sun hovered in a reddish-orange sky just above the peaks in the west. A chilly breeze swirled through the site and long, dark shadows groped their way toward the group. Travel was slow through the rocks until they reached the trail where they could make better time. Jer insisted on walking behind the stretcher. She kept her head bowed slightly, watching only the trail and the stretcher in front of her.

By the time they reached the aerodynes the sky was dark.

CHAPTER 20

RESOLUTION

Time Element 461.77.7.1.

I'd forgotten we brought body bags with us.

Lilea climbed the interdeck ladder to the Personnel Deck and went to her compartment. The sudden shock and mind-blocking numbness which engulfed her after Case's death had largely disappeared, and for the first time since returning from the western mountains she could envision in more detail what life on this strange planet was going to be like without the team leader.

"Bent," she called as she entered her compartment, but he didn't answer. She called his name again and looked in the bedroom. He wasn't around.

She sat down on the couch and stared at the com screen on the opposite wall. The screen was blank save for the current time, 461.77.7.2, in bright gold lettering in the upper left-hand corner. A blue "power on" LED glowed peacefully at the bottom.

Such a pretty color, that blue. Not much different from the blue you see of this planet from a distance.

She felt chilled. She called up environmental data on the com screen and checked the compartment's temperature and thermostatic settings. Twenty-two Tal. Not cool at all, but she crossed her arms over her chest, trying to maintain a little warmth.

Several thoughts trickled through her mind, but the memories that predominated were all about Case. She remembered especially the first time they'd met, on 459.685 at the meeting at SpaceComm Headquarters when they were told of their appointment to the Gold Team. As one of the few who held the second-highest spaceflight rank at SpaceComm, senior command pilot, Case wore four seven-pointed stars vertically on the sleeves of his flight suit, and with the extensive experience in space that title implied, he was the logical choice to head up the landing team. Yet, at the meeting when the ten of them were notified of their selection, he seemed just as surprised as she and Bent and the others, even though he was much higher up in the hierarchy at SpaceComm and certainly must've heard rumors.

She also remembered going through training with Case. She pulled from long-term memory an image of the five big simulator buildings on the spaceport with the facsimiles of the Blue Planet's surface built up inside, like a giant movie set. She, Case and all the others spent hundreds of T-sectors in those buildings learning how to explore an unknown planet. He taught her how to operate the runabouts because they were larger and so much more sophisticated than the ones she and Bent drove at home. Though he didn't teach her how to fly the aerodynes — that was done by a team of trainers at SpaceComm — he kept constant track of her progress.

She even taught him a few concepts about anthropology and paleontology, and how to look for artifacts of intelligent life forms. He seemed genuinely interested, going so far as to peruse a couple of e-texts on the subject during training. She was impressed at his attempt to understand her chosen field.

She visualized the mock-up control room of *Explorer* built within the Control Room Simulator Building on the spaceport, and she remembered the many subsectors she and Case and a trainer spent in that room learning how to fly the ship. She recalled the landings and takeoffs she made piloting the *real* ship under Case's tutelage. That was scary — nerve racking even — the first time she had to do that, especially the landing. Takeoff and insertion into orbit weren't so bad, they were almost completely automated, but then there were the landings. You can't imagine how scary it was, having to land that ship for real. Fortunately, she had to do it only twice, and Case was in the copilot's seat beside her the entire time, and she didn't have to do a great job — just good enough to get the ship on the ground — then she yielded the pilot's seat to someone else. And she was glad to, yet Case landed that ship time after time.

Her mind drifted to the aerodyne flight back from the grasslands with the cracked windshield, and of pulling back the heavy cloth Case had insisted on hanging in the cabin, and looking out the window to her right and seeing him flying Aero Two slightly ahead of her. She could still hear his voice through Aero One's headphones, "Land! Land!" and she said back as calmly as she could, "I can't. There's too much vegetation down there." He didn't argue. He accepted her decision to keep flying.

Whatever he was, he was at least fair and reasonable, though some memories seemed to belie that assumption. His dealings with Trea occasionally were . . . and here she searched for the proper term . . . heated. He and Trea never got along well, dating from an incident during weapons training when they were first issued the new electronic hand weapons. A stubborn pacifist, Trea at first refused to accept hers, though she was finally convinced by Jer and Col to wear it and learn to fire it or be kicked off the team. But since the team consisted of married couples, if Trea were kicked out, SpaceComm couldn't just add another zoologist. The entire Gold Team would be eliminated and the backup team, the Blue Team, would take over. Even after landing, she continued to refuse to wear it outside in spite of SpaceComm's direct orders and Case's bellowing at her to go back and get it.

I'm surprised SpaceComm didn't do something about their relationship. It got pretty tense at times.

Then Case's decision to go to the mountains so soon after the quaking—was there an element of rashness in that decision? She didn't think so. He could have easily overruled Bent and said no, let's wait a short time, but his argument to the team was simple and, in hindsight, appropriate: we were sent here to explore this planet. He explained his reasoning during the meeting the lightime before the Mountain Team left. "We knew it would be dangerous before we landed here. We can't just sit here, afraid to go out because something might happen. The shaking out there is only one incident, and there will be many more incidents, I'm sure. If we let them influence the way we explore this planet, we'll wind up afraid to leave *Explorer*. That's not our mandate, people. We are here to explore, and that's what we will do."

Besides, his death had nothing to do with the ground shaking, so maybe he was right after all.

But to Lilea, her relationship with Case was more than just the memories of their interactions. He was the one who got them here. His decisions in spacecraft operation—governed by more than forty years of experience in spaceflight—were invariably right on the money. He made most of the small decisions which guided *Explorer*, and yes, it's true the ship was primarily controlled by computer, but there were the myriad adjustments, corrections, opinions, and compromises the spacecraft commander had to make T-sector after T-sector during the flight, just to get them to this little speck of blue and white and green and brown.

He was the one who picked this landing site, so well chosen in the middle of the desert. He made the final decision to forego the original Prime Landing Site, a half-anthan north of Site One, because of the heavy sand that covered it, and his caution seemed justified. This site was much closer to the hills and potentially dangerous, but it was a hard site and safer for the ship, and he put it down so effortlessly, with a barely noticeable thump. He was the one who got the aerodynes and runabouts going, and he maintained and repaired them. He was the one who worked so hard leveling and smoothing the runway.

This was really his expedition and he'll always be known as the leader, even though he was killed leading it. *But more to the immediate point, what are we going to do without him? Who's going to take over and run this expedition? Jer?*

Lilea paused in her reflections. *Yes, she will. She's second-in-command.*

Then she turned to her recommendation to SpaceComm about continuing the exploration. Would it be yes, or no? To now, she'd always answered with a resounding "Yes." But now?

Yes, I think so. It may be difficult, but we can do it.

She left her compartment to look for Bent.

Time Element 461.77.8.0.

Lilea found Bent, Jad and Col at the base of *Explorer* digging a grave. They dug it northeast of the ship, about twenty links from the runway and not far from Aero One in its parking space. When they finished, all four took the elevator to the Medical Station on the Entry Deck.

No one spoke as they rode up in the elevator. When they reached the Medical Station, the men helped Dell place the body in one of the dark blue nylon body bags. Lilea waited outside, and as the four men carried the body the short nine links across the Entry Deck to the airlock she turned away, preferring not to watch as the group passed by.

So sad, and so utterly unnecessary.

At precisely 461.77.10.0, they lowered Case's body into the ground. Everyone except Jer gathered around the grave.

"Where's Jer?" Lilea whispered to Bent as the service began.

"I don't know," Bent whispered back. "She may be watching. She asked us to dig the grave here so she could see it from her window."

The short, simple funeral gave each person an opportunity to say a few words about Case, to praise some proper and fitting attribute of his personality, or to relate a suitable tale or anecdote. They raised a prayer to the Great Sun God Arteamos and they sang the dirge for the dead, the *Gor-Tenvos*. Then they filled in the grave and made their way back to the ship.

CHAPTER 21

GATHERING

Time Element 461.78.1.3.

"It's those goddamn boots we wear." Bent spoke quietly, but Lilea could hear the anger as it infiltrated the sadness in his voice. "They're too slippery. They don't have enough traction. They're made for the dry sand on Anthanos. They're not made for mountain climbing." Lilea reached over and took his hand. It was shaking. She squeezed it and he squeezed hers back.

As the pinks and oranges of the sunset were splayed out on the high streaky clouds in the west, and a warm dry wind swirled around the landing site, the team retreated to Mina and Dell's compartment to listen as Jad and Bent described in precise, horrifying detail what happened on that mountain. Several brought chairs from their own compartments. Mina served steaming hot jell juice—the colorless form without the bitter kell extract that turned the mixture a bright red and supplied caffeine and other stimulants. Hers was non-fermented for those who preferred it, but a small amount of the distilled form, the *khus-jell*, which someone had smuggled on board was also available.

Alcohol? The sharp, sweet aroma of the khus-jell drifted through the compartment. Lilea looked around for the source—yes, there it was. Col was heating some in the microwave in the food prep area. "On board a spaceship?" she said. "That's totally against regulations. Case wouldn't approve." She wanted only to make a joke to ease the tension in the crowded compartment, but as soon as she said it, she realized it sounded mocking.

"I'm aware of that, but at this time, why not?" Col replied, his voice dry and sharp. "I need it. It helps settle my nerves." He pulled the cup from the microwave and slammed the door. The loud clap startled Lilea slightly, and she watched Col even more closely.

Col's pleasant personality had vanished. Never outgoing and extroverted like Trea, he usually had a smile and a ready "Hi" for anyone he met around the ship or outside. But he'd turned distant. He took the cup of steaming hot juice over to the small table in the food-prep area. He sat on the table because the two chairs had been brought into the living area, and though he faced the group and was a part of the discussion, he was definitely separated from it.

Lilea admired Col above anyone else on the landing team, even more than Case. To her, Col represented the best of what scientific exploration was capable of becoming. Col didn't own the nasty temper of Case, his was a much quieter demeanor. With his slightly balding pate and stooped shoulders and tendency to a pot belly, he certainly didn't look the part of a first-class explorer, and his delight in spending time in the food-preparation area of his compartment didn't help either. But Col was endowed with a wonderfully insightful intellect which no one else on the team had, not even the cerebral Jad. Lilea enjoyed listening to Col talk—he always had fascinating stories to tell—even if he did occasionally use big words she didn't understand.

I guess he's really feeling the loss of Case. After all, Col and Case were close friends. Col was probably closer to Case than to any other man on the team. And now that Case is dead, Col's best friend is gone. She turned back to the conversation.

"Why did he fall?" Dell asked. "What was it that actually made him fall?"

"I don't know," Jad said, shaking his head. The tall, lean and lanky Jad had always had a tendency to slump down in his chair and throw his long legs out into the center of whatever conversation he was a part of, and this time was no different. Normally, Jad remained calm and cool in any situation he found himself, and his body language stayed quiet, if not downright motionless. But now he fidgeted more than usual. He'd slump down for a few microsectors, and then he'd pull himself up and sit hunched forward, his elbows on his knees, or he'd lean back in the chair and lift the front two legs off the floor. He shifted between those positions as the conversation continued, squirming restlessly, changing something— arms, head, torso, legs—as though he couldn't get comfortable. As he spoke, a trace of weariness infiltrated his voice. "He was last in line. Nobody saw him fall, but from the condition of the trail I guess he hit a slippery spot and his foot went out from under him. I slipped a few times myself."

"That heavy pack Case was wearing might have contributed," Bent said. "If that pack shifted when he slipped, it could have pulled him over. You know, before he could correct—"

"He fell more than five hundred links," Lilea said. "That's what it looked like to me."

"More than that," Dell said. "Maybe a thousand. Did you notice his body was several links away from the base of the cliff? I looked over the area just before we left, and I noticed his body was farther from the cliff than you would expect if he fell straight down."

"W-what do you mean?" Mina asked.

Dell took a big gulp from the glass of juice he held in his hand. "His body probably bounced after he hit the ground. Bounced or rolled. He probably landed on his back because his pack was crushed and a lot of stuff came out. I bet he turned and put the pack below him as he fell. To try to cushion the fall. But his head still hit some rocks." Dell stared at the floor and shook his head. "He couldn't avoid all the rocks."

"Do you think he had enough presence of mind to turn like that as he fell?" Lilea asked.

"I bet he did. That's not something that can be taught. You just have to be the type of person to do it automatically. That's what Case was."

The room became quiet for a few nanosectors when Lilea spoke. "I can't believe he's gone. It's like he'll be coming through the door any time now."

"I know what you mean," Trea said. "Jer's going through hell right now. I saw her about a subsector ago, but she wanted to be left alone."

"I gave her a mild sedative," Dell said. "She's probably sleeping, which is the best thing for her right now."

"Did she seem all right? Was she in touch with reality?" Lilea asked. "Or was she out of it altogether?"

"She's quiet and a little depressed," Dell said. "But that's normal in this situation. Actually, I think she's handling things pretty well."

"How are we going to redistribute his duties?" Wila asked. "Who's going to maintain the aerodynes and runabouts? He knew them better than any of us."

"The equipment maintenance will fall on us," Dell said. "We'll have to call up maintenance instructions on ship's com and make any repairs ourselves. That also goes for routine maintenance. As for the other stuff, Jer is officially in command now, and she'll take over most of his duties."

"That's going to be difficult for Jer to do right now," Trea said. "She's been devastated by Case's death. I don't think we should expect her to do everything he did right away."

"Actually, as far as the ship's systems are concerned," Col said from his seat at the table, "Jer knows those as well as Case." Everyone turned to look in his direction. "Especially environment, but even navigation, computers, engines, all the others. She *is* a Command Pilot." His voice turned hard, almost angry, and he poked the air with his finger. "She still outranks all of us and it's incumbent on us to not forget that. Undoubtedly she will be promoted to Senior Command Pilot when we return."

"This is the best reason I can think of why all of us were trained to fly this ship," Lilea said. "At least we know we can get back."

"I-I'm not worried about Jer getting us b-back," Mina said. "I-It'll be a long time before we have to r-return to *Star Voyager*. S-She should be back to normal by then."

"I'm sure," Dell said. "But we need to get back to work. Be sure and send out your reports. Kal will want a report from each one of us about this."

CHAPTER 22

JER

Time Element 461.85.2.0.
When they pressed the door-announce button, Jer answered. "I thought someone would be by sooner or later." She invited her three visitors in.

Dell and Mina took seats on the couch, and Lilea sat in one of the chairs from the food-prep area which Jer had placed opposite the couch, on the other side of the low table between them. A large backpack, its top flap torn almost completely off, sat in the corner next to the bedroom door. A pewter serving carafe and three cups were settled in a brass tray on the table as though Jer had intended to serve a warm beverage. But she made no effort to offer her guests a drink. She remained standing, refusing to sit in the one chair still available, and she turned away from her visitors, looking out the window in the food-prep area, her arms at her side, her fingers gently tapping the table.

Lilea scanned the compartment. The cleanliness of the compartment and the neatness of Jer's uniform reflected the care she always took of herself and her surroundings. That was so unmistakable in her uniform—clean and neatly pressed, with her trademark—and distinctly non-regulation—pale blue handkerchief poking a touch above the top of the left breast pocket. Jumpsuits, like all Anthanian clothing, were permanent press, and most on the team wore theirs straight out of the washer-dryers on the Life Support Deck, Deck 7, one level above Personnel. Jer's meticulous nature required an additional pressing.

"You must have already sent a report to Kal," Jer said, still looking out the window.

"Yes, I did," Dell said. "We've already received a reply. At 84.7.1. You can access the reply on com any time you want."

Jer nodded.

"Kal was angry."

"Angry?" Jer turned toward Dell and took a few steps toward her guests. "That's not like Kal."

"Perhaps angry is too strong a word. But he had questions about the expedition."

"Questions? What kind of questions?"

"About the conduct of the expedition. Why you were hiking on a narrow trail with a steep drop-off to one side, and why you were hiking on a trail that was wet and slippery, and why you didn't use a safety line. And why Case carried such a big pack. He wondered why you didn't postpone the trip because of the quaking in the area. Questions like that."

"I see." Jer turned back to the window.

"Kal will want to hear from you."

Jer didn't answer immediately. She remained still, staring out the window.

"Jer," Lilea said. "We're worried about you. You haven't come out of here in eight T-sectors. We were wondering when you can come back and join us."

"I don't know. I have a hard time getting up enough courage to leave. It's as though I've lost my security, my protection. I'm afraid to go out."

"You shouldn't be. You know we're all a part of the same team. Everyone is looking forward to seeing you back at work. I bet if Case were here, he'd insist on it."

"I know. But Case isn't here. He's gone forever, and I can't just ignore that."

"No one is asking you to ignore that," Dell said, "but we do need you back at work. If we were still back on Anthanos, you could take some time off to get over Case's death. That's standard SpaceComm policy. But we don't have that option here. Can you come back this T-sector? We've got several projects planned that are going to require aerodyne flights, and we need someone on Comm. How about it?"

"It's so hard to get up the courage to go out that door." Jer stared at the floor for several nanosectors, apparently lost in thought.

"How about in the next lightime, in two T-sectors," Dell said, "and working at Comm. You know that position better than anyone. We'll need someone reliable there."

"Well, okay, I'll try it. But I don't know how long I'll last."

"I'll bet you last a full shift," Lilea said.

"L-Lilea and I will be over at z-zero-zero."

"All right, I'll be ready. I'll try it." Jer turned back to the window and her three visitors left.

Early the next lightime, at 87.0.0, Lilea and Mina pressed the door-announce button on the jamb next to Jer's door and entered when she said, "Come in."

"Jer, are you ready?" Lilea asked.

"Yes, I'm ready," Jer called out from the bedroom. "I'm just finishing up here."

They left the compartment and climbed the ladder to Deck 2, the Communications Station near the top of the ship. Jer took her seat at the main comm computer and called up the title list of the most recent activity. She started screening the list.

"My, you guys have been busy." Eventually, she came to the entry that contained the medical and firsthand witness accounts of Case's death, including the images Dell made during his brief autopsy. The nondescript title, "Medical Report, 461.83" gave little information, but then she checked the size—85 MB. "That's a large entry," she said. "What is that?" She marked the report by touching it on the screen.

"Jer, are you sure you want to open that report?" Mina said.

Jer hesitated. "No, I guess I don't." She lingered at the entry, but continued down the list.

"Are you going to be okay here?" Lilea asked. "We need to get back to work, and we want to be sure you'll be all right."

"I'm sure I will be," Jer said, and Lilea and Mina left the deck.

"I forgot about Dell's report being on the comm computer," Lilea said as they reached the Command Deck, two decks below. "I hope she doesn't open the report and read it. It could push her back into seclusion."

CHAPTER 23

SWIRL

Time Element 461.89.2.0.

"What is that?" Col asked.

Lilea stood across from Col at the central table on Geo, scanning several probe images. Wila had downloaded them from her atmospherics computer over the past few lightimes and printed them out on plastic sheets.

"I've been monitoring atmospheric conditions over the water southeast of here for about twenty T-sectors now," Wila said, "and I've got these images from the probe. I download one or two each lightime. I've had the probe scan areas in the large body of water out to the east of this continent, and there have been some very interesting things going on." In the middle of one image a large left-hand swirl of clouds lay centered about a hundred anthans east of a prominent peninsula at the southeastern corner of the continent.

Lilea picked up one image and examined it closely. She was intrigued that a large group of clouds could take on such an unusual rotating structure, but she didn't have any more idea what the white, puffy, swirling cloud bank was than Wila.

I wonder if it's a storm. If it is, and it's that big, it could be dangerous . . .

"This large cloud group has been migrating east-to-west," Wila continued, breaking Lilea's concentration. "That's unusual from what I've seen since we've been on this planet. Most cloud groups move west-to-east. If it continues to go in the direction it's been going, it'll cross this peninsula," —she pointed to it on the image—"into the southeastern body of water. It's headed for that island you're going to. The way it's drawn out into a swirl like this, there must be winds inside it, but the probe can't estimate wind speed. I think you should take a look at it."

Col's trip to the little island had been scheduled for 461.151. A vaguely crescent-shaped island about six anthans long but only about a half-anthan wide, it lay a short distance off the southern coast and it attracted Col's attention early in planning for the expedition. It seemed to be composed entirely of sand. The probe had taken close-up images and he'd become fascinated by the vegetation along the interface between the island and the sea.

Images of the pounding wind and water during the gorge return flight flooded back into Lilea's mind. "Surely you're not suggesting we fly into it, if it is a storm."

"Storm?" Wila looked directly at Lilea, and then turned back to the images. "No, no—not if it's a storm, but I can't tell what it is from these images, and I can't understand why it's moving retrograde. I just think someone should take a look at it."

"I am curious," Col said. "But that's an excessively long flight from here. Do you really think it's a big storm?"

"I'm not sure . . . I just thought . . ." Lilea said. "If it is, I don't want to have anything to do with it."

"I certainly don't want to either," Wila said. "Perhaps we should wait a while . . ."

"Right," Lilea said. "Remember, in the reply Kal sent after Case's death, he asked so many questions, especially why they didn't use more safety precautions on the hike in the mountains. What he was really telling us was to be more careful, to use all the safety precautions we can. Kal will go ballistic if he finds out we flew into or near another storm."

"Undoubtedly, he would," Col said, "but if there's something as curious and dangerous as a big storm, I'm sure Kal would realize it is incumbent upon us to check it out. We don't have to experience it directly, but we could skim the outer edges and still maintain a modicum of safety."

"We tried that before," Lilea said, "and we got sucked into the storm. I'm not sure this is a good idea."

"It may not turn out to be a storm," Wila said. "It may be just a large group of clouds, and may not be dangerous at all."

"We'll see," Col said. "I'll talk to Jer about getting one of the aerodynes. Lilea, will you be joining us?"

"Oh, well . . ." Lilea was surprised by Col's invitation. It never occurred to her that she would actually be invited to go out there and *look* at it. What in the name of the Great God Arteamos was Col thinking . . . but on the other hand, it could be exciting. She understood and accepted Col's argument that things like this should be checked out—after all they *were* on this planet to explore it. And besides, Col is a top-notch pilot, and he certainly wouldn't do anything reckless, like flying into it, if it is a storm. So she agreed to go. "Okay, I guess so."

"Good." Col turned to Wila. "Keep me informed about where that thing goes." He tossed the image he'd been examining back on the table.

"Okay." Wila took the images back to her desk where she slipped each into a clear plastic sleeve and placed the sleeves in a loose-leaf binder.

Lilea left the deck, images of the clouds lodged in her mind. So surprising it was that she would be invited to go on a non-scheduled trip, especially one weather-related, and in a small way, that bothered her. If that was a storm, she would prefer to leave it alone. On the other hand, if it wasn't, it could turn out to be a productive trip to a portion of the continent no one had visited yet, perhaps even resulting in seeing some intelligent natives. So, over the next several T-sectors, she visited Wila's desk several times, flipping through the images, paying close attention to the newest ones, watching as the whorl of clouds lumbered its way across the peninsula and poked a few cloudy tentacles into the southeastern ocean. She found the phenomenon interesting, though in a strictly scientific way, but secretly she wished it would turn around and head back the other way.

Time Element 461.95.2.0.

They took off at 95.2.0 in a freshly refueled Aero Two. Col piloted, and Trea sat in the right hand seat, Lilea behind her. Wila sat behind Col, her electronic notebook on her lap.

But to Lilea, the idea of spending five to six subsectors in an aerodyne was not a comforting thought. She and aerodynes hadn't gotten along too well together lately. Three of her last five flights in an aerodyne had been—to put it mildly—unsettling, and those memories kept popping up in her mind as the time drew near to leave. Flying back from the gorge, flying the damaged Aero One back from the grasslands, bringing Case's body home from the mountains—these did not add up to a delightful time in the air, and her second thoughts about going on this expedition never diminished, even to the time she climbed aboard. The painful look on Bent's face when she told him she was going did nothing to allay her fears either, but once she accepted Col's invitation she couldn't back out. She tried to explain that to Bent, but he wouldn't buy it. He never said anything directly to her, but the return trip back from the grasslands must have been on his mind.

Immediately after takeoff, Col called up the latest probe image on the aerodyne's main com screen and activated the ITS. The eddy of clouds now lay entirely west of the peninsula, a huge billow of white that filled the eastern half of the ocean, still headed in a straight line slightly south of west, directly for that little island. A small orange dot popped up on the screen to indicate the ship's position, telling Col exactly where he was with respect to the ground and the mass of clouds. A thin yellow line developed behind the dot, the flight path of the ship.

Col took the ship southeast to the coast, and then turned east to a route parallel to the coastline. He would not fly over the water.

That's good.

Flying over large areas of water had been forbidden by SpaceComm. Had Col taken a direct route to the clouds over water and had there been an emergency, he might be forced to put the aerodyne down in the ocean, an eventuality no one on the craft was prepared to handle. He took the approved course and stayed over land so that should an emergency arise, he would have solid ground below.

After three subsectors of smooth flying, headed east at three anthans, the northern edge of the cloud bank lay directly ahead. A dark line of clouds jeered at them. "I can feel the wind on the ship," Col said, but maintained his heading. As they flew, the winds picked up, buffeting the craft more strongly.

Col, I think you should get out of this. I don't like those clouds — what was that?

The first drops of water began to strike the windshield. In a perfect display of randomness they came, *splat . . . splat . . . splat*, hard enough to be heard inside the cabin. At first, only one or two arrived per nanosector, but they picked up frequency and pelted the ship more strongly as it flew east. A frightening familiarity about this storm welled up inside Lilea — the water and the buffeting, the same panicky feeling growing stronger and stronger with each drop. She started breathing heavily and went over some of the breathing exercises from *Star Voyager* to calm herself.

"I think you should get out of this water," Lilea said to Col, an edge on her voice. "It's obvious this is a storm." She licked her lip where the tiny scar remained and glanced at her right hand. No blood — no, of course not — but her knuckles had turned white from her tight grip on the armrest. She looked through the front window into the heart of the clouds and an image of the exploding windshield hit her so hard she had to close her eyes.

"Agreed," Col replied. "But what do you think would happen if we went higher? It's conspicuously evident this *is* a big storm. Do you think we could get above it? We've got plenty of fuel."

"I don't know, but I'd rather get out of it altogether. Could you, maybe, turn around?"

"It might be worth a try." Trea seemed so calm in her seat in front of Lilea, those large drops of water splashing the windshield directly in front of her. "Wila, what do you think? Do you have the altitude of the clouds?"

To Lilea's immense relief, Col swung the ship left 200 degrees to get away from the water, and then turned to hear what Wila said.

"Yes . . ." Wila mumbled, running through a datalist about the storm on her notebook screen. ". . . here it is. The probe's interferometer put the top of the clouds at slightly more than 4.5 anthans above the water level. Above that looks like quiet air."

"Four-point-five anthans? We could make that easily." Col seemed almost flippant about it.

"Are you going to try?" Wila asked. "Do you think Jer would approve?"

Col pondered a nanosector. "Maybe we should ask her." He contacted Jer at Site One and explained what he wanted to do.

"Col," Jer said, her voice coming through the speakers in the cabin. "I'm surprised . . . I mean . . . are you trying to kill yourself and everyone in that aerodyne? You were only supposed to go out and take a quick look at it. We don't really know what it's like on top there."

God, yes. We don't know much about —

"Wila, what do you think?"

"Well, the interferometer —"

"We've got plenty of fuel and plenty of time," Col said, "and we need only to ascend a little more than one anthan and we should be on top of the storm. We could easily go up much higher. If anything happens we can descend."

Descend? Back into the storm? No damn way. Let's get our ass outta here. Lilea gripped the armrests even more tightly.

"Wila," Jer said, "are you sure?"

"It is clear air —"

"Okay," Jer said. "Go ahead, but be careful. Don't fly into any water."

"Affirmative," Col said, "I'll contact you when we reach the top of the storm."

Col banked the ship back around and pushed the throttle to **CLIMB 2**. A heavy pulse hit the aerodyne as more fuel poured into the engine and the ship jerked forward and upward at almost forty degrees. Visibility dropped to zero as the ship entered the clouds and the turbulence increased.

Lilea sat back in her seat and kept her tight grip on the armrests, but she held her eyes open, forcing herself to stare through the window to her right. Total whiteness surrounded the ship—*My god, that looks so familiar. In the name of the Great God Arteamos, let's get out of this.*

Then, with no warning whatsoever, at an altitude of almost five anthans, the ship burst out of the clouds into still, quiet air.

"Wow!" Trea said. "Look at that."

"Very occipital." Even Col's voice sang of astonishment.

They sat on top of a huge mass of clouds that stretched as far as they could see in almost every direction. Only to the west was any green or brown of solid land visible, and the brilliant yellow-white orb of the afternoon sun hung splendidly in the western sky. The clouds below appeared puffy white, almost benign. Lilea let out a sigh of relief, and the tightness in her face and hands began, slowly, to fade. Instinctively she wiped her hands on her jumpsuit, but, mesmerized by the whiteness out her window, she grabbed her camera and snapped panoramas. To her left, Wila did too.

"Jad will want to see this."

Col leveled off at five anthans, reduced the throttle setting to **CRUISE**, and adjusted trim. He checked the time recorder on the ship's control panel: 461.95.7.2. "It's getting late," he said. "It's imperative we head for home soon. We're still four to five subsectors from Site One."

"We don't need to leave for a few millisectors," Wila said. "Let's take some readings first. This may be the only time we get above a big storm like this. We should take advantage of it." Trea reached forward and touched a few markers on the central com screen, starting the cameras in the nose of the ship and activating the infrared thermal imager and the long-wavelength imager that would penetrate the clouds to get information about the makeup of the storm.

"Could we get a little higher?" Lilea said. "I'd like to get some wide-angle views."

With the ship out of danger—for the moment—and the apprehension of flying in and through a storm past, Lilea kept her camera pointed out the window. "That's one huge storm," she muttered as she snapped image after image. "Think of the power in that storm. I hope it doesn't come our way."

"What?" Wila turned toward Lilea, surprise on her face. She appeared to start to say something, but Col interrupted and she turned back to look out the window to her left.

"I can take us up to six anthans if you want," Col said. "Or even higher. It will be imperative we ascend to that altitude for the trip home anyway."

"Six anthans will be fine."

Col trimmed the wings to climb, and leveled off at six. The entire storm was laid out below them as a big, white counterclockwise swirl, and Lilea clicked several wide-angle images. "Okay, I've got enough. We can go home now."

"We can make up some time by flying most of the way at this altitude," Col said. "In fact, I think I'll go even higher where the air is thinner." He took the ship to seven anthans and banked left to a westerly heading almost directly into the sun.

Lilea reclined her seat back about 50 degrees and settled down for the trip home. Her heartbeat had dropped slightly in the few millisectors they'd spent in the quiet air above the storm, though it didn't return to normal. But the quickening of her heart and the residual tightness in her chest had nothing to do with the panic of facing a terrible threat. Now she was riding a wave of exhilaration, almost euphoria, after meeting and conquering the big, nasty storm. Nothing serious had happened, no one was injured, and the aerodyne flew flawlessly. This would be the way of the expeditions in the future, she was certain of that. Case's death was a mere anomaly, a short, though distressing blip on the expedition's timeline. Everything seemed so obvious now—they would get through the rest of their time on this planet without another death. There might be setbacks, perhaps even some consequential ones. But they could conquer the obstacles and learn to live on this planet.

Wouldn't that be great? She leaned forward and snapped one more image of the receding clouds.

Let's hope so.

CHAPTER 24

PATH

Time Element 461.97.6.0.

"Jad! Jad!" Wila yelled as she slid down the interdeck ladder onto the Personnel Deck.

Jad, still in his compartment near the end of a short break, had just slipped his feet into his boots, getting ready to return to the Astronomy Deck, and he could hear her yelling as she ran to their compartment door.

Now what does she want?

"The storm *is* coming toward us!" she bellowed into the compartment as she opened the door. She ran into the bedroom.

"What are you talking about?"

Wila's face was ashen and she was out of breath. She seemed scared, scared like he hadn't seen in her since . . . well, he had seen her this scared once before, but it was back on Anthanos and he couldn't remember when.

"I just plotted the position of the storm. It's turned north! And now it's headed directly for us here. I'm not kidding. Come see for yourself."

Wila left the compartment and ran to the ladder. Jad followed.

Lilea stuck her head out of her compartment on the other side of the deck. "What's going on?" she asked, perhaps wondering a little about the commotion.

"Lilea, you've got to see this!" Wila yelled as she started up the ladder. All three climbed two levels to Geo Sciences and went immediately to the weather station. The latest image of the storm glared at them from the weather graphics screen.

"I've been plotting the position of the storm twice every T-sector," Wila said, pausing to catch her breath. "Each time I plot it, I put a yellow dot at the center of the storm. I'm using a visual estimate of the center around which the clouds are swirling. That's how I measure the position of the storm." Wila turned to the graphics computer keyboard. She instructed the computer to display all the indicator dots at once, superimposed over the latest image, to chart the progress of the storm. "See? All these dots form a straight line that shows the movement of the storm—almost due west, straight toward that little island." She hit a few more keys.

"But this time . . ." Wila's voice quivered faintly. She hesitated and took a deep breath. "When I estimated the center of the storm and compared it to the last reading . . . look! The storm's turned north. And look at this! When I drew a line from the previous position and extended the line onto land, it points directly to Site One here."

"It does seem to be headed this way, doesn't it?" Lilea said.

"'Seems to be?'" Wila swung around to face Lilea. "What do you mean *seems* to be — "

"We should notify Jer," Jad said. "She should know about this."

Jad opened the comm link at the Weather Station. He described the latest image from the probe, and Jer decided to see this change of course for herself. Col and Trea, working one level above in Life Sciences, also came down. Everyone crowded around the Weather Computer, surveying the series of little yellow dots on the screen, and the red line between the last two dots that pointed directly to the little yellow seven-pointed star that denoted Site One.

But Jer studied the images most intently. She leaned over and put her hands on the desk in front of the screen. She traced the path of the storm laid out by all those little yellow dots, but she also switched back to earlier images, retracing the storm's path image by image, as though trying to discern future movement of the storm through details of its past life. She flipped back to the most recent image, and for several microsectors studied Wila's line of projected movement. Then she straightened up.

"It's too early to tell exactly what's going to happen," she said, still staring at the screen. "We need more images. But, if this storm is coming this way, maybe we need to start taking precautions now." She turned to Wila. "How long will it take this storm to get here?"

Wila took in a deep breath. "At the rate it's going now, it'll take eight to ten T-sectors."

"That's still enough time to get things ready. There is a procedure for emergency liftoff and all of you are familiar with it, but it's designed for emergencies that arise in less than one T-sector, so it doesn't apply here . . . but we may have to execute it if the storm comes this way."

"We should get ready for a liftoff," Wila said. "It wouldn't hurt."

Jer hesitated for a few nanosectors, probably going over alternatives in her mind. "I hate to give an order for emergency liftoff unless it's unavoidable. Let's wait for the next image. Let's make sure it's really coming this way before we lift off."

Most of those at the Weather Station agreed with Jer's decision. Outwardly, even Wila accepted it, at least for the present. The little group broke up leaving Wila at her workstation staring at the graphics screen.

Jad ascended three levels to Deck 3, the Astronomy Deck. He sat down at the main telescope control complex and activated the solar telescope. He ran through the primary sighting-in procedure, slipping in all the filters and blockers that prevented the intense sunlight from damaging the ultrasensitive photodynamic sensors of the imaging array, preparing to visualize the sun's corona. But as he down-modulated the lights in the room and stared through the binocular eyepiece at the heavily shielded sun, that line of little yellow dots stuck solidly in his mind.

Time Element 461.98.3.0.

The third meal was finished. Jad placed his dishes in the ultrasonic cleaner beside Wila's. He added a packet of detergent and closed the top cover, activating the unit. It filled with water and a barely audible high-pitched squeal came from inside.

Wila hadn't said much during the meal, apparently lost in thought. Jad tried to get her to open up, but all she talked about was the storm and how it seemed to be headed this way. As they sat on the couch, a couple of cups of warm jell-kell on the table in front of them, Jad pulled up on the com screen several of the corona images he'd just taken, but Wila seemed less than interested.

"There's something else, too," Wila said. "I've been having a dream. It's almost a nightmare."

"What?" Jad turned and looked at Wila, concern in his mind. She'd never had nightmares before. He paused the com display. "What kind of dream?"

"The first time I had it was during the darktime before we left on the trip to the gorge, but I didn't think too much about it at the time. Then I had it again before the grassland trip, and before the trip west when Case was killed, and the last time before the trip when we flew out to examine the storm. It's like I have the dream just before every major expedition away from the ship."

"What do you dream about?"

"You remember the T-sector we were told we'd been put on the Gold Team? And Case and Jer had a get-acquainted party for all of us later that T-sector? It was out at their house. There was this old guy in white clothes we met when we were walking up the sidewalk to their house, and he talked to us. Remember him? He was real tall, and he started talking to us. Right there on the sidewalk. Right out of the blue he just started talking. Almost yelling. He followed us up the sidewalk to their house. He kept saying how dangerous the trip would be. He told us not to go. I remember he said that several times. He said we didn't know what we were getting into. He said we were putting our lives in . . . in, I think he said 'great peril' on this expedition. Remember him?"

Jad took a few nanosectors to search his long-term memory. He had a vague recollection of a tall man in white clothes talking to him out on the street somewhere, but he couldn't remember the time or place. He probably didn't think it important enough at the time to induce his mind to put the encounter in long-term memory. People rarely talked to Jad on the street, and when they did, he frequently dismissed them and, usually, forgot about them. His tall, brooding persona turned people off, and they usually left him alone. Talking to strangers made him uncomfortable, and he rarely made eye contact with anyone he encountered unless he knew them personally. He preferred it that way. "Yeah, I sort of remember him. I remember the white clothes. I remember Jer was upset because he talked to each couple as they arrived, and—I remember we talked about him and we didn't know how he knew we were all on the Gold Team. How *did* he know? He was just an oddball, kind of nutty, but he wasn't—"

Wila interrupted. "And then several T-sectors later I saw him again in front of our apartment on the Spaceport. Remember? Just after I came back from jogging. You came back later and I'd shut up the apartment and locked the door and closed all the windows because he scared me so much." Wila turned away from Jad and stood up. She walked over to the food-prep area and stood in front of the little dishwasher. "I was so afraid he'd see me inside. My dream is all about that guy. I can't get him out of my mind. It's about what he said, but he says it over and over and I can't get what he's saying out of my head. 'Don't go. Don't go. It's dangerous. You don't know what you're getting into.' Over and over." She turned back to Jad. "And remember, then he said some of us would not return."

Jad nodded. "I remember the look on your face."

"That's what scared me the most. About not returning. He was *right*. Now Case won't be retuning. He was right."

At first it came to him slowly, but when Jad remembered the fear on Wila's face and how she was so scared she almost barricaded herself in the apartment, he recalled what she'd said about the old man. "Yeah, I remember that guy. But he was just some crackpot who didn't know what he was talking about. How would he know if some of us wouldn't return? He was just guessing. All he was telling us was that this is a dangerous mission. We knew that. SpaceComm drilled that into us lots of times. Especially before training. They made us sign that release form, remember? All about how spaceflight is dangerous and anything can happen, and we have to follow the rules, and all that. I think we decided he was some old-timer in spaceflight. He may have worked at SpaceComm. Or had family that worked at SpaceComm. That's how he knew we were on the Gold Team. I wouldn't worry about him. He's probably harmless. Just some nut—"

"I wish I could believe that." Wila picked up her cup and drained the last of the juice. "If Case won't be returning, who else is there? Who else won't be returning?"

"I think you're just concerned about the people on the expedition. That's natural, I am too. I'm always apprehensive when my friends go off on an expedition. All of us are. But that's part of exploring the planet. You remember the mental health lectures we had?"

"Of course, I'm concerned." Wila looked directly at Jad. "But I think this goes farther than that. There's something more to it than just concern, but I can't put my finger on it."

"More to it? Are you saying you think the old man had something to do with the disasters?"

"No, he's thirty-five light years away. He probably doesn't have anything to do with this planet. It's just that I have this feeling. A really weird feeling . . . that maybe something else . . ." She poured more juice into her cup and placed it in the microwave.

Jad thought about what Wila'd said, but he couldn't understand how her dream could raise such an unusual reaction in her. She'd never said anything about 'weird feelings' before. Wila rarely reacted irrationally to unknown situations, and her use of the phrase bothered him. He hoped her anxiety would go away eventually, it could turn into panic if left unattended. If he changed the subject she might feel better. "Let's just wait for the next several images of the storm. Maybe it'll go somewhere else."

"Maybe." Wila pulled her cup from the oven and took a sip. Lost in thought—again—she perhaps was trying to convince herself that the storm wasn't a direct threat. "Maybe," she said again, then drained the juice in her cup, set it on the counter and went into the bedroom.

Early the next lightime, T-sector 99, Wila climbed to Geo and retrieved the latest image from the probe, taken only a millisector earlier. She carefully and exactly plotted the "center" of the storm, and, yes, it had turned north. The point she used to plot the storm lay about forty anthans north and a little east of its previous position, and it was definitely going to make landfall along the northern coast. It wasn't headed toward Site One any more at all.

Wila called Jad who came down from the Astronomy Deck, and she notified Jer who came up from her compartment. Both looked over the latest plot.

"That takes care of that worry," Jer said. But Wila didn't appear relieved.

"Still, it might turn back west, though," she said.

Jer frowned at Wila's comment. "Nonsense. Let's just hope the storm continues north or, if it turns at all, it turns east."

It continued north. The storm made landfall during T-sector 101, then slowed down and turned east. By 461.105, as little more than a loose agglomeration of smaller storms, it drifted over the heavily-forested south-eastern region of the continent, and by 109, the remnants of that once mighty storm had faded into oblivion.

As Jad looked over the image of the storm on 109, his eye, by now very familiar with its vague crescent shape and light tan coloration, wandered south to the little island. What he saw confused him at first, and he wondered if he'd picked up the wrong image. The time element all images were taken was always printed on the back, and he flipped the image over.

No, it was the latest image, taken only a few subsectors earlier.

Where's the island? It should be right here. Why doesn't it show up — oh, good god.

He took the image up one level to Life Sciences to show Col.

CHAPTER 25

EARLY YEARS

Time Element 457.999.9.1.

Lilea swung open the heavy metal door to the Research Laboratory of the Anthropology Department on the third floor of the Sabean Museum of Natural Science. The lab was quiet, most of the faculty and students who worked here had left for the New Year's holiday. Her hands were grimy from the damp, loamy soil that lay several links under the sands at the Qelvet dig site and she went to the sink a few steps from the door. She slipped her identity card into the waterflow card reader which automatically activated the recorder. As she measured out enough hot water to moisten her hands, and squirted out a dollop of cleanser, the recorder reminded her that she'd exceeded her water ration limit for almost 100 T-sectors now. She hadn't expected to go to the dig site this T-sector, but with Bent off the planet, and in the excitement of finding so many new artifacts, she went anyway. That dark soil was so hard to clean off she had to scrub with plenty of hot water. She was far enough over her ration that the Office of Water Conservation would send her a Memorandum of Reprimand, and that would go on her record and she'd have to pay a fine, but as she began to rinse, her attention was diverted to the scuffling of feet near the back of the lab toward the Director's office. That would be Torena. Lilea rolled her eyes.

Oh, god, what now?

She finished rinsing.

"Mr. Uvos," Torena whined in her usual suck-up voice. "Lilea just came in and I *actually* saw her running the water. The *hot* water."

"Lilea!" Uvos bellowed. "Come in here."

Uvos was a little man, planted firmly in the obesity of a satisfied life, with bright red hair that circled his head in a curly U. His thick nose, a vivid crimson due to a skin ailment, mirrored his hair and gave him a comical lollypop look. Sweetness wasn't his disposition though, his mouth always seemed to be turned down in a perpetual sneer. Tarkuu like Lilea, but a racial variant with skin even more pallid than hers, over the last year his face had become more pinched and drawn than usual. At ninety-five years old he rarely went to dig sites anymore. He stayed in his office and relied on his students and staff to discover and excavate the newer sites, like the Qelveticos site Lilea had discovered.

He'd built this laboratory, indeed the entire building, from the ground up. Lilea'd been with him since 452 when she joined his laboratory after receiving her third level degree in anthropology, the highest degree in her field. She'd helped design the lab, and he relied on her to work with the Office of Design and Construction on most of the details. She was lucky to be able to work with such an eminent professor even though lately he seemed more crotchety than usual.

"Yes, Mr. Uvos." Always 'Mr. Uvos.' No one would *ever* address him by his first name. "I just—"

"Never mind. Torena says you were running the hot water. Isn't your regular quota used up by now?"

"No, sir, I just got back from the Qelveticos dig and I stopped to wash my hands. I waited to wash when I got in. I'm keeping track of my ration. I'm still within . . ."

"The dig? Why in the name of the Great God Arteamos did you go all the way out to the dig site? There's nobody else there. It's New Year's."

"Yes, sir, but I got so excited about the latest heads, I—"

"Never mind. Torena, get back to work and stop bothering me with minor details. Lilea, sit down. I've been going over this report you submitted on last quarter's findings at the Qelveticos dig." Uvos picked up his electronic notebook and looked carefully at the screen. "You dug up quite a few new arrowheads. About fifty."

"Sixty-three."

"Right. Sixty-three. At least that's what you called them. But I looked at the pictures you took of them, and they certainly don't look like Qelvet heads." He put the notebook down and focused on her in a dyspeptic glare. "Dammit, we've been over this before. Qelvet workers shaped their heads from the center outward. These are clearly peripherally derived. Look at the way the flaking process overlaps. Can't you tell by now? Only the Toens people started their heads peripherally. And they were on the other side of the damn planet. Everybody knows they didn't have any contact with the Qelvet. Delete this damn report and reread the texts I've written about arrowheads. Get your facts straight first, Kalatarian, then rewrite it."

"But Mr. Uvos, I explained that discrepancy. These arrowheads were found at a lower level than the original ones. I radiocarbon-dated the fire pits at the same level and it shows they're older. By several hundred years. These heads are earlier, and I think the Qelvet started like the Toens did, peripherally. Later, they went to center-out. The Toens never made it that far. They were overrun by the—"

"Yes, yes, yes, I read your hypothesis, but it doesn't cut it with me. A shift in arrowhead processing like that would go along with major lifestyle changes within the community, and there's no evidence the Qelvet did anything else different. The pottery Torena is studying is consistent with a stable communal life pattern. From all levels. Now get on the stick, Lilea. Your work was pretty good until now, but you've gotten sloppy lately. Your faculty—"

"But if they're not Qelvet heads, what are they? And why—"

Uvos held up a hand. "Let me finish. Your semiannual review is due in a few T-sectors and your rating is already down. I wouldn't want it to get any lower. Those earlier heads are probably an earlier civilization, but clearly they're not Qelvet heads. We're here to study the Qelvet people. We'll get to other civilizations later."

"Yes, Mr. Uvos." Lilea stood and retreated to the main laboratory. *Well, that was fucking humiliating.*

Torena sat at her workstation off to the left, her back to the door, shards of Qelvet pottery scattered across her desk and the nearby workbench. She was examining one piece under a low power microscope but didn't look up as Lilea sat down at her workspace, across the room and out of Torena's view.

Good old Torena. She can't do anything wrong and I can't do anything right. Some of those pieces do show changes in construction — I saw them when she first pulled them out of the ground — but they're so subtle she wouldn't know that if they hit her in the ass.

Lilea activated the com terminal at her desk and the on-screen memo told her she had two new messages, the first from Bont with a few details about the expedition he'd been on to the sixth moon of Shaltous—"I should be back 458.095."

Oh, god, finally. I can't wait for him to get back.

The other message came from Spaceflight Command. They were looking for anthropologists to undergo basic spaceflight training because they were considering sending an anthropologist to the Blue Planet. ". . . the possibility of intelligent life . . ." the notice said and Lilea's eyes brightened considerably. This was the announcement she'd been waiting for. The probe images started dancing around in her head — deserts, mountains, forest, grasslands, they all sang to her.

I can't imagine anything more fantastic than being the one to find intelligent life on that planet. I wonder what they'll look like.

When she wrote her adulthood Commission near the end of tertiary school group about what she wanted to do with the rest of her life, she speculated about the possibility of intelligent species on other planets and even mused about their appearance and intelligence. She desperately wanted to be the first to actually see and study them. But SpaceComm had never had any use for anthropologists — until now. With only twenty people to be selected for two teams, she didn't think she had much chance with a puny six years' experience.

Probably a lot of anthropologists will apply. Miserable odds. But it could give me a chance to take the basic training and get out there in space with Bent. He's always enjoyed it. I've never gotten anything less than a 9.8 rating in this job. It's time for me to get my ass outta this lab.

CHAPTER 26

NORTH

Time Element 461.121.0.0.

By T-sector 121, the hot season was well underway at Site One. The lightimes were warm and dry, the darktimes joyously cool. The showers had begun, too. Whether as minuscule as a few drops or intense as a cloudburst, they rarely lasted for more than a millisector. Like the brief downpour that occurred the first lightime the team was on the surface, they were just enough to soak the ground and give the plants a little moisture. But a few millisectors later, any remaining surface water had either evaporated or percolated into the soil, and the ground was dry again. Occasionally, a larger storm would come through and the wind and water would pound against the ship for several microsectors, threatening to blow it away. But the clouds would dissipate and the sun would come out, radiating its warmth and brilliance over the entire area, as though to apologize for the brief interlude of dampness.

Lilea spent most of her time after T-sector 115 preparing for her survey flight. SpaceComm had allowed her to put only one survey flight on the Expedition Planning Calendar, and one landing flight to check out what the survey found. If she needed more flights, they told her, she could arrange to use the aerodynes during off periods. That was the best they could do. She'd have to work out a schedule when she got to the planet. The preliminary flight was scheduled for 125, now rapidly approaching. She turned her attention north. But where up north?

Ever since she saw the first animals around the landing site, and especially the predatory animal at the gorge, she knew that creatures of substantially more intelligence than those could exist on this planet. After all, lower Anthanian species evolved into higher forms, why couldn't the same happen here? True, that wasn't a scientific reason to believe they would, but it was her main working hypothesis. That's why she was sent here—to look for them.

She first thought of the "mounds" on the ice near the North Pole. The probe had taken an image of several small dots that stood out from the surrounding ice by their round, smooth, regular nature. Seven little mounds, arranged in a rough circle. She'd wanted to visit them ever since she first saw them, and during the ten T-sectors *Explorer* was in orbit before landing, she imaged the area again, and they were still there. Two things argued against that trip, though. It would be a long flight, eight subsectors at four anthans, and it would put the ship out of range of the homing signal Jer could send from *Explorer*. She could use the ITS, but SpaceComm frowned on flying so far from Site One without both navigational aids. But more significant to Lilea, the ice up there appeared so rough and uneven that finding a landing site would be virtually impossible, so she turned her attention to another part of the continent.

Most on Anthanos who had seen the "mounds" assumed, as she did, that they were housing for intelligent beings. And if they are, she reasoned, then those creatures may have begun to spread out, and migrate away from that area. She used the early Anthanians as an example of just such a migration when they migrated toward the terminator as the sun baked the hot side. On the Blue Planet, the only direction they could go would be south. They may even be living south of the ice. So she selected an area at the southern end of a large rift in that huge expanse of ice up there . . .

Time Element 461.125.3.0.

. . . and Bent piloted.

They loaded a cooler of food and drinks into the racks over the rear seats in Aero Two and she and Bent and Dell took off north. Though it was Lilea's expedition which gave her the right to pilot the craft, she decided to let Bent fly. Sitting in the pilot's seat brought back certain memories, memories she would rather not deal with now. She'd have more time to scan the terrain below.

Yet, by the time Lilea slipped into the front right-hand seat of Aero Two, most of the apprehensions of previous flights were forgotten. She looked forward to this trip, and the anxiety and tension that characterized her previous trips had largely disappeared. She was upbeat now, almost euphoric. This was her expedition—her mission. She was in charge and everything would turn out all right. After all, this was just a survey flight to check out the terrain and look at the situation. What could go wrong?

The flight took almost two subsectors. The probe hadn't made close-up images of most of this area, and she wanted more detail than the existing pictures could provide. An almost total lack of cloud cover had given them good flying weather and a bright, unobstructed view of the surface all around. Farther north, a starkly beautiful brilliant white blanket covered the surface almost everywhere as several glaciers snaked through the hilly landscape, terminating in rough edges of raw, blue-white ice. A large river coursed through the naked terrain.

But the river had become a torrent. Spread out almost a half-anthan wide with ghostly white meltwater from the vast areas of ice to the north, it swept east for hundreds of anthans, finally emptying into a huge lake well out of sight beyond their right wingtip.

Only barren and rocky terrain lay south of the river. Rough, heavy ridges towered above the surrounding landscape, and impassable valleys cut vicious passages through the area. Stony peaks seemed to jut from everywhere, and spiky mountain ranges surrounded by bouldered, pebbly flatlands lay in a crazy patchwork over the surface. From their vantage point three anthans above, they could make out only large features, but with a vision aid they got a detailed look at the rocky ground, but no one saw any good landing sites. Bent took the aerodyne north across the river and reached the selected area at the extreme edge of the ice. He circled for several microsectors while everyone scanned the ground.

"Coordinates indicate this is the right area," he said.

"Keep a sharp lookout," Lilea said. "If you see anything that looks promising, we'll image it." But the terrain below was as rugged and formidable as that south of the river, and Lilea's optimistic attitude began to fade.

Bent put the ship on a careful east-west search pattern, each leg progressively south of the previous, making twelve passes, from the edge of the glaciers to the river. Lilea activated the high-resolution cameras and long-wavelength interferometers in Aero Two's nose, and then she and Dell scanned the ground using vision aids while the cameras imaged the terrain. She labeled this image set "125 A."

"Take some images of the area south of the river," Lilea said as they finished the last leg of the imaging runs. Bent banked left and crossed the river, putting the ship on a west-to-east heading. But only then, as they examined the terrain through the increased magnification of the vision aids, did Lilea and the others really begin to comprehend the magnitude of the river as a barrier to land travel.

"If we want to explore north of the river, we'll have to land north of the river." Lilea shook her head as her hopeful attitude faded even further.

Bent repeated the east-west pattern south of the river and Lilea gave this image set the designation "125 B." Then she exhaled a deep, weary sigh. "Why don't we look at these pictures back at *Explorer*, and see what we can find. Let's go home."

"Works for me." Bent swung Aero Two south, entering airspace over the northern edge of the boreal forest. "We've covered everything from south of the river to the edge of the ice."

They landed at 125.9.3. Lilea downloaded both sets of images from the aerodyne's computer and printed them on high contrast plastic sheets for everyone to examine at the next meeting of the North Team around the central table on Life Sciences.

CHAPTER 27

IMAGES

Time Element 461.126.0.0.

The images were not encouraging. Everywhere was hilly, rocky ground, or ice, or glacier. Rivers, creeks, and streams of all sizes cut through the area in sinuous, torturous paths, running into and draining hundreds of lakes, ponds, pools, and puddles, merging into larger and larger rivers that themselves merged into the one huge river that had been so dominating from above.

Lilea's little expedition to the north had attracted considerable attention among the rest of the landing team, and everyone not involved in the survey flight came to the meeting. That wasn't unusual—everyone was vitally concerned about every expedition, even the ones they were not a part of—but this expedition attracted more than usual attention because it was the first to use a preliminary survey flight, and the images were the main attraction. Col and Trea drifted over from their workstations to the central table just to see them, and Mina and Wila joined their husbands in scanning the images for landing sites. Jer stopped by occasionally, though mostly she flitted in and out, making her regular inspection rounds of one or another segment of *Explorer*'s equipment. The images were passed around the table and almost everyone felt obliged to comment.

"Wow," Trea said when she picked up one of the images. "There's not much here. What are you looking for?"

"Any indication of intelligent life—towns, lights, cultivated fields—anything." Lilea didn't bother to look up from the image she held in her hand. "But we also need a place to land nearby. About four thousand links long."

After several microsectors of briefly glancing at some of the images, Col and Trea returned to their workstations, and the North Team turned quiet, settling down to intense inspection. They passed the images from one to another as each scrutinized the sheets, some closely, others superficially. Lilea used an 8X magnifying glass to scan each 15 X 20 decilink image in detail. Bent called up the images on one of the com screens at the central table, scanning each electronically, and Jad instructed the Life Sciences computer to examine all images for flat areas at least four thousand links long, using the interferometer elevation data. While he waited for the results of the search, he picked up one of the printed images and scanned it with a magnifier. His voice shattered the silence a few microsectors later.

"Hey—what's this?"

"What?" Lilea said, raising her head. "Find something?" She looked over at the image he held in his hand as he peered through the magnifier.

"It's too regular to be natural," he said. Several others squinted at the image.

"What number is it?" Bent said.

Jad flipped the image over and read the number on the back. "117, set A."

Bent brought the image up on the com screen and scanned it. "What part of the picture are you looking at?"

"Just above the center line, about a third of the way in from the right-hand side. See the little ring of brownish dots?"

Bent squinted at the screen. "Oh, yeah," he mumbled. "Let's enlarge it."

He touched the screen in the vicinity of the little ring, and a yellow box followed his finger, outlining the ring. He removed his finger and touched the marker **EXPAND** at the bottom of the screen and the outlined area filled the screen. Lilea left her seat and stood behind Bent, staring at the image over his shoulder. Each enlarged dot was a round to slightly oval blotch, a mottled tan to brown color with occasional patches of lighter brown and amber, even white in a few odd places. Arranged in an almost perfect circle, the twelve splotches filled the screen. A bluish haze covered the upper right corner of the image.

At first Lilea didn't attach any significance to the blotches, and thought they might be a natural formation. But their arrangement was too regular to be natural, unlike so many things she'd seen on the probe images. After staring at the screen for several nanosectors, thinking of and discarding one possibility after another, one word flickered into her mind—village. At first she dismissed it, figuring—*it couldn't be*. But as she stared at the screen, she categorized in her mind all the reasons it could be, and when all the evidence came together in one convulsive, sobering rush, she understood what this image contained, and, more importantly, what it meant. Her eyes opened brilliantly wide, her jaw dropped, and her heartbeat shot up twenty points.

"Wait a damn microsector!" she shrieked. "It is! It's a village!"

"How can you tell?" several people said.

"Yes!" Lilea exclaimed and pumped a fist in the air. "Yes! Yes!"

"How can you tell?" came the chorus again.

"Each of those round things is a housing unit." She circled one of the brown spots on the screen. "And look here! There's smoke coming from . . . somewhere . . ." She pointed to the haziness. "They're using fire for something, maybe for warmth or cooking. Can we get the air temperature? Was that recorded?" she asked Bent.

"Yes, it was," Bent replied. "We took complete surface readings."

"Get it, get it," she said, tapping Bent on the shoulder. She turned back and leaned over the table to get a closer look at the screen. "Yes, I'm sure of it." Then she noticed something else on the image. "Uh-oh," she said. "Animals."

"'Animals'? Did I hear 'animals'?" Trea left her workstation and strode over to the central table. Col came right behind, and Jer dropped in from the Command Deck.

"There's a barricade around the village." Lilea pointed to a thin tan to yellowish ring encircling the village. "They may be having trouble with animals in the vicinity."

"The air temperature at the surface when we took this image was 5 Tal," Bent said, reading the number off the screen.

"That's not that cold. They use fire—that shows a moderate level of sophistication. They're not crude cave dwellers. They may be hunters, or they may be into farming, though I don't think they raise many crops in this terrain. The presence of the barricade shows they took some time to build the village. This is a permanent village, or perhaps semipermanent. They may be nomadic, but I would expect them to be there when we get there." Lilea picked up the original image from the table. "Look—the village is situated in a shallow valley. The valley's closed on three sides, protecting them from, well, from something. Perhaps from predators, maybe from invaders from other villages. Maybe from the weather. I will need to get up there to be able to tell for sure."

"But where are you going to land?" Bent said. "We still haven't found a landing site."

Lilea's heartbeat dropped back twenty points. "Oh, crap. You would bring that up."

Lilea stared at the screen as the terrible, hard feeling of disappointment tightened her chest. She remained quiet for several nanosectors. No one else spoke. Several drifted away, returning to their regular duties. The nanosectors became a microsector.

She shook her head. The village had to exist—the image had been taken only a few subsectors earlier. It was a short flying time away and with a good landing site she was ready to leave at next light. But the last step of the flight—landing—continued to elude her.

I can fly up there but I can't land. I can't believe that part is still missing. So near and yet so far. Damn.

"Well," she finally said, "if we can't land in the vicinity of this village, maybe we can find some other villages near where we could land. That's a big area up there. There must be other villages. Maybe we could go back and take more images and find a village or a village complex near where we could land."

Jer shook her head. "Maybe you could, but maybe not." Lilea turned and stared at her, a feeling of dread poking her belly at what she feared Jer was going to say. "That could take a lot of time. You could be imaging hundreds or even thousands of square anthans just to find one village near a place where you could land. Then you'd be using a lot of liquid hydrogen fuel. It would take time to scan that much area. That would monopolize an aerodyne for much too long and intrude on the next expedition."

"I just had a thought," Jad said. "Would it be possible to land on top of one of the glaciers? The surface seems smooth. It's probably hard enough to support the weight of an aerodyne. We've landed aerodynes on the ice packs on the dark side on Anthanos. What about trying it here?"

"I could go for it," Bent said, but Lilea hesitated.

"That's true," Jer said. "Aerodynes have landed on ice on the dark side of Anthanos, but there are two important points you have to remember about those landings. In the first place, the landing sites were found by explorers on foot first, and then secondly, they were smoothed off and prepared by land vehicles. Here, on this planet, neither of those is being done for you. Besides, have you looked closely at the top of those glaciers? They're not that smooth. They just look smooth from a distance. I'm not sure I want to be responsible for giving an order that would allow you to land on ice like that."

"There's another problem, too," Lilea said. She brought up a large-scale image on the com screen and measured the distance from the nearest glacier to the village. "The village is still more than forty anthans away. Not only that, but we'd have to get off the glacier and walk to the village. That's too far to look for intelligent beings that we're only going to observe. And if something happened, and we'd have to retreat . . ."

"We would probably have to cross water somewhere along there, too," Dell said. "And we're not equipped to cross large bodies of water."

"It seems to me that this expedition has become much more complex than we all imagined at first," Jer said. "You really haven't been able to come up with any landing site at all, let alone a good landing site, and that's going to be the first thing you have to have before you can do any research on these people. Let's end this meeting now and let the North Team take more time to look at the images in detail."

Lilea sat down at the table and stared at the screen.

Time Element 461.126.3.7.

At Jer's comment the meeting broke up and most left the Life Sciences Deck. Only Lilea remained at the table, her mood deteriorating. The delight of finding the village had evaporated like water on the desert floor. She'd been cautiously optimistic while reviewing the images, holding out hope they could find a good landing site, but the lack of anything in the vicinity of the village had brought her to the brink of discouragement. Then, to have her idea about widening the scanned area get shot down even before it left the ground, well that pushed her even closer. The last straw was Jer's order terminating the meeting.

Slowly and reluctantly she gathered up the images. She thumbed through them one more time, putting them back in rough numerical order, though she did that only to appear she was still working while everyone else left the deck. When she finished, she stood and crammed the images into a plastic folder. She stomped over to the ladder and descended to her compartment. Outside she appeared cool, but inside she seethed.

She met Bent at the Personnel Deck, and he walked with her to the door. She said nothing as they entered their compartment, but after the door was shut ensuring their privacy she hurled the folder of images across the living room into the food-prep area.

"Goddammit!" she yelled, and stormed into the bedroom. The folder hit the outside wall just below the window, sending the images flying over the table and floor.

"Hey! What do you think you're doing?" Bent picked up the images and put them back in the folder. "Those are important pictures. It took a lot of work to make them. What the hell's the matter with you?" He went into the bedroom to find Lilea pacing back and forth beside the bed.

"Now we have to spend even more time looking at the damn images to try to find a landing site. That could mean the whole trip is postponed indefinitely. I was looking forward to making a landing soon. Now we have to wait even longer."

"Well, you heard Jer. This expedition *is* getting complicated. I'm sure she's concerned that we can't find a landing site. I certainly wouldn't want to try landing on that terrain up there. She's right. We need to do more work on this. We can't just go up there and land like we do around here."

"I bet Case would have let us go, or at least find a way out of this."

"Oh, come on. Now you're unbelievable. If Case were here he would've done the same thing. He wouldn't want to land up there either. You know that as well as I do."

Lilea didn't say anything. She sat down on the bed and crossed her arms over her chest. She stared at the blank wall directly ahead.

"I know you're frustrated at not being able to go north, but you have to face the reality of the situation. There may not be any place to land up there. Any place we can land may be too far away or on the other side of the river. This isn't Anthanos where we can land anywhere we want. This planet is a lot more complex and a lot more frustrating. I know that just as well as you. So face it, chula, some things we want to do may not be possible. We may have to let the next explorers check out the intelligent beings on this planet."

"Oh, no! Oh, no! Don't tell me that!" Lilea was almost shouting as she stood to face Bent. "I didn't come all the way to this damn planet just to be told I can't do my job—that I can't do what I came here to do. I'm going to find a way to get up there and examine that damn village if I have to walk the whole goddamn way up there myself!"

"That will be hard to do. Take Jer's advice and look at the images really carefully and see if you can find something. We haven't had a chance to look at every one of them. There are more than three hundred fifty of them."

"That will take a while." Lilea sat down on the edge of the bed and folded her arms across her chest again.

"Take as much time as you need. Besides, Jad and Dell and I will be helping you. You're not the only one frustrated and inconvenienced by this situation. That's the way things are around here, chula, so get used to it."

Lilea sat quietly for a few nanosectors. She hated when Bent called her "chula." It usually meant "young girl" or "young lady," but it could also mean "immature girl," and she knew damn well Bent was using it that way, but she was too furious about the images and Jer's termination order to make a big deal of it right now.

"All right, all right. I'll look at the damn images, but I don't think there's much chance we'll find anything. You saw the terrain up there. There's not much there."

"I realize that, but do the best you can."

CHAPTER 28

PLANNING

Time Element 461.127.8.3.

Fatigue. This wasn't the exhaustion of hard physical labor. Rather, it was the mental weariness of long subsectors spent hunched over hundreds of images of the northern landscape. So bleak was the area they found almost nothing. They did find several more villages scattered across the terrain north of the river which led Lilea to exclaim, "I was right, they are migrating down from the north." A few more landing sites appeared farther to the east where the landscape opened up and became smoother. But the terrain near the villages was just too rugged and harsh, the ground too rocky and scraggy, the surface just a little too unforgiving, and neither Lilea nor Bent nor Jad nor Dell found anything that even vaguely resembled an acceptable landing site near a village.

Lilea and Bent took their third meal and joined several others on the catwalk to watch the sunset.

The sky had been overcast for most of the lightime, and water had fallen from the clouds just before the team assembled on the catwalk. The storm moved largely east, and the sky cleared in the west just before sunset. The setting sun illuminated the high clouds with a deep crimson and scarlet. It cast a dull reddish hue on the mirror-like *Explorer* and the surrounding landscape, and etched dark purple and black shadows into the hills to the south. With the air temperature at 20 Tal, a light, cool breeze swirled out of the west.

To the south and east, a line of dark clouds still covered the horizon, and Jad stood at the far end of the catwalk, apparently fascinated by the flashes of lightning that lit up the clouds.

"Is the lightning any danger to us?" Lilea asked.

"We should be okay," Jad replied. "Lightning is strictly cloud-to-cloud. Or within a cloud."

"Didn't Seth predict the lightning, too?"

"Not only that, but he predicted real turbulence in the atmosphere," Wila replied. "Especially with the all the moisture in the air, and the stratification of the temperature from pole to equator, and the rotation of the planet. His predictions were right on. Most of the time."

As Jad watched the flickering in the clouds for a few more micro-sectors, Lilea glanced down at the landing site. Another stream of muddy water, somewhat more intense than the one she'd encountered the first T-sector, had surged out of the hills and was splashing against the landing fins at the bottom of the ship. She pointed it out to Bent.

"The water builds up in the hills. When there's enough, it flows out."

She watched the stream for a few more nanosectors, and she and Bent rejoined the others at the center of the catwalk.

A warm, inviting evening, the ambience cried out for a concert.

Mina, the only musician on the team, brought her nanoro to this little gathering. At nineteen decilinks long, the nanoro had a light tan slender body, slightly wider in the center than at each end. Only the player's right hand operated the metallic keys that opened or closed the various stops, the left hand merely held the instrument as the player blew past the plastic reed at the top. It had a plaintive sound, a somewhat wistful, almost melancholy timbre, perfect accompaniment to the setting of this lightime's sun. While everyone watched the colors fade from the sky, Mina played softly one of her own compositions. To this one she gave the simple name, "Largo."

Lilea and Bent stood on the catwalk beside Trea and Col. The orange-red sun sat directly atop one of the low flat-topped hills in the distance, and to Lilea it resembled the sun of her home planet. "I wish we had colors like this on Anthanos. In some respects Anthanos is so dreary compared to this place."

"Anthanos is dull," Trea said. "And there's so much variety here, so much to see and do. It seems like every time I turn around there's something new. I'm seeing so many new animals I don't have time to examine them all. Col feels the same way. I'm even getting used to the regular cycle of light and dark. We've decided to apply to be on the next team that comes to this planet after we get back. That's how much we like being here."

"Exactly," Col said. "Before we landed I said I thought one trip here would do it for me, but I'm beginning to change my mind. Too occipital."

Lilea didn't respond. She heard what Trea and Col said only peripherally. She'd left the colors of the sunset, and the images of the northern terrain were flipping through her mind like pages in an electronic notebook. Image after image popped up—the villages, the terrain, the brown earth and the lighter rocks, the rivers and streams that so often bisected a particularly intriguing area—but on all of them it was the same thing: no landing sites. The terrain was just too rocky or hilly, or too wet.

I came thirty-five light years to get to this planet, but now I'm stymied by a distance of three to four hundred anthans. I can't even get close to the natives to get a quick look, let alone a good look. There's got to be a way up there.

As she thought more about it, a new plan formed in her mind.

Time Element 461.128.2.2.

"Yes, but are you going to be able to land?" Jer said.

She and Lilea sat at the central table on Life Sciences, looking at several probe images of the terrain south of the ice. This time Lilea had chosen an area about seventy-five anthans southeast of where she and Bent had surveyed earlier.

"The probe images show subtler terrain," Lilea said. "It's not as rocky or hilly. I'm hopeful I'll find a landing site. Maybe I can find some definite indications of intelligent life, like arrowheads or pottery or stone tools. I'll look for a village, but if I can't find one, I'll land where I can and look around."

Jer scanned the images again, a rather noncommittal look on her face. "Who's going with you?"

"Just Col. Bent's staying here to install some recorders."

"Wasn't this supposed to be your landing flight?"

"Yes, it was." This flight had been planned to give her a chance to land at a site she selected from the results of the survey, but without clear results, she decided to reverse the process. She'd land, *then* begin to explore, pending Jer's permission, of course.

"Okay," Jer said, hesitantly. "But be careful. Take your weapons and don't stray too far from the aerodyne. Remember, we need the aerodynes after this. If you don't find anything, it may be a while before we have more openings."

"All right," Lilea said, much more relieved at getting Jer's permission for the flight than upset about this being the last chance she would have to mount any sort of expedition for at least thirty T-sectors.

CHAPTER 29

NORTHERN PLAINS

Time Element 461.129.2.3.

Below Aero Two were low rolling hills with an occasional stony ridge jutting up here and there as if placed deliberately to frustrate a pilot looking for a place to land. At first the rocky terrain dismayed Lilea, though she noted with some anticipation that the rocks seemed to be smaller and didn't dominate the landscape as they did in the vicinity of the large river to the northwest.

She made several passes over the area at one anthan, high enough to prevent the noise of the aerodyne's engine from startling any intelligent life forms on the ground, but close enough to give her and Col a good look at the area. She circled an area that had several likely landing sites. One good site stood out, reasonably rock free and flat, running slightly west of north-south, and about 3500 links long, enough for landing and takeoff.

"That looks good," she said. "Let's go down and see what we've got."

She tapped **LANDING 3** on the Engine Power Dynamics screen to slow the craft to a barely perceptible glide, lowered the flaps, trimmed the elevators, and dropped the skids. The ship bounced and jerked along the rocky ground, and finally came to a stop in front of a small pile of rocks. She left the reactor active to provide power, and contacted Mina, on duty at comm, to tell her they'd landed. She and Col dropped to the ground. Col knelt to sample the vegetation.

The intense ebony black soil nourished a short straw-to-green-colored grass in scattered clumps and tufts. Between the tufts grew a moist patchwork of hardy, yet colorful, ground-hugging plants, some flowering, some not. Scattered among the vegetation were the rocks—millions of them of all shapes and sizes, pebbles to boulders, singles to large clusters, all a light gray to chalky white. The rocks covered everything, extending as far as they could see, even as far as the low hills on the northern horizon. The perception in Lilea's mind as she scanned the area was a region of uncompromising ruggedness. She glanced up at the sky.

The sun shone brilliant in the bright azure sky and warmed her against the cool breeze that came from the northwest. "Feels good." But though she was bundled in a toasty jacket and exposed to the warmth of the sun, she still felt chilled. She looked around at the landscape again, letting the breeze bathe her face. "This is a cold place." She shivered a bit and fastened her jacket securely. "We're not that far south of the ice. It must be cold here all the time."

Col nodded, donning gloves after stuffing several specimens of plant life in small plastic bags. He stood and pointed west toward a dark grayish band that stretched across most of the horizon. "We've got several sub-sectors before the clouds come in." Lilea glanced in that direction, then she and Col grabbed their backpacks from the passenger section and began to hike northward.

They traveled easily along the rocky ground. The soil was damp though not particularly muddy, and they stepped comfortably from one large rock to another. Lilea examined the ground as she walked, looking for anything that might have been made by an intelligent species. As they continued north, they crested a low rise and stopped to survey the area. A line of hills lay in the distance, about an anthan away. As they started down the rise, she went back to watching the ground. That was when she noticed the footprints—an oval depression in the soil with several smaller depressions arranged in a partial semicircle around it. She pointed them out to Col and made several images. *Intelligent?* The footprints headed north.

After several thousand links, the footprints turned east and led toward a large outcrop of rocks and boulders a few hundred links away.

The terrain had become more rugged. Small flinty stones and pebbles covered most of the surface, and Col and Lilea were now treading over rocks almost entirely. The footprints had disappeared except in the occasional spot where the animal stepped on soft soil. As they neared the rocks, they stopped and scanned the area. They'd lost the footprints altogether and Lilea was unsure where to go. She finally decided to turn north again, but as she turned the corner around several large boulders she heard a rustling noise—a sort of scratching sound. It came from above, on top of the boulders. She looked up and came face to face with the animal that had made those footprints.

Undoubtedly the animal detected Lilea and Col long before they saw it, and it took a high perch, probably to ambush its prey. It opened its mouth with its two huge dagger-like teeth flashing in the sunlight, and let out an explosive roar. Lilea screamed and jumped back so violently her foot slipped on some loose talus and she fell backward onto the rocks. Col immediately drew his weapon and ran forward. But he'd taken only a few steps when the animal turned toward him. Crouched as if to spring, it let out another tremendous roar.

"Look out!" Lilea scrambled to her feet and drew her weapon, but Col fired first. With his weapon set at level 1, a wire-thin electron beam shot toward the animal, hitting it just below the left eye. Lilea fired too — her beam struck the animal on its right side. The animal shrieked and jumped backward, slipping off its perch, falling to the ground on the north side of the rocks. It pawed at its face, screeching and howling in ear-piercing screams. After a few nanosectors it scrambled to its feet, and shaking its head furiously from side to side, turned and ran east, whimpering and howling as it ran.

"What the hell was that?" Col yelled as the animal fled.

"I don't know, but it sure scared the hell out of me. Did you see those teeth? Good god, what an animal." Lilea knelt on the ground, trembling and breathing rapidly, finally rising to lean against the rock pile to steady herself. Her hands shook so badly she had difficulty putting her weapon back in its holster. The safety was automatically set when holstered, and she didn't like holding it in her hand any longer than necessary. She took several deep breaths to try to calm herself and break the cycle of rapid, shallow breathing. After a few microsectors, the tension began to drain from her body, and she took a couple of swallows from her water bottle.

"You okay?" Col's hands shook, too. "I hated to do that, but it seemed a definite threat. Trea will be most upset."

"Yes, I'm okay. But let's stay here for a few more microsectors. I want to let it get as far away from us as possible before we continue."

"Eminent thinking."

Col and Lilea watched the animal as it ran. It had retreated to flatter ground and could run a little faster, but it kept swinging its head from side to side and it favored its right side as it ran, falling frequently. It finally disappeared behind some boulders about a quarter-anthan away.

Time Element 461.129.4.2.

Lilea and Col stayed at the rocks another millisector to give Lilea's heart time to stop palpitating. She briefly considered returning to the aerodyne, but decided she didn't want to lose the time she'd gained by coming this far, and decided to continue on.

"Let's go north," she said.

Immediately ahead of them stretched a low range of hills, several hundred links high and covered with the same whitish-to-gray-to-tan rocks that were all around them. As they approached within about a hundred links of the hills, they stopped to survey the area.

"What time is it?" Col asked.

"Four, two."

"How far do you estimate we've gone?"

"Probably no more than one anthan. We have plenty of time."

"I'm ready if you are. But where do you propose to ascend these hills?"

"I don't know. Let's look over here." Lilea pointed to her right. "There seems to be some sort of trail here."

They walked over to the end of what seemed to be a trail, but what was really little more than a narrow dividing line running up the side of the hill between the boulders and large rocks. Lilea studied the trail.

"I don't like the looks of this," she said. "It's pretty rugged. It might be an animal trail, but I think something else has been using it. Look how some of the rocks have been pushed aside. I think we ought to stay off it."

"Do you think intelligent creatures are using it?"

"It's entirely possible." Lilea scanned the ground in front of the trailhead. "See? Here? This large rock has been pushed aside. That's something more than just animals. Let's look for footprints." She started an intense survey of the surface near the trailhead when the glint of an odd color caught her eye. "Hold on, what's this?" She picked up what looked like, at first glance, a dark stone. Unlike the light color of the rocks around, it had a deep brownish-black tint and a shiny, glassy surface. Around five decilinks long and three decilinks across, one side of the rock was tapered to a fine edge.

"That's a rock," Col said.

"No, it isn't. This is more than just 'a rock.' Someone's been working on this rock. See, here, someone's chipped away at one side of it, trying to form a sharp edge. Probably a spearhead. Actually the beginnings of a spearhead." She pointed to the tapered edge. Several small arc-like areas, remnants of fragments chipped off the rock, lay next to one another along one edge. "Those flakes were done purposely."

"How can you tell?"

"I've seen this kind of thing on Anthanos. I recognized the technique these intelligent creatures were using right away. Early Anthanians did the same thing to make spearheads or arrowheads. They take small chips off the edge of the rock. This type of glassy rock makes a sharp edge when they chip it this way. I've studied this a lot."

"Intelligent creatures?" Col raised an eyebrow. "Are you saying there *are* intelligent creatures around here?" His right hand went to his weapon, and he looked around in every direction, undoubtedly nervous at being spotted by natives using their trail. "Perhaps we should be heading back, or at least away from this trail."

But Lilea heard only part of what Col said. She turned to scan the ground near where she found the spearhead. She pulled off a glove and ran her hand over the dark soil, feeling for fragments that might have been flaked from the rock. She remained for almost a millisector, gradually widening the search area around where she first plucked the stone from the ground. "It's possible the spearhead-maker worked on this rock here, at the end of the trail," she said. "Maybe he sat on one of the rocks nearby." She picked up, examined, and discarded several other tiny rocks and fragments, but she eventually, and somewhat dejectedly, came to the conclusion that no chips or flakes were present—at least not in this area.

"I have no doubt intelligent creatures have been using this trail," Lilea said as she stood. "We should be careful. They may be back at any time." She slipped the partially completed spearhead into a pocket of her jumpsuit.

They began again to walk west, paralleling the hills. Lilea surveyed them constantly, looking for an accessible route to the top so she could see the other side. She wondered where the trail went, but as they walked, her mind kept returning to the spearhead, and a feeling of self-satisfaction swelled within her chest.

I knew it! I knew I'd find something sooner or later. Now I've got something solid—not just images of a village—to show that there are intelligent creatures on this planet. This'll go over great on Anthanos. The spearhead's consistent with the images of the villages. Not highly sophisticated, but intelligent enough to make weapons and use them for hunting. Could be dangerous. That's also consistent with the lack of cultivated fields.

As they continued to walk west, Lilea turned more of her attention to the hills. They were almost un-navigable. Rocks and boulders jutted from everywhere.

"If natives are using the trail, there must be something important beyond the hills," Lilea said. "Like a village or community of some sort.

Let's see if we can get to the top." They'd gone about two thousand links beyond the trail when they stopped. "This is far enough. We should be able to scale this hill without being seen."

Lilea took the lead scrambling up the hill. They crawled over and around the rocks, hopping from one boulder to another, carefully and deliberately making their way to the top.

As they reached the summit, Lilea cautioned Col not to raise his head above the top of the hills to prevent being seen by something below. In their bright blue-green jumpsuits and jackets, they would stand out in stark contrast against the light-colored rocks and dark soil that made up the hills. Lilea crouched behind a small boulder and peered around it into the valley beyond.

"Damn," she said, and stood up.

The valley floor was flat and, oddly, almost rock free. Another row of hills lay a few hundred links beyond, but nothing like a village met Lilea's gaze as she scanned the valley. Far to her right, the trail ran down the hill they stood on, over the valley floor, and up toward a low pass on the hills beyond. They saw no animals or other creatures.

Col made a 400-degree sweep of the area with his vision aid. "I can see the aerodyne from here," he said, looking south. "No one seems to have come across it." He turned to look east, the general direction from which they'd come.

Suddenly he motioned to Lilea. "Get down! Get down!"

CHAPTER 30

VISUALIZATION

Time Element 461.129.5.5.

"Look over there," Col said, gesturing east. Lilea grabbed her camera. From behind the rocks about a quarter-anthan away came two upright, bipedal natives, one behind the other, a long pole slung from the shoulder of one to the shoulder of the other, an animal suspended by its feet from the pole. Lilea started her camera and ran the magnification to 100. The natives wound their way across the flatland to the trailhead and began to ascend.

"There they are," Lilea whispered. "I knew when I found the spearhead we'd see some of these people sooner or later. It was just a matter of time." Her heart pounded in her chest, her fascination at the sight of these aboriginal people so intense she barely noticed when, in trying to squat behind a large rock, her foot slipped on some loose stones and started a noisy cascade of rocks sliding down the hill. The second native glanced momentarily in her direction but he had to return his attention just as quickly to carrying his load over what must have been a frustratingly rocky trail.

They were dressed in skins, dark and furry against the cold, and wore boots of the same skin. Each had a dark pouch of some indefinable material slung from one shoulder across their chests so the pouch rode at hip level. Col's vision aid gave him an estimate of the height of the lead native. "Seven and a half links. These gentlemen are exceptional."

"That's as tall as Jad."

Lilea increased the magnification on her camera to 150 to get a close-up of the lead native. Bareheaded and clean-shaven, and fair and light of skin, his dark black hair fell down past his shoulders. His slender build also reminded Lilea of Jad, yet her overall impression was that within those skins there dwelt a substantial muscular build. The second native was shorter, about seven links, and a stockier build. He wore a full dark beard and a hat made of the same fur as his clothing. He might have been older than the first. Even under the weight of the animal on their shoulders they both walked upright, not giving in to the load.

"They're good-looking," Lilea said. "Rough, hardy. Well suited to this clime."

"Were you expecting something else?"

"No, I didn't have any real preconceived . . . they do remind me of early Anthanians of about ten thousand years ago . . . their use of natural materials like animal skins and spears . . . they've probably only just started using fire . . . I can't see them domesticating any animals . . . yet . . . I'll need to study them further."

Col followed the two natives closely as they inched their way up the hill. "I notice that the pole they're carrying the animal from is really two poles, and there are sharp points at the end of each. I gather those poles are really spears, but now they're using them to carry their prey."

"I see that." Through the telephoto lens of her camera, Lilea focused on the animal—pale tan or tawny in color with indistinct stripes across its back. "Doesn't it seem to you that there's something familiar about that animal?"

The animal's left side faced them. As the natives carried it up the rocky trail, the head swung back and forth. Huge fangs flashed in the sunlight.

"There's a lot of blood on its head," Col said. "It appears as though there's a wound on the head somewhere."

"That's just it. That animal we encountered. You shot it in the head."

"Are you postulating it's the same animal?"

"It could be. It ran back in that direction. Maybe it died and they found it."

"Or they found it wounded and finished it off."

"Possible." Lilea returned her concentration to the natives as they made their way slowly up the hill and over the top. They carried the animal down the other side, across the flat land between the hills, and up the other side, finally disappearing over the pass. Lilea stopped the camera.

"If that was the animal we shot," Col said, "I wonder what those two beings thought to themselves when they found it. The wounds we gave it wouldn't be like anything they'd ever seen before."

"They might not have paid much attention. They might've thought it fell and hit its head on a rock, or something. These people probably don't have the sophistication to tell much about different types of wounds. What time is it?"

"Six, one," Col said as he glanced at his personal chronometer.

"What would you think about going down the other side of this hill, and up the other hill and looking over it to see where those two went?"

Col didn't say anything right away. A painful version of 'you're kidding' crossed his face. "I think not. We're limited in time. It's just past the midpoint of this lightime, and we should be returning to the aerodyne."

"Why? There's plenty of time before it gets dark. We can make it up and back in one subsector."

"It's not the dark I'm worried about. It's what might happen if we get to the top of that hill. There may be many more creatures on the other side. You said yourself we shouldn't approach them."

"I'm not going to approach them. I just want to see what's on the other side of that hill. There may be a village down there. The type of their living arrangements would tell me a lot—"

"If there is a village, there may be many more of the natives, and I certainly don't want to get caught by them at the top of a hill looking down on them."

"Col, I think you're afraid of them."

"No, I'm not afraid of them individually, but we could get surrounded if they see us at the top of that hill. If there is a village over there, there certainly will be more of them. If anything happened, we might have to dispatch several of them just to get away. Besides, if two natives returned with a dead animal, more may reappear from hunting, too. We could get caught out in the open, like, down there." He pointed toward the land between the hills.

Col's caution was beginning to irritate Lilea. She looked at the flat land below and the hills beyond. "Well, Col," she finally said, "you can stay here if you want, but I'm going down and look over the top of that hill and see what's over there." She removed her daypack and stuffed her camera inside. She started down the side of the hill, swinging her pack onto her back.

"Have you noticed the wind is picking up? And it's getting colder, too." Col pointed west. "Clouds are approaching."

Lilea stopped. She looked at the clouds in the west and checked the wind. The sky was still clear overhead and the sun cast crisp shadows over the rocky terrain. The clouds were now only a few subsectors away from blanketing the area, and the breeze had intensified. "I see what you mean." She turned and looked at the hills to the north. They beckoned to her. She looked back at the clouds. "I think I can make it over to the other hills and back before the clouds move in. I'll keep in contact with you by Pers-

Comm."

"Are you quite sure you want to do this?"

"Yes," she said, without looking back. "It should take me only a half-subsector."

Time Element 461.129.6.4.

Lilea worked her way to the bottom of the hill as rapidly as she could, occasionally slipping on loose talus. Still, it took her more than a millisector. She crouched behind a boulder at the edge of the valley and scanned it, east and west. She saw nothing, but before she stood, she pulled out her PersComm and contacted Col.

"Do you see anything?"

"No. Everything is clear."

Lilea, conscious of how visible she must appear in her bright blue-green jacket and jumpsuit against the speckled black and white terrain all around, darted across the valley, hunching down at another boulder to contact Col.

"See anything?"

"Nothing. Everything's still clear."

Lilea was about to tuck her PersComm in her left thigh pocket when a familiar voice came from the speaker. "Lilea? Lilea. C-Can you hear me?"

"Mina? What are you doing on comm?"

"Your P-PersComm communications are going through the aero-dyne to us. J-Jer is also listening."

Oh, that's right. I left the PersComm matrix in relay mode at Aero Two. Everything is being passed to Explorer.

"Lilea? What are you doing? Where are you going?" Jer's voice sounded inquisitive, not concerned.

"I'm getting ready to climb this hill and see if I can tell where the natives went."

"Natives?" Jer's voice jumped. "What natives?"

"We've seen two natives. They went over these hills. I'm at the base of one hill and I'm going to the top and see if I can tell where they went. There may be a village there."

"Col, where are you? Are you at the base of the hill too?"

"No, I'm situated at the top of a hill to the south. I'm observing Li-lea."

"Lilea, have any of those natives seen you?"

"No, but I really need to get going. There are clouds coming in."

"Okay. Contact me when you get back to the aerodyne. But be careful."

"Okay." Lilea slipped her PersComm into its pocket. She looked up at the hills. This would be a formidable task. These hills were higher by two to three hundred links than the ones from which she'd just come, and they looked just as rocky and treacherous—in many places even more so—and no ready trail existed. She would have to clamber over rocks and boulders all the way, and that would take time. It would be a challenging climb, but she could do it. But could she do it within the half-subsector time limit she'd given herself? She'd used almost two millisectors just getting to this point.

She started out, working her way up, maneuvering over and around the rocks. She swallowed hard to choke down her feelings about the climb: the excitement at being able to see a village close up, yet mixed with a little trepidation at being exposed and solitary on this hill. Col did have a valid point—if the natives saw her she could be trapped. Or killed.

Slowly she made headway up the hill, but she concentrated so much on getting to the top she lost track of time. About halfway up, her Pers-Comm beeped.

"Lilea, it's getting late," Col said. "The clouds are moving in. I think you should get back."

"Just a little more. I can make it."

"It's later than you think."

"Lilea," Jer's voice said again, but this time with a trace of unease. "What's going on out there? Why is Col saying you need to get back?"

"Lilea," Col said, "it's taken you three millisectors to get halfway up that hill. At that rate you'll utilize another three millisectors to get to the top. The clouds are increasing and the wind has picked up. We should repair to the aerodyne."

"Lilea," Jer said, "I can't see what's going on, but I think you should listen to Col."

Lilea didn't say anything right away. She stopped climbing and looked toward the top of the hill. She looked down at the route she'd taken and compared the two distances.

"I can make it. It's not that far."

"It's farther than you think." Col now had an edge on his voice. He spoke more rapidly than usual, running his words together. "You're only about halfway. By the time you get up there and take a look around and get back here and by the time we get back to the aerodyne, the clouds will be here and we may be stuck here for the darktime and who knows what it will be like next lightime."

"It sounds like he's right, Lilea," Jer said. "I suggest you do what he says."

Lilea checked the distance to go and the distance she'd come. She scanned the clouds and felt the wind. The western horizon was covered in thick, gray, billowing clouds, but as she stood on this hill she couldn't tell if they held the threat of dumping water on her and Col. The wind had picked up, steadily from the west now, not in feeble gusts as before. The temperature recorder on her PersComm showed a drop of 4 Tal over the past subsector.

She glanced toward the hill where Col stood. Even in his bright jacket, he was a small, dark speck against the sky. She came to the agonizing conclusion he was right.

She turned back and looked at the top of the hill on which she stood. The thought of being able to stand up there and look down into the valley on the other side made her heart jump. There must be a village — or at least some sort of living area — over there. It was a solid fact in her mind. Why would the natives struggle to carry that animal over two hills if there *wasn't* a village or a cave or *something* there? They had to be taking that animal *somewhere*. The temptation to continue climbing was so strong.

But, no — she couldn't. She didn't want to get stranded here. Col waited for her to return, and she couldn't force him to stay in a potentially hostile wilderness like this. If the clouds came in, they could be trapped here until the next lightime, or even longer. They could be stranded with only the food and water they'd brought with them. She had to get back.

"Okay," she said. "I'm coming back." She turned the PersComm off but held it in her hand.

She said it but she didn't mean it. She turned and looked uphill and made a rough estimate in her mind — only a few hundred links and she'd be standing on the top. Then she could take a quick peek at the valley below.

That's all I want. Just a quick peek.

"Crap. I was so damn close."

She stood on the side of that hill with anger building in her chest. To be ordered to return when she had almost reached the top of the hill brought out the fury in her — so close, so damn close — and she hurled the PersComm against one of the rocks at her feet.

"Goddammit!"

The unit smashed against the top of the rock and the plastic outer casing cracked and split into several pieces. The rest of the unit skipped off the rock and shattered against another rock farther downhill. The keys splintered off and the bottom half of the case came to rest against a small boulder about twenty links away. The power source, cracked and useless, fell to the ground nearby.

Oh crap, what did I do?

As a state-of-the-art communications device, a PersComm cost more than 2000 monetary units. They were so much more powerful than the little sonotic device they used back on Anthanos. PersComm signals were relayed to *Explorer* through a runabout or aerodyne comm system that could be as far as thirty anthans away. She'd be fined by SpaceComm for the full price when she got back. What was worse, Jer would have a fit when she found out she'd destroyed a valuable piece of equipment, and her inability to control her anger would go on her record. She'd never hear the end of it. Extra units were available on *Explorer*, but they were replacements to be used only in case of accident or malfunction, and bashing one against a rock didn't seem sufficient justification for requisitioning one of the replacements. But it was too late now, she'd have to face the consequences. Col probably saw her throw it anyway.

"I was so damn close." She gathered the pieces of the PersComm and stuffed them in her pocket, and scrambled down the hill. After about a millisector, she reached the bottom, and without looking left or right bolted across the valley and vaulted onto the southern hill. She scampered up the hill as fast as she could, reaching Col by 129.7.2.

Time Element 461.129.7.9.

Lilea and Col made their way back to the bottom of the southern row of hills, headed for the aerodyne. They saw no other natives like the ones carrying the animal in spite of carefully looking in all directions — especially to their rear — as they walked. When they arrived at the landing site after more than a half-subsector's walk, they approached the ship cautiously, sneaking up on it to avoid surprising any natives or animals which might have come across it in the meantime. From the crest of the slight rise that overlooked the landing site, they scanned the area, but saw no one. They hustled back to the ship and inspected the takeoff area. It didn't look good.

Shadows disappeared and reappeared as white, puffy clouds moved across the sun.

The line of travel the ship would take in getting airborne carried it over rocky terrain. It was smooth enough, and no worse than the landing, but Lilea had something else in mind.

"If we take off north, we'll go right over the area where we saw the natives, and there won't be enough distance to gain altitude. If there is a village beyond that second row of hills, we'll fly right over it. We could bank left or right just after takeoff, but they'll hear us. If we could just turn the ship around . . ."

"We can't use the jacking wheels," Col said. "The surface is too rocky and soft. But we could start the engine, and then both of us push vigorously on the right wing tip and try to turn the ship around. Remember them showing us that?"

"I remember." Lilea never liked that maneuver, even when Space-Comm showed them how to do it. "It usually takes four people. I'd have to get out and push. The pilot is supposed to stay in the pilot's seat whenever the engine's running."

"I realize that, but one person pushing won't provide enough force. Two people will be essential."

Lilea considered the plan for a nanosector. She didn't have any alternative, and the sky was clouding rapidly. "Okay, let's try it." She entered the craft on the left side and started the engine. She advanced the throttle just far enough to move the ship about one link per second, then grabbed her sound balancers and jumped out, running over to help Col push. She could barely reach the wingtip, seven links off the ground, but together the two of them were able to force the ship into a broad left-hand arc of almost 200 degrees, bringing it around to face a relatively flat area which would make a serviceable "runway" for takeoff. Lilea jumped back in on the right side, and throttled the engine back.

She shifted to the left-hand seat and Col jumped in behind her while she hurriedly ran through the pre-takeoff checklist. She advanced the throttle and the ship began to slide awkwardly over the irregular terrain. Slowly it picked up speed, bumping and jerking along the ground, finally lifting into the air.

She took the ship to four anthans, and then circled back toward the area they'd explored on foot, and activated the cameras in the nose. She flew over the two rows of hills, capturing several images through a fortunate gap in the clouds. She hoped it would show a village or some other group of dwellings where these natives made their home.

After the imaging run, she set the ITS to fly the return vector, and then pulled some food from her pack to curb the growling in her stomach.

As they flew, she called the images up on the com screen, and when she examined the area beyond the second line of hills, she found, sure enough, a village of eight "huts" in a circle nestled into the eastern end of the valley. The flat terrain on which the village lay was wide open to the west—a perfect landing site directly in front of the village.

"Fan-damn-tastic," Lilea said, and pumped a fist in the air. "I knew there'd be a village there. There had to be. Now I have a known village with a good landing site, and I can come back to study these people."

The feeling of pride and excitement of a job well done swelled up in Lilea's chest, and she unzipped her jacket. Never before, not even on Anthanos, had she had such a good T-sector of solid accomplishment—discovery of a village with a good landing site nearby, a spearhead she could show everyone, and full-motion images of the two natives carrying the animal. She almost couldn't settle down enough to fly the ship.

"Mina!" she yelled into the microphone. "I found it! I found a village! And it has a good landing site nearby."

Comm was silent for a few nanosectors. "Lilea, wh-what are you talking about? Wh-where are you?"

"We're on our way back to Site One." Lilea's thoughts came so rapidly she couldn't speak fast enough to get them all out in any coherent order. "I imaged the area over the hill and I wanted to get to the top of it before the clouds started closing in and there's a village on the other side. Now I can come back and meet these people and study them. It's fantastic!"

"That's great," Mina said.

"Is Jer there?"

"I'm here," Jer replied. "I heard about the village. It's great. I'm glad you found what you were looking for. But did you say *meet* them?"

"Ah, well, maybe not meet them, but at least study them. Put me down for an aerodyne flight sometime in the future. I'm coming back."

"Okay, I'll see what I can do."

Lilea terminated comm and settled back in her seat. With the ship on autocontrol and flying the return route on ITS, she wasn't constantly occupied with the tedium of flight, and she had plenty of time to think. She couldn't help it. Her mind had erupted with visions.

CHAPTER 31

PERSCOMM

Time Element 461.135.2.8.

Like the others on the team, Lilea'd been allowed to design her own work station on the Life Sciences Deck, and she filled it with drawers and cabinets containing hundreds of cells, chambers, and cubbyholes to store the variety of specimens she expected to collect. She removed the spearhead from the only locked drawer and placed it on the stage of a low-power microscope. She frequently pulled it out to admire it as much as to examine it. The spearhead fascinated her as did no other early Anthanian artifact she'd ever found, and she had a collection of more than fifty items at home, many of them similarly constructed spearheads and arrowheads. In the microscope she could discern in considerable detail the sequence of events the spearhead maker had taken to get to this point. She estimated he'd taken about ten chips off the edge before he stopped. But why had he stopped? Had he been interrupted? Did he lose interest? She couldn't tell, he still had a lot of work to do to bring the stone into any real semblance of a spearhead. But those few flakes were enough to tell her what he was trying to do.

And why had he dropped it at the end of the trail? Was he in a hurry to attack some passing animal? Or was the reason merely as prosaic as a hole in the bottom of his pouch? He certainly wasn't working on it on the trail—she would've found chips on the ground near where the spearhead lay, so he must have done the work somewhere else and lost it moving along the trail.

Lilea had become so absorbed in examining the stone she almost didn't hear Jer call her name. She looked up from the microscope and turned around as Jer strode over to the workstation from the interdeck elevator, her electronic notebook in one hand.

"Lilea, I just got notified that you removed a replacement PersComm from the electronics rack on the Storage Deck. It says you signed it out. Is that right?"

"That's right."

"Why did you take a replacement?"

"Oh . . . uh . . . mine got broken on the trip. To the northern plains."

"But I read your report about the trip. You didn't say anything about your PersComm being broken. What happened?"

"Uh, I slipped and fell when I was coming back down the hill. I bashed it against a rock. That is, my foot slipped and I tripped over a rock and bashed the PersComm. It was in my pocket where I always keep it. It got smashed."

"But you didn't put that in the report."

"No, I didn't think it was important enough to put in the report."

"But the destruction of equipment should always be reported. Also, if you were injured, you should report it. Can you send out a supplemental report and describe the accident?"

"Okay."

"Thanks. And I'd like to see the broken one. Maybe it's repairable."

"Oh. Okay."

Jer hurried away, headed to some other part of the ship.

CHAPTER 32

STRUCTURE

Time Element 461.138. 2.3.

Lilea sat at the little table in the food prep area, her electronic notebook open in front of her. In the twilight of the early darktime, the water of a sudden intense storm splashed in waves against the window, and she occasionally turned and glanced outside. Brilliant lightning and crashes of deep rumbling interrupted her as she scrolled through the images. She tried to concentrate on making some sense of what her encounter with the natives in the north meant in terms of intelligent life on this planet, and the storm kept diverting her. But as she worked, her attention was drawn more and more to Bent, sitting on the couch in the compartment's living area. The lightning, but most especially the noise, seemed to spook him. He winced constantly at the flash and boom, much more so than she did, and he played the same short movie on the com screen, over and over. He'd played it three times since the storm began. Finally, he stopped the movie in the middle of the fourth play and left the compartment. He left the door slightly ajar and she heard him climb down the ladder to the Entry Deck one level below.

Lilea returned to her notebook, playing the full-motion and individual images of the natives. She didn't like the term "native" and wanted a better name for these people. After all, she reasoned, every species, plant and animal, on the planet was "native," even these, probably the most intelligent species. She searched for a word that would designate them uniquely. But what? Sophisticated? Intelligent? Sentient? Undoubtedly all were true, but those were individual traits, not the all-encompassing word she wanted. The best term she could come up with was derived from the Anthanian word "humanos." It meant "a relative," but referred to a distant relative. An "omanos" was a close relative, like a first cousin. Like most Anthanian terms that had the suffix "-os," both had to do with friends or friendship, or referred to a fellow traveler. The Great God Arteamos was a friend of Anthanos, which likewise, was a friend of the God. They traveled the galaxy together. So she decided she'd call them "humans." Granted, they weren't *really* relatives in a genetic sense. They evolved on different planets and that meant their evolution and genetic material were unquestionably different. Yet in a larger sense, they *were* relatives. They inhabited the same sector of the galaxy, and that made them, in her mind, distant cousins.

With that out of the way, she wondered about the "humans" themselves. The fact that they look like us — or rather, we look like them — she mused, tells us something about the evolution on our planets. They took parallel routes — the cephalization, the general physical structure, the microscopic cellular organization — there's a common thread here.

I'll have to get some genetic material to find out. I definitely will have to go back to that village.

Now she conceived a whole series of experiments — not only going back to the village and getting a sample of their genetic material, but analyzing it and comparing it to Anthanian. Her brain took off as the excitement of new knowledge built in her chest. Trea and Mina had already worked out the structure of the basic genetic material of many of the animals Trea had caught, and it turned out to be considerably different from Anthanian, though there were a few points of intriguing similarity. There certainly would never be any crossbreeding between them. But at the cellular level, they noted many more points of similarity. After all, as Trea put it, a cell is a complicated organism — so many things have to happen inside a cell for it to survive, and she wasn't surprised they'd be similar to Anthanian cells. And the tissues and organs of the two were even more alike. Lilea agreed with them that the final organisms built of these cells, tissues, and organs would *have* to be similar. Divergence was probably impossible and her images bore that out. *Maybe it's a common thread among living organisms developing on different planets. At least within this sector of the galaxy.*

As she hurriedly typed her ideas into the notebook, Bent returned to the compartment. The front of his jumpsuit was sprinkled heavily with drops of water, as though he'd stood in *Explorer*'s main entry door while the water splattered him. He must have remained there for a millisector or more to get that wet. He said nothing and entered the bedroom.

CHAPTER 33

VORTEX

Time Element 461.155.3.7.

Col picked a landing site in a broad valley between two rows of low hills. The flat, straight valley, almost three hundred links wide and running northeast-southwest, was long enough for a landing and later takeoff. A thin ribbon of dark green vegetation, outlining a narrow stream, hugged the north side of the valley, and left plenty of room for the aerodyne south of the creek.

Col, Dell, Mina and Lilea had left in Aero One, headed for the northern plains, several hundred anthans east of where Lilea and Col spotted her "humans." Not on the Expedition Calendar, Col put this trip together to sample the vegetation in this part of the continent, almost due north of the grasslands they'd explored earlier. But this region wasn't grass. On the probe images it appeared as a great swath of grayish-black, a region of low, rolling hills and vast plains, the same dark soil that Lilea and Col had visited earlier, with the same interminably cold, blustery winds that swept off the ice to the north. From orbit, Trea had imaged vast numbers of animals, large and small, in this area and wanted to study them, but at the last millisector — and for reasons Lilea never understood — she backed out of the expedition. Lilea grabbed the aerodyne's empty seat.

Col set the aerodyne down in a northeasterly direction and allowed it to slide to a stop. As the team members opened the door and stepped out, they were met with an icy breeze whistling down the valley from the northeast, right in their faces.

"I checked the outside air temperature," Col said. "It's 8 Tal."

The cool air penetrated the thin fabric of Lilea's jumpsuit as she dropped out, and she joined the others in retrieving heavier jackets from the aerodyne's cargo hold through the access door on the ship's left side. She turned to examine the landing site.

The ship had come to rest on the north side of the valley, its left wingtip above the little stream. Lilea walked forward of the aerodyne and scanned the terrain. The hills that formed the valley rose about twenty links above the floor, running straight and parallel for several thousand links, finally tapering at their northeastern end to the level of the valley floor. She walked around to the right side of the ship, the southern side, and climbed to the top of the hill.

Stretching endlessly from where she stood was a random pattern of low hills and hillocks, none more than twenty to thirty links high, and covered by the same scrawny vegetation. A monotonous, unvarying land, it had little to recommend itself to intelligent life, except perhaps for the presence of the animals. A herd of ten to twelve large animals, adult and young, ambled by about a thousand links away. She was fascinated by their long furry coats, their elongated snouts, and the huge, sweeping, in-curved tusks. No animals like that ever existed on Anthanos.

I remember Trea's images. I remember thinking that intelligent beings could hunt them. I'll get some images of them and show them to Trea when we get back. Maybe I'll find something here. But this place is still cold. I don't know why, but I dislike this place. I'll be glad to leave.

But she was interrupted by Mina's voice from behind her. "Lilea. Can you g-give us a hand with the shelter?"

Time Element 461.155.8.0.

They erected the shelter on a small level plot about 200 links behind Aero One at the base of the southern row of hills. Putting it in the usual position would have put it on top of the stream. A power cord, stretched its full length, ran from the aerodyne, and a small portable solar power unit sat on the hill behind the shelter.

The first they knew about the approaching storm was the heavy, thudding noise in the distance. When Lilea and Dell left the shelter to check on it they were greeted by a long row of dark, ominous clouds advancing from the west and northwest. The breeze had picked up and the air temperature had dropped—down to 4 Tal by the thermal recorder at the entrance to the shelter. The storms reached the campsite around 155.11, about a subsector before dusk.

"We should put the solar unit back in the cargo hold before the storm hits us," Col said. "It might get blown around."

Dell agreed to help, and while they unhooked and disassembled the solar power unit and took it back to the aerodyne, Mina joined Lilea outside the shelter's airlock, watching the approaching storm. When she first heard the noise, Lilea wondered if the storm would bring just water, or balls of ice, or perhaps something more exotic, but as she studied the approaching band of dark gray clouds, she noticed something more—something very unusual—about the sky.

"Do you see it? The air is a funny green color. Sort of grayish-green. I've never seen that before. I wonder what it means?"

"I don't know." Mina's eyes darted around the sky. Her face had turned pallid, her breathing heavier. She blew on her hands to warm them. "It's weird, almost creepy. Maybe we're going to get another ice storm. We'd better get inside."

Col and Dell met the ladies at the shelter, but as Dell neared the shelter he spoke. "I just remembered, my notebook is still in the aerodyne. I want to start writing up some notes about our trip. I'll be back in a micro-sector."

In the safety of the clear plastic entrance airlock of the shelter, Lilea and Mina watched as Dell trotted toward the aerodyne, and as the first drops splattered the ground, he sprinted the last fifty links. He reached the aerodyne just before the deluge began and jumped in through the right side door. Lilea and Mina retreated to the shelter's interior.

Around 156.3.3, the roaring began. At first it was a low rumble in the distance that sounded like the thundering noise they'd heard during storms at Site One. But this noise didn't blast and fade out as Lilea was familiar with, instead it was one long, slowly appreciating rumble. Lilea slipped into the airlock to look through the clear plastic. A band of deep, dark clouds—unusually and unnervingly dark—stretched like a malignant curtain across the western sky, so reminiscent of the clouds they flew into returning from the gorge.

I'm glad I'm on the ground and not in the sky. Still, looking at the clouds she felt a twinge of misgivings. *What are they going to bring now?* Then she saw the worm.

Dipping from the clouds about a half-anthan away appeared a black, writhing, whirling cylinder, maybe twenty to thirty links wide at the base. It undulated as it moved, a squirming, wriggling channel from sky to ground, darting over the surface from southwest to northeast on the far side of the northern row of hills. As she watched, the base of the vortex vaulted the hills and landed squarely in the valley in which they were camped.

"Mina," Lilea yelled back into the shelter. "Come here and look at this!"

Mina and Col joined her in the airlock. "What is that?"

Light rain pelted the clear plastic of the airlock, but they could see the general outline of the swirling mass headed in their direction. But more importantly to Lilea, it was the debris the storm was kicking up—grass, soil, rocks and the like—that alarmed her beyond her initial misgivings. As the funnel came nearer, Col—obviously also now beginning to understand the power of this unusual phenomenon—yelled, "That thing could be dangerous and it's coming right at us. Perhaps we should leave."

Lilea ducked back into the shelter. Mina yelled back at her.

"Lilea! Where are you going?"

"I'm going to get my camera."

Lilea grabbed her camera and ran to the back section of the shelter and raised Dell on the comm link. "Dell!" she bellowed into the microphone. "There's a storm coming! Get out of there!" She dropped the microphone without waiting for a response and ran through the front door of the shelter right behind Mina and Col without re-zipping the front door or the airlock door. She followed them around the shelter and up the hill and down the other side. Only a few nanosectors after they left the shelter into what was now a drizzly rain, the writhing cloud struck the shelter and sent it and everything in it flying. In panic, they sprinted across the plains.

"Get down! Get down!" Col yelled when the roaring increased, and they fell to the ground and lay face down for several microsectors until the roaring faded away. Cautiously they raised their heads, exhaled, and retreated to the valley.

As they crested the hill, the first thing Lilea saw was Aero One and it didn't seem to be damaged. But the shelter was gone, and in its place a broad trail of debris ran up the valley almost to the aerodyne. Clothes, boots, the computer display, two sleeping bags, food containers, the fan heaters—ripped from their place at the rear of the shelter and damaged beyond repair—were spread in a wide swath over the ground. The computer keyboard lay on top of the southern hills, opposite Aero One. The power cable lay on the ground, ripped from the shelter but still attached to the aerodyne at its far end.

"Oh, my god," Lilea said, but the others remained silent. They stood at the top of the hill as they surveyed the area.

"What the hell w-was that?" Mina said. "It was like some sort of whirling cloud, sort of like a vortex in the air. How c-could that be possible?"

"It was so powerful," Lilea said. "It just picked up the shelter and threw it away—where is the shelter, anyway? I don't see it."

"All our stuff. All our food, c-clothes . . . everything's been thrown away like so much t-trash. Even the emergency s-system is gone."

"Unbelievable." Col's face had turned almost white, yet he seemed to be sweating. He wiped his mouth with his hand. "I would never have postulated that the atmosphere could produce such a tremendously powerful storm. And so compact, too."

They stayed at the top of the hills for almost a millisector, not knowing what remnants of the storm dallied in the valley, perhaps waiting to send them flying into the sky, too, just like the shelter.

What was that? Was it a part of the storm? Will it return? Lilea looked to her right, up the valley, but the wriggly cloud had disappeared. The rain had stopped, only the dark, spawning clouds remained, still covering the sky, rolling and boiling in the murky dusk, still threatening and ominous. *Are there more of these storms? What happens if it returns and hits the aerodyne?* Lilea scanned the horizon, but she saw nothing that resembled the storm.

"We must leave," Col said. "Immediately. Grab what you can, and we'll take off within the millisector."

"Col, we can't leave now. It's a two subsector trip, and it'll be dark in a few millisectors."

Col glanced at his wrist chronometer and nodded. "Ah, yes. True." He wiped his mouth with his sleeve. "Trea will be exceedingly upset." He said nothing more as he crept down the hill. Lilea followed, joining Mina in retrieving what they could. Col picked up the end of the power cable and coiled it over his arm as he walked toward Aero One. Only bare wires protruded from the end of the cable where the plug had been ripped off when the shelter had been sucked into the vortex.

Lilea set her camera on a small clump of grass above the shelter site and began gathering clothes and utensils as she walked, following the trail of debris, not far behind Col.

Col unplugged the cable from the side of the aerodyne and opened the right side door. Lilea could hear the alarm — the double bonging alarm of a minor emergency — that had been activated when the cable was ripped from the shelter. She wasn't concerned, it was the expected response by the ship's computer to the abrupt removal of the cable, and she went back to picking up debris. But she kept one eye on Col as she worked, and — she thought this a bit odd — instead of returning to help salvage debris, he walked around the front of the ship, visually sweeping the area as though looking for something. He looked under the aerodyne, and then jumped over the stream and walked up the hill on the ship's left side. He surveyed north and west of the campsite, then turned and scanned the valley in which the aerodyne rested, northeast and southwest. Her curiosity grew into unease as Col trotted down the hill, across the valley, and up the southern hill. He stood on a small knoll, staring east at some unidentified point on the distant plains.

"Lilea! Mina!" he bellowed and waved a "Come on!" gesture as he sprinted down the far side of the hill.

Lilea's heart jerked and her unease grew into concern. Now she understood the importance of the alarm she heard when Col opened the door, and that sudden realization startled her. Had Dell been in the aerodyne, *he* would have shut off the alarm. She didn't know why he didn't, and she wasn't sure what Col was doing, but she understood he had some serious intent. Col was not given to practical jokes. "Mina! Come!" she yelled and ran over to the hill.

Mina still salvaged near the shelter site. She apparently hadn't heard Col's yell, but she came running at Lilea's call.

As Lilea reached the top of the hill, she saw Col running east, and she projected her gaze in front of him to see where he was headed. There, several thousand links away, she saw it—a dot of color—the same bright blue-green color of the team's jackets and jumpsuits. It was so small and so far away, but it couldn't be anything else. Mina saw it at the same time and gave a sudden gasp. She looked briefly at the aerodyne, and with the sudden realization of what that little dot of color meant her knees buckled, but she managed to start running after Col. Lilea took off behind her, deep dread aching in her heart.

"Dell! Dell!" Mina shouted as she ran. "Oh, my god, no! Please, no!"

Col was the first to arrive at the body. He picked up Dell's hand to feel for a pulse.

CHAPTER 34

DELL

Time Element 461.156.3.8.

Dell's body had come to rest in a misshapen, contorted posture. He lay on his right side, his right arm wrenched behind his back, his left arm across his chest. Both legs were badly twisted and undoubtedly broken. The right side of his face lay buried in the black soil—his neck was probably broken, too. A deep gash across his forehead disappeared into the hairline. His left eye was still open, a look of terror on his face. Mina knelt and tried to talk to him.

"Dell," she said softly through the tears streaming down her cheeks. "Can you hear me? Can you hear me, darling?" She brought her face close to his and kept whispering to him, "Dell, can you hear me? I love you, darling, I love you. Can you hear me? Please tell me you can hear me."

As Lilea arrived, Col stood over the body but made no attempt to resuscitate him. At first she thought she understood his meaning, but then she noticed that his face, pale and thin, trembled and quivered, and sweat poured from his forehead. His breathing was heavy and he wiped his face with his sleeve. "I believe he's . . . ," he mumbled. Then, without any explanation, he turned and bolted toward the aerodyne.

"Col—" Lilea watched as he disappeared over the hill. *Where's he going? I hope he comes back with the first-aid kits.* She turned to Mina and knelt beside her and put an arm around her waist. "Sweetheart, I don't think Dell can hear you anymore."

Mina said nothing. She pushed Dell onto his back and tried to straighten his legs. She spoke to him as if he might eventually respond, and as she sobbed tears fell onto his face. She pulled a handkerchief from her pocket and began to wash his face, to remove the dirt and tears that streaked his face.

Where is Col? Is he going to bring the first-aid kits? They'll have resuscitation equipment in them. Maybe I should try CPR . . . at least some chest compressions . . . maybe he can still breathe. Lilea picked up Dell's left hand and felt for a pulse. Like Col she felt nothing. She tried one chest compression, but something cracked, or crunched, when she pressed down on the sternum. It didn't rebound like the dummy's chest did when they taught her CPR. "Oh, no, his rib cage is crushed. I can't . . ."

She sat back on her heels, and Mina rested her head on Dell's chest. Lilea stayed beside her, trying to comfort her. She put an arm around Mina's waist and spoke to her as best she could, but she didn't know what to do or say.

So much had happened so quickly. Almost on a whim, she'd been picked up by some unknown, unseen force and dropped squarely in the middle of the death of a good friend and fellow spaceflight explorer without being aware of the events taking place. It happened so quickly it was disorienting, and Lilea found herself wondering how she got here. Nobody ever got killed by storms on her planet. Anthanos was so quiet, so smooth, so sedate. But that was of secondary importance. The memory of the storm was put on hold while she dealt with Dell's death.

With the storm's passage, the wind had died down, but the temperature kept dropping. The sun hung low in the western sky, edging out from behind the clouds, and the reddish-orange light cast long, eerie shadows of the two mourners across the bleak landscape, giving the scene a grim, funereal appearance that reflected the mood of the two women.

Lilea decided to let Mina have her time to cry. She could do nothing now other than to try to comfort Mina. She relaxed her hold on Mina's waist, waiting for Col to return. The emptiness of grieving overwhelmed her.

What do you say to someone like this? How do you comfort them? She'd have to say something to Mina, to say something to make her feel better, something to make everything okay. But she was so empty. She felt frustrated by her inability to express her thoughts.

She raised her head and looked around at the deserted landscape. Several animals ambled by but they were too far away to make out any detail, and she didn't have the telephoto capability of her camera to investigate them—it was still sitting on the clump of grass at the shelter site. She looked toward the hills to the west which concealed the landing site. Only the tip of the aerodyne's tail projected above the hill to let her know they were not alone.

They were so exposed and vulnerable out here in the middle of the plains, the cold, forbidding northern plains, the plains she disliked from the moment they landed. They weren't even near the landing site anymore. They were on a conspicuously flat region with no hills or undulations close by, and the vast openness just made the isolation even worse.

As she knelt beside Mina, details of the storm and the death of Dell began to coalesce in her mind. How did Dell end up out here? *He must have been picked up by the vortex and carried out here, but how did he get out into the path of the storm? The aerodyne wasn't damaged. That could only mean he wasn't in the aerodyne. He must have been outside. But why did he get out in the path of the storm? Why didn't he just ride out the storm . . . oh god —*

The realization why Dell was not in the aerodyne hit her hard. *She* was the one who told him to get out. *She* was the one who called him on the comm link and yelled at him, "Get out of there!"

"Oh, my god," she said, blurting out a whisper, still conscious of Mina's presence. She stood and turned away. Her heart pounded and an aching tightness gripped her chest. She now realized what had happened—he'd jumped out of the aerodyne right into the path of that vortex. *Oh, god, that means I killed him. Oh, no, that can't be right. The vortex killed him, that's what killed him. But if I hadn't called him and told him to get out, he'd still be alive. The vortex was coming, it would have killed us if we hadn't run. It seemed the right thing to do at the time — but, my gosh, if I hadn't said anything, he'd still be alive.*

Tears welled up in her eyes and trickled down her cheeks. She turned to face north, looking out over the barren terrain. A pack of seven or eight small, four-legged creatures, two to three links high at the shoulder, appeared a short distance away, barely visible in the dark. They reminded her of the animal at the gorge, but without the bushy tail. The pack stopped, looking her way.

Oh, god, what have I done? Will Mina ever forgive me?

Beyond the small animals, a herd of the large, wooly creatures paraded across the darkened horizon, at least a half-anthan away. The reddish-orange sun now sat directly on the hills enclosing the landing site, and the black shadows of the two mourners stretched almost infinitely across the desolate landscape. The air temperature still drifted downward, and Lilea fastened her jacket snugly from waist to neck and jammed her hands in her pockets. She watched the animals, but her thoughts returned to the storm and her call to Dell. Abruptly she was interrupted.

"Lilea."

Mina's voice was pale and thin and seemed far away. Lilea turned back. Mina still knelt on the ground next to Dell's body. She'd stopped crying, but tears and dirt streaked her face.

"Lilea, can you help me g-get Dell's body back to the aerodyne? We need to get him back to the l-landing site. He should be b-buried there."

"Sure, baby, sure," Lilea said, kneeling back down beside her. "Let's wait for Col to come back. He'll help us take Dell back."

"Where's Col?" Mina asked, looking around.

Lilea hesitated. "He went back to the aerodyne, probably to contact Jer. They're going to bring the stretcher." Lilea looked toward the aerodyne and the campsite, and was relieved to see Col walking toward them, carrying several things.

"I found one of the daypacks," Col said when he arrived. "Lilea, I think it's yours." He seemed calmer, but his hands trembled as he handed her the daypack. It had her initials on it. A few morsels of food and a plastic bottle of juice remained inside.

"Mina wants to take the body back to the aerodyne."

"Yes, I brought a shelter half for that purpose." Col wiped his mouth with his sleeve. "Let's, uh, place the, uh, body on the shelter half and drag it back. I don't want to spend the night out here without a shelter. Even with a weapon. Another one of those storms may come around again. I've seen an eternity of storms."

"I know what you mean." Lilea glanced at her chronometer, 156.4.2. "It's unnerving out here. I don't want to spend any more time out here than I have to."

As the dim light of twilight slipped away, Col pulled out two high-intensity lamps, and while Lilea held the lights, Mina and Col spread the shelter half beside Dell's body and slid him onto the sheet. As they started toward the ship, Mina insisted on helping Col pull the sheet.

Lilea trained one lamp on the ground immediately in front to see where she was going, and with the other she illuminated the landscape much farther out, keeping the hills in view. But as they walked, a new problem had developed.

The pack of smaller animals had circled in.

Perhaps they knew death had invaded this little group — maybe they could smell it. Lilea could keep them away with the lights. When she focused a beam on one or two of them they ran off. Their eyes sparkled brilliantly when hit by the lights, but when she took the light away they returned. She continued to swing the light at them, one side to the other, keeping them at bay long enough to get back to the camp site.

"Get away from here! Go away! Get out of here!"

It took almost two millisectors to drag Dell's body to the aerodyne. Once at the ship, Lilea and Col hoisted the body to shoulder height and placed it in the cargo hold. Mina held the lights while the animals circled, growling and snarling, but as soon as the cargo door was closed, she gave the lights to Lilea and entered the aerodyne and curled up across the two back seats. When two of the animals approached Lilea from behind, fangs bared, nipping at her calves, the frustration and melancholy welling up inside boiled over, and she pulled out her weapon and blasted the nearest one. "Get away from me!" she yelled.

Her weapon was set on level 1, but the collimation control at the front of the weapon had been partly deactivated and the electron beam spread over a narrow angle. It struck the animal in the face and the fur on its face burst into flame. The animal let out a raspy squeal and fell to the ground, rolling around, yelping and whimpering, trying desperately to extinguish the fire, and all of a sudden Lilea felt so sorry for it. After the flames were dampened it ran off, wailing as it ran, whipping its head from side to side, its fur still smoking and sparkling in places. The electron beam had undoubtedly scarred the animal's corneas into opaque uselessness, and, unable to see where it was going, it tumbled into the creek. That killed the fire, but it struggled to extract itself from the mud at the bottom. It finally ran off with the rest of the pack behind.

Col and Lilea entered the ship and closed the doors against the cold. "Did you talk to Jer?" she asked. "What did she say?" She set her weapon on the floor at her feet.

"Yes, I did." Col sat slumped in his seat, staring out the front window, his voice flat and unemotional. "She was as stunned as we. I talked to Trea, too."

"Is Jer going to bring the stretcher?"

"I don't know. That decision wasn't made. After I told her about Dell, she couldn't talk. She was overcome."

"Maybe you should call her back."

Col didn't move for a nanosector, then, wordlessly, he activated the comm link with *Explorer*, and Jer responded. "We've moved Dell's body back to the aerodyne. Do you want to bring the stretcher in the other aerodyne?"

"Yes. I still want to come. Someone will leave at first light. Will you be okay?"

"Yes. We'll see you then." He deactivated the comm link, then turned down the lights. He advanced the thermal regulator to take the chill out of the air and Lilea reclined the back of her seat and closed her eyes.

CHAPTER 35

RETURN

Time Element 461.157.1.0.

The aerodyne faced northeast, and as the sparkling rays of the dawning sun peeked over the southern row of hills, they seeped through the side window, illuminating and warming Lilea's face. She woke with a start, but realized immediately where she was. Col still lay asleep in the seat to her left, and she turned around to check that Mina was resting quietly. She opened the door beside her and stepped out. She strapped her weapon on, closed the door as quietly as she could, and walked across the valley to the southern hill to survey the plains.

The rising sun, brilliant and yellow in the intensely blue sky and crisp air, hovered about 20 degrees above the horizon, and the air that tickled her face was chilly and pleasantly fresh. She scanned the area around the landing site and noticed a few more items left from the shelter. But most urgent to her now was her camera, and she walked back to retrieve it, still sitting on the clump of grass at the base of the southern hills.

She used the long-range capability of the camera to scour the area again and located several more pieces of equipment and one more backpack several thousand links away. She even found the remains of the shelter to the northeast. She saw several large animals in the distance, but to her immense relief none of them were headed toward the aerodyne and none seemed to have large, prominent front teeth. She walked back to the ship and told Col what she'd found.

"I'm going to pick up the backpack," she said. "It might have some food in it."

"Hold on," Col said. "We shouldn't go walking around out here alone. It's too dangerous. We should stay together. Mina can stay here. She'll be safe here."

"I'll go with you," Mina said from the back seat. "I-I didn't get any sleep during the d-darktime, anyway."

"How are you feeling?" Lilea asked as Mina dropped from the ship.

"Okay, I guess." Mina shrugged her shoulders. Tears still streaked her face and her short brunette hair, normally well groomed, was tousled into an untidy mess. Her clothes, mussed and dirty, were stained at the knees.

Col activated the ship's homing signal, then joined the ladies. They climbed the southern hills, and down the other side toward the backpack.

Their trek was quiet and deliberate. They stayed together, three people, yet separate. Only rarely did anyone speak. Col did tell the women that Wila, Bent and Jad had left Site One in Aero Two, and they would be here in about two subsectors, but he said nothing else. He repeatedly turned around to check behind them as though he expected something to come over the hill after them. He drew his weapon and advanced the power setting to a higher level — Lilea couldn't see exactly how high — up from SpaceComm's required setting of 1 for undrawn weapons.

Lilea was so deeply conscious of Mina's presence as they walked. She wanted to be able say something to Mina, to be able to make the pain go away, to anesthetize her best friend to the distress and grief she must be going through now. But this was new to Lilea. She had no experience in grief counseling. Except for the death of her father, killed in an accident on the fourth moon of Tekaa on 432.208, her sixth birthday, and, more recently, for the death of Case, Lilea had not known the death of a family member or a close acquaintance. Case was the first friend of hers to die — and so horribly too — on either this planet or Anthanos. And though Case was not a really close friend, his death hit her in so many ways. But she got through it and went on, just like the rest of the team. She learned that Jer was in command now and the exploration of the blue planet continued — no other alternative was available.

Now death had struck again, taking down a close and valued friend and physician to the team and husband to a dear friend, a friend she'd known since college. She felt so empty, unable to say what she wanted, to relay her deepest respect and sorrow to her friend, though that probably wouldn't make Mina's pain any easier anyway. So they walked in silence, eyes straight ahead, focused only on the items from the shelter, walking in perfect step with one another, picking up one item at a time, holding each as though it was the Emperor's golden chain, the signature of his office, collecting and carrying, until they arrived back at the aerodyne.

At least no vicious animals circled about.

They found the shelter, Col's vision aid and a backpack. The vision aid had been damaged beyond repair, and the shelter was hardly better. The fabric was largely intact, but the heavy polypropylene cloth had been ripped and torn, especially where the fan-heaters were jerked away when the vortex lifted it into the air. Col crawled inside and found several sleeping bags, some clothing and one of the weapons.

Later, they found the coolers lying in a depression at the bottom of the southern hills, beyond the site where the shelter had been erected, and on the other side of the hill. They'd come open on impact, and food packages were scattered over the ground. They gathered as much as they could, threw it in the coolers, and brought them back to the ship. Col and Mina entered the aerodyne, taking advantage of the warm air inside to remain comfortable until Aero Two arrived.

But Lilea shrank back. Aero Two was still a subsector away, and the thought of sitting in Aero One staring out the front window sounded tedious, even boring. She wanted to be outside, to be active, to take her thoughts with her wherever they led. It was in her nature to explore, to invade the wild areas wherever she found them. There was so little of that on Anthanos and so much of it on this planet that she had to get out and explore—that was her, that was Lilea. Only if you dug down below the ubiquitous sands of Anthanos and explored the past by finding the artifacts of civilizations of long ago could you do much real exploring on her planet, and that worldly limitation contributed, at least in part, to her becoming an anthropologist. It was important to her.

But this planet had so much to explore, so much that called to her. Even this region, the place she disliked from the moment she stepped out of the aerodyne, needed to be explored. She still wondered if intelligent beings could be hunting the large animals, and she wanted to look into it. A little extra time was available. Why not? The area didn't seem so forbidding in bright sunlight. But she did realize that in her desire to walk away, she was avoiding having to talk to Mina about Dell's death. Yes, there was that. She couldn't sit in the aerodyne for another subsector without talking to someone. She decided to hike back down the southern ridge.

"I can't just sit here anymore. I'm going to walk around for a while."

"That's not a good idea. We should stay together." Col's face was pained, possibly at Lilea's refusal to join them in the aerodyne. But most likely he was still upset at the events of the past T-sector, and Lilea thought briefly about canceling her walk.

"I'll be okay. There aren't any animals around. I've got my weapon and PersComm."

"All right. Be careful." Col nodded. He seemed to relax a little, his face not so strained. "Stay within sight."

Lilea grabbed her camera from the front seat and closed the door. She hiked back to the top of the southern hill and walked southwest again. She passed the site where the shelter had been, and the depression where they'd found the coolers. As she walked, she removed her weapon from its holster and advanced the power level setting to 4. That was as high as she dared go. She still hated those damn weapons, and that included being afraid of what might happen if — for some obscure reason — it discharged in its holster. The safety was automatically engaged when the weapon was holstered, but — *you never know what might happen.*

The wind came fairly steadily from the southwest now, chilly, but not biting, nippy but not icy, meeting her almost directly in the face. She kept her head down as she walked, watching the ground, carefully noticing where she placed each foot. Occasionally, she would raise her head and look for animals, especially to her rear, but the area remained clear.

She enjoyed the invigorating air. As she walked, she came to a slight rise along the southern ridge, and she stood on the hill scanning the plains, using both the still and full-motion capability of her camera to image the terrain 400 degrees around. She ran the telephoto to 50**X** to survey the horizon. Several herds of the large, wooly animals appeared, well to the south.

So peaceful. She powered down the camera and continued walking. As she walked, she again made a mental comparison of this planet with hers. Her planet fared better this time, but she was still confused. Life on her planet was so easy, so simple. With a life expectancy of more than 100 years, an Anthanian could expect to accumulate a vast amount of knowledge and experience, if not wealth, before passing on. But on this planet, with its storms of water and wind, of ice, of whirlwinds, of vicious animals, of ground that moved under your feet, and god-only-knows-what-else, life expectancy must certainly be lower. Much lower.

Those two natives carrying the animal couldn't have been much out of their twenties, if that. Case was sixty-three when he died, and he's barely considered middle-aged. This planet has so much going for it. It has so much to offer that Anthanos does not. Except for the ice on the dark side, Anthanos is desert and not much else. I could easily imagine coming to this planet to live.

But there's a dark side to this planet. There's a terror here, too. I've seen it. I've seen predatory animals devour smaller animals. I saw another large animal with huge teeth that almost attacked me. Only because Col fired first am I standing here right now. I owe my life to Col.

She came to the end of the ridge where the hill gradually tapered to the surrounding level. She turned around and looked up the valley. *I prob-*

ably shouldn't be so far from everyone. She walked back up the ridge and reached about the halfway point when she heard a familiar sound, a faint high-pitched roaring with an underlying deep-bass throb. It came from the south, over her right shoulder, the unmistakable roar of a liquid hydrogen-fueled fission rocket engine. Her heart skipped a beat.

Lilea waved as Aero Two made one low pass over the area then landed at the far end of the valley, coming to rest several hundred links behind Aero One. Lilea ran to Bent's arms as though she hadn't seen him in twenty years.

"Jer persuaded Trea to stay behind with her," Wila told Lilea and Col. "I think Jer was afraid to stay by herself."

Jad and Bent strapped Dell's body to the stretcher and placed it in the cargo hold of Aero One. Mina remained in Aero One and Col and Lilea re-boarded and left for Site One immediately. Aero Two followed a couple of microsectors later.

The men prepared a grave next to Case's, and by the official time 461.157.11.0, Dell was placed in the ground. Everyone gathered around and said goodbye to their good friend.

Mina attended, but said nothing.

Time Element 461.159.2.3.

"You killed him!" Mina's stutter always disappeared when she got angry.

She stood outside Lilea's door on the blue carpet that circled the Personnel Deck. Lilea, bewildered and confused, listened as her best friend bellowed at her.

"I just realized—when you went back into the shelter to get your camera, you called Dell on comm and told him to get out of the aerodyne and he jumped out and ran right into that storm. *That's* why he was outside. *That's* why he was killed. I heard what you said but I didn't connect it until now. It was *you.* You drove him out into that storm. You killed him!"

"No, no, Mina, listen—well, yes I did call him, but—"

"If it hadn't been for you, he'd be alive now—you killed him."

The noise, Mina's incessant loud talk and yelling, had attracted others. Jad opened his door but stayed in the doorway, listening. Col and Trea came from their compartment, around from the other side.

"What's going on?" Trea said.

"She called Dell on comm and he ran out right into the storm."

"You mean—"

"Yes, when we were on the northern plains. She called him —"

"Lilea." Col turned to her. "I do recall you ducked back into the shelter. What did you do? What is Mina talking about? Did you —"

"She killed him!"

"Mina, hold on. Wait a millisector." Col's voice was calm and composed and it seemed to quiet Mina. "Let her talk. I suspect there's more to this than that."

"Yes, I did call Dell on comm, but I went in to get my camera and I picked up the comm link and yelled at Dell to get out of there. I thought he couldn't see the storm because it was coming at the aerodyne from the rear. I thought it might hit the aerodyne. We were running and I thought he should, too. I couldn't tell. I had no idea. Mina, I'm sorry. I didn't realize he'd get picked up, I mean, by the storm. Honest."

"I see. Yes, we were getting ready to run. It was imperative we leave the shelter."

"I didn't do it on purpose, Mina, believe me. I would never do that."

"Mina," Trea said. "It sounds like it was an accident. Col told me all about that storm. How could Lilea have known that he'd run out into—"

"It was an accident. Honest. I didn't know. It was the vortex that killed him."

"But you drove him out into it. I'll never forget that."

"I understand, but I didn't know —"

Mina didn't say anything, but she dropped her eyes. The glare was gone, the glare that had shot bolts of pain and displeasure into Lilea's heart. Mina turned and walked back to her compartment.

"I'm concerned," Col said. "She may remain angry for a substantial amount of time."

Lilea couldn't reply. What was this? Her best friend now accusing her of killing her husband? That made no sense. She didn't know what to say to Mina's accusations. It was the vortex that killed him, but Mina didn't appear to accept that. She was too angry to understand. *This damn planet is placing one obstruction after another in front of us and now it's come between friends. It's killed two people already. When and where will it end?*

"I hope she'll be all right," Trea said.

"I've known Mina for a long time, but I've never seen her get angry like that. I think she'll be okay." Lilea returned to her compartment and to her notebook. But she couldn't concentrate with Mina's outburst so fresh in her mind.

CHAPTER 36

MEETING

Time Element 461.161.11.0.
Lilea knocked on Mina's door as quietly as she could. Afraid of re-kindling Mina's anger, she spoke her name in slightly more than a whisper. "Mina?"

A click from inside—the sound of the door being unlocked. An angry voice on the other side of the door. "Come in."

Lilea cautiously opened the door and stuck her head in. "Mina, I just wanted to see how you were doing. Jer has called a meeting for 162.2.8."

"I know. I saw it on comm."

"I wanted to see if you were going." Lilea stepped into the compartment and closed the door behind her. "I think they may have heard from Kal about . . ."

Mina stood in the living area of the compartment, but faced away from Lilea who remained just inside the door. Mina spat her words out in a vitriolic spasm.

"I know what the meeting's about. I'm not going. I'm going to stay here and get some sleep. I haven't gotten much sleep in the past six T-sectors. I'm tired."

"I guess you are." *At least she's talking to me. I was afraid she'd still be angry about the com link call.*

"Please leave me alone."

Lilea glanced into the food preparation area of Mina's compartment. It was clean and neat. She didn't see any evidence that Mina had prepared a meal in the last several T-sectors. "Have you been eating anything? You need to keep your strength up. You know Case's directives. He'd be—"

"What I eat or drink is none of your business. Or Case's. He's dead anyway." Mina turned and faced Lilea. Her voice rose. "Just like Dell. Leave me alone. Go to the damn meeting without me. I've got a lot I want to think about. I'm so tired of this place."

"Okay, baby. I'll tell Jer." Lilea left the compartment, and as soon as the door was closed she heard behind her the distinctive click of the locking mechanism. That was unlike Mina. Nobody locked their doors on *Explorer*.

Lilea had known Mina longer than anyone else on the team, even longer than Bent. They met in college and roomed together for two years. Lilea considered Mina one of her best friends, but she'd never known Mina to get angry. Mina always projected an impression of the cautious, methodical researcher—calm and cool, even detached. Setbacks in the lab never seemed to bother her, she shrugged them off as though they didn't matter, though deep beneath that gentle exterior Lilea knew they really did. Like Jad, Mina could be quiet and taciturn, even enigmatic, opening up only to Dell and to close friends, such as Lilea. Yet Lilea and Mina got along well and maintained their friendship after graduation and through spaceflight training. Perhaps that was because they were scientific buddies—both understood instinctually the consequences of their research.

Certainly Mina was within her rights to forgo this meeting. Passing up a meeting to take sleep time was not unheard of, though when Case held meetings, especially a regular meeting, he usually insisted on all team members attending, sleep time or not. But Mina's refusal seemed to carry a second meaning, a meaning Lilea couldn't put her finger on. It might have been simple anger at the death of her husband, but she might have been trying to tell Lilea something more, something she wouldn't—or couldn't—convey verbally.

What did she mean by, "I'm so tired of this place?"

Time Element 461.162.2.8.

They took their usual seats at the center table on Life Sciences for the meeting, waiting for Jer to arrive. Lilea and Bent sat in their usual seats, but both seats beside her were empty, and one would be so permanently. She tried not to look at them.

The room was unusually quiet for a meeting. The only sound was a gentle hum from several of the instruments on the workbench that circled the periphery of the room—incubators, sterilizers, glassware washers, a nucleic acid analyzer that Trea had activated just before the meeting.

Jer was the last to arrive, sliding down the interdeck ladder from the Communications Deck at the top of the ship. "I contacted *Star Voyager* as soon as I heard that Dell had been killed," she said as she reached the center table. "I described the circumstances of his death, and I asked Kal to decide how best to utilize Tac for the rest of the time we're on the surface. I just got Kal's answer. He says Tac and the rest of the medical staff on *Star*

Voyager can communicate with us as they have been, but he said he would send Tac to the surface in the Rescue ship only if there's a serious emergency, like an aerodyne crash, or an outbreak of a disease that incapacitates most or all of us. The main difficulty with that scenario is that it would take forty T-sectors for *Rescue* to reach us here, and by that time any disaster may have played itself out."

"Sending *Rescue* would terminate the mission altogether, wouldn't it?" Col asked. He had both hands folded on the table, but his hands shook slightly, like a faint quivering.

"Yes, it would," Jer said. "But Kal says that's the best they can do under the circumstances. There's no mechanism for sending a new physician to the surface after the death of the primary."

"Why would sending *Rescue* terminate the mission?" Lilea asked. "If *Explorer* is still flyable, when *Rescue* returns, can't *Explorer* stay on the surface?"

"It terminates the mission because SpaceComm regulations allow only one rescue mission. They figure if things get so serious they have to send *Rescue*, then the entire exploration should be over. Besides, when *Rescue* gets back, there isn't enough liquid hydrogen fuel remaining at *Star Voyager* for another trip. If something else happened, we'd be without rescue capability from that time on. Remember? They told us that at the beginning of training."

Lilea nodded her head. "Oh, that's right. I do sort of recall . . ."

"That's why he's reluctant to send *Rescue* unless there's a big emergency," Col said. "The longer he waits, the longer we can work."

"But there's a little more to Kal's reply," Jer continued. "I'll read what he has to say. 'Even though the team voted to stay on the surface until four or fewer active team members remained before returning to *Star Voyager* prior the end of the scheduled 500 T-sector exploratory period, SpaceComm regulations do allow me the option of terminating the mission early if the physician is incapacitated.'" Jer stopped reading and looked up. "He says he wants to know how we feel about continuing. He wants some feedback. Do you want to stay and continue without Dell, or do you not want to take the chance and return?"

The room grew silent. Lilea held back. She wanted to speak, to say, "Yes, I would like to stay." She certainly wanted to return to the village up north. That trip burned in her mind and ached in her heart. Leaving the surface without having an opportunity for a return trip was not an option—even the discussion of it horrified her. But she also wanted to hear what the others had to say. Would they be willing to stay and continue to work in spite of the hazards of exploring what had become a dangerous planet, especially without the physician?

Several nanosectors passed and no one spoke. "What do I tell Kal? Yes, or no?" Jer studied the group but no one returned her gaze.

Lilea's heart beat faster as the desire to speak built up inside. The others were struggling with an answer as much as she and perhaps some wanted to say, "No—let's go home." But that's not how she viewed the planet. It sounded corny and perhaps a little sentimental, but she believed in the work they were doing. This could be the planet they would eventually colonize, and that was important to her. She *really* wanted to be on the expedition that made that determination. She didn't want to be on a mission that had to be aborted because people were killed. "Yes," she blurted into the silence, and most turned to look at her. "I would like to stay. I still want to go back to the village. I think it'll be important for this expedition. Kal's right, we did vote to not leave unless four or fewer remained. We have to try." The silence returned. "It's more important now than ever." Lilea paused to let her words sink in. "When we left Anthanos, there wasn't any other option. As far as we know, this may be the planet we colonize. We have to learn as much as we can about it." Several people shifted uncomfortably in their chairs, and silence returned to the room.

"I agree with Lilea," Col said in a low, but clear, voice. "I also have considerable work to accomplish."

"I do, too," Trea said.

"I've still got specimens to examine," Bent said. "And more recorders to place."

Jad mumbled, "Okay," and nodded his head. Lilea glanced over at Wila, but only out of the corner of her eye, without turning her head. Wila sat at her usual place, beside Jad at the far left of all the team members around the table, but she'd turned even farther to her left, her hands folded in her lap, looking down at the table as though she was deliberately trying to avoid having to express an opinion. Jer seemed not to notice.

"Okay," Jer said. "I guess we're staying, unless Kal calls us home. He has the authority to override your opinion, but my guess is he won't. I think we're here for a while."

"That's good," Lilea said as the meeting broke up. She started to express her sense of relief to Bent, but as she turned toward him she saw Wila march directly to the interdeck ladder and descend.

CHAPTER 37

DREAM

Time Element 461.176.9.5.

"Ooh, damn! God, I hate that."

Wila sat upright in bed. Jad woke and reached over to the small table on his side of the bed and touched a yellow button. A pale yellow light in the ceiling came on, giving the two sleepers a subdued tawny cast. He sat up beside her. "What happened. That dream again?"

Wila nodded. She turned and sat on the side of the bed, her feet on the floor. Shivering, she covered her face with her hands.

"Same thing? That man in the white clothes?"

Wila didn't say anything for several nanosectors. "Yes." She removed her hands from her face. "Only this time he's more insistent. He keeps saying the same thing over and over, 'Don't go. Don't go. You don't know what you're getting into. Some won't come back.' Now he's yelling. It's like he gets in my face and yells at me. I don't know what to do anymore. It happens just before each expedition."

"I think you're just nervous about the expedition. We all are."

Wila turned around to face Jad. She knelt on the bed, her pale face illuminated in dark shadows by the light. "I know I'm nervous about the expedition, but there's more to it than that. It's like this guy is trying to tell us something. He's trying to tell us not to go. Like something's going to happen."

"Wila, it's just a dream. Okay, okay—it's not a dream, it's a nightmare. But that doesn't mean anything—"

"Jad, I had the same dream just before they went north when Dell was killed. It meant something then." She pounded both fists on the bed.

"You couldn't tell that someone was going to be killed. Neither could that guy in your dreams. You've had the same dream before each expedition. You're just nervous about them. That's all."

"I wish I could accept that. This dream and the one before the north expedition were different. They were stronger. The guy is yelling at me. 'Don't go! Don't go!' I can't take it much more." Wila turned back around and sat on the edge of the bed. She rose and slipped her feet into a pair of pink slippers and walked into the food-prep area of the compartment where she drew a drink of water from the chilled water tap.

Jad said nothing when Wila left the room. Her outburst surprised him. She'd never reacted this strongly to her dream before. In fact, she hardly mentioned the dream before the north plains expedition and he thought maybe it wasn't bothering her anymore. But he noticed she was unusually quiet when they went down to ground level to see the North Plains Team leave, and he wondered about that. She didn't wave to the departing aerodyne as she usually did, and she left the runway before anyone else, returning to their compartment to stay for several subsectors before going to the meteorological station on Geo. That was so unlike her.

When Wila returned to the bedroom she knelt back on the bed. She stared Jad in the face, anger and exasperation in her eyes. "Jad, don't go on this expedition to the mountains. I'm really afraid something is going to happen."

"I have to go. I'm already committed. I have to help Bent —"

"Make up an excuse. Tell them you have to finish the corona studies. Tell them you have to start the surface imaging, or calibrate the neutrino detectors. You've always been fascinated by that ringed planet in this solar system ever since the probe imaged it on its trip here. Start imaging it. Do something! But don't go!"

"The corona studies are finished. I've completed all the readings and made all the images, and sent the results out. The neutrino detectors are already calibrated and the discriminators set, and I've started imaging the solar surface. The computer monitors the sun every lightime. I've already put the segregation delineators and spectrum analyzers online, and I'll check them when I get back. There's nothing more I can do. Sure, I could start looking at the ringed planet, but . . . and I will eventually, but I'm looking forward to the trip. It's a chance to get out and see the mountains of this planet. I showed you the trip we laid out. We're not hiking on any narrow trails next to a steep drop-off like we did when Case was killed. Our route is easy and safe."

"I know, I know. But other things can happen."

"Like what?"

"I don't know — I don't know!" Wila yelled, and pounded the bed again. "Maybe the ground will quake again, or a storm might come up."

Jad hesitated. "Sure, but that's the chance we take. We knew that when we agreed to come here. Listen —"

"Maybe Col will postpone the trip . . ."

"No, I don't think Col will postpone the trip just because of your dream. He and Trea have been looking forward to this trip for a long time. They put it on the Calendar before we left. You don't know that something is going to happen. Only your dream tells you that. You had the dream before you flew out to examine the storm and nothing happened."

"I had the dream before the trip to the western mountains and something happened, and I had the dream before the north trip and something happened. People were killed! I even had the dream the night before we went to the gorge and you almost passed out from the heat. You came this close to dying from heat stroke. That's what happened—"

"That's because I didn't drink enough water. That doesn't—"

"I can tell you right now that something is going to happen this time. I know it! That guy in the white clothes told me. And it may happen to you—again. *Please* tell me you'll drop out of this trip."

Wila looked Jad straight in the eye, silently pleading and imploring, but he remained quiet. Dropping out of the mountain expedition was out of the question. He would look like a coward, afraid to go on any more expeditions because of his wife's dreams. That would be unacceptable, to Jad and to SpaceComm.

"I can't drop out. It would look too suspicious. I'll go anyway. I bet nothing'll happen. You'll see. Everything will be fine."

Wila didn't say anything and that wasn't the response Jad was hoping for, but at least the argument was over. He lay back down in bed and stared at the ceiling and the little light. He had to admit in his own mind that in one respect Wila was right, something *could* happen. But he wasn't prepared to admit the old man in her dream was capable of predicting it.

That was the odd thing about Wila's dream. She took the old man at his word, even though his predictions were nothing more than vague generalities.

That old man has never been specific about what's going to happen. Never. He just says we don't know what we're getting into when we go on these little trips. Or that someone "might not" return. Vague generalities, that's all they are.

Jad pressed the button to extinguish the light and closed his eyes. But he didn't go right back to sleep.

Time Element 461.177.10.2.

"Okay, sounds good to me," Jer said. "But there are a couple of other things." She sat at the center table on Life Sciences, her notebook in front of her with details of the upcoming expedition to the mountains northeast of Site One on the notebook's screen. Everyone else sat in their usual places around the other side, Jad and Wila at the far left. The seat beside Mina remained empty.

Wila had been unusually quiet all this lightime. She clearly didn't get much sleep the darktime before, and she did little work at her workstation on Geo. She seemed lost in thought. Jad looked in on her a couple of times before this meeting, but she refused any of his offers of help, and said she'd be okay. At 177.10.0, they ascended to Life Sciences.

Jer droned on for several millisectors, finalizing the details and minutiae of the expedition. Then her voice turned from pedantic to serious. "I would like to have you check in with us here three or four times during each lightime. I want to be able to keep in touch during the expedition. Does anyone have a problem with that?" She glanced around at the others.

"Eminent idea," Col said. The others shook their heads.

"But there's another aspect of this expedition I think we need to consider. It's an issue I don't like to bring up, and it may be difficult to talk about, and it may even scare some people, but it's a topic we need to get out in the open. It's the issue of danger to those on the expedition. We've had two deaths so far. I'm very concerned about the possibility of more occurring on this . . . on the time we're on the surface. Now we're proposing to go into more unknown territory and we don't know what's going to happen. Let me ask those of you who are going into these mountains: are you satisfied it's safe enough?"

Jad scanned the others around the table. He sat the way he usually did, slouched down in his chair, his hands in his pockets. He was surprised Jer had brought this subject up and he had a definite opinion, but he didn't want to be the first to say something. He rarely did. Always quiet, cautious, and analytical, he kept his opinions to himself until the time came to make himself heard.

The room remained silent for several nanosectors until Trea spoke.

"No, I guess not. But we can't just sit here and wait for our time on this planet to expire and then go back. I think we have to go whether we like it or not. I'm looking forward to this little expedition." Trea smiled at the others around the table. Her eyes had a kind of sweetness in them, a sort of twinkle that Jad had seen only a few times before.

It isn't a "little" expedition. It's four lightimes and three darktimes on that mountain.

"I am, too," Lilea said. "We were sent here to do a job, and we have to do it. They're depending on us to come back with some answers. Whether we like it or not, this has already become a dangerous expedition."

"But don't we know enough already?" Wila said. She held her hands out in a supplicating gesture and shrugged her shoulders. "We've already found out a lot about this planet. We know it will be dangerous, that much is certain." She leaned forward in her seat. "This planet has already killed two people. Isn't that enough? Why stay and risk more being killed?"

"I question whether we have accumulated sufficient data about this planet," Col said. He stared directly at Wila. He didn't appear angry, but he leaned forward and tapped the table. "I challenge the view that we know enough so that Anthanos can decide whether this planet is acceptable for colonization. More than three hundred T-sectors still remain in our tenure here. We have a complete exploration schedule that includes numerous expeditions to other areas of the planet. I believe it is incumbent upon us to stay the allotted time. That means—"

"But now we know it's much more dangerous than we thought when we left," Wila said. She threw a hard look at Col, and then slapped one hand on the table. "We've done all we can. It's not up to us to make the decision for the people back on Anthanos."

"I disagree," Col said. He shook his head and a brief, angry look flashed in his eyes, a look Jad couldn't recall ever seeing on Col's face. "I propose we *haven't* done enough."

"That's not all true," Bent said, turning to look at Wila. "I know I still have several things I want to do while we're here. I still want to plant more charges. I don't want to leave just yet." He turned back to the others at the table. "I'm looking forward to the expeditions that have been scheduled with longer hikes. Maybe a hike of six to eight lightimes rather than the four we're going on now."

"I don't want to leave now either," Lilea said, glancing toward Wila. "I've got several more things I want to do, especially go back north. I know that's dangerous, but that's something we have to put up with. The longer we stay on this planet, the more we'll learn about it, and the more likely we'll be able to live here safely. This planet has so much to offer, we can't just run away from it."

"But isn't it enough to know that people have been killed?" Wila said. "Why risk it?"

"Wila, please . . ." Jer said, not pleading, real anger in her voice.

"But we've got *work* to do," Lilea said.

"Quite," Col said. Trea nodded.

"But what else is out there?" Wila asked. "Why don't we just leave? Why risk it?"

Jer turned and made a cutting motion with one hand. "Wila, give it a rest. We can't leave early and that's that."

Wila didn't seem to get the message. "What would happen if we just blasted off and went back to *Star Voyager*?" Jad sat forward in his seat and put a hand on Wila's arm to quiet her. She was getting angry and worked up, and he would have to rein her in or face a backlash from Jer.

"Oh, god," Jer exclaimed, rolling her eyes. "If we went back early without Kal's permission he'd be furious with us and we'd never hear the end of it. That's totally against regulations. Not only that, we might be kicked out of SpaceComm for being cowards. They might even court-martial us for dereliction of duty."

"Do you think they'd really kick us out?" Wila asked. "Even after all we've done?"

"Yes, dammit, I do."

A quiet tenseness surrounded the table. Jer shut her notebook and left, taking the elevator to the Command Deck one level above. Wila scowled at her as she walked across the deck, though she remained quiet. Jad squeezed tighter on Wila's arm. Trea and Col glared across the table at her. The anger in the room that seethed just beneath everyone else's skin at Wila's insistent questioning of the expedition frightened him. It could divide the team at just the time they needed to remain close and unified.

"Yes, I think they would," Lilea said, breaking the silence and nodding slightly. But her voice was calm, disarming.

CHAPTER 38

NORTHEASTERN MOUNTAINS

Time Element 461.179.5.3.

"A walk in the park." Col brought Aero Two in from the south and set it down on the emerald surface of the valley. The ship came to rest a few hundred links from a small sand dune, just off to the right. While Col finished with the final checklist and made the obligatory contact with Jer, the rest of the Mountain Team opened the doors and dropped to the ground.

A warm, gentle breeze drifted in from the northwest. Jad stood near the aerodyne's nose and surveyed the area of the landing site. North and west from where he stood were stands of several different types of trees, and a faint but pungent aroma wafted in on the breeze. To the east, his right, stood the mountains, still white-capped, majestic and dignified. He stared long and hard at the mountain's most prominent peak, and a face, etched within the rocks and ice of the mountain, seemed to ogle back at him. A nose, a slightly downturned mouth, two somewhat cockeyed and off-center eyes—but a face nonetheless, the face of a man. The white that capped the peak gave him an aged look and in his mind Jad dubbed him 'The Old Man of the Mountain.' Lower down, between the aerodyne and the mountains, lay a large area of inviting pale tan sand. He decided to investigate. He pulled his high-def spectrographic camera from his daypack and walked over to the edge of the nearest dune. Trea came right behind.

"Except for the mountains in the distance and the vegetation in this valley," she said, "this could be the warm side of Anthanos."

"The breeze would be a little cooler at home." Jad squatted and picked up a handful of sand and let it trickle between his fingers. The sand was dry and fine, not like the coarse, hard-packed sand that made up the Lifezone on his planet.

"That doesn't really make much difference. It still reminds me of home."

"You sound a little homesick." Jad stood up and began scanning the mountains to the east using a wide-angle setting on his camera.

"A little. But don't get me wrong, I still enjoy being here. I wouldn't mind going home, but I could stay here for a while, too." As Trea spoke, she took off her boots and socks and rolled up her pant legs to about mid-calf and stood barefoot, working her feet into the sand. "The sand is a little cooler than I remember from home. Much finer too."

"Yeah, I noticed that."

Trea continued to squirm her feet into the sand, raising one foot slightly and letting the fine grains trickle between her toes. She walked around for several nanosectors, absorbed in the sensation of the sand on her feet. She didn't say anything further, but to Jad, glancing occasionally in her direction, she seemed lost in thought. He didn't want to stare at her as she played in the sand, so he took spectrographic readings of the mountains, though he'd sneak a quick glance at her from time to time, watching as she amused herself in the sand. He'd been busy for a few microsectors with his readings when Trea abruptly walked back to the edge of the dune and put her socks and boots on.

"I guess it's time to get back to work," Trea said as she strode back to the aerodyne.

Jad heard what she said only tangentially. He finished his readings a few nanosectors later and followed Trea back to the aerodyne.

"Let's start getting things unpacked," Col said when Trea and Jad arrived. "Trea and I will set up the shelter and intruder perimeter. Jad, you and Bent make the security sweep."

After the shelter was set up, Col headed north into a large stand of white-barked trees — they seemed to fascinate him more than most others. Trea took the opposite approach. All she did was stand in one place — she picked a spot near the front of the shelter — and the animals paraded before her, attracted perhaps by the water in the creek about two thousand links north of the camp site. The animals didn't seem disturbed by the presence of visitors to their domain, nor by the click of Trea's shutter, though they did stay several hundred links from the ship as they strolled past.

By 179.11.3, all four members of the mountain team rendezvoused at the shelter. They prepared and ate their third meal of this lightime, and, as requested, Jad contacted Jer. They sat around outside the shelter in the cool evening air and checked and loaded the last items in their backpacks, preparing for the hike. When they finished, they watched the sun go down behind the mountains in the west and retired for the darktime.

They rose at first light. After gobbling down their first meal they shut off all power from the aerodyne to the shelter, except to the coolers. They locked the shelter and contacted Jer to tell them of their impending departure, and flung their backpacks on their backs and set off on the longest hike so far in their exploration of the Blue Planet.

Time Element 461.181.1.0.

Col and Trea led the way.

The cool wind swept off the mountain directly in their faces as they traveled northeast over the sand headed for the narrow valley that would take them upward toward the imposing white-capped peak. They found the valley easily. It was the only one in the vicinity through which a stream meandered down its entire length. A narrow animal trail paralleled the stream, snaking its way up the valley at a comfortable slant, taking them immediately into the forest.

"Absolutely magnificent," Col said several times as he walked. "Positively occipital."

Jad was eager to be hiking again and the walk invigorated him. He'd pressed the details of his last hike — when Case was killed — solidly into his long-term memory where it belonged, and the elation and euphoria of the present trip was substantial enough to prevent those memories from reappearing. He watched the trees as he walked, he watched the trail, and he watched Bent directly in front of him.

Jad's good physical condition and the moderate grade of the trail gave him an easy walk. He carried the heaviest pack of the four. The hand drill, drill bit, and drill bit extensions used to drill into the surface to place the seismic charges were strapped securely to the outside of his pack, though Bent carried the charges themselves. No one else was allowed to handle them. Those tools, plus the usual equipment of sleeping bag, shelter half, food, water and clothing gave Jad a pack of more than two dekakrill. Ahead of him, Bent plodded along, though he kept up with Col's pace. His breathing had become heavy already, though it wasn't the labored breathing and panting that might indicate Bent was pushing himself too hard.

Behind Col, Trea, like Jad, walked easily. Apparently enjoying her walk, she sang quietly to herself the *Dolotolo*, an Anthanian hiking song. With its easy, regular rhythm and smooth recurring beat, hikers used it as a march on Anthanos to stay together over the flat, unchanging sands where visible landmarks were scarce.

Occasionally, Col would ask the team to stop while he examined some odd plant along the trail. By the time of this trip, Col understood the difference between what he called "flat-leafed" and "needle-leafed" trees, and he could distinguish differences within each group. But, as on the valley floor, his attention was occupied by far by the large number of white-barked trees. He made videos of the leaves as they quivered and danced in the slightest breeze, and he collected leaves, both from the ground and from the trees themselves.

"It would be judicious to rest here," Col said at the third stop. "It's two-two. We've been hiking for a full subsector. Let's get some rest."

Time Element 461.181.2.2.

They'd come to a small clearing in the forest, shaded by the over-hanging branches of several trees. The breeze had faded and the sun, rising above the mountains behind them, had raised the air temperature. Jad dropped his pack and sat down on a small log in the shade next to the trail. Trea sat on a flat rock to Jad's left and a couple of links in front of him, and Jad, still intrigued from the previous lightime's encounter, again began to study Trea.

It wasn't all that surprising that Jad hadn't noticed Trea in any strong, calculating way until now, their paths hadn't really crossed until they began Gold Team training. Jad could remember seeing Trea and Col occasionally at the Sabean Spaceport before their selection to the Gold Team, but he made nothing of the encounters at the time—he saw people from all areas of SpaceComm. Even during training as the Gold Team, and later during the 700 T-sector voyage to the Blue Planet, Trea and Col seemed to remain separate from the rest of the team. Col associated with Case mostly, and Jer and Trea became good friends.

But now, thrown together in this little group, closely united in a trek up the mountainside to study the planet, and for the first time that Jad could recall, he and Trea sat together. Like all in this group of hikers, Trea had rolled the sleeves of her jumpsuit up past her elbows revealing her slim, lithe, muscular arms, and Jad began to appreciate the attractiveness of this woman. Her deep reddish-brown hair which she kept short, her long, graceful neck visible above the collar of her jumpsuit, her cute oval face with the ultramarine eyes, the long eyelashes and the splash of freckles across her cheek and nose—there was an allure to this woman. At only about a decilink shorter than Jad, she was taller than Col by several decilinks. But more to Jad's liking, she loved to run, too. Jad and Trea had so much in common he found himself wondering if they could have made a life together.

As he sat watching Trea, another image intruded into his mind. He recalled when *Explorer* was in orbit just before landing, and Trea, using the telescope on the Astronomy Deck, had taken images of animals on the surface. "Look what I got!" she cried when she brought up the pictures on the com screens at the table on the Life Sciences Deck during one of the regular meetings. Her face beamed with an enthusiasm and excitement Jad had seen only rarely in her. Those images represented a vitally significant time point in the mission, the first clear look at large animals on the surface, and he made a mental note of them. Part of that notation was Trea's glowing face.

As she sat on the trail, Trea reached into her pack and pulled out her electronic notebook. She scanned the pages containing images and notes on the animals she'd seen, including those from the previous lightime, and Jad was impressed by the suppleness of her fingers as they flew across the pages, animal after animal, image after image, datasheet after datasheet. The carpal muscles in her forearm—well-developed as a result of the hand and grip exercises SpaceComm insisted everyone do—flexed and rippled as she worked her way through the book. When she finished she returned it to her pack and removed a cereal bar from her food bag and took a few bites. She finished with a long, cool drink from her water bottle.

Then Jad caught a glimpse of Trea's thigh. The leg of her jumpsuit had been pulled tightly around her right thigh, accentuating the massive running muscles she'd developed over a lifetime of jogging. Though Jad had known Trea for more than two years now, and was well acquainted with her bright auburn hair and her deep blue eyes and the cute freckles dotting her childlike face, he had never appreciated so much her engaging good looks—especially her magnificent thigh muscles—as much he did while she sat next to him on the trail.

But the image of the handsome Trea beside him awakened something else in his mind, a vision of his first girl friend and first love Taeni, and he redirected his thoughts from Trea to reflect on the young woman who lived only four houses down the street from him as a boy.

CHAPTER 39

TAENI

Time Element 431.086.5.7.

Jad stood in the backyard of his house in Till, a small town of 2500 inhabitants, not far from the major metropolitan area of Doserovos in the southern hemisphere of Anthanos. The street in front of his house ran directly toward the sun, and from his backyard he could point his solar measuring equipment directly at the sun, sighting down the other back-yards in the neighborhood to take the solar measurements he enjoyed making as a hobby. Turning around and looking in the opposite direction, he could point his telescope at the darkest region of the sky near the horizon and pick out stars and planets. On this T-sector, he'd mounted his homemade reflecting telescope on a tripod firmly anchored to a cement patio, and had just focused on the largest planet in his solar system when Taeni came by.

"What're you looking at?" She sniffled slightly.

"Shaltous." Jad looked up from his telescope. "Wanna see?"

"Sure." Taeni bent over slightly to peer through the telescope's eye-piece. "It's colorful. It's got lots of colored bands."

"Those represent different levels of the components of the atmo-sphere of the planet. It's mostly just a big ball of hydrogen and helium with some other stuff, but it rotates on its axis real fast and the winds have swished the different components into horizontal bands."

"Oh, I see." Taeni straightened up and looked directly at Jad. Dressed in a typical Taeni outfit, dark blue shorts and a pink blouse, her below-shoulder-length dark sienna hair rustled in the breeze. But her voice turned to a chilling whisper. "Jad, there's something I need to tell you. We're leaving Till. Dad says we're moving into Doserovos." Her words came tumbling out all at once, as though she couldn't hold them back.

Jad looked Taeni in the face. He'd never seen her like this, tears streaking her cheeks, her eyes puffy and red. "What? Why? Will I be able to see you?" His first thought was annoyance. He wondered if he'd have to travel into Doserovos to see her.

"No. Dad says he doesn't want me to see you anymore. This is the last time I'm allowed to talk to you. I've . . . I've been promised to another man."

Another man? Is that what she said? Another man?! Now the annoyance turned on him, wrenching his chest, and he exploded. "Is he crazy? What is this? You can't get married. You're only sixteen."

"Dad says we're going to get married when I'm eighteen."

"But when you get to be nineteen, you can marry whoever you want."

"I know, but Dad says I have to go with this man. He says he promised this guy."

"That's stupid!"

Jad collapsed into a small chair next to the telescope. Totally blindsided by this revelation, he couldn't think though he knew he had to do something. He and Taeni were committed to each other. They had their future all worked out and it was going to be so lovely. Marriage—attend the university in Doserovos—raise a family—go jogging together every other T-sector—run in long races. Taeni was so into jogging. At sixty-five decilinks she was just Jad's height, and her thighs absolutely bulged with running muscles. They were so right for each other. But now he had to deal with this stupidity of her father promising another man his own daughter.

No one did that anymore, though it wasn't unheard of either. Most of Jad's friends from school were allowed to pick their own mates, and his parents allowed him to. Yet now, Taeni's dad had reached back into the past and pulled out this old marriage convention that permitted parents to select a mate for a daughter coming of age. Back then, hundreds of years ago and even more, this type of arranged marriage was common, a way to maintain the purity of the group. As each of the various racial groups that constituted advanced intelligent life on this planet migrated toward the terminator from the hot side, they wanted desperately to maintain their racial integrity. In the conflicts that inevitably followed the forced inter-mixing of the races, arranged marriages were seen as a way to keep a daughter from marrying outside the group.

But the groups were well integrated now. It worked for several thousand years, but now many families had begun to let their daughters marry the man of their choice. Besides, Taeni and Jad were in the same racial group—they were both Lakuu—and, well, Jad just had to do something. He jumped out of his chair.

"Taeni—let's run away together." He took her hand. "We could go somewhere until you're nineteen. Then we can get married without any-one's permission."

"No, Jad. It won't work. They'll just find us and bring us back. And you know what they'll do to you when they find you."

"We could go to Sabean. It's a big place. They won't find us there."

"No, Jad, we can't live together without getting married. They'd never let us—"

"Taeni, all you have to do is hold out for a little more than two years. You're almost seventeen—then it's just two years. Then we can get mar-ried."

"No, Jad, *no*. It won't work, that's too long. They'll find me. And then it'll be even worse." She jerked her hand free of his.

"Crap, Taeni, I don't believe this! Is this a joke?"

"No, Jad, I'm sorry. I have to get back." A tear trickled down her cheek and she brushed it away. She turned, about to leave. He grabbed her arm.

"What if I talk to your dad?"

Her head spun around. "No, Jad, no! Don't do that! He's made up his mind. Don't make this any harder than it already is. Please—I have to get back." She wrenched free of his grip and took off running over the hard compacted sand that composed the adjoining backyards between her house and Jad's. She was out of sight in less than a microsector.

"Taeni! Wait!"

He never saw her again.

But as he sat beside the trail looking back over the last time he saw Taeni, Jad knew that his memory of the event may not be entirely accu-rate—after all, even long-term memory can suffer some degradation of details after thirty years—so perhaps he was less than completely clear about some of the minor details. But he remembered the significant parts, and the feelings of despondency and dejection that boiled up inside him as he watched Taeni run home, and the anger and frustration he felt when he knew he would never see her again could still explode in his mind now with as much clarity and sharpness as it had so long ago.

Yet, there was so much of Taeni in Trea.

Jad went on to college in Doserovos several years later as he'd planned hoping he would run into Taeni there, but he didn't.

He did meet Wila at college in Sabean where he moved to do grad-uate work in astrophysics, and they began a fond relationship right away. Wila'd already taken an interest in running, and he was delighted to see her thighs actually develop strong, robust running muscles. Wila was a definite antidote for Taeni, and he eventually thrust Taeni's image into long-term memory where it belonged, and rarely did he bring her likeness out to savor the relationship.

Only when Col called the group to resume hiking did Jad stop his daydreaming and return to work. He had to poke Bent to wake him up.

As they hiked, they entered the darkest part of the forest.

CHAPTER 40

VALLEY

Time Element 461.181.4.8.

About five millisectors after they started, the trail petered out. Large trees with trunks several links in diameter encompassed them in a chilly thicket, and Col called a halt and dropped his pack. "According to the route, we're to proceed due east from here. We'll have to travel by compass heading. My compass indicates that we should hike in that direction."

He pointed toward a particularly dark and gloomy region of the forest, and then returned his electronic compass to a small pocket on his backpack. He and Trea headed out, directly into the blackness. Bent and Jad and followed. Within a few steps they were totally engulfed by the cool darkness of the inner forest.

Visibility was limited now, only several hundred links in any direction. The forest closed in all around them and a panic rose in Jad's throat. Such a new feeling, nothing similar to it on Anthanos at all. No forests existed there to get lost in, no dark, funereal thickets that could engulf a person and conceal him from everyone else. Scary, and dangerous too, not being able to see what was around the next tree. Jad wiped his forehead with his sleeve and put his head down and followed Bent. The gloom seemed to infect the others, too, as a hush fell over the group. Trea stopped singing.

"I hope we know where we're going," Trea muttered as she and Col stopped to don jackets. Jad tacked a marker, a small square of aluminum painted yellow, to a tree. He placed it on the east side of the tree so it would be visible on the return trip. About two millisectors after they resumed hiking, and after placing nine or ten more markers, they came to the meadow. Col led them in a short trip around.

About a thousand links long and three to four hundred links wide, the meadow was completely encompassed by the forest. "I remember visualizing this open area on the probe images when our trip was in the planning stages," Col said. "But it was just a green spot. I was at a loss to explain its composition. Seeing it up close like this, it's magnificent."

"Quite a contrast to the darkness of the trail," Trea said.

"It's so green," Jad said. "You only see this much green in the hydroponics gardens at home."

Jad continued to stare at the meadow, impressed by how the forest seemed hesitant to enter and colonize it. Several trees at the edge had fallen over into the green, and their silver-gray trunks, denuded of bark after many years of decay, lay like spikes half buried in the green of the meadow, as if to hold it together. But what impressed Jad most about the meadow was the brilliant green of the vegetation. Sunlight bathed the meadow as he had not seen the sun since they entered the forest after leaving the sand. The low broad-leafed plants that covered the meadow like a brilliant green blanket—vaguely reminiscent of Anthanian plants— caught and reflected the sunlight, saturating his eyes with viridian and malachite. Around the circumference of the meadow stood the trees of the forest, their brown, gray, and white trunks and green canopy overhead contrasting in color and texture and elevation, and perhaps even a little in nobility, with the vegetation in the meadow below.

They lingered at the meadow only a microsector and walked on. Slowly and carefully they headed toward the peak, following the precise direction of the compass, blazing their own trail, marking a tree every few hundred links. Their path took them uphill, steeper and steeper, until after five millisectors of trudging through heavy woodland, the forest thinned out and they found themselves on the south ridge of a huge valley.

"Oh, my!" Trea exclaimed, and everyone stopped walking.

"Wow," Jad said.

Jad's vision aid gave him the dimensions of the valley, one-half anthan from ridge to ridge and more than two anthans to the eastern end. The team stood about two hundred links below the top of the southern ridge, and looking down they could see the stream as it trickled through the valley floor almost three hundred links below. Several low trees and bushes sprouted near the stream and a few isolated trees had taken hold on the slopes, but by far the most prevalent ground cover on the sides of the valley was a pale straw to light green grass.

At the far end of the valley the ground rose sharply—and heavily forested again—leading upward toward the peak, now a prominent white-capped massif looming directly above everything.

They took off hiking again, upward toward the crest of the ridge. A breeze drifted down the valley directly in their faces, and the sun, almost directly in front of them, hung brilliantly warm in the clear eastern sky. They stopped at a large red-barked tree and dropped their backpacks and removed their jackets. Col made wide, sweeping images of the valley.

By 181.5, they were back hiking.

They started east, gradually advancing up the ridge toward the top, and ran across another narrow trail only a few links from the summit of the ridge. They followed the trail, and when they'd walked for about three millisectors, Bent stopped and set his pack down. They'd come to the approximate midpoint of the ridge.

"This will be a good place to detonate one of the charges."

Time Element 461.181.5.7.

Jad unstrapped the portable drill, a four-link long auger-shaped drill bit, and a four-link extension shaft from the outside of his pack. He handed them to Bent who walked up the hill to the top of the ridge where he drilled a hole the full distance of the bit and extension. From a bright yellow carrier strapped to the outside of his pack he carefully removed one of the coal-black seismic charges.

A cylinder two links long and five decilinks in diameter, the charge had a hollow front end to shape the blast, directing it downward. Bent pulled a spool of black cable from his pack and screwed one end of the cable to a pin at the rear of the charge.

"That dinky thing is going to send a seismic signal to the recorder from here?" Trea screwed up her face in amazement.

"That's the idea," Bent said as he lowered the charge down the hole. He ran the cable its full 250 links back along the trail to where the others stood, and connected the other end of the cable to his electronic notebook. "Okay, everything's ready," he said.

Jad pulled out his PersComm and contacted Wila. "Is there any activity now from the northernmost recorder?"

"No, nothing. It's quiet now."

"Okay, here we go. Standby. We're going to ignite."

It wasn't so much the noise as it was the vibration in the earth all around. Jad felt it as an immense muffled 'thud' as though a large meteor had hit the ground, and the vibrations shuddered through the earth as he had never felt before. They reminded him of the rapid-fire vibrations he experienced when strapped to a couch on *Explorer*'s Command Deck as the big ship roared into the void of deep space. With the explosion, a geyser of rocks, dirt, smoke and sparks erupted from the hole, sending debris a hundred links into the air, showering everyone with dust and pebbles. Birds screamed in the few trees on this side of the valley, and a black-and-brown bird, otherwise busily rat-a-tat-tatting on the side of a tree farther down the slope, stopped briefly, but resumed its effort several nanosectors later when all turned quiet. A spark landed at Trea's foot and she stamped it out. The only part of the charge to survive the blast—the end plate with the attached cable—was hurled high in the air and landed well behind the group.

"My god, I could feel that through my feet," Trea said as she brushed the dirt from her hair and clothes. "I didn't realize a charge like that could pack so much power in it."

"That's the idea," Bent said.

Jad contacted Wila again. "Did the recorder feel that?"

Wila remained silent at her end of comm. "Feel what? Did you ignite?"

"Yes, we did. Did we get anything?"

"Nothing's appeared so far." A trace of disappointment pervaded Wila's voice. "But it may take several nanosectors before the impulses reach the recorder."

Five more nanosectors elapsed. "Nothing," Wila said. Jad relayed the information to Bent.

"It should take only a few nanosectors for the impulse to get there," Bent said and shook his head. "If there isn't anything by now, there never will be. Tell Wila to send the tracing anyway."

"Okay. Send it to Bent's notebook here."

"Here it comes." In less than a nanosector the tracing appeared on the notebook screen.

Jad looked at the tracing, a horizontal black line near the bottom of the screen, superimposed over a grid of faint blue squares. The line ran exactly along the baseline of the graph, almost taunting him and Bent as they stared at it. The tracing covered a millisector of time, and the displacement of the line by the charge should have appeared toward the left side of the graph. But the black line just sat there, straight and long. The notebook had placed a small red arrow just above the line at the exact moment of detonation, and Bent magnified the line beyond the arrow. Any tiny displacement would have been magnified, too. Yet even then nothing appeared, no tiny upward thrust of the line to show the seismic waves had reached the recorder, no peaks and valleys to indicate miniscule vibrations of the crust near the recorder's probe. Jad stared at the black line and the line stared back.

"What do you think it means?" Jad asked.

"It means my first impression is probably right," Bent said. A slight smile crossed his lips. "I've been suspicious since I saw the first probe images—the crust isn't solid rock like Anthanos. It may be porous, fractured, heterogeneous—probably all three. At home, in the rock under the sand, this charge would've been felt easily by the recorder. But this type of event, where nothing shows up, happens like when we set off a charge in sand. Sand muffles the shock waves and they won't travel more than a few anthans, but in solid rock, the seismic impulses will travel a thousand anthans. The results I got from the quake made me suspicious the crust was fractured, but I wasn't sure. Now I'm even more convinced."

"Are you going to set off any more charges?" Col asked.

Bent didn't reply right away. He stared at the notebook screen for a microsector more, an intense, thoughtful look on his face, then stood up and closed the notebook and slipped it into his pack. "No. Too far away from the recorder. Let's get the equipment together. I bet you want to get going."

They collected and repacked the tools of their little study and slung their packs. A wisp of blue-white smoke still wafted from the hole, and Bent scraped some dirt and rocks back into the hole with his foot. He rejoined the team as they set out along the ridge.

Time Element 461.181.7.0.

They traveled east along the ridge into a forested region at the head of the valley, and the white-barked trees returned, giving the forest an illusion of light and openness. Jad began tacking markers on the trees. Col seemed fascinated by the trees, especially the way the bark split into a semicircle to reveal a dark "eye" which seemed to watch the team as they walked. He made several images, and on rest stops made it a point to examine them more closely.

"I don't like the way the 'eye' is watching me," Trea said.

Jad snickered to himself. He couldn't tell whether Trea was joking or serious. He decided she must have been serious. *Yeah, right, like those plants are going to harm you in any way at all. That's one thing Taeni was not. Paranoid.*

After they'd walked about an anthan, the forest thinned out and Col stopped and pulled out the probe image map of the preplanned route. He'd traced the route on the map with a red marker. "The lake shouldn't be too far," he said, pointing upward toward the peak in the distance. "But we're in for a substantial climb. The lake is at the base of the peak, and once we reach it, that's as high as we go. From there we return downward."

Here the terrain went sharply upward, and the surface was covered with dark gray boulders — boulders bigger than a runabout and as small as a runabout's wheel. A few small trees and bushes sprouted amidst the rocks, but otherwise very little green color was visible. Jad's impression was of a huge leaden rock pile stretching upward, almost out of sight.

By carefully stepping from one rock to another they made their way up the mountain. Col led them in a zigzag route beside the creek whose waters gurgled over the rocks that made up its bed to their left. They passed through the timberline in the ascent, yet when they reached the top of the boulder field they still hadn't arrived at the lake, lying stubbornly above them.

They rested for a millisector, and then turned to confront their next challenge. They stood in a desolate environment, facing a further climb of several hundred links over a desert-like surface strewn with craggy rocks and pebbles that jutted from the dusty soil, making travel more hazardous than the climb they'd just endured. The only plants that existed here were a few scrawny specimens, low to the ground, warped into gnarly shapes by forces Jad couldn't imagine or conceive. A ground-hugging grass dotted the surface here and there, but the tan soil that made up the greatest part of the surface lay exposed almost everywhere. The breeze kicked up the dust and sent microscopic grains into their eyes.

Jad eyed the terrain with trepidation. The ground was suspiciously familiar, like a vast rocky desert, but more forbidding and hostile than deserts he was used to. It looked too much like the surface of that trail in the western mountains when Case was killed, and he was increasingly apprehensive about the coming climb. But he said nothing to Col. He noted one important difference between this area and the western trail. Here the soil was dry — no wet spots peppered the ground. But the mountain they were on was much steeper than the trail out west. He tried to put the best face on this predicament. *If we take our time, we can make it up this slope.*

They filled their water bottles with cold, crystal clear filtered creek water and set off again, hiking in another zigzag pattern.

They reached the lake in about eight millisectors.

"Oh, my gosh, how beautiful," Trea exclaimed.

CHAPTER 41

LAKE

Time Element 461.181.10.1.

Jad's vision aid measured the lake at three hundred links across. Tan to silver-gray rocks surrounded the lake everywhere, and a small island of angular rock protruded from the water near the center. The reflection of the gray of the rocks gave the lake a lustrous mirror-like finish. To the north and east, the mountain ascended almost vertically toward the rugged peak that had been their goal. White still covered the apex, and several large patches of ice lay in the shadow about half way up the north side of the mountain. Near the lake, a few small trees grew twisted and contorted close to the ground, and clumps of scraggly grasses grew in odd places over the surface.

To Jad, who'd never seen up close a body of water larger than a swimming pool on Anthanos, any water sitting out in the open like this, even one as small as this one, was an enticing sight and he stared at it for several microsectors.

I should've brought my swimming trunks.

Here they dropped their packs. The time was well past the midpoint of the lightime, and they hadn't stopped yet for the second meal. Trea pulled out the portable stove and boiled some water to make hot jell-kell, and Jad contacted Jer, watching as Bent pulled a few small plastic boxes from his pack. He walked over to the west side of the lake to collect specimens.

They erected their shelters five links apart on a flat area south of the lake. Jad unrolled his sleeping bag inside his shelter and dropped his pack on top. He pulled his camera from the pack and picked a spot near the water where he made spectrographic readings of the terrain around the lake.

"I'm going to take a quick dip in the lake before the air gets too cool," Trea said.

Trea disappeared into her shelter and emerged a millisector later wearing a two-piece swimsuit and carrying a towel. She walked gingerly across the stony surface to the edge of the lake not far from where Jad was imaging, and tested the water with her toe. "Brrrr. Chilly." She crossed her arms over her chest in a mock shiver.

She folded her towel and set it on a rock beside the lake. She squatted at the lake's edge and splashed some water on her chest and legs, then stood and walked in. Moving cautiously, she felt her way with her feet along the rocky bottom. When the water reached her waist, she took a deep breath, dipped under the surface and swam under water forty or fifty links. She surfaced near the center of the lake and swam to the little island and climbed onto the rocks. She sat there for a few microsectors, then jumped into the water and swam back to the campsite.

By the time Trea returned, the wind had picked up and the air temperature was dropping. The sun hung low on the western horizon—a bright tangerine-red disk poised just above the western mountains visible through the haze that had settled over the distant peaks. Reds and oranges permeated the haze, spreading color across the horizon. A chilly wind whirled around the campsite, and the men donned jackets. Trea grabbed her towel and ran back to her shelter. She dried off and disappeared inside and re-emerged two millisectors later fully dressed in jumpsuit, boots, and jacket.

Jad watched Trea's swim with deepening interest. He even snapped an image of Trea sitting on the rock. This was the first time he'd seen her in a swimsuit, and a revealing one at that. He hadn't even seen her during the 700 T-sectors of Gold Team training on Anthanos even though Space-Comm required swimming as a part of physical exercise. Col and Trea, perhaps because they'd been in a different training class from the others, used Swimming Pool No. 2 on the Spaceport. Jad and Wila used Pool No. 1, two anthans away on the other side of the Spaceport since that was the pool to which their training class had been assigned. But now here she was, this slim, attractive, blue-eyed, auburn-haired woman with the slender expressive arms and full muscular thighs, flaunting her loveliness in front of Jad and the others—well, not the others as Jad found when he looked around. Col was examining some reddish-orange glob growing on the rocks around the lake, and Bent was . . . well, Bent was off somewhere gathering rocks, so perhaps this swim was meant for Jad's enjoyment all to himself

What's the matter, Col? Don't you appreciate the attractiveness of your own wife?

Jad savored the display. He noted the rippling of Trea's thighs as she walked to the water's edge. He watched as she squatted and splashed water on herself, and as she carefully entered the water and slipped beneath. He followed her through the camera's lens after she surfaced and climbed up on the rock. He captured an image of her sitting on the rock, and watched as she jumped off and swam back to shore.

But Trea noticed something, too. She watched as Jad took her picture. In fact, she smiled for the camera.

She didn't wave to the camera; no, she didn't go that far. In the image her hands were down at her side—perhaps she needed to balance herself on the rock—and when she returned to the lakeshore, she didn't say anything to Jad about taking an image of her in a swimsuit, but she definitely knew he had done it. She seemed okay with it.

Jad called up the image on the camera's view screen and it was exquisite. Trea sat in a small depression in the middle of the rock, turned slightly to her left, but centered perfectly in the image. She looked directly into the camera's lens and smiled broadly. Her dark red hair seemed a little darker because it was wet and clinging to her forehead. Her petite breasts were covered adequately by the top of her swimsuit, and her right thigh with its magnificent running muscles, still moist from the lake water, glistened in the golden light of the evening sun.

There was so much of Taeni in Trea.

Time Element 461.183.0.3.

The next lightime dawned bright and clear. The wind had died down during the night, but the air was still chilly, around –5 Tal. Jad woke as Trea, as usual, was the first one up and started water boiling on the stove. As they rose, each hiker fixed some hot jell-kell, consumed a meal, and started packing. They took the shelters down and packed them away, filled water bottles with filtered lake water, and brought out and consulted the maps.

At 183.2.2, they set out and followed the stream down to the area of the rocks where they turned left and made their way back to where they'd left the rocks on the ascent. Now they still had to negotiate the boulders, but in the reverse direction. Stepping up from rock to rock required force and energy, it was exhausting and time consuming. Stepping down from one rock to another required a finer touch and good balance. Col led.

They took more than a subsector to reach the bottom, now back in the forest. They stopped for a short rest and water break, and then searched for the markers on the trees. When they found the first one, they resumed hiking, and after another subsector followed the markers until they found the trail where the forest ended at the head of the valley.

Again the valley was spread out before them, and again they stopped to admire the arresting view. They bathed in the warmth of the sun, and the cool breeze from the west felt dry and relaxing as it swirled over their faces. Trea and Col made several images of the valley while Bent took a short hike down to the waterfall at the head of the valley to take samples.

They picked up the trail and followed it along the ridge. Jad led, walking easily. He was relaxed, almost happy-go-lucky. He enjoyed the breeze and the walk, and the expedition seemed to go well. Col got lots of specimens, Trea'd imaged some interesting animals in the vicinity, and though Bent got nothing from the seismic charge, he got plenty of specimens.

All things considered, this was a good trip. It looks like we'll get out of these mountains without anything happening. Wila will be relieved.

Walking at the end of the group, Trea started singing the *Dolotolo* softly again as they walked, and Jad also hummed the melody, but quietly to himself, lest someone be able to tell he couldn't carry a tune.

They passed the spot where they'd set off the seismic charge, but continued without stopping. Just before they left the ridge, Trea turned around, probably to admire the valley one last time.

That's when she saw something unusual.

CHAPTER 42

URSUS

Time Element 461.183.5.9.

"What are those?" Trea wondered aloud, and the group stopped and turned around. Jad saw immediately what she pointed at, and a wave of concern gripped his mind.

From farther back up the ridge, two dark brown furry animals scampered toward the group. The men drew their weapons. Trea's weapon remained in its holster.

The animals bounded down the hill like a couple of playful youngsters, but stopped about twenty links short of the team. They sniffed the air and the larger of the two stood on its hind feet as though to get a better view of these visitors to his home valley.

Trea held up one hand. "Don't shoot. They look like juveniles. They may not be dangerous."

Jad relaxed only imperceptibly. He remained wary of the animals and he watched them closely. The animals hadn't made contact with any of the group, perhaps they were merely curious. Jad and Bent kept their weapons tight in their hands, but Col returned his to its holster. Trea crouched in front of them and made several images, and as she stood and returned her camera to her pack, Col said, "It would be prudent for us to leave. They may turn vicious."

They edged their way down the hill toward the forest, carefully watching the animals.

As he walked, Jad became aware of a sound behind him—a rushing sound—a thumping sound. He couldn't identify it. He started to turn around to investigate, but a sudden deep, rumbling blast shattered the quiet of the valley and *wham*, he'd been slammed flat on his back and thrown a few links down the hill. "What the hell?" he yelled and looked up. More roaring came from down the hill. But besides the throaty, deep-pitched bellowing there was something else, over and above it. It seemed a higher pitched sound, like screaming—a man's voice, shrieking, coming from the same direction. Jad jumped to his feet, his weapon still in his hand. He threw off his pack. "What the hell's going on?" Bent jumped up too, and there's the rump of a huge brownish-black animal just down the hill—it must be seven links high and it's howling.

"What is that?" Bent yelled.

The screaming continued. *Where's the screaming coming from?* Then it stopped. "Trea! Where's Trea?" Jad yelled. She was up the trail a few links, just getting to her feet, her weapon still in its holster.

"Where's Col?" Bent yelled. Jad saw boots—boots underneath the animal—boots on feet that were gyrating around in panic.

"It's got Col!" Jad yelled. "Shoot at it!" and he fired at the animal. Bent fired too, but their weapons were set on level 1 and they produced only a benign puff of smoke as the electron beams singed the animal's backside. The shots did nothing to stop the huge animal from continuing its attack.

Trea started screaming. "Col! Col! Oh, god! What's happening?"

"Trea! Shoot at it!" Jad yelled several times, but she never drew her weapon. She seemed dazed, and Jad wondered briefly if she comprehended what was going on. "Trea! Goddammit! Shoot at it!"

Jad and Bent fired several more times at the animal, but the attack continued. They ran around to the front of the animal—Jad to the animal's left, Bent to the right—and fired again, hitting the animal in the head. Those shots didn't do anything either.

"Col—where's Col?" Trea yelled, several times. Still, she didn't draw her weapon.

The animal continued its attack, its huge teeth embedded in Col's face and neck.

"Get out of here!" Bent yelled. "Stop it! Stop it!" He fired several times, but nothing happened.

Jad's weapon was still set on level 1, and with the thumb of his right hand he flipped the power level control upward. It stopped on 6 and he fired again, hitting the animal squarely in the head just in front of the left ear. The loud crack and bright flash of light startled him and he jumped back as the weapon discharged. But that shot worked.

The animal stopped its attack and slowly lifted its head. Its muzzle was saturated with Col's blood. Bent fired another time, hitting the beast on the neck behind the right ear, and it let out a faltering, stuttering roar. It turned its head slightly toward Jad. Blood oozed from its ears and nose, its bloodshot eyes gyrated around in their sockets, and its entire body trembled like a leaf in a stiff breeze. A crimson, swollen tongue hung limply from its open mouth. A raspy, grunting sound came from deep within the animal's chest and its breathing was heavy and intense. Bent raised his weapon as if to fire again.

"Don't shoot!" Jad yelled. He held up a hand toward Bent. "Let it get off Col!"

Slowly the animal turned to walk away. It turned to its left, toward Jad, stepping over Col's body, dragging its huge right hind clawed foot across Col's legs. Jad stepped back a few paces but kept his weapon aimed at the animal's head. It took two or three more steps and stopped, shaking uncontrollably and grunting painfully. Jad cautiously backed up several more steps. Without warning, all four legs of the animal collapsed and it rolled down the hill like a giant brownish-black fur ball, tumbling and bouncing side-over-side, end-over-end, landing face down in the creek with a tremendous splash. Birds flushed from the trees and bushes nearby. Jad turned back to Col. Bent was opening a first-aid kit.

Col didn't move—blood had splattered everywhere. His lower jaw and neck were a mass of red, torn, bleeding tissue. Blood poured from open veins and spurted into the air from torn arteries. His breathing was labored and difficult, and air bubbled sporadically from his shredded larynx.

Jad drew a handkerchief from one pocket and placed it over Col's neck, trying to stop the bleeding, but blood poured out so much faster than he could stop it. He grabbed the first-aid kit from his pack and pulled out a large bandage and laid it over Col's neck. "I can't stop the bleeding! Where are the clamps? Get the clamps!"

Trea dropped her pack on the trail and ran over to Col, kneeling beside Jad on Col's right side. "Oh my god, Col! Oh, my god!" Then she screamed. She'd seen the injuries, the terrifying, horrifying injuries. She stood up, backed up one or two paces, and with her hands covering her mouth, screamed again. She turned around and vomited, then fell to her hands and knees.

Jad was only vaguely aware of Trea screaming "No! No! Oh, god, no!" over and over. He looked for Col's pack—*It should have the first-aid kit with the clamps.* There it was, a few steps up the hill. It must have been thrown off when the animal first hit him. Bent pulled the cardiomonitor from his first-aid kit and strapped it to Col's left arm, but the unit beeped slowly and irregularly.

"Get the blood volume expander!" Jad yelled, and he grabbed several hemostats and began clamping bleeders. Bent pulled out a plastic bag with the light tan powdered blood volume expander and poured an eighth-trilink of sterile water into the bag. The powder dissolved immediately and Bent started an IV in Col's left arm. He held the bag in both hands, pumping the solution in as fast as he could.

Jad stopped the bleeding from Col's neck, but worried he was too late. "He's already lost a lot of blood. Get another bag!"

Bent retrieved another bag from Jad's first-aid kit, but before he got the water in, the cardiomonitor stopped beeping and spat out a high-pitched squeal.

"Goddammit!" Jad yelled, and he started pounding on Col's chest. "Intubate him!" Bent grabbed the tracheotomy tube from a first-aid kit.

"Where do I put it?" Bent said. "I can't see the trachea!"

"Look where the air is coming from!" Every time Jad pressed on Col's chest a bubble of air escaped from the torn trachea. Bent slid the tube in the opening and put the hand pump on the other end. He tried to force air into the tube but it wouldn't stay in place. It kept slipping from the wound and he was getting frustrated trying to reinsert it. The cardiomonitor continued to squeal.

"I can't keep the damn tube in place!" Bent yelled. "I can't—"

"Get the PCS!" Jad yelled back. "It's in my pack!" Bent grabbed the portable cardiac stimulator and placed it on Col's chest. Jad stopped pumping as Bent activated the instrument. Once, twice. Nothing. The cardiomonitor continued to squeal.

"Shock him some more!" Jad yelled. "Pump in the expander!"

Bent hit the big red button on the PCS that triggered the shock. Again—again—again. Repeatedly he hit the button, shock after shock, time after time, as many as fifty or sixty times—almost the limit of the power source in the unit. Except for one or two weak beats immediately after each shock, Col's heart refused to pump again.

"Get some more expander!" Jad yelled.

"That's all there is. There's only two bags."

Exhausted and discouraged, Jad sat back on his heels. It seemed useless to continue, nothing they'd done had made any difference. He shut off the cardiomonitor. His hands were covered in blood and he instinctively wiped them on his jumpsuit. He had to quit. He couldn't continue. Col was almost certainly dead.

Bent tried to keep going. He picked up a bag of regular IV fluids, unwrapping the tubing, pushing the needle into the IV. "We can't quit now," he yelled and he started pumping the bag. "Maybe he just needs more fluids. Shock him again!"

"He's lost too much blood." Jad stayed sitting on his heels, feeling nothing, not pain, not relief, not resignation. He looked at the body in front of him, a mass of blood-stained blue green, all of it torn, shredded, and ragged. Like an old uniform to be discarded. He was an outsider now, merely watching everything unfold, a horror movie he was not even a part of. Life could never survive within that body. It would be useless to continue. "He's dead. There's nothing more we can do. His heart won't beat."

"We have to try," Bent said. "Shock him again!"

"It's no use." Jad stood up beside the body.

Bent dropped the bag of IV fluids and he too stood up. He said nothing. He just stared at the carcass of the botanist/explorer in front of him.

Jad covered the body with a shelter half from Col's pack, then stood quietly beside it for several microsectors. In the solitude of that lonely valley his mind reeled and staggered.

Time Element 461.183.7.8.

Jad was absolutely stunned and shocked by the savagery of the attack—it defied Anthanian comprehension. Nothing like this ever occurred on Anthanos where all the animals were held in zoological parks and few animals were wild enough to attack a person at all, let alone with such ferocity and viciousness. It was unthinkable, it was unimaginable. Yet it had occurred, and the fury and anger grew inside.

He looked for the animals that had started the attack, but they were no longer around. He turned to the attacking animal, half covered by water in the creek, still unmoving.

"You bastard!" Jad yelled, his anger at the animal increasing exponentially. He grabbed for his weapon, still hanging by its cable from the power pack on his belt, and fired five rapid shots at the animal. Still set on level 6, the weapon belched out five brilliant eruptions, hitting the animal, the water, and the hillside beyond. This time Jad did not flinch.

"My god! What the hell is this? What the hell are we doing here?" He tried to throw his weapon away, but it stayed cabled to his power pack. He ripped the power pack belt from his waist and hurled the entire unit down the hill. "I can't believe this! Is this really happening? Are we thinking about colonizing this planet?"

Jad turned and faced away from the animal. His outburst had relieved some of his frustration but he still raged inside. He wondered what to do next, but he couldn't think. Frustration mounted within—there was nothing he could do. He wasn't able to save Col's life any more than he could have saved Case's life. He'd now been party to the death of two highly respected members of the landing team, and the frustration inside tore him apart. He was tired of the Blue Planet, and he wanted only to leave.

Welling up within him was a tremendous desire to run. Running was his medication, his purgative. It helped him deal with the trials and uncertainties of life by giving him time to think, time to ponder a response. But that was out of the question here. He couldn't just abandon Col's body and Bent and the backpacks strewn on the side of the valley. He would have to make do.

He picked up his backpack and repacked it. He collected the equipment from the first-aid kits and shoved everything into his pack. He picked up Col's pack, closed the top cover and took it back up the hill. He set both backpacks on the trail next to Trea's.

Trea!

"Where's Trea?" Jad asked, almost yelling. He scanned the valley, up toward the top of the ridge, down to the creek below. "Trea!" he yelled. He looked east toward the forest they'd just left, and west toward the forest they were about to enter. He strained his eyes to see beyond the darkness at the edge of the wood.

"Bent! Where's Trea?"

Bent didn't answer, he seemed dazed. He stood quietly, staring at the shelter half covering Col's body.

"Bent! Where's Trea?" That was the second time he'd addressed Bent, and still the geologist gave no response. Jad became concerned and he wondered if Bent was in shock. Had the terror of the attack pushed him over the edge into a bear-pit of insanity? Jad walked over to Bent and placed a hand on his shoulder.

"Bent? Are you okay?"

Bent stirred slightly. "I don't know where she is," he said in a voice drained of emotion. "Maybe she ran back toward the campsite." He turned and walked up the hill.

Back toward the campsite and the aerodyne. Of course. That's the most logical direction for her to go. "I'm going to go see if I can find her," Jad said. "Will you be okay here?"

Bent sat down on the side of the hill just below the trail next to his pack. "Okay," he said, placing his head in his hands.

Jad took off at a fast trot across the side of the ridge onto the trail to the forest. Ah—now to run again.

But soon he lost the trail. He found the markers and followed them until he came to the meadow. He assumed Trea had already passed, but as he started to circle it, he saw her in the vegetation near the center on her hands and knees, still vomiting. He ran over to help her up.

"Leave me alone!" she yelled as Jad touched her arm. She pulled away from his grip and stood, then took off running across the meadow. In the soft soil and heavy vegetation she couldn't run very fast, and he caught up with her and grabbed her arm.

"Trea. Wait . . ."

"Stop! Stop!" Trea yelled through constant sobbing. "Let go!" She jerked free of his grip and fell to her hands and knees. She vomited again.

"Trea. Let me take you back to the aerodyne."

"No! No! I can't stand it! I've got to get away!"

"Get away from what? What are you running from? Trea, you can't keep running."

"I can't stand it! I can't stand it!"

Jad helped Trea to her feet, but she wrenched free of his hold again and struggled to run across the meadow. Jad hesitated to run after her. He decided to let her run, figuring she would exhaust herself sooner or later. When she came to the edge of the meadow, she sprinted into the forest. Jad followed, but the route she took wasn't familiar. She was south of the ascent trail, headed into a different valley. He tried to catch up with her, but she continued to run amazingly fast through the forest.

"Trea!" Jad yelled after her. "You're going the wrong way!" His yelling had no effect. It was as though his voice was muffled and dampened by the vegetation all around and she couldn't hear him. Or didn't want to hear him. For whatever reason, she continued to run.

No creek ran down this valley and she ran easily over the dry soil. She ran and ran, skimming, almost gliding down the valley, through the underbrush and past the trees. Sometimes she would get tangled in the shrubs or bushes—she even fell once, but she got back up and kept running. Soon the humid forest thinned out and in the open terrain of the lower valley she could run even faster. Jad decided to let her run.

Maybe she'll run herself out.

But Trea was one of the best runners on the team and if she wanted, she could keep running almost forever. She might get lost or injured, though, and he had to stay with her. He could also hear his PersComm beeping, but he couldn't stop to answer it. He wanted to keep Trea in view.

When she came to the dry sand at the bottom of the valley, her pace slowed and Jad caught up with her again. She fell in the soft sand, but this time when Jad tried to help her up she offered no resistance.

"What are you running from?"

"Col's dead, isn't he?" She was still crying.

Jad hesitated, taken by surprise at Trea's question. He was hoping he could keep the answer from her for at least a short time, but he nodded. "Yes, he is."

Trea fell to the sand sobbing uncontrollably. "Oh, god, no! Why? Why?"

"Let me take you to the ship."

Jad helped Trea to her feet and persuaded her to walk to the aerodyne. They reached the shelter around 183.8.8. By this time, a lightime and a half after the team had left and turned off the power to the inflation fans, the shelter had collapsed inward. Jad restored power to the fans, but when he opened the shelter's airlock door, Trea refused to go in. She sat on the ground near the aerodyne and continued to weep. She also continued to vomit, but her stomach was empty and she brought up nothing. Jad gave her an injection of an antiemetic from the aerodyne's first-aid kit.

Then he called Jer to tell her of Col's death, but he found out Bent had called earlier, around 183.8.2, and now all they wanted to know was how Trea was.

Time Element 461.183.8.2.

"What is happening here?" Bent said to Lilea through his PersComm link to *Explorer*. She listened carefully, not interrupting, letting him talk. He'd called intending to tell them only of Col's death, but when they found out Col was dead and Trea had run away, they demanded to know what had happened. They wanted all the details—why it happened and what led up to it, and what happened afterward. Bent described the attacking animal and the two animals they'd seen before the attack, and told them about what they did to try to save Col's life but that it didn't work, and then he told them about Trea's running away though he and Jad didn't actually see her run away, and he told them about Jad running after her to try to find her, and now he sat alone on the side of the hill with Col's body, and he had to stay there and make sure nothing happened to it.

After the anger and confusion and rage over the death of another member of the Gold Team had died down on *Explorer*, Lilea returned to speak to Bent privately. She sat on the couch in the living area of their compartment using the comm unit of the compartment's computer. And Bent, after sitting so quietly for so long on the side of that valley vented his anger and frustration in her direction.

"I can't believe this is really happening," he said. "First Case, then Dell. Now Col. What is happening here? What kind of planet is this? Are we supposed to be thinking of living on this fuckin' planet? I don't think so. I don't think I would ever want to live on this goddamned planet. That attack was so vicious and so savage. I've never seen anything like it. Only in those god-awful science-fiction movies where they have all those vicious monsters. It's so useless and savage. I can't get the image of Col lying there with his neck ripped open out of my mind. I've got his blood all over my hands and I can't get it off."

"I don't know, darling." Tears streamed down Lilea's cheeks. "I don't know why this happened."

Oh! What Trea must be going through right now.

Lilea wanted to let Bent have his say, to let him talk. He'd just witnessed a hideous and gruesome attack, an attack that must have damaged his psyche and turned his mind inside out with horror and revulsion. He had to relieve the pressure of that horror, he had to purge and cleanse his mind of the terrible impressions and images the attack had produced. She knew what he was going through because she'd gone through it too, when she was only ten years old and she watched as her best friend in the whole world—Titi was her name and she was the most wonderful friend a girl could have—was struck and killed by a drunken driver in a speeding runabout. He was driving manually, not in autodrive as the law required, and he didn't even stop and try to help, and it sent Lilea swirling into grief and despair. Her mom encouraged her to talk about it and she brought it all out, about how she felt and what Titi meant to her, and she cried and cried for five T-sectors. But it helped, and when she emerged from it she was able to deal with the reality that her friend was gone forever, so now she wanted to do the same for Bent. She listened quietly as he talked, making a comment only when he paused, perhaps to catch his breath or think about what to say next.

"I wish I could give you an answer, darling. But I can't. It is so useless and senseless. I just don't know what to say."

"My hands are shaking, and I can feel my heart pounding. I don't want to stay here. I just want to go back to the aerodyne and get the hell out of here. But I can't. I can't just leave Col's body. Jad hasn't come back and I don't know where he is."

"Jer's trying to contact him. But he doesn't answer his PersComm. We don't know why. I'm worried."

"Who's next?"

"What do you mean?" Lilea asked, startled by the non sequitur. She'd stopped crying and dried her eyes with a handkerchief.

"Who's next? It's either Jad or me. We're the only two men left."

"Oh, no, darling, that doesn't make you next. I don't—"

"Is something trying to kill off the men on this expedition? There's just Jad and me . . ."

"Oh, no, nothing's trying to kill off the men. I don't believe that and I know you don't believe that either. Please tell me you don't believe that."

The comm link was quiet for a few nanosectors. "No, I guess I really don't believe it. But I wonder."

Bent sounded quieter now. He seemed to have calmed down and he didn't breathe so heavily into his PersComm microphone. Lilea would agree that it could appear that the men on this expedition were being targeted if you didn't look too closely at the details of each person's death, but that wasn't the way it really was. No, these were merely accidents of nature — random events — freak incidents. She couldn't visualize any connection among the deaths of the three men, and that meant she didn't believe Bent's hypothesis. She rejected it absolutely and unequivocally.

"These have just been terrible, horrible accidents," she told Bent. "I don't think anyone is trying to kill you. This is just how things are on this planet. Things were like this millions of years ago on our planet with all the animals and everything. You know that. We just have to accept it. That's all."

"I know that. But it's just so hard to believe that when we've seen three people on this expedition get killed so . . . so brutally and so harshly. It's almost like something else is going on. Something has to be causing it. I can't put my finger on it. I just don't know."

"I don't know either, darling." Lilea's heart sank. When she terminated comm she ran into the bedroom and sat down on her side of the bed, and as several tears trickled down her cheeks, she wondered about her recommendation to Spaceflight Command.

I don't know. Three people killed — violent storms — quakes in the ground — vicious wild animals . . . it doesn't look good.

CHAPTER 43

AFTERMATH

Bent opened the left rear door of Aero Two. "Jad, where's Trea? Didn't you say you left her here, lying across the middle seats?"

"Is she gone?"

"I don't see her."

"Maybe she's in the shelter."

Jad entered the shelter and called Trea's name. He separated the curtains that defined the four sleeping areas, and he checked the back room where the com panel sat on the floor. "I don't see her," he said as he stepped outside. "I wonder where she went."

"She's not outside either. I looked all around."

"She may have wandered off. I hope nothing's happened to her."

"We'll have to find her before we leave next lightime. The sun's going down. That means now."

"All right," Jad said, pointing, "I'll go north, you go south. Contact me if you see anything."

"Okay."

Jad circled the shelter and headed toward a clump of trees north and slightly west of Aero Two. A lustrous green grass covered the valley, and about two thousand links north of the aerodyne a small stand of several types of trees had taken hold in the moist soil beside the creek as it trickled off the mountain. Jad covered this area when he and Bent made the security sweep the first lightime, and the thicket enclosed by those trees seemed a secluded niche where Trea might have gone to be alone.

Trea's absence from the campsite didn't bother Jad and he wasn't overly concerned. She might be feeling better and just went out for a walk. His concern, actually more of an annoyance, came largely from not finding her near the campsite this close to sunset.

As he walked, he stretched the muscles of his upper arms and shoulders. This lightime he and Bent had brought Col's body down off the mountain and placed it in the cargo hold, strapped to the stretcher, still covered by a shelter half. Then they returned to the valley and brought down the backpacks, and the exertion had left his arms and shoulders sore.

I'm not made for heavy lifting. I'm a runner, not a weight lifter.

Jad's mood was better now. His anger had subsided, in part because of the exercise. It alleviated his frustrations and took his mind off Col's death. He'd been so concerned about returning the body and the backpacks he didn't have time to stay angry. But as he walked toward the trees, he couldn't help but review the events of this lightime. A sense of frustration and dark foreboding chilled his spine and tightened his chest. He felt afraid, not so much for himself, but for the expedition and for everyone else on the trip.

He entered the grove of trees near the creek, checking carefully as he walked, looking for anything that might indicate that Trea had passed through. He called her name as he wandered among the trees and emerged on the other side near a dam made of thousands of seemingly randomly placed sticks, and the pond backed up behind it. As he approached the pond, he surprised a brownish animal busily gnawing at another small tree, and the animal scurried for the pond, slapping its wide, flat tail on the surface with a loud *sploosh* as it dove beneath.

Jad scanned the dam and the pond. The murky water yielded nothing recognizable. But as he turned to his left and looked down at the narrow stream that trickled from the bottom of the dam, he saw a streak of familiar color several hundred links away. Just a spot of color but he recognized it immediately. His first feeling was relief—he'd found Trea. He exhaled slightly and the tightness in his chest dissolved, but he wondered why she was lying in the creek bed. What was she doing?

"Trea? Are you all right?" He received no answer.

Jad jogged a few steps along the bank of the creek, shading his eyes against the brilliant setting sun. But after he'd gone about thirty or forty steps he knew immediately—"Trea!" he yelled. "Bent! Bent!" He sprinted along the bank of the creek toward the color, yelling Bent's name over and over, in his panic leaving his PersComm in his pocket. When the bank became too narrow to run on, he jumped out into the creek and ran down the creek bed, splashing through the cold, muddy water, soaking his boots and jumpsuit. The creek bed was almost ten links wide here, but the water was a shallow trickle, a few decilinks deep.

"What the hell. Trea! Are you okay? Answer me!" She lay face down in the creek. "Bent! Bent!"

She wasn't moving. He grabbed her right arm and pulled her out of the water. Her face was covered with mud, and mud matted her hair and soaked the front of her jumpsuit. He didn't stop to try and find a pulse, he shoved both hands under her arms and dragged her to the bank of the creek, through the trees that lined the creek bed, and back onto the grass of the valley. He dropped her face up.

"Bent! Bent!" Bent came sprinting across the valley.

"I found her in the water! She's not moving. Get the first-aid kits!" Jad started CPR.

"Get the water out of her lungs first!" Bent yelled as he ran.

Jad rolled Trea over onto her stomach and lifted her at the waist. A small amount of dirty water trickled from her nose and mouth, but as he pumped her chest about five or six more times, she spat out a lungful of water and began coughing and choking and gagging.

"Trea! Are you okay?" Jad yelled. "Trea? Can you hear me?"

Trea didn't answer, she vomited another mouthful of water and tried to rise onto her hands. "Leave me alone," she cried in a hoarse, gurgling snarl. "Leave me alone!"

My god, the relief! The absolute ecstasy of relief at the sound of her voice that shocked Jad as though he'd been splashed with a bucket of cold creek water—the bliss of hearing Trea speak once again, knowing she was alive and going to be all right. Jad exhaled a heavy sigh and stood up beside Trea, still lying in the grass, still gasping and hacking at water left in her lungs. He didn't know what to say until the realization hit him and he understood what Trea had done.

"Trea, you stupid bitch! What did you think you were trying to do?"

Time Element 461.186.1.0.

They washed Trea's face and cleaned her jumpsuit as best they could. She refused to put on a clean, dry jumpsuit even though she had one in her backpack, now stashed in Aero Two's cargo hold. All she wanted to do was lie in the aerodyne, across the middle seats.

"I gave you an antiemetic," Jad told her before he closed the door. "That's the last of the eight doses in the kit."

"Thank you." Trea's voice was a raspy whisper. She coughed and spit up.

Jad removed the empty vial of antiemetic from the subdermal injector and picked up the half-empty vial of pain reliever he'd had to remove from the injector to insert the antiemetic. He locked all four doors of the aerodyne from the outside. Trea certainly knew how to open the doors from the inside, but Jad hoped she would stay inside and sleep until next lightime.

All he wanted to do now was to get back and see Wila. She was right, something *did* happen. As he stood outside the aerodyne in the cool evening air, he shoved his hands into his pockets, and then slipped away toward the shelter. A thin glow of scarlet still permeated the sky behind the mountains to the west, punctuated here and there by a few random puffy clouds. Wila'd started naming the different types of clouds, but he couldn't remember what name she'd given to those.

As Jad reached the left wing tip, he turned around. He gazed upward at the shadowy peak that had dominated the lives of the four explorers these past several T-sectors. Bathed in the faint blood-red glow of the sun, the Old Man of the Mountain seemed to be laughing at him.

He entered the shelter. *Wila must be beside herself now. At least she doesn't know about Trea trying to kill herself. I need to get some sleep. The sooner I get to sleep, the sooner this T-sector will be over and we can leave and get back to Site One.*

He instructed the aerodyne's com system to notify him if any of the doors of the ship were opened during the darktime, and then entered his sleeping bag. A subsector and a half elapsed before he fell asleep, but he slept until first light.

Trea stayed asleep until Aero Two reached Site One, when she was able to walk, with help, to her compartment.

They placed Col's body, still wrapped in a shelter half, in a body bag and laid it in the ground next to Case and Dell at 187.10.0.

Neither Trea nor Wila attended the funeral.

CHAPTER 44

MEETINGS

Time Element 461.192.0.0.

"Getting Trea to go back to work may be more difficult than getting Mina to go back," Wila said. She sat in Jer's compartment burrowed into one corner of the couch with her arms crossed over her chest the way she so often did at these unofficial meetings. Lilea sat in one of the chairs from the food-prep area opposite the couch. She watched Wila carefully as she and Jer talked. They'd been discussing Trea's severe reaction to Col's death, and Mina had gone down to pharmacostorage in the Medical Station on the Entry Deck to retrieve an antidepressant prescribed by Tac. "Trea is so sensitive," Wila continued, "this is going to really knock her down. The vomiting may be part of that."

"But Trea's also been the most vocal about how she likes it here on this planet," Lilea said. "Maybe that'll help her get back to working."

"I'd be afraid the sight of anything having to do with this planet now will just bring up memories of Col's death," Jer said. "I wouldn't be surprised if she doesn't want to have anything to do with this god-forsaken planet ever again. I mean, this place is in some ways so dreadful. I don't know, I mean . . ." She shrugged her shoulders.

Wila nodded. "I know what you mean. I guess we'll have to wait and see how she takes it."

"Getting Trea to go back to work is not the only problem we have," Jer said. "Mina went back to work only nine T-sectors ago, and now we've got two more members of the team out, one dead and one unable to work. That means all biological work is halted, except for Mina's micro work. There's only six of us still working, and I'm not so sure about Bent and Jad right now." Her voice rose, her eyes narrowed. "I'm at my wit's end. I don't know what to do anymore. When I signed on as Vice-Commander, I had no idea it would come to this. Sure, I knew it was a possibility, and I even thought that one or two people might be injured, maybe at the most one person would be killed, but . . . god, I never imagined anything like this. Especially not the space surgeon, too. I've been on expeditions to most of the moons in our solar system, and a few people were killed, but never as many as this."

Jer broke eye contact with Lilea and Wila and looked down at her notebook sitting on her lap. She closed her eyes and released a long, slow breath. A look of desperation, born no doubt from the pain and heartache of losing not only her husband but other friends on the team, spread painfully across her face. She made short, chopping motions as she talked. "How can we get anything done when people are being killed like this? It's got to stop. I'll be so glad to get off this damn planet." A bright drop of blood appeared on her lower lip where she'd bitten through.

"Jer?" Lilea leaned forward in her chair. "Are you all right? It's okay. We're all in this together."

"I'm okay." Jer raised her head and addressed her visitors. A tear dropped from her eye, and she pulled out a handkerchief and wiped her face. "I'm sorry. I should be able to control my frustrations better." She wiped her lip and went on. "How are Bent and Jad doing? I mean . . . are they . . . have they been able to get back to work?" Jer turned to Lilea. "How's Bent doing?"

"He's still awfully shaken up," Lilea said. "He had to take a sleep injection last darktime, and he hasn't left the compartment since the funeral. Right after the attack he spent 184 on the mountain, then in the shelter during 186 before they returned. At first, I was worried about him because he stayed in bed during 189, but he seems to be doing better now. He actually went out into the living room and picked up the probe atlas and began looking at it again. But that's all he seems to do. I've tried to talk to him, but he doesn't say much."

"Jad's the same," Wila said. "He took a sleep shot too, but he doesn't really like to take them. I don't think he got much sleep, though."

"I feel sorry for these guys," Jer said. "They were both there when Case was killed, and then they saw Col die, and they were the ones who had to try to revive both of them. It must be difficult for them now." She shook her head.

"It is," Lilea said. "Bent keeps talking about 'who's next?' He's beginning to wonder if something or someone is trying to kill off the men on this expedition. I have a hard time accepting that, but still, you wonder if there's something going on. We've seen so damn many movies that show these people-eating monsters and other vicious and sinister life forms on other planets that we've become conditioned to think if we visit another planet there will automatically be something there that will attack the expedition and drive it away."

Jer smiled faintly and nodded. "I know what you mean. I've seen some of those."

"Jad's mentioned the same thing about 'who's next?' I think he's getting scared to stay here. He's always enjoyed working here, but after Col's death I can't tell if he'll ever go back to work. I think he wants to go back to Anthanos. He just keeps staring out the window. Sometimes he picks up his camera and scrolls through the images. I can't tell if he's looking for something, or just trying to pass the time, but it's getting to me just watching him go through this. What's worse, he's not running either. He used to run up and down the runway every lightime. He likes to run so much, but he can't bring himself to leave our compartment. He says memories of the attack keep running through his head."

"Bent said the same thing. He just keeps looking through the probe atlas. I don't know whether he's planning something or just trying to avoid doing something. It's like Col's death was more than he could accept. Case and Dell's deaths he handled pretty well, but when Col died, that was too much. It was Case all over again, but with blood and gore. Now he's retreated inside, emotionally and physically. God, I hate this." Lilea tossed her arms in the air. "I keep wondering why it's all happening."

Lilea didn't cry. Jer had called this informal meeting to discuss the recent events and she steeled herself against an emotional outburst, but she could feel the wetness in her eyes, poised to spill over at the least further emotional trauma.

"It sounds like they're withdrawn," Jer said. "Tac gave me the name of a mood elevator if they need it. Do you think they'd take it?"

"Maybe," Lilea said.

"Jad might, but I don't think so."

"Well, if you can get your husbands to go outside again, maybe you should take the expedition that was scheduled for several T-sectors from now. Col and Trea set up a short trip to the northwest of here, to the rocky coastline on the western edge of this continent. Trea won't be going, but the rest of you might still want to go."

"I don't know about that. It might be hard to get Bent to try something now."

"Jad might not want to, either."

"Why don't you talk to them and suggest that the best way to get over Col's death would be to get back to work, the same as we've been telling Trea, and even Mina before? If necessary, tell them about the mood drug. We've got to get back to work."

"Okay," Lilea said.

Wila nodded and the meeting broke up.

Time Element 461.192.4.5.

Bent sat at the foot of the bed poking through the probe atlas. Lilea sat down on the near side, turning so she could see the atlas over his shoulder. "Jer says there's an expedition planned to the northwest in several T-sectors. Let's go on that expedition. I'll bet Jad and Wila would be willing to go, too. It would be good for you to get out and get back to what you enjoy doing."

"I know about the expedition." Bent flipped several pages toward the back of the image book. "I saw it on the calendar. I was looking at the area Col planned to go."

"Where?"

"Here." He pointed to the shoreline on one of the images.

Lilea looked at the large-scale image of the area, and then flipped a few pages further to examine some close-ups of the same region. "It's pretty rocky in this area. Do you think you could find a landing site?"

"There isn't much. We may have to make a preliminary trip and take some high resolution images before we try to land."

"Why don't you and Jad take one of the aerodynes next T-sector? I bet Jer would approve."

"I'll think about it." Bent closed the atlas. He set it on the bed between himself and Lilea, as though putting something symbolic between them. "I'm not sure I'm ready to go on another expedition now." He didn't look at her, his voice sounded hesitant and resigned.

"That's just it." Lilea pushed the atlas out of the way and scooted over beside him. "I think it would be good for you to go out soon. You can't stay here for the rest of the time we're on the surface. Your job takes you outside. Jad can do some of his work behind a telescope, but even he has to get out every now and then. You need to start working outside again or you'll never get anything—"

"I know, I know." Bent's voice rose. "It's just that I'm still scared that if I go out, something will happen. Already, three men on this expedition are dead, and I can't shake the thought that either Jad or I am next."

She put her arm around his waist. "Sweetheart, you know how I feel about that. I know you well enough to know that you must realize these deaths are all unrelated. Just because three have been killed doesn't mean more will be."

Bent didn't answer at first. "Yeah, okay," he said, his voice faint and unconvincing. "But it's one thing to make that realization, and another to actually believe it."

"I understand that. But I think you need to try. Why don't you talk to Jad sometime next T-sector? Wila says Jad's having the same thoughts. He's also having the same difficulty getting out. Maybe if the two of you go on an imaging run it'll help."

Bent stayed quiet a few nanosectors. "All right, I'll talk to him, but don't expect us to go flying off next lightime. We may have to make some plans first."

"I'm sure you will." Lilea's heart leapt even though Bent still sounded unconvinced of the necessity for the trip. At least he was thinking about it. He went into the living area of the compartment and composed a short message to Jad, and sent it over the ship's internal comm system.

Time Element 461.193.0.0.

Jad didn't take a sleep injection this past darktime. The one he took earlier gave him a headache and left him dizzy and groggy when he rose at first light. He wanted to be sharp for his meeting with Bent, but without the injection he didn't get much sleep. Visions of Col's mutilated body, the animal, the vivid shots from the weapon that left him with five luminous afterimages, and of Trea and Wila, and even Taeni, came swooshing through his mind like an endless video as he lay in bed, and he wasn't able to find the 'off' button to shut it down.

He pulled down Bent's message as soon as his comm monitor beeped. He thought he knew what Bent had in mind, but he wasn't sure he wanted to have anything to do with that expedition.

Bent pressed the door-announce button the next lightime at 193.2, right on schedule.

"I take it you got my message," Bent said. "I just wanted to see how you felt about a trip northwest."

They sat across from each other at the table in the living room.

"Wila and I talked about this trip before we went to bed," Jad replied. "I can't say I want to do anything right now. I've got several projects I need to work on. I'm finishing some planetary studies, and there are some solar studies I want to start."

As Jad spoke, the bedroom door opened and Wila stepped into the living area. She wore a regular jumpsuit but she was barefoot, and she crept behind Bent, headed into the food-prep area. Bent barely acknowledged her presence.

"I realize the stability of the sun is extremely important," Bent said. "But I wonder if we — that is, you and I — aren't using things like this as an excuse to avoid getting out. There are things I could be doing inside — I've got lots of rocks to examine — but I've thought about this a lot in the past few T-sectors, and I think we need to get out and try to get over the loss of the others. Lilea and I talked about this during last darktime, too, and she's right. I would hate to see you stay here and not get out at all. We've done a lot together, and we should still do some more. I'll need your help."

"That was Col's trip. What were you going to do? You can't use charges there."

"Right, I can't plant charges, just examine the terrain, take samples, make images and spectrographic recordings, all that. We should be gone only three lightimes, and spend two darktimes in the area. After that, you'll have plenty of time to do astronomy. How about it?"

Bent leaned forward and put his elbows on his knees. He looked directly at Jad, a look of almost pleading on his face.

An uncomfortable feeling welled up in Jad. He broke eye contact and looked down at the table between them. "I don't know. That's awfully rugged terrain up there. I'm not sure I'm ready to go on another trip yet. So much can happen."

"Sure, it's rugged terrain and a lot can happen, but I think it'd be worse if we just sat here and did nothing for the rest of the time we're here. We still have a mandate to explore this planet."

"I'm not . . ." Jad said, but paused when Wila began to slice some fruit. Jad glanced briefly in her direction, and then turned back to Bent. "I'm not planning to do nothing for the rest of the time. I can do a lot from the Astronomy Deck while I'm here. In fact, I'm behind in —"

"I realize that," Bent interrupted in a rush of words. He sat back in his chair, gesturing as he spoke. "But what I'm concerned about is the possibility that if we don't do something now, we may never get out of this ship again. The longer we wait the harder it'll be to get out. The Expedition Calendar is mostly useless now, and we need to get as much done as we can in the time we have left."

"Well, yeah." Bent's arguments had an effect on Jad. He had to admit that Bent was right, that with three members of the team dead and their contributions to the exploration irrevocably lost, major changes in the schedule would have to be made. Now could be a good time to make those changes. Someone should take the trip or the opportunity will be lost. But Jad still had reservations, and his hesitation came more from the danger of the trip, not the necessity for modifying the Calendar. A trip to the north-west would mean getting into an aerodyne and flying a long way, and landing, and exploring unfamiliar terrain, and there was always the potential of a crash landing and vicious animals and another quake or storm . . . *Who knows what could happen?*

It would be so nice, Jad decided, to be able to sit here and study the sun from the safety of this sturdy, stable landing ship. But if he did that, soon—quite soon—everyone would realize what he was doing, and he would look like a coward, afraid to face the world around him while the rest of the team was out doing important work. To Jad, that would be un-acceptable. But there was more than that.

Bent was the one who'd argued for setting the cutoff value so low, at just four team members remaining before returning. SpaceComm had called a meeting before the team left Anthanos to discuss what Case called a 'cutoff value.' The whole thing was Case's idea. He wanted a guideline on how many people should be out, either dead or unable to work, when they would quit what they were doing and return to *Star Voyager* before the end of their scheduled 500 T-sectors. SpaceComm refused to make the decision. They called the meeting and dropped it into the team's lap. A lot of proposals were thrown around—five out and five left, three out and seven left—but Bent argued for just four members remaining before an early return. Jad never liked setting the limit that low and he remembered being annoyed that it was the geologist—the guy he was supposed to be working with—who argued for that level. Yet, when it came time to vote, he voted for the low limit. He voted for it because everyone else did, and he didn't want to be seen going against the majority. He also remembered that Trea vocally opposed that level. She didn't seem worried about her image or her standing within the team and he admired her for that. She argued for a cutoff much higher, only two out and eight left, but in the end they voted her down, even pressured her to change her vote so they could tell SpaceComm the vote was unanimous. Now Bent was using some of the same arguments on Jad he'd used in the meeting when that topic was discussed, and Jad was stuck with what he believed was an unreasonably low level, and he had to go along.

At its most fundamental level, Jad didn't disagree with Bent's argu-ment that it was important for Anthanos to learn as much as possible about the Blue Planet before the team returned. After all, Anthanos was his planet too. It was his society and his people, and he owed it to them. And that made a difference to Jad.

"All right. I'll go, if Wila will go, too." Jad glanced over at Wila in the food-prep area. She stood near the sink, running vegetables through the digital slicer. She pressed a button on the top of the slicer and it buzzed and whirred, slicing the vegetable into thin slivers and slinging them onto a plate. She didn't answer immediately and she didn't look at Jad. She followed the vegetables with some fruit and watched as the slices spilled from the discharge chute onto the plate. For several nanosectors the only sound in the room was the whirring of the slicer and the faint *plip-plip-plip* as the slices hit the plate.

"I'll go if Lilea goes." She kept watching the slicer.

"Good. Lilea wants to go, too. I'll talk to Jer about it. We'll have to make an imaging run before we can find a landing site, but we can do that in a few T-sectors."

"All right," Jad said. "If you get one of the aerodynes ready, I'll go on an imaging run. That'll allow me to wrap up some of the planetary studies I started."

"Okay. That sounds good. I'm looking forward to it."

They made the imaging run on 461.195.

CHAPTER 45

NORTHWEST COAST

Time Element 461.201.5.2.

Aero Two faced north, resting on the smooth, soft sand of the back-shore about thirty links from the dark forest off the right wingtip. The waters had receded to almost their maximum, and a cool, crisp breeze drifted out of the northeast. A faint scent that Lilea didn't recognize—moist and aromatic—hung in the air.

They unloaded most of the supplies, including coolers and personal equipment, and set up the shelter in the shade of several enormous trees, placing it this time just outboard and behind the right wingtip. Bent and Jad made the security sweep of the beach and reported the area clear. Mina—who'd taken the one empty seat at the last millisector—grabbed some of her sampling bottles and sauntered out toward the ocean.

Lilea hiked north along the beach, paralleling the line where the forest met the sand. She wanted to make a detailed examination of the forest by walking in a short distance, perhaps several hundred links, but that would come later. First, she decided to examine the interface of the forest with the shoreline. She started by making broad, sweeping images of the beach and forest, capturing everything in wide-angle views with little or no close-up detail. Later she took close-up images of some of the native animal life, including many of the birds in the air and along the shore. Most of the land animals darted away before she could get a good picture, though. When she'd gone about 500 links up the beach, she turned right and headed toward a thicket of eight or ten trees.

Two slim, white-barked trees formed a natural doorway through the thicket into the forest, and she plunged immediately into near darkness. A sudden spasm choked her throat, and she steadied herself against one of the trees. But as her eyes adjusted to the dim light, she relaxed. With two or three more steps she'd entered a world so enormously different from anything she'd ever seen that at first she didn't know how to proceed. Green surrounded her. Leafy ground cover rose to her waist and even shoulder, and rough-barked trees towered above her. A strange scent invaded her nostrils, perfume like, yet pungent and sharp. Thin shafts of light pockmarked the ground deeper in the forest, the light reflected back to her as a brilliant yellow-green. Nothing on Anthanos could match this. She'd been into the forest surrounding Site One, but it was more open and airy, without the oppressive feeling. She took about ten cautious steps farther in and turned right, carefully keeping the ocean in view as she edged south through the shadowy glade. As she worked her way through the underbrush, picking apart the intertwining branches of the low trees and bushes, the leaves of different shapes and sizes made sharp whishing sounds as they brushed against the slickness of her jacket.

The terrain interested Lilea. The vegetation, the shore, the ocean — she tried to put it all together in her mind and imagine a human population living in this area of the continent. It seemed so logical and proper for an indigenous people to live in the forest with its lush production of vegetation for food, or perhaps to exist by obtaining subsistence from the sea, but she found no evidence of humans in this region.

As she walked, she became more comfortable in the wildwood. The surf to her right assured her of civilization only a few steps away, yet here she was, up to her waist in vegetation, darkly immersed in living plant life. So infinitely different from anything on Anthanos. Even the simulations of forested areas in the simulator buildings never approached the intensity of color and density of vegetation in this part of the continent. She scanned the ground for artifacts, she examined the trees for carvings or engravings, and she looked for trails in the area, but came up empty. She consoled herself with the thought that this is just a preliminary survey of the area.

I'll go farther in later. I'll see if I can talk Bent into going with me.

As she left the forest in the vicinity of the shelter, she found that Mina had returned, placing several small glass vials containing water samples in a carrying case. "The water's chilly," she said as she closed the case. "But it m-might make a refreshing swim. Anyone want to g go with me?"

"Sure," Wila and Lilea said, and changed into swimsuits and ran out to the beach.

Time Element 461.202.0.3.

All five of the Northwest Team sat outside the shelter enjoying their third meal of this lightime. Not a whisper of a breeze in the crisp, cool air ruffled the fabric of the shelter. The bright orange-red sun hovered about 30 degrees above the horizon, dancing over Aero Two's tail. A few high, thin clouds speckled the sky above the sun, and caught and scattered the oranges and pinks of the fading sunlight, shooting intense streaks of color across the western horizon. But more than the sunset, what occupied Lilea's interest now was the advancing edge of the water as it crept closer and closer to Aero Two's left skid.

"Why is the water coming up like that?" Lilea asked.

"The one moon of this planet," Jad replied.

"The moon? Get serious. How can the moon affect the water?"

"It's relatively large for a planet this size. It has a definite gravitational effect on the planet. Especially the oceans. It pulls on them, and they appear to rise. Those two puny pieces of rock that circle Anthanos aren't large enough to cause any effects like this, so we've never seen this. But we don't have the large oceans, either."

"How much farther will the water come?"

"Not much farther. I've made all the calculations and it shouldn't come much farther."

"You mean you *hope* not much farther."

"Whatever." Jad ignored Lilea's little quip and dug into a plate of *totsovos* — thin slices of the fruit of the totsos plant, steamed, then fried in a special wine-red fruit sauce which Mina had devised in her own kitchen. He seemed much more interested in piling food into his mouth than participating in a conversation.

The water continued to approach the ship and by around 202.0.5 it had advanced to within forty links of the left skid. But it came no farther and Lilea breathed a quiet sigh of relief.

When the sun had dropped to about 10 degrees above the horizon, Jad jumped up. "I'm going to take some images of the sun," he announced, and from Aero Two's cargo hold pulled his camera case — almost a small trunk — containing his spectrographic camera and all manner of paraphernalia, including a tripod. He walked to the front of the aerodyne and attached the camera to the tripod and fitted the lens with a funny-looking silvery filter. "The change in color of the sun as it descends through the atmosphere will tell us something about the composition, refraction and reflection of the dust particles," he explained. "The atmosphere on Anthanos is clean, but this atmosphere has a lot more suspended particulate matter." He peered through the camera's viewfinder and aimed it directly at the setting sun. As he tinkered with the camera, he kept up a constant chatter about the dust in the atmosphere, about particulate size and composition, reflectivity and refractivity, and so on. Lilea looked around at the others. Only Wila showed any interest in what he was doing.

Lilea leaned over and whispered to Bent, "How would you like to take a walk along the sand? Just the two of us?"

"Okay," Bent whispered back.

They had to slip behind Jad and his camera, but he didn't seem to notice—he was totally immersed in his little project. When they'd walked several hundred links south along the beach and were out of earshot of the others, Lilea whispered. "For someone who didn't want to leave the safety of *Explorer*, Jad seems to be enjoying himself."

"He's doing what he likes to do," Bent said. "He's a stargazer. He likes to visualize the sun. And this is a new sun for him to image. He's in his element."

Lilea enjoyed their little walk along the sandy beach, but they couldn't go far. The deepening crimson of the setting sun and the lengthening twilight shadows forced them to return three millisectors later. Jad was still imaging the last remnants of the sun, still pattering on to a bored Mina and a now somewhat less interested Wila about the dust in the air and the light from the sun. Someone had activated a lantern and set it on a small stool in front of the shelter. It produced a soft ring of light around the campsite as they admired the sunset.

Just enough to keep away the demons of the dark.

CHAPTER 46

EXPLORATION

Lilea woke earlier than usual this T-sector feeling unusually light and sunny, almost giddy, but she couldn't understand why. She felt warm too, as though she had a fever, and she went outside to cool off. But she put it out of her mind as she and Bent prepared for their trip into the wooded area behind the shelter. She viewed the walk as an opportunity to discover if intelligent species — her "humans" — lived in these woods, and that was far more important than any mild discomfort she might have.

Within about a hundred links of the beach, the heavy undergrowth thinned, and they found walking easy, almost a pleasure. She activated the compass in her PersComm and set a direct easterly course. After walking perhaps two hundred links farther, out of sight of the beach and out of earshot of the surf, Bent began marking the trees with the yellow markers.

Beyond those first three hundred links, the light from the beach faded and they were enveloped in a dim wildwood, the sunlight tempered by the broad canopy above. They passed huge trees, the trunks of which reached ten links or more in diameter. Other more slender trees also shaded their route, and curtain-like growths hung from branches higher in the trees. They flushed out several small animals as they walked, and Lilea snapped as many images as she could. She stopped occasionally to examine tiny flowers on the forest floor.

Too bad Col and Trea aren't here to see this. This is why they set up this expedition in the first place.

They came to a stream where the forest parted and let the sunlight sprinkle the ground. They crossed at a gravel bar that had formed at a bend in the creek. Bent took a few stones from the creek and slipped them one-by-one into small plastic bags which he dropped in his daypack. Then they continued on, plunging back into the dusky forest again.

Lilea usually led, looking for signs of intelligent life, but she had little luck. As she'd done before, she checked the trees for carvings or other expressions. Occasionally, she would run across a narrow trail. Invariably it would run only a short distance, and then fade away, and she would resume cutting her own route through the forest.

She checked the ground and she checked the banks of the stream, and she looked skyward for any sign of aerial displays. She found scat, but thought it was probably animal, and couldn't have come from any intelligent, upright beings like the ones she saw in the northern region. She assumed — even without any good reason for thinking so — that humans were not likely to drop directly on a trail. In her mind, that wouldn't be like them. Certainly, they would be considerably more circumspect about their waste.

Overall, she found nothing. She did find a small stick which, on first glance, looked as though it had been carved by an intelligent hand, but when she examined it more closely, she found no, it hadn't. It was just a natural twig from a tree, twisted during its short lifetime into an interesting and unique form. If she looked at it in just the right direction, it took on the likeness of an Anthanian figure. She decided to keep it as a souvenir of this expedition and slipped it into the pocket of her jacket.

She was disappointed, certainly, at not finding anything because she'd made such a big deal about it being so right for intelligent life to exist, even thrive, here. But she was in too good a mood to let disappointment spoil the hike. They turned and started to hike back to the campsite.

I would usually be a little upset at not finding something. But it's funny, I don't feel that bad. That's unusual for me.

Around 203.6.4, they stepped back onto the beach a few links north of the shelter.

Mina'd already started the second meal, water boiled on one burner of the stove. From a box of food supplies she pulled out a large flat pan, like a round griddle but with an edge about one decilink high, and set the pan on the other burner. Onto the pan she dropped *zlor*, a thick, flat, bread-like pancake seasoned with heavy aromatic Anthanian oils and spices. As the zlor-cake began to warm, Mina sliced and dropped onto the cake *lateania*, a round, green vegetable with a sharp, spicy odor. As the zlor popped and sizzled on the hot griddle, the peppery fragrances from the oils and the lateania drifted out around the campsite.

A cool breeze wafted in from the south, and as Lilea approached the campsite, the tangy aroma hit her like a tart punch to the nose. She took a deep breath and the feelings of euphoria seemed, thankfully, to ebb. The breeze dried her forehead and cooled her fever.

As soon as the food was ready, Mina sliced the zlor-cake into six parts, and she and the others grabbed a plate and began to eat.

"Col would have loved this area," Lilea said as they sat in a circle enjoying the meal. "When Bent and I entered the heaviest part of the forest, we felt so alone, so cut off from everything. It was almost surreal."

"This was really Col's trip," Bent said. "He planned it on Anthanos before we left because he knew from the probe images there would be a lot of vegetation to investigate. But now . . ." He shrugged his shoulders.

"That brings up something I've been thinking about," Wila said. "Without Dell and Col and Case, what's going to happen to this expedition? How is it going to affect the next one? What are they going to think if we go back and say the planet killed thirty percent of our group? Are they going to want to come back here?"

"I don't think they'll look at it like that," Lilea said. "I'm sure they'll be sympathetic to the fact that we couldn't do anything about them. The deaths, I mean."

"I still have my doubts. I can't help wondering if anyone would want to colonize a planet as dangerous as this one."

"Wila has a good point," Bent said. "They may have trouble getting people to volunteer for the second trip. Would you volunteer if you knew several people had been killed? If I weren't on this team, and the team came back and told us that three out of ten were killed, I'd have second thoughts about volunteering, too."

Lilea listened as Bent spoke, and a bit of uncertainty, even confusion, formed in her mind. She remembered the meeting when Bent argued so passionately for setting the low cutoff limit. It seemed so simple then—just wait for six people to be out, either dead or unable to work, and then return to Anthanos before the 500 T-sector limit. But now, was he questioning his decision? His last statement spun over and over in her mind. "Second thoughts?" What did he mean by that? It sounded as though his involvement with the deaths of Case and Col had led him to change his mind—or at least question his decision. Maybe he found it harder to deal with the deaths of three people on this expedition than he assumed from a comfortable seat in that plush conference room at SpaceComm Headquarters. *I certainly wouldn't be surprised if he did.*

"Maybe we shouldn't worry about it," Jad said. "It's not our problem. We've done the best we can." He plopped another bite of zlor-cake in his mouth and washed it down with a swig of jell-kell.

"I think the Assembly will be awfully hesitant to send another team here," Wila said. "After all, three people have been killed in only 200 T-sectors. One death I can accept, that's an accident. Two deaths is a tragedy. But three deaths — that's a pattern. I can't get it out of my head that someone or something is behind it all. Any exploring we do from now on may be unnecessary."

"Oh, no," Lilea blurted out. Wila's comments appalled her. "I don't think anything we do from now on is unnecessary. I think we need to find out as much as we can about this planet. I think the Assembly and the Science Council and SpaceComm will look at the whole picture and make a decision based on everything we've done. At least I hope they will."

"But what is there to look at? People are being killed on this planet. Why would anyone want to come here to live. It's a death trap."

"We may just have to accept the deaths as a price to be paid for living here. I bet we can learn to live here."

"I sure as hell don't want to live somewhere I could be killed in a split nanosector. Anthanos isn't like that. It's so warm and nourishing. It's damn cold here. I'm so ready to go home."

"I wonder if we'll *ever* find a planet just like Anthanos. We may have to pay a small price to live somewhere else. It's just that —"

"Small price!? Lilea, thirty percent isn't a —"

"Why don't we get going?" Jad said. He stood and stepped between Wila and Lilea and set his empty plate on the rock next to the stove. Then he finished off the last of the jell-kell in his cup and set it on the plate. "I want to go farther up the beach. I want to get some pictures of the large rocks that are isolated out in the water before we have to leave."

"You go on ahead," Bent said. "I'm going to get a look at the cliff that starts several hundred links north of here."

Time Element 461.203.7.1.

The cliff started about a quarter-anthan north of the campsite.

"It appears to be a discontinuity," Bent said when he and Lilea reached the first rocks in the sand that marked the beginning of the cliff. "It looks as though the rocks that form the cliff continue down into the ground, forming a fault line of some sort. I wish I had some charges and six or eight recorders, I could map the fault line. It would be interesting to see where this line of rock goes." He seemed to be mentally tracing the rock line as it disappeared into the earth, perhaps trying to image it in his mind as it descended deeply below the beach. He pulled his camera from his backpack and began snapping images of the rocks at the beginning of the cliff, then walked north to image the rocky escarpment as it rose higher and higher above the sand on which he stood.

Lilea relaxed near a large boulder partly buried in the sand, waiting for Bent to return. She took a number of images herself, of Bent as he examined the cliff line, and by pushing the camera's telephoto lens to 50X, of Jad, Wila, and Mina as they marched out of sight farther up the beach. She imaged the ocean and sky, took full-motion studies of the surf, and then turned around and snapped pictures of the forest. When she finished, she stood on the beach gazing out over the ocean. She took out her handkerchief and mopped her forehead.

"It's interesting," she said to Bent when he returned. "This is the largest body of water on the planet, and here we are standing on the edge of it. It looks so calm and peaceful."

A gentle breeze slid off the water, and Lilea closed her eyes and let it swirl through her hair, ruffling her curls like a light, stroking massage. After a few nanosectors, she looked north along the beach, but the others were mere bits of color, almost out of sight. She snapped one final image as they disappeared around a big boulder, three-quarters of an anthan away.

Her feelings of euphoria had moderated somewhat during lunch. She attributed that to the aroma of the spicy vegetables, but now those feelings returned. With their return, a new sensation had developed. She was having thoughts of sex, intense prurient thoughts, unusual for her, thoughts that rarely entered her mind unless Bent was making advances. The warmth returned too, perhaps a fever. Her vagina was wet, and her breasts throbbed with a sensuality she enjoyed only when they were well along in their lovemaking. A flush had developed on her arms, and she assumed her face and chest were flushed, too. But Bent hadn't said anything about sex since before the trip to the mountains when Col was killed. He certainly was in no frame of mind to make sexual overtures, and she accepted that. *He'll come around sooner or later, and I'll wait.* Yet the sexual feelings she had were real and intense, so unusual for her out here involved in prosaic scientific pursuits. Were these feelings a delayed reaction to the unusually long time since their last encounter?

Maybe they are. But we've gone this long before, and even longer. I've never had feelings this intense outside of lovemaking.

She turned and looked at Bent. He stopped imaging the rocks to watch her.

"What are you looking at?"

"Oh, nothing." She turned back to face the ocean. "It's just so peaceful here." For several nanosectors she watched the waves gently roll in over the sandy beach, savoring the cool breeze. It assuaged her fever and dried her perspiration. She turned back to face Bent. He had a sly grin on his face.

He set his camera on a small rock at the base of the boulder and walked over to her. "Your face is flushed. Do you have something in mind?" He put his arms around her and she wrapped her arms around his neck.

"Let's go over here," she said, motioning for him to come over behind the boulder. She pulled a waterproof covering from her daypack and spread it on the sand behind the rock. She glanced up the beach to check on the others—still out of sight. "Come on, let's do it. They won't be back for a while." She opened her jumpsuit. Her crimson breasts and abdomen pulsated as she began breathing heavily. She watched the fullness growing below his waist.

He knew exactly what to do. He took his jumpsuit off and she shed hers. He dropped his shorts and she stripped off her panties. She lay down on the poncho and he lay on top of her, penetrating her to the fullest depths imaginable. She wrapped her arms and legs around him, pulling him to her, locking him over her. They lay together for several millisectors, their passion and excitement swirling through and around and between them, taking her to a height of ecstasy she'd experienced only rarely before. It pleased her, it exhilarated her, it satisfied her. It relieved her fever and lessened the euphoria. She relaxed and Bent withdrew.

"I love you," he said.

"I love you," she said, and it was finished.

CHAPTER 47

NORTH RETURN

Time Element 461.205.11.4.

"It does take a load off my mind," Bent said. He and Lilea sat at the little table in the food-prep area of their compartment. The iridescent smell of baked *kielkus*—a light, fluffy pastry filled with vegetables in a smooth, velvety sauce—permeated the compartment, but Bent just picked at his food. "I will admit I was afraid I was next, or maybe Jad was."

"See? I knew you could do it." Lilea watched Bent carefully, concerned that he was not eating. Kielkus was a favorite of his, and he usually devoured it.

"It does make it a little easier now knowing that we did it. We actually went on a trip and came back alive without anything happening."

"I'll bet Jad is relieved, too." Bent just shrugged his shoulders. "You don't seem too convinced."

Bent didn't respond immediately. "A little."

"What do you mean?"

"We're less than half way through the exploration. We still have a lot of other trips to take. There's a lot of potential for something to happen." Bent's voice was cloudy and dark, his face somber. He put his fork down and pushed away from the table. He didn't rise, but stayed in his chair.

"Bent, stop it." Lilea reached over and put a hand on his arm. His hesitancy alarmed her. "You know I don't believe that."

"I know you don't, but I'm not sure I don't. There've been so many things happening. Not just the deaths, but other things—the storms—the animals—the accidents—things that would never happen on Anthanos."

"That's a part of life on this planet. We have to put up with it."

"It's like a monster. Just waiting to jump up and grab one of us. It's lurking just below the surface. And it seems to like men." He stood, but stayed beside the table, looking out the window. He appeared to be scanning the outside, looking for something. An underlying agitation seemed to be churning inside him but he held it in check, at least for the moment.

"Bent, there's no monster out there. The only monster is inside of you. You have to look inside to fight this monster. The only thing you have to be afraid of is inside you."

"But what's SpaceComm going to say about all the deaths?" His voice rose slightly. "Are we wasting our time going through the motions of studying this planet when it's not colonizable at all?" His hands and arms were tense and fidgety, his face strained.

"No, I don't think so. We talked about this on the beach. Remember?"

"I remember. But I also remember we didn't come to any conclusion."

"What do you mean?"

"I mean . . . I just mean, why don't we get our ass off this fuckin' planet? Maybe it's time to go home and look for another one." He turned and walked into the living area and sat on the couch. He picked up the remote control and ran through the main menu on the com screen, trying to find something to watch, probably, Lilea thought, to take his mind off the concern and anxiety at being one of only two men left on the Gold Team. He'd seemed so relaxed and easy on the beach that Lilea hoped he'd gotten over these difficulties, but that may have been due to the fact that, like Jad, he too was in his element, and he'd repressed the fact that three men had been killed. Now, in the comfort and safety of their compartment in *Explorer*, the apprehension returned.

Lilea didn't say anything right away. She tried to eat, but her appetite was rapidly disappearing. "You were so excited about coming to this planet when we landed. You couldn't wait to get to the gorge out there. You couldn't wait to go on the mountain trip. You still have lots of seismic charges to place. Where's all that excitement? Why don't you —"

"Mountains?" Bent exploded and Lilea gasped. "Every time I go into one of those mountains, somebody gets killed. And the gorge? I can't even get down into it — there's no fuckin' way down."

"You and Jad got down —"

"That was only about one tenth of the way down. Maybe less. I need to see what's at the bottom. Ever since Case was killed Jer told me not to even think about trying that again. I can't walk in, the walls are too close. And we didn't bring any boats."

"What about the charges? You've always said —"

"Those seismic charges aren't worth shit. I'm not getting any readings from them at all. They don't work here. They're too small. On Anthanos, the crust is solid. A seismic signal travels a long way. Here the crust is too damn heterogeneous. It fragments the signal, and without more re-corders, I can't get any systematic data." Bent's voice rose, almost to a shout. Even through his dark skin, Lilea could tell his face was flushed—she knew how to read his signs. "Don't talk to me about getting results on this damn planet. All I've got are a bunch of rocks in my bench up there." He flipped the remote control across the room. It rattled to the floor under the screen.

"Bent, please, don't. Those rocks have always been important to you. And all the chemical analysis. And the seismic data. You've got lots of seismic data. Maybe you can—"

"Maybe—*maybe*." Bent threw his arms in the air. "Maybe isn't good enough." He turned to face her. "I've got to get results, dammit, don't you understand? I've got to get *something*. Something I can work with, some-thing I can be proud of. I got lots better results at home. Or on the moons of Tekaa. I knew where every damn deposit of yttrium and scandium and all those damn lanthanides were on those moons. I could find them in my sleep. But here . . . " He retrieved the remote and shut down the com screen. But he kept staring at it, his face blank, his voice empty. "I hope I sleep better this darktime. I haven't slept well in several T-sectors."

"Didn't you sleep well in the shelter last darktime?"

He'd turned quieter. "No. I slept better than the darktime before, but I was still worried about the flight back."

"You could take a sleep injection."

"No. Don't need to. Don't like to."

"Okay."

Bent did seem to sleep soundly this darktime. When Lilea awoke around 204.8 and glanced at the time display beside the bed, Bent lay still beside her, breathing heavily, a good sign he was asleep. He woke in a better mood, too, and after a good first meal he ascended to Geo to begin a detailed examination of the fifty or so specimens he brought back from the northwest coast. Getting back into his element . . .

Lilea slept better too. The unexplained euphoria and sexual feelings had begun to dissipate during the three subsector flight home from the beach, and they continued to fade after arrival. When she rose early on 207, she felt normal—well, near normal—but still upbeat about the trip. The lack of any signs of intelligent life in the forest near the beach still didn't bother her, she continued to take it as an indication the "humans" hadn't migrated that far south.

Time Element 461.209.0.0.

Lilea sat at the table in the food-prep area of her compartment, revisiting the images in her camera of her trip to the northern plains. She interfaced her camera with her notebook, scanning the images on the larger screen. She downloaded all the info from Aero One's computer which showed the terrain in the vicinity of the village, and she paid meticulous attention to the area west of the village where she planned to land. It was flat and obstruction free, and that fact more than anything was what made this expedition possible. But there were several difficulties with that scenario.

Land next to the village? And just walk up and say hello? Well, no, that won't work.

Lilea desperately wanted to meet these people, but a face-to-face meeting raised its own special dangers. She and her party — Jer would never allow her to go alone — would be armed, of course, and they could probably shoot their way out of any danger, but was that a sincere way to introduce yourself to a new race? That offended her sensitivity toward them, and she wanted nothing to do with that.

Then there was the problem of communication. How would she communicate with them? Hand signals? Don't be ridiculous — that would never work.

She returned to the problem of landing. If she landed from the west, the village and the hills farther east would block her takeoff — and possible escape route. She considered landing from the east, passing over the hills and the village. But that would put the aerodyne a long way from the village, and she would pass directly over the village at a low altitude, and the noise, the terrible screaming of the engine, might frighten the humans. They might scatter or barricade themselves in their village, or even attack. No, she would have to land from the west. Quieter, certainly, but still problematic.

The more she thought about the flight, the closer she came to an alternative.

"Didn't SpaceComm tell you not to approach any of these 'humans' of yours, just observe them?" Jer asked around 209.8, when Lilea presented her plan for the northern return flight. They sat on the Life Sciences Deck at the center table.

"Not in so many words. They didn't say I *couldn't*. They just wanted me to stay a 'reasonable' distance from them. They didn't say what 'reasonable' was, they left the final decision to me."

"I think you ought to respect SpaceComm's wishes and stay away from them, unless you can't avoid it. Leave a clear path to retreat." Jer flipped through the description of the flight plan on the screen of Lilea's notebook. She took her time, carefully going over all details of the trip. Her face betrayed little emotion as she scanned the various pages.

It was to be a brief flight, up and back in one lightime.

"I'm concerned about safety more than anything. This could be dangerous. You don't know much about these humans. You know they carry spears, so they can be dangerous. There's a real potential for disaster here, and with the deaths we've had, I don't want to send someone into a chancy situation without good reason."

"I'm concerned about safety too. But we'll be wearing weapons, and we've got the aerodyne to retreat to if they start to become belligerent. Since all I plan to do is land at the site I landed at before, and observe them from the top of the hills south of their village, there's less likelihood I'll be seen or get caught."

"All right. Take at least two others with you and don't stray too far from your plan."

"Okay." Lilea's heart jumped at Jer's approval. "Why don't you go with us? It'll get you out of the ship for a while."

"I don't think so. I've got too much to do." Jer pushed the notebook back to Lilea. "What'll you do if the village isn't there anymore?"

Not there anymore? The question jolted Lilea. She hadn't considered any alternative to the flight, and had she, *that* alternative would have been the last thing to enter her mind. Her planning had been based on the assumption the village would still be there. But there was a fair chance the village might not exist now, almost a hundred T-sectors later. A nomadic people could easily have moved on by the time she arrived.

Lilea mulled over the question in her mind. Come home without landing? Try to find another village? Land and examine the site of the village anyway? To her, only the third alternative was acceptable. Coming home without landing would be giving up. Trying to find another village would be too time consuming and would use precious liquid hydrogen fuel. Landing and investigating the site of the village would at least give her the opportunity to collect specimens of human life, perhaps small discarded pieces of pottery, tools, or hunting instruments.

"I'll still land and investigate the site."

"Okay. Be sure to wear your weapons."

CHAPTER 48

VILLAGE WHITE

Time Element 461.213.0.2.

"What is that white stuff?" Lilea glanced down from the pilot's seat in Aero One as it headed north toward the village. "Where'd it come from?"

From an altitude of two anthans, the surface had taken on a mottled appearance. Large areas of brilliant white, interspersed with meager, irregular pockets of grayish-brown soil covered the terrain in almost every direction.

"I assume it came from the clouds, like the water," Wila replied from the second row of seats. "Like Seth said. That's the only place it could have come from."

"Are you saying, like, like, f-frozen water?" Mina asked.

"Sort of."

"You pulled down images from the probe before we left," Bent said. He sat beside Lilea in the front seats, but turned to talk to Wila behind him. "Didn't they show the white?"

"No," Wila replied. "We only looked for cloud cover. There's clouds coming in from the west, but we've got clear sky for most of this lightime."

The team flew in silence for another subsector, carefully examining the terrain below as they flew. Around 213.2, the valley of the village came into view.

"There it is," Lilea said. "I recognize the two rows of hills."

Lilea made one imaging pass over the valley at two anthans and brought up a close-up image of the village site on the main com screen. She and Bent examined it carefully, and Mina and Wila leaned forward and squinted at the screen from between the two front seats. The brilliant white valley floor, smooth and uninterrupted, glistened in the late morning sun.

"Where's the village?" Bent asked.

"I don't know. Let's go down for a closer look."

Lilea circled down to one anthan and throttled back to **CRUISE SLOW**. She trimmed the wings and made a leisurely pass down the valley, scanning it intently, looking for any sign of the village. She flew the full length of the valley, but no group of huts came into sight.

Damn. The village should be there. Where is it?

"We should be able to see it," Lilea said. She called up on the main computer screen the image she'd taken on her previous trip. She checked the landmarks in the image—the trail going over the two hills, a tall peak farther north, a lone tree on a hill that marked the eastern end of the valley—and correlated them with the landmarks beneath her craft now. "Everything's here," she said. "The landmarks check out. We're in the right place."

"But there's no village," Bent said.

"Th-they're gone. They've moved on."

Frustration gurgled up in her throat, but Lilea remained quiet. She wanted to avoid looking discouraged in front of the others, but the irritation and disappointment she'd experienced when she bashed her Pers-Comm against the rocks returned, and she wanted to throw her hands in the air and scream, "Why did you have to pick this time to move on?" But expressing her frustration in front of everyone else in the aerodyne—*certainly not*—that would be embarrassing and totally unacceptable. She shook her head almost imperceptibly, and went back to piloting the aerodyne.

"Well," she said after she calmed down, "let's examine the area anyway." She swung Aero One back around to the western end of the valley and made another pass, this time at 1000 links.

White covered the entire area creating a smooth blanket over the valley floor and the hills on both sides. It draped the huge tree at the eastern end, turning it dappled green and white, looking for all the world like a huge candle that might provide illumination to the entire valley. Patchy whiteness covered the tops of the rocks and boulders on the hillsides.

I'll bet that white stuff isn't too thick. Like, maybe, only one or two decilinks. I'll bet I can land it.

She made another right bank to swing back to the western end of the valley. "I'm going to take it in."

"What?" Bent said. "You're going to land on this?"

"Hold on." Wila leaned forward, sticking her head between the front seats. "You don't know how deep that stuff is."

"It doesn't look that deep. I bet it's only a few decilinks deep."

"I don't think so," Bent said. "You don't know anything about it."

"Why don't you measure the stuff with the nose instruments?" Wila said. "That'll give you the depth and composition and temperature."

Oh, yes, I could do that. Lilea pressed a few markers on the aerodyne's main com screen and made a second pass over the valley at 500 links, barely grazing the top of the tree at the end of the valley. She banked right again and brought Aero One back around to the western end.

Lilea read the results from the com screen. "The interferometer says it's around one link deep on the valley floor, but there are places where it's up to two links. The thermographic imager says it's minus twenty-two Tal. It's cold, but not too deep."

"What does the s-spectrographic imager say?"

"Pure water."

Wila leaned forward from her seat in the rear of the ship and looked at the numbers on the screen. "I notice the interferometer shows it's real porous. It's not solid, like ice. Like it's light and fluffy."

"Do you think I can land on it?"

Wila paused. "I think so." But there was a trace of doubt in her voice. "I think the ship will drop down through it and hit the ground below it."

"Okay, here we go."

Time Element 461.213.4.1.

Aero One rested in a flat plain. To the south and east, hills of two to three hundred links high, and on the north, a small mountain of several thousand links enclosed the plain in a U-shaped basin, open only to the west. The big, lone tree stood straight ahead, looming over the valley. A blanket of white covered everything, including the abundant trees on the hills to the north. From the pilot's seat Lilea could make out the trail as a mild depression in the whiteness as it meandered over the southern hills into the village area.

While Lilea and Wila went through the post-landing check, Mina and Bent, conscious of the outside temperature of 22 Tal, displayed in bright flashing yellow digits on the com screen, opened their backpacks and pulled out heavy clothing, including jackets, hats, gloves and boots. And when the checklist was complete, all four dropped to the ground into the above-ankle-deep whiteness. Lilea gasped when the bitterly cold air hit her face. She watched her breath condense into swirling white clouds as she squatted to sample the white powder near the ship. It slipped easily between the thick fingers of her gloved hand. Toward the rear of the aerodyne, the parallel tracks the skids made during landing stood out prominently in the white. Underneath the ship, the heat from the engine had melted some of the white stuff, and the water trickled over the dark, exposed earth in tiny, sinuous rivulets.

Now Lilea began her examination of the abandoned village. From her pack, she pulled out an image of the east end of the valley and shuffled through the white powder to the village's approximate position. The computer had inscribed triangulation marks on the image and she took intermittent readings with her theodolite until the readings matched those on the image.

Now I should be in the center of the village.

But almost nothing remained of the dwellings. A few pieces of wood covered with white lay scattered on the ground throughout the area, and several poles, stuck in the ground at odd angles, jutted from the cover in various places. She assumed the poles were structural members of the huts, but without a thorough examination of the area when there was no impeding blanket, she couldn't be sure.

She squatted and brushed some of the white from the ground around one of the upright poles, and came across a few pieces of bone. These could give her some of the genetic material she was looking for to examine her humans.

But what kind of bone are these? From some of the animals we see all the time on this planet? Or could they be from 'humans'? I'll sort them out later.

She put the bones in a plastic bag and stuffed the bag in a pocket of her jacket.

From the high-definition images of the village, she'd measured the diameter of the huts at twenty to twenty-four links. By triangulation, she estimated the center of one hut, and stepped off twelve links, which should take her to the edge. A few more steps and she was back near the center of the village. She brushed away more white. Many odd pieces of wood lay on the ground, some blackened by fire.

Sweeping away more white, she came to an area of dark earth about five links in diameter which she took to be a fire ring, perhaps the central cooking area of the village. She picked up several more artifacts, small pieces of bone and slivers of wood, and stashed them in several more bags.

But there was just too much of the white material, and it was too cold and too deep to work in for long. After a subsector of squatting or kneeling in the subzero temperatures, sweeping the white away with the small broom in her sampling kit, and carefully foraging for exquisite, delicate items, she was exhausted. She frequently had to remove her glove to pick up the tiniest pieces, and the fingertips on her right hand had grown numb. Her legs were cramped and stiff from squatting for so long. She stood at the edge of the village and surveyed the work she'd done. Though she missed the humans, she'd put in a good T-sector's work, entirely worth the flight up here. She concentrated so hard on her work she didn't hear the voice behind her.

"Lilea."

Lilea slipped her pack from her back and pulled out her camera. She decided to image the site, to record it and the work she'd done.

The voice came again. "Lilea." This time she turned. Wila stood behind her, a vision aid hanging at her neck.

"There are clouds coming in from the west." Wila pointed. "We need to get out of here."

Lilea looked toward the west and north where heavy dark clouds dominated the horizon. She looked at her time recorder—213.5.4—near midpoint of this lightime.

Several options went through her mind. *If we stay, we can set up the shelter, and there'll be plenty of power for the fans and heaters. But the temperature will go down, maybe as far as 25 or 30 below zero, maybe even lower. That's not too cold for the sleeping bags and heaters to provide enough warmth. But what about those clouds?* She looked back at the sky. Heavy clouds, threatening and dark, draped the western horizon. Though the sun lingered about thirty degrees above the clouds, it soon would be engulfed and the temperature would quickly go down.

"We need to get out of here." Wila's voice cracked and it had a distinct edge on it, as though she was giving an order. She kept looking at the hills surrounding the basin, her face white and tense. "Now."

"Are those clouds going to bring more of it?"

"I don't know, but I wouldn't be surprised if they do. I think it's entirely conceivable that if we get too much more of this stuff, it may keep us from taking off. Besides"—and Wila lowered her voice—"we're being watched. There's someone out there. I know it. I feel it. This place scares me. We need to leave."

Wila didn't point to any particular place from where she thought someone might be watching, but Lilea scanned the hills around the landing site anyway. She didn't see anything or anyone, and she didn't feel she was being watched, but she'd been so engrossed in her work on the remains of the village that almost anything could have happened and she might not have been aware of it. She certainly wasn't interested in humoring Wila, either. Wila's solid ability to read the weather impressed her, and she took seriously her word about the possibility of new white cover. She made up her mind to leave this inhospitable place much more because of the weather than Wila's feelings. She didn't want to be stranded here.

"Okay," Lilea said, "let's get out of here. We'll have to turn the ship around. Tell Bent to use the jacking wheels. The ground is hard enough under this white cover. I'm going to take a few images of the area."

Bent pulled the four jacking wheel units from the cargo hold and attached one pair to each skid. With a pumping motion on a hydraulic arm on one side of each jack, he lowered the wheels, raising the skids about three decilinks, just enough to clear the ground. With two people pushing hard on each wing tip, gaining leverage from the long slender wings, they rotated the ship in place. When it was lined up with the projected takeoff run, they raised the jacking wheels and dumped them in the cargo hold.

CHAPTER 49

RETURN

Time Element 461.213.6.5.

By the time Aero One left the ground, the sun had been almost fully engulfed by the clouds and the air temperature had begun to drop. From the pilot's seat, Lilea watched as small, white specks hit the windshield, melting immediately. She pointed them out to the others.

"Little flakes of frozen water," Wila said. "I wish I could collect several of them."

"They've made those in the lab at home," Bent said. "But I don't think anyone ever thought they could occur naturally. They sure as hell would never occur naturally on Anthanos."

"That's one thing I like about Anthanos." Lilea couldn't see Wila sitting behind her, but Wila's voice had a rambling nostalgic air about it, and she talked slowly and wistfully. "The Lifezone is always nice and warm. This planet is so damned inconsistent and changeable, but Anthanos is nice and stable. You always know what the weather's going to be. Here, you can't tell what's going to happen from one T-sector to another. You actually have to look out*side* to see what the weather is. You can go from having a bright, clear blue sky, to having clouds and water coming out of them, to high winds, then back to clear sky, all in about one subsector. I still haven't gotten used to that and I don't know if I ever will. And this alternating from light to dark and back again is getting me down. I'm getting so I hate it. I'm ready to get back to Anthanos where things are more predictable."

Wila seemed to prattle on forever, but Lilea tuned her out. She was too excited to care. Inside, Lilea was exhilarated, flying much higher than the craft she was piloting. Her heart pounded and she could barely sit still. She was so preoccupied in reviewing the evidence she'd just collected—especially the trinkets and artifacts that told her so much about the inhabitants of the village—that she missed one visual checkpoint along the route and almost missed a second. But she remained calm enough to fly the aerodyne home following a vector provided by Jer, and she put the expedition aside long enough to put Aero One down on the landing strip at Site One at 213.9.7.

"Come over about 214.0, and we'll have a little celebration," Lilea told everyone as they rode up in the elevator. "Tell Jer and Jad. And Trea, too, if she wants to come."

"I can't believe it," she blurted to Bent after they'd closed door to their compartment. "I actually got to see the village! This is so great! Now I can go home and tell everyone I examined a village of humans. I actually got to do what I came here to do."

"That's good," Bent said. "I'm glad you did."

The euphoria was back, but this time she could see a reason for it. And with the euphoria came another familiar feeling.

"Those weren't the best conditions, though," Bent went on. "All that white . . ."

"Well, yeah. I would've liked it better if that stuff wasn't covering everything, but at least I got to collect some artifacts. All those pieces I picked up, and the spearhead I got will make a nice collection for the museum at home. This is so damn fantastic!" She paused for a few nanosectors, walking around the compartment, unable to settle down. Bent stood at the bedroom door, watching her, but only just barely. He seemed preoccupied.

"Speaking of fantastic . . ." She went over to him and curled her arms around his waist, a coy smile on her face.

"Again?" Bent unwrapped her arms and pushed her away.

"Bent . . . what?"

"You've been so damn horny lately. If I didn't know better, I'd say you were entering your fertile period. But you couldn't be. You took the anti-pregnancy vaccine before we left, and the booster before we left *Star Voyager*. You shouldn't be having a fertile period. That booster's supposed to last a year, isn't it?" He turned and entered the bedroom.

"Yeah, but it just prevents pregnancy." She followed him. "It doesn't stop me from having sex. When everyone leaves after the party . . . how about it?" He didn't reply. "Bent?" "What . . . ?"

"No. Don't feel like it."

Time Element 461.214.6.0.

Lilea stayed awake for at least a subsector after retiring, staring at the little red light over the bed. She insisted SpaceComm change the light from yellow to red because it reminded her of sleeping in her bedroom on

Anthanos. But it wasn't the demons of the dark that kept her awake. The sweet, penetrating odor of the khus-jell had swept through their compartment during the little party, and it lingered a short time until the ventilation system swept it away. But it was something more than just the odor that prevented her falling asleep.

Everyone came to her party—Jad and Wila, Jer, Mina, everyone except Trea—stopping in for at least a few millisectors to congratulate her and admire the artifacts she'd found. She even brought the spearhead down from her workstation and displayed all the items on the table in front of the couch so everyone could see them. Among those who came by there was an unspoken realization that her discovery of humans in the north—first the images, now the solid evidence—was a real accomplishment and it justified her place on the team. She wasn't just Bent's wife anymore. She was a real contributing member of the team.

But the hubris in her chest wasn't what kept her awake either. It was the fact that Bent drank so much of the khus-jell. That was something he rarely did, and it bothered her. She couldn't remember him drinking that much. He drank small amounts of wine sometimes, during meals or afterward, or before bed (he preferred the *dhus*-wine, fermented, not distilled, from a winery in Sabean), but never as much as he drank this time. He didn't get drunk—after all, the khus-jell was in short supply because Col had brought only a few bottles in his personal luggage, and that was the funny part because Jad brought it over and she wondered where he got it. Trea didn't come, and Jad didn't drink—his healthy, exercise-intense lifestyle would never permit it—and it kept her awake until 214.8 just thinking about it.

CHAPTER 50

COLLISION

Time Element 461.221.2.2.

Jad sat in the front right-hand seat as Aero Two roared off the runway at Site One. Lilea and Wila sat in the two middle seats, chatting between themselves. He tuned them out and started scanning the surface below for emergency landing sites.

Bent was headed for Recorder 2, installed on a large rocky plateau — a treeless island in the midst of the forest north of Site One — overlooking a prominent river. Finding a place to land in the vicinity of Recorder 2 would not be difficult. Bent took Aero Two beyond the site, looking for a landing site a hundred anthans away, but the terrain, heavily forested and forbidding, white-capped and ominous, was devoid of any place to land at all.

Bent made several passes over the mountains at four anthans. "There's not much here," he said. "Let's go south."

They passed over another river, and several potential sites appeared within the forest beneath them. Like the plateau on which Recorder 2 had been installed, these were also flat-topped, largely barren but covered to various degrees with scrub vegetation, sitting well above the forest like tan jewels jutting up from the green vegetation around. Bent picked one, circled, and then made a west-to-east pass at 500 links.

"We should be grateful these flat areas are present all over this part of this continent," he said as he began his landing run. "They make good landing sites. Chest restraints."

From an altitude of 500 links, the landing site Bent picked appeared free of vegetation and large rocks, but when the ship touched down, the rocks seemed to burst out of the ground, throwing themselves in front of the aerodyne's skids. He brought the ship in from the southwest, and it jolted, jarred and jerked over the surface for almost a thousand links. Jad subconsciously reached up and checked the latch on his chest restraint buckle.

I hope the skids don't get damaged.

As the aerodyne skidded along, the rocks largely disappeared. But as the ship slowed slightly, the right skid slammed headlong into a large rock. Bent had already shut the engine down so the cabin was quiet, and the skid didn't make much noise when it struck, just a mild 'thunk', but the collision threw the skid several links into the air. The nose and right wing shot upward, jostling everyone against their seat belts and chest restraints. "Look out!" Jad yelled. The ship took a sharp jerk to the right and came to an abrupt stop. The left wingtip dipped so low it grazed the ground. The aerodyne held that position for a split-nanosector before it righted itself, and the right skid came down hard, smashing into the rock with a loud *whack*.

"My god, what the hell was that?" Jad opened the door beside him and looked down. The skid sat on a large, flat-topped rock slightly aft of its midpoint, raising it off the ground about a link. While Bent shut the engine down and ran through the checklist, the others jumped out. They gathered on the ship's right side, staring at the skid.

"Should we push the ship off the rock before we start exploring the area?" Lilea asked.

No one answered.

Wila knelt before the skid, running her hand over its upper and lower surfaces. She examined the forward and aft suspension struts, and pulled and tugged at the skid, but it didn't move. "It doesn't seem to be damaged. I can't find any cracks or fractures. This skid is almost pure titanium. It's strong enough to take almost anything." She pounded on the skid with her fist as though that was supposed to prove its hardiness.

"What worries me," Jad said, "is there may be damage to the suspension system up inside, where the strut is attached to the retraction arm." He knelt and crawled under the ship, poking his head into the retraction well. He waited a few nanosectors for his eyes to accommodate, but there was still too little light to see well. "Too dark. I can't tell anything."

"I'll get one of the lamps," Lilea said.

"No, wait. Leave it. We don't need to do anything now." Bent's voice was strident, almost harsh. He waved his hand in front of his chest in an obvious 'no-no-no' gesture while he spoke. "The engine'll push the ship off the rock. We can do that when we get ready to leave. In the meantime, we need to set the charge." He turned and walked around the rear of the ship, headed for the cargo door on the other side.

Lilea screwed up her face and mouthed the word, "What?" and went after him. "Bent . . . wait."

Jad shook his head. *What is Bent up to? Yes, I guess it won't hurt to leave the ship like this, but . . . shouldn't we . . . anyway?* In spite of his hesitancy and vague unease at Bent's attitude, he went to help Bent remove the drilling tower.

They carried the drilling equipment several hundred links north and began to drill, but the maddeningly rocky surface forced them to try three different locations before they could get a hole the full twelve links without running into rocks that stymied the drill. Bent placed a charge and connected it to his portable notebook and ignited it as he'd done before. Again, Jad felt the recognizable thud of explosion, and again he watched as the blast of debris discharged from the hole, showering everyone with dust, dirt, and stones. A couple of sparks landed on his jumpsuit, but he brushed them off before they could burn.

"Wow!" Lilea said as Bent plopped the drilling equipment in the cargo hold. "You told me how powerful those little charges are, but I didn't really believe it until now." She bent over to shake the dirt from her hair.

"That's the idea. But it's getting late. It's already 221.9.4. We should set up the shelter and spend the darktime here."

They erected the shelter at the usual spot, though the left wing tip now sat only about five links off the ground, instead of the usual eight.

As the darkness engulfed the camp after the third meal, a chilly northwest breeze swirled around the camp site. Wila slipped a hand under Jad's arm and rested her head on his shoulder. Lilea donned her jacket and watched as Bent retrieved the information from the Geo computer at *Explorer*.

"Hey!" he exclaimed, and a broad grin crossed his face. "I got something." Lilea leaned over to glance at the screen and Jad came around from the other side. "It's not insignificant, either."

It wasn't. A tall, spiky peak less than a nanosector after the charged ignited, it faded away in an irregular descending sawtooth wave, falling back to zero in a few nanosectors. "Incredible!" Bent said. "We'll try farther south next lightime." He entered commands into the notebook and brought up equations and discriminators, he ran the peak through data processors and system integrators, and plotted points on a graph. After a subsector, he closed the notebook and entered the shelter.

By 222.3, when the temperature dropped to 10 Tal, Lilea and Wila decided to retire.

Jad followed Wila into the airlock, and as he zipped the airlock door behind him because he was the last to enter, Wila whispered to him, "Did you contact Jer and bring her up to date?"

"No. Bent did when he pulled down the tracing. Over a subsector ago."

"Did he tell her about the aerodyne striking a rock?"

Jad shook his head. "I don't think so."

Time Element 461.223.1.0.

The next lightime dawned sunny and cool. The temperature was 2 Tal when Wila rose and started water boiling for the first meal. Jad came outside two millisectors later. He'd had a restful darktime's sleep, and was anxious to get going, looking forward to the next flight and hike. *Let's see . . . Bent wants to fly south from this site and land and . . . hold on a microsector. Land? Will the aerodyne be able to land?* He stepped around the shelter and looked at Aero Two, still sitting canted on the rock. But he couldn't do anything about it right now, and he returned to the front of the shelter where Wila was preparing lumyon.

At 223.2, Jad removed a high intensity lamp from the tool kit in the cargo hold and focused it up inside the skid well. "I don't see any damage to either the skid or the suspension system," he said to Bent who joined him standing nearby. "But that doesn't mean there isn't any. I'm concerned the skid might not retract normally. There may be damage to a strut or re-traction arm. Once we get back to Site One we can take off the access panels and—"

"Let's get it off the rock, first," Bent said. "Then we can make a decision."

Decision about what? The decision is already made—the regs say a dam-aged ship goes back to base. You don't question it. You don't have to "make" a decision. Jad started to say something but Bent climbed into the pilot's seat, closed the door, and started the engine. Slowly the ship began to move, the right skid grinding and grating as it inched its way across the rock. But the left skid slipped more easily across the sandy surface beside the rock and that skewed the ship about ten degrees to the right by the time the skid dropped off. Bent shut the engine down and came around to the others.

"What do you think we should do?" Lilea asked.

Bent didn't answer immediately. He stared at the skid, apparently considering his next move. "It looks okay. I think we should try it."

"Are you going back to Site One?"

Bent shook his head. "If skid retraction is okay, then I think we can trust it."

"But there could be damage in there. Inside, where you can't see it."

"I don't think so. If there's damage, retraction won't go. We weren't going fast enough to damage anything. I'll bet it's safe. Even Jad didn't see anything—he said so."

"Hold on, all I said was that I couldn't see anything because it was dark—"

Bent didn't bother to listen to Jad, he just continued talking. "Those struts and retraction arms are heavy duty. They were made that way just for this expedition." He turned to Wila. "Isn't that right?"

"Uh, yes, they are heavy duty . . . but there's still a limit to how much they—"

"Doesn't matter. Hitting that rock wouldn't have damaged them that much. They can take a whack like that. There's probably nothing wrong. Let's get loaded and try it."

What the hell do you think you're doing? There could be damage in there, in the dark where you can't see it. Are you going to fly this ship—possibly damaged, with us in it, too? What in the name of the Great God Arteamos . . . It wasn't the collision with the rock in the first place that worries me, it's when it came down hard on top of the rock—that could have damaged something inside . . .

But no one said anything more and Jad joined the others loading the ship, and then boarded. But when Lilea climbed into the front right-hand seat, she had a funny look on her face, sort of a grimace, perhaps an expression of puzzlement. Bent restarted the engine and the ship jumped into the air. When he ordered skid retraction at two hundred links, everything seemed normal.

"There! See, I told you," Bent said. He made a point of tapping the little in-motion display on the com screen of the skids entering the retraction wells. "We should be okay."

Jad watched it too, leaning forward from the left center seat to get a good look at the screen. *There still could be some damage. You really ought to go back to Site One.* But he didn't say anything. Not a good idea to criticize the leader of your little exploratory team, especially in front of the others.

As Jad looked up from the screen, he saw Lilea turn and glare at Bent. An angry look flashed in her eyes, and she crossed her arms tightly over her chest. Jad settled back in his seat to enjoy the flight.

Next stop? Who knows?

CHAPTER 51

LEAVES

Time Element 461.223.2.8.

As Bent took the aerodyne south, Jad's mind wandered from Bent's decision and turned to watching the terrain below. The pattern of plateaus poking up here and there above the forest began to dissolve and the terrain took on the unbroken forested appearance they were so familiar with. They passed over a prominent white-water river in a curved, tortuous channel near where the forest thinned out, and a good landing site appeared on a plateau nearby. Bent circled twice.

The site lay at the southern edge of the forest, and, like the region they'd just left, covered with many small to mid-sized rocks, each primed to do its utmost to frustrate an aerodyne landing.

"What do you think?" Bent asked. "Want to try it?"

"I haven't seen much else," Wila said. "This region is either too heavy with vegetation or it's too rocky. I would go ahead."

"Are you sure you want to do this?" Lilea said. "What about the retraction system? Do you think it'll hold? Shouldn't we go back to Site One? The runway there is smooth. If you hit another rock . . ."

Bent shook his head. "It'll be okay. There's nothing wrong."

Lilea shook her head, a sullen look still on her face. Her eyes narrowed into daggers of pain and displeasure. She took a deep breath and let it out, and seemed to tighten her grip on her camera. Then she turned and looked out the right side window, apparently to scan the ground as Space-Comm required. She kept her camera cradled securely in her lap.

Bent made another slow pass over the site at 200 links and went around for a landing from the south. He lowered the skids—still normal—and set the ship down lightly on the dusty surface.

"What'd I tell you?" he said when the ship came to a stop. But Lilea didn't say anything. She jumped out.

Time Element 461.223.5.6.

"Good landing," Jad muttered as he opened the door to his left and dropped to the ground. He walked around to the right side of the aero-dyne and looked at the skid. It still seemed normal. The ship wasn't canted to one side like it might be if something were broken inside, and the retraction arm was fully extended. He reached into the retraction well and ran his hands over the suspension struts as well as he could in the cramped well, but he didn't feel anything unusual. He wouldn't be able to determine if anything had been damaged until they got back to Site One where he could take the access panels off and get a good look at the entire retraction mechanism. He stood up and perused the landing site.

Aero Two rested on a bluff overlooking the river to the west. Many of the plants growing in this area were similar to those around Site One, and he half-expected to turn around and see *Explorer* in the distance. To the east, about a thousand links away, the forest started at the bottom of a gentle slope, running upward toward a broad ridge in the distance.

The bluff was flat and wide open and Jad could understand why Bent chose this site. He pulled his vision aid from the aerodyne's cabin and walked west. After a few hundred links, he came to the edge of the bluff where it dropped almost vertically into a broad canyon. Coursing through the center of the canyon was the river, a white, churning, frothy mix. Beyond the river lay another plateau, it too as flat as a zlor cake, shimmering with mirage on top. His vision aid computed the distance across to the bluff on the other side at more than two anthans.

He examined the far plateau with its panoply of earth colors—reds and tans, umbers and blacks, grays and greens. He ran the magnification to 100 and scanned the top. Several animals grazed on the meager vegetation, and some seemed to be staring at him.

He lowered his vision aid and looked around at the plateau on which he stood. Lilea and Bent were retrieving their backpacks from Aero Two's cargo hold, and Wila walked toward him, holding her camera.

"Magnificent terrain," she said. Jad grunted a vague acknowledge-ment and returned to surveying the land. Despite the incident with the rock, Jad's mood had risen. He more and more appreciated this planet and its varied landscape. He liked it more than any of the moons of the outer planets in his solar system, most of which he'd visited at least once. This planet was so varied, so fascinating, and so interesting, and he didn't have to wear a bulky pressure suit to walk around on it. It had a stable sun that was so appealing to examine. But it had its drawbacks too, dangers that could rise up and strike down a visitor with no warning whatsoever, even rocks that seemed magically to rise out of the ground and throw themselves in front of an aerodyne's landing skid and send it careening off in a different direction. Rocks like that didn't exist on Anthanos because its terrain was little more than a smooth sandy surface and it always presented a good landing site.

But mixed with his admiration for the planet was a hesitation, an anxiety, a vague fearfulness which he couldn't ascribe to any one factor — not to any incident or death in particular. He feared more for *Explorer* and the people he was with, and for the expedition itself. That was how he felt after the death of Col, but now gaining much more prominence in that unease was Bent, and most especially his attitude during the last few T-sectors. Jad's first impressions of Bent, dark and unfavorable, were returning. In spite of being an excellent geologist, he still turned Jad off. Bent could be pushy sometimes, and that, more than anything, contributed to Jad's apprehension.

I still think we should have returned to Site One.

Jad and Wila tarried at the edge of the plateau a few microsectors longer, and then returned to Aero Two.

"Where do you want to set off the charge?" Jad asked Bent as he pulled his backpack from the cargo hold.

"I haven't decided. It's still early. Let's take a walk and check out some sites." He pointed toward the forest slope and swung his pack on his back. Then without any order or directive for the others to follow, he set out for the hill.

"Do you want to set up the shelter first?" Wila yelled after him as she and Lilea hoisted their overnight backpacks and raced to catch up with the striding Bent.

"No," Bent replied over his shoulder. "We'll spend the darktime in the forest."

Jad lingered at the ship, using his PersComm to notify Jer of their intent to enter the forest, and then he too sprinted after them. Shortly after they started out, Bent began marking trees with the markers.

Time Element 461.223.5.8.

The still, cool air felt good on Jad's face. The trees of this forest were largely the needle-leaved variety, though they also hiked past an occasional stand of the white-barked trees. Compared to the eastern forest, the trees here were set well apart and little undergrowth impeded them as they walked. Sunlight streamed through the forest, warming the air around them, and they could see hundreds of links in all directions. Jad didn't feel as closed in as he had in the other mountains. He enjoyed himself, the grade was easy and he remained relaxed. He had no sense of the dark, gloomy nature of that other forest. The dry air and gentle slope made the walk exhilarating.

His sense of relaxation seemed to infect the others as well. Even Lilea had broken out of her frustration with Bent and was her talkative self again. She and Wila jabbered easily, talking mostly about Anthanos and what they were going to do when they got home. The confrontation with the rock seemed to have been forgotten (or suppressed temporarily) and no one was injured, though damage to the retraction system was still possible. *Maybe Bent's right and there is no damage.* Overhead, huge flocks of birds blackened the sky, honking and squawking in a raucous symphony, almost drowning out all conversation.

But as they journeyed deeper into the forest, an unsettled feeling engulfed the group. Conversation dwindled, and everyone looked around as if to say, "There is something wrong here."

Lilea was the first to spot it. The leaves on the trees, especially the white-barked variety, had changed color. Few of the green leaves that greeted the team when they traveled in the other mountains still remained. They stopped and studied them.

"Aren't these leaves supposed to be green?" Lilea asked. She watched as a few leaves drifted to the ground. "They're changing color and dropping off."

Jad saw it too—huge swaths of color: crimson and orange, yellow and gold.

Most of the leaves were a brilliant yellow or gold, but a few stands stood out in a deep *dhus*-wine red. Once the team saw what was happening, they had little difficulty spotting the leaves drifting lazily from the trees and settling on the ground.

"My gosh," Wila exclaimed. "You don't suppose these plants are dying, do you?"

"It certainly looks like it," Lilea said. "Look how the ground is covered with these fallen leaves."

"Have we brought some sort of disease to these plants? Are we responsible for this?"

"I don't see how. We haven't been to this part of the continent before."

"But Site One isn't too far south of here. Maybe some of our germs have been carried by the wind up here and infected these plants."

Lilea shrugged her shoulders. "That's possible, I guess, but it seems farfetched. How could the germs of people infect foreign plants?"

They stood in the forest for several microsectors watching the leaves, though under Bent's prodding they turned and walked on. The falling leaves interested Jad only mildly. He appreciated the importance of Anthanian germs infecting native plants, and he liked the colors, but his feeling was, *What's done is done. We can't undo it.*

"We should take some of these leaves back to Anthanos," Lilea said. "Someone there will want to examine them."

Lilea and Wila gathered up some of the leaves and stuffed them into plastic bags. Bent and Jad continued into the forest, and the women had to scurry to catch up.

They hiked east for almost another subsector, marking trees as they went. Their route took them out onto a ridge which turned north. The slope steepened and the white-barked trees gave way to more of the needle-leafed variety. Around 223.6, they crested a rise near the summit of the ridge. From here they could look downward through the forest in all directions. Bent decided to stop for a meal, and Wila and Lilea dropped their packs under an imposing tree with deep, furrowed gray-black bark. As the women relaxed, Bent and Jad hiked north another 300 links and stopped in a shallow dry swale near a stand of white-barked trees.

"We'll set off the charge here," Bent said, looking around. The area was clear for about fifty links in every direction, so they swept away the leaves in an area about three links in diameter and drilled a hole and placed the charge, running the cable back to where the women sat. After the explosion, Jad and Bent restored the notebook, drill, and accessories to their backpacks, and all four hikers swung their packs and set out. By 223.8, they were hiking south, back down the ridge in the direction they'd come.

By 223.10, with sunlight rapidly disappearing from the sky and the horizon turning a deep scarlet in the west, they made camp on a level plot of ground in the vicinity of several magnificently endowed red-and-gold-leafed trees. By 224.0, they'd set up their personal shelters, taken their third meal and watched the sunset. Bent brought out his notebook and had Jer send the tracing of the charge. His expression, so upbeat in anticipation of another peak that would indicate the recorder felt the charge, slid painfully from his face as he looked at the straight line along the bottom of the screen.

"Nothing," he said, and gave a small sigh. He tossed the notebook into his and Lilea's shelter and lay down on his sleeping bag. Lilea entered a few microsectors later and closed the entrance flap. Jad and Wila entered theirs, and as Jad removed his jumpsuit he began to listen to, and really hear for the first time, the howling and wailing of many of the animals deep in the forest. In the cool air of the darktime, the winds carried their sounds through the trees almost unabated, as though they stood right outside the tent.

By 224.4, everyone was asleep.

They had no idea of the maelstrom surging toward them.

CHAPTER 52

CONFLAGRATION

Time Element 461.225.0.1.

"What's going on?" Bent fastened his jumpsuit as he stepped out of his shelter. He'd put his boots on, but Lilea slipped out right behind him in stocking feet. Jad was already standing outside his shelter.

"All this smoke," Jad said, pointing north. He pulled his camera from his backpack and made a few quick images. Wila joined him.

"Jad, what is this? I'm scared."

A dense white smoke filled the sky and drifted down into the camp site. The acrid odor stung Lilea's nostrils and burned her eyes. She wasn't completely unfamiliar with smoke—on Anthanos, house fires did occur, even occasionally gutting an entire house, leaving nothing but a blackened shell.

"Where's the smoke coming from?"

"North of here. The forest must be burning."

"The forest burning? How—?"

Fleeing south through their campsite came the animals, animals of all descriptions and sizes—small animals that scurried along the ground, hoofed animals similar to the ones she'd seen around the landing site, other animals with flat, spread-out paws and sharp teeth they bared at her as they passed. Jad, Bent and Lilea drew their weapons, set on level 1, and fired randomly at them to keep them from coming into the camp site. Behind them were the huge animals, similar to some she'd also seen at Site One, the ones with the long, muscular extension of the face that Trea decided was the animal's proboscis, but without the wooly covering, lumbering through the forest, shaking the earth as they moved, snorting and trumpeting in a thunderous shriek as if to say, "Get out of my way, the fire is coming. Go—go—go."

Jad fired at several of the larger animals. He set his weapon set on level 2, and later on level 3. It did little harm to the thick-skinned animals, but with the sting it produced they swung around the team as they passed.

"What does all this mean?" Lilea holstered her weapon. "Is there any danger to us?"

"I don't know," Bent said, "but we should be careful."

Through the heavy canopy of trees about two thousand links north of the grove where they'd camped, tiny flickers of red, orange, and yellow became visible dancing along the tree line. This was such a new and frightening concept Lilea didn't immediately know how to react. Without the huge stands of vegetation on Anthanos, a fire like this could never occur, and her mind, free of precedent, spun over different possibilities. *Does it spread around, or does it stay in one place and burn itself out?* She even briefly considered that it might expand exponentially and take over the entire continent. *Explorer* could be engulfed.

Lilea ducked back into her shelter. She jammed her feet into her boots and zipped them up, and grabbed her camera on her way out. She made a few quick images of the smoke, but only a few microsectors after she left her shelter, the fire itself erupted into sight about a thousand links north, crowning through the trees. Tree after tree exploded in flames. A wind, caused by the suction of the hot fire at the top of the forest, swirled around the team as they stood in the campsite, transfixed by the sight. The wind hurled burning embers from the flaming trees hundreds of links in all directions, onto other trees, down to the forest floor and onto the shelters and the team, watching and wondering. Jad started yelling.

"Let's get out of here!"

"Lilea! Run! Let's go!" Wila shouted. As she ran, she grabbed Lilea by the left arm almost knocking the camera from her hand. Jad and Wila took off, following the tree markers as they ran, with Lilea a few strides behind.

The fire ignited the trees like candlewicks. Faster and more furiously the trees became engulfed, one after another, exploding into flames, crackling and snapping, spitting red-orange embers on the forest floor behind them as they scrambled through the forest. They made the turn without hesitating when the ridge swung west, running past the site where Lilea and Wila collected leaves. Jad set a generous pace, but not so fast the others couldn't keep up. When the winds and the sound of the fire subsided in the distance, he stopped. He turned around to check on the fire, blurting out almost immediately, "Hey! Where's Bent?"

Lilea, all out of breath, didn't immediately comprehend what Jad said. She assumed Bent was right behind her. She stopped and leaned against a big red-barked tree for a split-nanosector to catch her breath. "What?!" She turned around.

"Bent!" she bellowed, and visions of the panic and fear the Blue Planet had so often visited on the team shot through her mind. Now the terror was on her, sitting squarely on her shoulders, and the thought that Bent was "next" horrified her. She'd so often said to him, "No, I don't think you're next," and she didn't want to be proven wrong. She'd do everything she could to prevent that from happening. She yelled his name several times, and when she didn't see him coming down the ridge, she ran back toward the fire, determined to find him. "Bent! Where are you? Oh, god—No! No! No!"

"Lilea!" Jad and Wila yelled almost in unison. "Wait! Don't go back! Come back here!"

Lilea ran for several thousand links, her heart pounding in her chest well beyond what was needed for the running she was doing.

"Bent!" she yelled over and over. She'd gone almost three thousand links up the ridge when she saw the unmistakable blue-green color of a jumpsuit coming through the forest. Just a small dot in the distance, but it could only be Bent. Searing embers pelted the ground all around him. He ran as fast as he could toward her, carrying something in one hand, yelling and gesturing as he ran.

"Keep going! Keep going!"

Lilea didn't have time to be glad she found him. She turned around and ran back down the ridge. Bent caught up with her, but stayed behind her as they ran. When they reached Jad and Wila, they turned around to check on the fire, now a raging, blistering orange-red inferno almost an anthan away. That's when Lilea saw the back of Bent's jumpsuit. The suit had been burned at the upper back and left shoulder, and several decilinks down the back of his left arm. Remnants of his undershirt stuck to his skin, and several small areas on his back and shoulder were a brilliant scarlet. Soot, cinders, dirt and leaves covered his back.

"Oh, my god, Bent!" Lilea yelled. "What happened?"

"Something burning fell on the shelter when I went back in to—"

"'Fell on the shelter?' What kind of stupid logic possessed you to go back into the shelter?" Lilea brushed some of the debris from Bent's jumpsuit.

"I had to get the notebook. It's got all my data."

"The notebook? You idiot! You should've started running when we did! Does it hurt?"

"A little. Not too much."

"Did you get the notebook?"

"Yes." He showed her.

"You asshole." She slapped his right arm. "You scared the crap outta me like that."

"We need to get going," Jad said as he looked back up the slope. "The fire is still moving this way. Can you walk with us?"

"Yeah." Bent nodded. "I can keep up with you."

They started out again, walking briskly, staying together, sometimes jogging down the slope in the forest, until they reached Aero Two around 225.3. Lilea cleaned the burned area on Bent's back and sprayed some local anesthetic from the aerodyne's first-aid kit, then placed some bandages over the reddest areas. He said it felt better, and retrieved a clean jumpsuit from his daypack.

"Let's go," Bent said. "I'm ready to take off. We should get out of here before the fire reaches us here." He climbed into the pilot's seat. "Ow!" he yelled when he leaned against the seat back.

"Bent," Wila said. "You get back here. I'll fly."

"I can still fly." Bent seated himself hunched over, leaning forward in what must have been a cramped and painful position. He started to run through the pre-engine-start checklist.

"Like hell you can." Lilea put a hand on his right arm. "You can't fly like that. You and I will get in back."

Bent remained quiet for a nanosector, his face expressionless. But he stopped going over the checklist. "Okay," he said in a voice mixed with dejection and pragmatism, and opened the door and jumped out. He put his daypack behind his lower back to keep his upper back and left arm away from the seat. He said he was comfortable as the ship left the ground.

Once they were airborne, Wila circled the fire as Lilea snapped several images. Her camera and PersComm, Jad's camera, and Bent's notebook were the only objects, other than the clothes and boots they wore, saved from the campsite. Everything else — backpacks, shelters, food, the extra seismic charges, all their clothing — gone.

They arrived at Site One around 225.4.8.

CHAPTER 53

DISCUSSIONS

Time Element 461.227.10.3.

"No, I don't think you're 'next' at all," Lilea said.

Stripped to the waist, Bent lay on his stomach on the bed in their compartment while Lilea smeared a white antibiotic lotion on the burned area on his back. Mina had brought the lotion up from pharmacostorage. "I've told you that before. The only reason you got burned was that you went back into the shelter to get that notebook. If you'd started to run when we did, you wouldn't have gotten burned at all."

"Yeah, but I wouldn't have gotten the notebook. It has all my data."

"Oh, yeah, the notebook. I hope it was worth almost getting killed just to get the damn notebook. The notebook's backed up, anyway, why did you . . ."

"But I need it to work. Without it I can't set off the charges, or record specimens, or anything."

"Oh." Lilea placed the lotion dispenser on the table beside the bed and taped new bandages over the burn. She really wanted to yell at him about what he'd done by going back into that shelter, by not running when the rest of them did, and by not being with her when they stopped and turned to look at the fire. He deserved to know about that, about how it terrified her and about how she thought he was dead or dying, and how she visualized his body lying frozen in some ghastly disfigured position in the embers of the fire up there on that ridge. That's what he should know, but before she could say anything, his voice brought her back.

"But even if I did run when the rest of you did, that doesn't change the fact that the blaze was coming directly toward us. It's like, maybe something started the fire and sent it our way."

Lilea gritted her teeth, closed her eyes in frustration, and suppressed her desire to yell at him. "Well, I don't know how the fire got started, but maybe it was natural."

"Natural?" Bent turned and looked at her. "How could it be natural?" He pushed himself up on the bed with his left arm. A slight twinge of pain crossed his face. "How could a fire like that start naturally? What could cause a blaze to just flare up and begin to spread?" He shrugged his shoulders as he tried to stand next to the bed, but winced again. Lilea helped him—painfully—pull a T-shirt over the bandages. "It seems like the fact that we were in the vicinity couldn't be coincidence."

Lilea didn't answer. She had no idea how the blaze got started, but she wasn't getting anywhere trying to persuade him that it might have been a natural event. It's true, she admitted to herself, someone could have started the fire and directed it toward them. But why? Would the humans in the north start a fire like that? They might—but could they control a fire once it got started and send it their way? That seemed unlikely, but she did admit to herself she didn't have any evidence one way or the other. Bent's argument wasn't making much sense to her and she decided to end the discussion. She gave him a pain injection, and he lay back on the bed and closed his eyes.

As she left the room to leave Bent to his nap, a single thought went through her head. *Wouldn't it be nice if the ointment would make his head better too?*

Time Element 461.228.2.0.

Everyone except Trea assembled on Life Sciences for the meeting, the first team meeting since the return of Aero Two. Jad and Wila sat at their usual places at the far left side of the group at the circular table, and Bent, Lilea and Mina completed the group. Bent wore only a shirt over his bandages. A jumpsuit still put too much pressure on the burn.

Jer was the last to arrive. She came up in the interdeck elevator and walked over to her place at the table, opposite the others. She set her notebook down, then turned and glared directly at Bent.

"Why didn't you notify me when you hit that rock?"

Jer's sharp tone of voice startled Lilea and she looked up. This was so out of character for Jer, and Lilea almost said something.

"You know regulations require you to come back to Site One whenever one of the transports is damaged."

"Well, yeah," Bent stammered. "But the regulations also give us some leeway if the damage isn't too bad. We didn't think it was bad enough to return."

"But you couldn't tell how badly it was damaged."

"I figured if skid retraction was okay, it wasn't badly damaged." Bent shrugged his shoulders and winced as the undershirt scraped over the bandages.

Jer paid no notice. "What does skid retraction have to do with it?"

"If the skid or the mechanism was badly damaged it wouldn't retract normally. Besides, Wila said the mechanisms in these aerodynes are real heavy duty. We figured it could take a big 'whack' and still be okay."

Wila jumped. "What? Wait—hold on. That's not what I said. All I said was they *were* heavy duty. I never said they could take any whack and still, you know . . . there's a limit and I said so."

"But it wasn't okay." Jer's voice rose slightly. "Jad and Wila found a hairline crack in the joint between the forward strut and the hydraulic retraction arm. There was even a slight leak of hydraulic fluid. They had to replace the strut/joint assembly. That joint could have given out during any landing you made after you hit the rock. Especially a hard landing." Jer paused. "That's my point, we have to be more careful." Her voice rose even higher. "We need to stick to the rules no matter what." She stepped slightly to her right and pointed a finger directly at Bent. "If that skid failed, you could have been killed or injured and it might have been difficult to get to you." She paused and let her voice drop back to normal. "Next time, notify me and come back to the ship if anything like that happens again."

"But the skid could have given out when we landed here. There's just as much chance we could have been killed in a crash landing here."

"Bent—" Lilea said. She put a hand on his arm. He could have let the argument go, but he didn't, and his brusque attitude surprised her. This was unusual for him, he rarely took such a patronizing attitude with anyone, let alone the leader of his working group, and she grasped his arm more tightly, as though that would calm him.

"But at least you would have been here where we could have done something about it," Jer said. She turned away from Bent and retreated to her notebook.

"That doesn't make any sense," Bent muttered. Lilea winced.

Jer jerked her head up and turned back. She put her fists on the table and leaned over, scowling directly at him. "I beg your pardon?"

"What?!" Bent stood up, almost knocking his chair over. He scowled back at her.

Lilea jumped out of her seat. She put one knee on the table to get between Jer and Bent. "All right, you two—all right! Calm down—both of you." She held up two hands, one in front of Jer, the other on Bent's shirt. He resisted at first but took a short step back and returned to his seat. Jer stood her ground, fury and outrage on her face. Lilea's voice turned calmer. "Bent isn't going to violate the rules anymore. I can guarantee it. Now both of you sit down and act like intelligent people."

Still scowling, Jer returned to her place. A drop of bright blood appeared on her lower lip where she'd bitten through. Bent turned to his left, facing away from Jer. He crossed his arms over his chest and said nothing. In the awkward silence that followed, Jer dabbed at her lip and tried to continue with the meeting.

"Does, uh, anyone have any idea what caused the fire?" She stuttered slightly and a hesitation infiltrated her voice for a few words until she recovered. "Was it something we did, or is this normal?"

"It's hard to tell," Jad said. His answer came so promptly after Jer's question it startled Lilea. He might have been trying to help reduce the tension by changing the subject. "We don't know when it started. All we know is that it came at us from the north."

"Did you see the fire when you flew over the area just before landing?" Jer looked around at the others at the table.

"No," Jad said, shaking his head. "We didn't see anything."

"He's right," Wila said. "We would've noticed all that smoke right away."

"Bent?" Jer turned toward him. "You were piloting. Did you see anything?"

Bent turned in his seat back toward the table, and shook his head. "No, I didn't see anything." He threw his words out, callously and unemotionally.

"So it must've started after you landed."

Several nodded. "That's probably true," Lilea said.

"Do you think you had anything to do with the starting the fire?"

"Hardly," Bent said out of the side of his mouth, a sly, sarcastic smile on his face.

"Oh, no," Wila said. "I don't think so. What could we have done to start a fire? Something else may—"

Wila was interrupted by a familiar sound behind the group, a metallic click and a low whirring as the interdeck elevator began to descend. Bent and Jad turned in their chairs.

"What?" Jer said. "What made the elevator start?"

"It must have short-circuited," Bent said. "There's no one down there."

"No one except Trea," Lilea said.

"Trea?" Jer opened her eyes and turned to Lilea. "When you looked in on her before the meeting, was she ready to leave?"

"She didn't say anything. But she was dressed like she could leave any time."

The elevator stopped whirring. It had descended several decks. Jad left his seat and walked over to the opening in the deck through which the elevator traveled, peering downward.

"I can't see much. The curvature of the ship's hull . . ." He made a vertical 'curving' motion with his hand and walked back to his seat. The whirring started again, and a few nanosectors later the elevator arrived carrying Trea.

To Lilea, that was unusual. The effervescent, irrepressible Trea never took the elevator. She always scrambled up or down the interdeck ladder, especially in her haste to get outside to see some of the animals that frequented Site One.

"Hi," Trea said quietly, stepping off the elevator platform. "I thought I should join the meeting." She smiled briefly and walked slowly to the central table, but instead of sitting in her usual location, to the far right of everyone else, she took a seat next to Jad. Lilea couldn't recall ever seeing her sit there before, though she did realize that seat was nearest the elevator. To reach her regular seat, Trea would have to walk halfway around the table.

"Hi." Jad nodded to her slightly when she sat down. Something strange hit Lilea about Jad's voice. There was a familiarity about it, the way you'd say "Hi" to a member of your own family, not to an outsider. It was almost as though he expected her to sit there.

"Hi," Trea replied, but quietly, almost whispering. She glanced quickly at Jad, smiled briefly, and then turned to the others.

Everyone stared at Trea. She'd lost several krill in weight over the last forty-two T-sectors and her face was pale and drawn, but she wore a neat, clean jumpsuit. She'd pulled her hair into a short ponytail and tied it with a pink ribbon. She did manage a slight smile, but there was no indication of the exuberant, high-spirited Trea everyone knew before Col's death. She sat quietly with her hands in her lap.

"Welcome back," Jer said. "It's good to see you."

"Thanks. It is good to be back." Trea's voice was steady, but low and quiet.

"We were just discussing the fire. We were wondering how the fire got started."

"I think I know how the fire started. I've been thinking about it."

"What do you mean?" Jer raised an eyebrow. "Let's hear your theory."

Trea leaned forward in her chair and spoke in a subdued, tender voice. "I've thought a lot about this ever since you came back. Lilea and Wila told me all about what happened, especially about the leaves falling, and they set off a seismic charge, and I got to wondering how a fire could have started. I didn't have any idea until I remembered the charge you set off in the mountains. I especially remember all the sparks that shot out of that hole. I bet some of those sparks started the fire. Lilea said there were a lot of leaves on the ground where you set off the charge. Col told me the leaves on this planet were full of cellulose which burns really easily when it's dried out. I wonder if the sparks started the fire in the dried leaves on the ground."

"That's impossible," Bent said, shaking his head. "I can't believe that. Those seismic charges have never started a fire before."

"That's right," Jad said. "The charges never started any fire when we used them in the mountains."

"Maybe not," Trea said. "But the charge you set off in the mountains wasn't around a lot of dried leaves. It was on that ridge, not near large vegetation."

"That's true," Jad said, "but we always filled up the hole and stamped out the sparks. I assume we did this time too, but I don't remember whether we did or not."

"No, you didn't," Lilea said. "You ran the cable back to where we were, and I remember watching the charge go off. You didn't go back."

"That's right," Bent mumbled, nodding. "We didn't fill the hole. We just left it. But there wasn't any need to fill it. It was just a hole in the ground. It would get filled sooner or later."

"Who told you to fill the hole after a charge is set off?" Jer asked. "Did you just decide to do it on your own, or is that standard procedure on Anthanos?"

"We just started doing it," Bent said. "Nobody ever told us. We don't use those charges on Anthanos. Those were made just for this expedition. The ones we use at home are much larger, and they fill the hole with heavy equipment. They wouldn't let me bring those charges on this expedition. They said it was too dangerous. But these puny charges are too small to send a signal very far through the crust of this planet. I'm not gettin' crap."

"Well, in any event, the damage is done. I suggest in the future we not set off seismic charges in any area where there is burnable material.

Either that or be careful to put out any sparks that come out of the hole." She paused and checked her notebook. "Do we know how much stuff we lost in the fire? Has anyone made a list?"

"Wila and I did," Lilea said. "There were several articles of clothing, especially cold weather gear, and other personal belongings, as well as one shelter for each couple, four sleeping bags, four backpacks, a small amount of food, Wila's vision aid, two first-aid kits, stove, water carriers, two seismic charges—"

Bent nodded. "I remember hearing those things go off as I ran."

"—all of Bent's specimens, all of our weapons, and a few other miscellaneous items."

"Most of that can be replaced from ship's stores," Jer said.

"Except the backpacks. We didn't bring any extra backpacks on this trip. The packs are pretty rugged, so there was no provision made for replacing those burned in a fire."

"What about Col's and Dell's backpacks?" Jer asked. "Can we borrow those?"

Trea nodded and Mina said, "Okay," and the meeting broke up.

Time Element 461.228.3.1.

Lilea turned to face Bent as he closed their compartment door. "You know, you really should apologize to Jer for what you said." She kept her voice low. She didn't intend to chide him or be critical, but in her mind she thought it important that Bent apologize, a small but crucial point to her. "You know good and well you should have come back after the damage to Aero Two. She makes good sense about what happened."

"Oh, crap." Bent's voice turned sullen and angry. He walked into the bedroom and Lilea followed, taken aback at his temper. He pulled off his shirt, getting ready for bed. "There was nothing wrong with the goddamn aerodyne. It was perfectly good to land anywhere. If I'd brought it back here and that skid had given out when we landed here, we could have been killed *here*. What difference would it have made? We all would have been dead. It's a stupid rule anyway."

"If you crashed here, you would have *been* here. Jer wouldn't have to send out Aero One and potentially risk the others who would have to go out and find us and land and pick us up. The only people left here were Jer, Mina, and Trea. They would've had to come out and pick us up. *That's* what difference it would have made."

"Yeah, well, Jer can kiss my fuckin' ass."

"Bent, please, don't . . ."

"You're the big flying hero around here. You're the one who flew the damaged aerodyne home from the grasslands. You're the one with all the wonderful artifacts that everyone drools over. I ain't got shit."

Lilea hesitated a nanosector, confused. "Bent, don't bring that up. That has nothing to do with it. When I flew that aerodyne home, I *was* flying it back here. Those are the rules and you know it. Besides, you —"

"I don't know any such thing."

"Is that what's behind this? Are you trying to be a big hero and fly a damaged aerodyne around? I know you better than that. That's not you. You've never taken risks like that. You've never been someone to do something that stupid. Or that dangerous."

"That's right. That's not me. I just wanted to make my own decision about this."

"Your own decision? What . . . ? I don't understand."

"I got a good result at the first site. I wanted to see if I could get the same from farther away, and if I did I would've had some damn good data and I would have been able to make something of it. I didn't want to have to come back here. Then we'd have to wait for the aerodyne to be repaired and that'd take several lightimes, and I didn't want —"

"But you jeopardized the rest of us —"

"Oh, crap, that's not true. No one was in any danger."

" —and for all your trouble, you didn't get anything. Serves you right."

Bent said nothing more. He stripped off his shorts and put on pajama bottoms. Lilea stayed quiet too, standing on the other side of the bed, waiting for him to respond. After a microsector, she could wait no longer. "Bent. Don't turn away from me. At least tell me you realize —"

"There's something else going on."

Lilea stopped, surprised. "What do you mean?"

"There's something about this planet. Like it doesn't want us here."

"Bent, please. You're beginning to sound like Wila. Don't tell me you believe we should just leave and go back home."

Bent's voice rose. He turned and faced Lilea. "At least if we went back home, I could get some decent results."

"Results? You're getting lots of results. You've got all those rocks and samples up there and you told me you're getting quake data almost every lightime —"

"Those are trivial. I need results from the charges —"

"Trivial?! Bent—those results are not trivial at all. You've said so your—"

"I need local results. I need to find out how stable the crust is and I can't do it with the puny charges they gave me. I can't get down into the gorge and I don't dare go up into the mountains. I can't work when the damn water's falling from the clouds, and now the fire comes and runs us out of there . . . it's like something happens every time I go out. On Anthanos we could go out anytime."

"Trea's right, the fire was caused by sparks from the charge. Nothing else caused the fire. You know that as well as I do."

"Those charges have never caused a fire. Anywhere. Not Anthanos, not here."

"Of course not. There's nothing to burn on Anthanos. The sparks just fall on sand."

"It's still possible someone or something started that fire, and . . ."

Lilea had gotten exasperated with Bent's insistence in not recognizing the role of the sparks in causing the fire, and she was becoming angry. It scared her, too. She'd never seen Bent this intransigent about anything. Ever. She almost never became angry with him. She hadn't in a long time, so long ago she couldn't remember when. Their marriage always seemed so harmonious, so compatible in spite of being from two different racial groups, two different genetic backgrounds. Others had warned her there might be consequences from marrying outside her group, but she ignored them and went ahead and married him anyway and she always felt she made the right choice. Yet now, this planet, this earth, this world, so different from her own, so unusual, so unlike any she or Bent had ever visited, was edging itself between them and it frightened her in a deep, fundamental way. She put her hands on her hips and stared directly at him. "You know damn good and well that's not true."

"Yeah, yeah, I know, the sparks. Okay, the fuckin' sparks I'll agree the goddamn sparks may have had something to do with the fire, but how can we work on this planet if we have to constantly be worried about fires? Or the ground quaking? Or water falling from the sky? Or people falling off mountains or being attacked by wild animals? I'm so tired of this place. I just want to go home. Or back to the moons of Tekaa."

"That's the way things are here." Lilea paused, trying to think of words that would convey her feelings, her convictions about this planet. "Remember the slithering creature I told you about? It ate the furry animal and I was so upset? That's normal for this planet. That's the real thing around here, I'm sure of it. And the storm that dropped the ice on Aero One? That's normal, too. I knew that before I took off. And the animals at the gorge? Bent, these things are just part of the—"

"That doesn't make any difference." Bent waved a dismissive hand at her, turning toward the bathroom. "Everything you say is 'natural' or 'normal' or something like that and I'm getting damn tired of it." He turned back to face her. "How can everything be so damned normal? This planet isn't normal. It's so fucked up I can't get any data that makes any sense. When I was on the moons of Shaltous or Tekaa, I could get all the data I wanted. And I didn't have to worry about getting killed either. Here all I can do is pick up rocks. Or set off charges that don't *do* anything."

"But all that seismic data—"

He closed the door to the bathroom, not really slamming it, but not a gentle tap either.

Lilea had nothing more to say. Nothing she'd said in the past fifty or so T-sectors had made any difference to Bent about her belief in what she called the 'normality' of this planet. He'd been the senior geologist at SpaceComm for two years before they left, able to get the important results from the other moons in their solar system. He was their go-to guy for geology, finding all the deposits of the rare precious metals that were needed to build the spaceships that brought them to this little orb of blue and green and white and brown. But on this planet, so dissimilar from any planet or moon he'd ever encountered, he couldn't get the data he wanted because the 'normality,' the highly complicated mosaic of factors that made up 'life' here always seemed to get in his way, and he reacted with anger and frustration. None of the moons of the outer planets had any life forms that interfered with his studies, or fires that swept large areas of the surface, or water that fell from the sky. There he knew how to find exactly what he wanted.

Oh, and did he really want to go home? Or was he just angry?

To Lilea, this was the worst thing that could happen. It put him at direct odds with her, and that was so different from anything that'd ever happened in their marriage. Now he was drifting away from her, taking his own route down a strange and difficult path toward an ending she could see only dimly, an ending she dreaded to think about. She wanted to say something that would turn him around and bring him back to her point of view, to bring him back into her world, a world of logic and reason. That's right, he was just being unreasonable.

She turned and left the bedroom and went to the refrigerator. She filled a plastic tumbler with jell-kell and dropped two ice cubes in the red liquid. She stood in the food-prep area sipping the juice, listening to the tinkle of the ice against the sides of the tumbler, staring through the window over the table into the blackness of the darktime. Her mind turned to the slithering creature and the furry animal, and she played the attack over and over in her mind, but she couldn't find a way to communicate the story's meaning to Bent. And that saddened her more than anything.

CHAPTER 54

SPICE SAUCE

Time Element 461.231.0.8.

"It's unlocked," Trea said, and Lilea and Mina entered. Trea stood in the food-prep area of her compartment, frying some vegetables on a small hot plate. A fragrant odor filled the room.

"How are you feeling?" Mina asked. She handed Trea a plastic bottle. "I b-brought some of my special spice sauce l-like you asked."

"Oh, thank you." Trea flipped open the lid of the bottle and skimmed a finger across the top of the viscous alizarin-colored liquid and licked the sauce off her finger. "Yummy!" She closed her eyes and brought a look of mock ecstasy to her face. Trea's exuberant personality was returning and her infectious smile made a momentary comeback.

"You seem to be doing better." Lilea allowed a tiny smile to creep up the edges of her mouth, but that was as far as she would let her emotions go.

"Oh, yes. I'm getting my appetite back. I'm even thinking about returning to work." She spooned a big dollop of sauce on the vegetables in the pan. Immediately a warm, spicy odor mingled with the scent of the vegetables, and Lilea's nostrils began to quiver.

"That's good." Lilea inhaled deeply. "You must have a lot of specimens backed up by now."

"I do." Trea put the remaining sauce in the refrigerator, and then turned to her visitors. But now the delight of idle chatter was gone, and her expression turned serious. She spoke in a low voice, almost whispering, as though someone might overhear. "Jad and Wila were here a few millisectors ago. Did you know she's talking about leaving early?"

"Y-Yes, we know."

"I couldn't believe it. I mean . . . I thought, my god, Wila, let it go."

Lilea's ears perked up. *Is Trea really saying what I think she's saying?* "We've heard it too. What do you think?"

"I don't think so. I've thought a lot about Col's death and I've come to the conclusion it was an accident, a terrible, horrible accident, just, you know, a chance encounter. I think it was a female animal. I bet those two juveniles we saw just before the attack were its young and it was just protecting its young."

"But that's such a . . . a vi-vicious way to defend your young. No animal on Anthanos would ever d-do that."

"But there were animals in Anthanian prehistory that would have. I've seen them. I've studied their bones and their habitats and their nesting habits. It wasn't that unusual."

Lilea nodded. "I've seen all that, too."

"Are you sure you're not reading into what happened your own interpretation of how extinct Anthanian animals would have acted in the same situation?" Mina asked. She jabbed the air with her finger as she talked, her voice hard and direct. She didn't stutter, her words came pouring out rapidly and clearly. Her eyes shifted rapidly between Lilea and Trea.

"Mina. What are you saying?" This was so new to Lilea, to hear Mina talk like that.

"I'm just saying I think we shouldn't judge events here on this planet by outside interpretation. Maybe there are other explanations for what happened. Like for what killed Dell and Col."

"Are you saying you agree with Wila?"

"I-I'm just saying there may be other explanations. We s-shouldn't eliminate every possibility."

Lilea eyed Mina suspiciously. She wasn't sure what she'd heard, but she didn't like it. But what Trea said next took her mind from Mina.

"I can't leave now. I've got so much work to do. There are so many animals out there. I want to continue where I left off. Col would want it. He enjoyed being here. Even after Case and Dell were killed, he wanted to continue. He wanted to come back on the next trip. I do too. I feel so much better now. I want to get out and run, but I'm still too weak to do much yet. Jad and I—oh, I almost forgot." She held out to her two visitors a small dish containing several brownish-black nuts. "Here, have some nuts. Col found these a few T-sectors ago. You have to crack them open with your teeth, but the nuts inside are delicious."

Lilea grabbed one and, after a couple of unsuccessful tries, cracked the hard shell open and extracted the sienna-brown nut inside. "We knew you'd come back," she said after she swallowed the nut. Now she had a big smile on her face. "Mina and Jer did, and we knew you could, too."

"I-I have to get back to work," Mina said, glancing at her personal chronometer. "Those bacteria won't analyze themselves."

Lilea left a few microsectors after Mina, and as she walked the circular hallway to her compartment, she replayed in her mind all that had just taken place, from the dippy look on Trea's face when she sampled the spice sauce to her flat dismissal of Wila's desire to leave early. That just made the smile on Lilea's face grow even bigger. But though the weight of Trea's antics temporarily displaced Mina's comments, she never completely forgot them.

CHAPTER 55

COMPLETE SURVEY

Time Element 461.235.1.8.

"I talked to Jad," Bent told Lilea. "I've given him my notebook. It has a complete diagram of where to set the charges. He knows what to do."

Mina had just left Bent and Lilea's compartment. At 235.0.4, she swabbed of a spot of bright red skin near the center of Bent's back, between his shoulder blades. He'd been complaining of more pain than usual since he woke, and Lilea called Mina who suspected an infection. She returned a subsector and a half later with the news. Lilea met her at the door to the compartment.

"This is one of those 'g-good news/bad news' things," Mina said.

"What's the bad news?"

"Th-the bad news is the burn is infected. I've isolated an Anthanian bacterium, known to infect wounds. The g-good news is it's susceptible to antibiotics, and I picked up this lotion from the Medical Station." She gave Lilea a plastic tube. "P-Put some of this on the whole burn every T-sector."

"I've been applying the other lotion you gave me."

"It's become resistant to th-that antibiotic. This one should work."

Lilea applied the lotion to Bent's back and arm, wiping it evenly over the burned area, putting a little extra on the central red area. Then she gave him a pain shot.

"Those pain shots make me sleepy," he said. He picked up the copy of the probe atlas he kept on the bedside table and opened it to the images of the gorge. "I'm going to find a route to the bottom if it kills me."

"I'm going to do some work outside. It looks nice out."

With Bent not feeling well and confined to bed, Lilea decided to try to finish her part of the Complete Survey Project. Each person was supposed to do a complete examination of the landing site, and she was still—ostensibly, anyway—looking for artifacts which could indicate the presence of intelligent life in the area. But after her thorough examinations shortly after landing, the chances of finding artifacts in this area were, well, nil, so she shelved the Survey for an indefinite time. After her discovery of humans in the northern regions she lost all interest in it. Later, with the appearance of cooler weather and Jer's restriction on travel up north because of all the white stuff that'd started falling, she worked up a plan to finish her part. Only the sandstone cliffs, about an anthan away, remained for a detailed examination. She waited for clear weather.

T-sector 235 had dawned clear and cool, around 4 Tal, but warmed as the sun rose higher in the sky. Lilea grabbed a lightweight jacket, her camera and sampling kit, an eighth-trilink of water, and walked across the deck to Jad and Wila's compartment. Wila answered her tap on the door.

"Trea and I are going out," Wila said. "We're taking Runabout 1 and going east. She wants to visit her 'special place.'"

"Her 'special place?' What's that?"

"It's a secluded place near a small creek about a half-anthan away, near the base of the hills. She and Col went there once, before he was killed. She wants to go back."

"I remember. Col mentioned that place to me. But I would have thought Trea wouldn't want to have anything to do with any place that reminded her of Col."

"I was surprised myself, but she says she wants to go, and I thought it would be good for her to get out and get some fresh air. She's been isolated here in this ship for almost 50 T-sectors."

"Has it been that long?"

"It'll do her some good to get out," Jad said. "I'm going down to the Equipment Deck and get some stuff. Lilea, can you give me a hand?"

Jad kissed Wila goodbye and she left, walking toward Trea's compartment. Jad and Lilea descended to Deck 10, Equipment Storage, two levels below Personnel, where he pulled out the drilling equipment — drill motor, collapsible drilling rig, drilling bits, extensions, cables, pulleys — and lowered everything to the surface using the winch that projected through the large exterior loading door on this deck. Then they descended to ground level and loaded the equipment into the cargo bins on the back of Runabout 2.

Time Element 461.235.3.7.

While Jad and Lilea loaded the equipment, Trea and Wila arrived at the surface. Jad kept a careful eye on Trea as she walked to Runabout 1 parked a few links up the slope from Runabout 2. Trea wore a jumpsuit and light jacket, but as she entered the runabout on the left side Jad noticed — again — how much weight she'd lost. She'd always been slender, like Jad himself, but she'd been muscular too, and her body fat index was the lowest on the team, save for Jad himself. But now, after almost 50 T-sectors of near total isolation in her compartment, and even though she'd begun eating again, she appeared wasted, down several krill. The vomiting, the inability—or outright refusal—to take solid food for the first ten T-sectors after Col's death, had all contributed to a distressing weight loss and emaciation. As she sat in the driver's seat before the door closed, Jad didn't see the robust muscular thigh he remembered from the mountains. Now her jumpsuit leg revealed little more than a slim, feminine thigh. She was a shadow of her former self, yet still a lovely woman, and the late morning sun accentuated the freckles across her nose and the highlights in her auburn hair. She wasn't as outgoing as she had been, though she smiled and waved a restrained "Hi" as she entered the runabout.

But Lilea's voice abruptly broke Jad's concentration. "Jad? Are you ready to get going?" She jumped into the right front seat of the runabout.

Jad backed the runabout away from *Explorer* and turned west, stopping briefly as Trea pulled Runabout 1 away from the ship, passing in front of him. Lilea waved, and Wila waved back, but Trea seemed intent upon driving and didn't acknowledge them.

Jad pulled down the microphone of the runabout's comm system. "Jer, Runabout 2. Do you read?"

"Reading clear. Carrier signal optimum."

"Okay. We're off." Jad initiated inertial tracking, and accelerated west.

As he drove, the images of Trea swirled in his mind, and he tried to concentrate on them. Trea's condition still surprised him, even though he knew she would bounce back. Her willingness to work outside for the first time in fifty or more T-sectors was good evidence of that. She'd been a great runner, just like him, and with a little training she could regain her former physique. He had a plan in his mind, a plan to help Trea get her running legs back. As the other dedicated runner on the team, he was the one to do it. He started working on the details of the plan—get Trea outside and back into running without Wila getting suspicious—when Lilea, annoyingly enough, decided she wanted to talk.

"Have you finished the solar studies?"

"Mostly, but I'm still collecting data." As he spoke, Jad tried not to take his eyes off the surface ahead. The gently undulating terrain required him to pick his way carefully around the vegetation, changing course every now and then for the occasional depression.

"What are you working on now?"

"I'm taking periodic images of the sun, the surface, solar flares, that sort of thing. This sun has a lot of solar flare activity. More than ours. I've been doing this for a hundred odd-numbered T-sectors now. That's more than SpaceComm wanted, but, what the heck. I'm getting ready to start core measurements."

"Did SpaceComm ask for those studies too?"

"Yeah."

Jad's curt answer to Lilea's last question seemed to quiet her, and she said nothing further. He concentrated on the sandstone cliffs, now directly ahead, looming over the runabout.

"Drop me here." Jad stopped the runabout and Lilea got out, walked over to the cliffs, and looked up.

"I'll be back to get you in about a subsector."

"Okay." Lilea waved and turned back to the cliffs. Jad spun the runabout 150 degrees and took off northeast, back to a preselected area where Bent had asked him to set off one of the charges.

Bent had installed all twelve of the smaller seismic recorders in a circular pattern around the ship, each about five hundred links from the huge rock on which *Explorer* stood. As he described it, the shock wave from each charge would strike that rock and ricochet back toward the various recorders, but part of each wave would travel through the rock and get diffused and modified, split into many thousands of parts, and from the entire pattern of return waves — and crunched by the computer on Geo — Bent could get an accurate picture of the rock and surrounding territory, much more accurate than the long-wavelength studies he took from orbit before landing.

Jad would set the first charge west of the ship, about an anthan from *Explorer.* Later, he would go north, then east of the ship, completing a triangle around Site One, setting off a charge at every place Bent had asked.

Jad stopped the runabout a half-anthan from where he dropped Lilea. He stepped out and studied the area. To the south were the hills, but the immediate area around him was only low vegetation and a few scrawny trees. Two anthans away to the north and west the forest encroached on this quiet patch of desert. Two shiny metallic objects also caught his eye, the neutrino detectors he'd set up shortly after landing. A faint rumbling from far away tickled his ears, but he paid scant attention.

He focused on the drilling.

CHAPTER 56

CLOUDBURST

Time Element 461.235.4.5.

Jad wrenched the collapsible drilling rig from one of the runabout's cargo bins and set it up a few hundred links north of the runabout. Then he lugged the heavy drilling motor over to the rig and hoisted it into position. He attached the six-link-long drilling bit to the motor, hooked it into the runabout's power supply, and energized the drill. He relaxed a little as the bit chewed its way into the earth, but soon he had to add the first extension. It was a sweaty job raising and lowering the drill just to add each extension.

I'm glad Bent doesn't want a core sample. That means I can use the smaller bit.

After he added the second extension, he stood at the runabout watching the drill spin. A chilly breeze came at him from the south. No, southwest. He turned and looked in the direction of the cliffs, and the breeze washed over his face in a satisfying nip. He could see Lilea as a dot of blue-green at the base of the cliffs. He watched for a few nanosectors as she walked around, occasionally disappearing into some shallow cavity in the cliff wall. He turned back to look at the drill—oops, time to add the next extension.

And so the process went, extension after extension.

Finally, with the fifth extension, the drill reached the full thirty-six links Bent wanted for these charges. Jad withdrew the entire bit, section by section, and removed the motor and rig. He was just about to remove the charge from its carrier when, from the other side of the cliffs, came the unmistakable sound generated by the lightning. They'd begun calling it '*yuo-tast*,' or 'lightning noise.' Just a muffled blast, probably several anthans away. He looked up, concentrating on the sky above the cliffs. Dark aggressive clouds had rolled in, covering the southern sky in a broad, gray blanket.

Uh-oh, we're going to get water again. I'd better finish this.

He lowered the charge in the hole, connected it to Bent's notebook and initiated a five nanosector countdown. The blast covered him, the notebook, and the runabout with dust, dirt, sand, and stones.

He rolled up the igniting cable and decided to pick up Lilea before the water came. He entered the runabout preparing to swing it around when, from the clouds over the hills south of *Explorer*, a huge lightning bolt split the still air. The flash of light momentarily blinded him, and the noise reverberated within the runabout and hammered at his ears as though he were inside a pounding bass drum.

"What the hell—"

The black clouds had completely engulfed the hills behind the ship, and the storm dumped huge quantities of water. It was moving slowly but noticeably toward *Explorer* in the distance.

Jad shook his head to clear the ringing in his ears and headed toward the cliffs. A few drops of water began to fall. Nothing heavy. A brisk wind hit the runabout head-on as he drove, hurling the water into the windshield with a sound like small pellets. Lilea had ducked into a miniature cave at the base of the cliffs. She waved to him, but without something to wipe away the accumulating water over the windshield he could see only a vague, constantly shifting blob of blue-green as he drove up to the entrance of the cave. He went as close as he could, swung the right hand door open, and she jumped in.

"Wow." She tossed her sampling kit and camera into the rear seat. "It's wet out there, and I didn't bring my waterproof cover." She smiled slightly and giggled a little, treating the water as though it were a minor inconvenience.

More lightning and noise pounded the hills south of *Explorer*, but with the hills heavily engulfed in clouds, Jad couldn't see the bolts. He saw only the light as it dissolved the darkness.

"Do you think there's any danger to us?" Lilea asked as Jad drove toward *Explorer*. "From the lightning, I mean."

"I don't think so." Jad shook his head. "Lightning is strictly within the clouds. I can't imagine it striking us down here. I've seen lightning on the giant planets in our solar system. It just goes from cloud to cloud, or within a cloud. We should be okay."

Jad seemed satisfied with his answer. After all, he'd just given Lilea the best evidence Anthanian science had to offer, and he felt secure and confident, talking within his field.

"Are you sure? Some of those bolts I saw struck the hills behind the ship. Are you sure they don't strike the ground?"

Another huge blast lit up the inside of the runabout. The sound seemed to turn eardrums inside out.

"There," Lilea yelled. "That hit the ground. I saw it."

"Oh . . . yeah," Jad said, as his theory collapsed around him. "I couldn't see . . ." He stopped the runabout momentarily. The water swept in almost horizontally now, a long, sweeping wave of wind and water. Then more bolts — noise — lightning — water pounding the runabout — water splashing — wind rocking the runabout. Wetness everywhere outside, but everything dry inside. Jad tried to drive east, but the runabout became bogged in the mud. The wheels spun and lost traction.

"I hope the water doesn't get into the wheel motors," Jad said. "It might short them out and we might be stuck here until this storm ends."

Lilea didn't say anything, and Jad kept trying to drive forward. But he couldn't see more than a few links ahead.

By now the storm had moved directly over *Explorer*, obscuring the ship altogether. One long curtain of blackness extended from the ship to the hills, punctuated by brilliant flashes of lightning and blistering cascades of noise.

"Maybe we should stop." Lilea sounded a little uneasy, as though the storm was making her nervous or apprehensive.

"Okay. We may have to wait this out. According to inertial guidance, we're only about a quarter-anthan from the ship."

Another brilliant flash of light was followed by another heavy blast. This time the burst was much closer to the runabout. Jad shook his head to clear the ringing.

"See?" Lilea blurted. "That bolt hit the ground. It had to. It was right out in front of us. They must've seen that at the ship."

The ship. Those two words, so innocuous in sound, so unobtrusive in meaning hit Jad hard, as though the bolt had struck him sitting naked in the runabout. He exploded. "Saw it at the ship? It might have struck the ship." He grabbed the microphone of the runabout's comm system and yelled into it. "Jer! Jer! Get out of the ship! Get out of there! Tell everyone to get out of the ship!" He waited for an answer. Several nanosectors went by but Jer didn't answer and Jad tried again. "Jer! Get out of the ship! Lightning could strike the ship! Get everyone out!" But only static returned his call. Five nanosectors — ten — still no answer.

"Jer, can you hear me? Jer, do you read?" Jad continued to call Jer's name over and over, but he received no return.

"Are you online?" Lilea asked. She checked the main com screen in the center of the runabout's console. "Yes, comm is open, the matrix is on-line. How come you're not getting a return?" She raised her head, her face drained of color. Her fair skin looked even more pallid than usual. A look of panic spread over her face. "Oh, no. You don't suppose . . . ?"

Jad said nothing. He stared straight ahead, out the window at the shroud of blackness that enveloped the ship. Slowly the veil rose. The hills south of the ship were almost clear now, clothed only in an indistinct haze.

Gradually the squall released its hold on the ship. As though being raised by an unseen hand, the curtain lifted. *Explorer* appeared, bottom first, but weirdly misshapen. It seemed crooked, or hunched over, or sitting at a funny angle. Neither Jad nor Lilea could see clearly through the drizzle that drenched the windshield. After several microsectors, when the water had dwindled to a gentle mist, Lilea opened her door and stood up.

She screamed. "It's tilted! It *is* tilted! Oh, my god! What happened?"

Jad got out too and stood beside the runabout in the open left side door. He looked at the ship, a quarter-anthan away, sitting on the landing site, tilted at a precarious angle to the northeast. He scanned the ship, top to bottom. "Look at the antenna. The low gain antenna on top. It's gone. It's melted away. A lightning bolt hit the top of the ship."

Lilea closed her door and took a hesitant step forward. "But why is it tilted?" Her face was still locked in a moment of horror.

Jad closed his door and walked carefully through the mud to the front of the runabout. He stood at the left side, wondering about Lilea's question—lightning—a bolt of electricity—the ship's computer—com control. "The navigational computer has been knocked out. All of the leveling pads in the fins are retracted. That means the one pad that was extended eight links is retracted. That would put it . . . and that means the other computers are out too . . . the communications computer . . . no wonder Jer couldn't . . ."

Jad was interrupted by a low roaring coming from the hills south of the ship. Out of the opening in those hills, the opening that led directly to the ship, came a wall of water, water that must have built up in the troughs and valleys of the hills behind the ship since the downpour began more than a subsector earlier. As soon as the water accumulated it began to move, and it took the only route available—through the narrow opening that led directly toward *Explorer*. All that water—several million trilinks—swelled out of those hills in one immense, boiling, churning wave. In a mere instant it crossed the two hundred links from hills to ship.

Near the base of the ship were two dots of color, the bright blue-green of jumpsuits. The water was confined largely to the rock-hard sur-face between the hills and the ship, and only a few steps to either side was safety. But will those people get out of the way in time?

Who are they? Do they see the water?

Jad took several steps forward, yelling. "Get out of the way! Get out of —"

Lilea saw the water too. "My god," she gasped as the water hit the ship.

CHAPTER 57

WATER

Time Element 461.235.5.8.

No, the water didn't knock *Explorer* over—it didn't possess enough energy to do that. But when it collided with the ship it engulfed the two dots of color and at the same time there came a short but intense screeching sound. The sound was carried all the way to Jad and Lilea standing in the desert a quarter-anthan away. It was a grinding sound of metal against rock as the ship rotated slightly. Jad watched as the right lateral fin shifted position when the water slammed into it, and the upper medial fin—the fin that overlapped the groove in the rock—dropped more than a link. The ship groaned and creaked and moaned as it tilted even more, and the lower medial and right lateral fins rose slowly and ominously from the surface. Then the ship seemed to hesitate. It held that position for, at most, a microsector. And as Jad watched in the absolute horror of what he knew was about to happen, the upper medial fin, now carrying much more weight than it had been designed to hold, buckled and crumpled like a piece of aluminum foil. Silvery streams of molten sodium exploded in a blast of metallic lightning from the heat exchangers in the fin, and the ship went over, all the way over.

It hit the ground with an earth-shaking roar that rippled and danced through the ground and reverberated through Jad's feet like a gentle massage. Undoubtedly, the seismic recorders in the vicinity of the landing site also felt the shock, all twelve dutifully sending a complete record of *Explorer's* collapse to the Geological Computer, its circuits long silenced. The ship landed, in one last ironic blow to the expedition it housed and transported, directly on top of the graves of Case, Dell, and Col, and not far from Aero One parked in its usual place on the east side of the runway. A huge crack—it would have been vertical were the ship still standing—opened along what was now the upper side of the ship, from the Entry Deck to the engine bell at the bottom.

Lilea screamed and started running, yelling at the top of her voice. "Oh, my god! Bent's in there! Bent's in there! We've got to help them! Jad, we've got to help them!"

Jad hesitated for a nanosector, not sure what to do. He continued to watch the ship, lying on its side, belching smoke and steam. Steam? White billowing clouds of condensed moisture formed above the ship, and a plume of some steamy liquid spurted skyward from near the bottom. Jad stared at the clouds, unsure of what caused them. The plume stopped momentarily, and then began again intermittently, sometimes shooting vertically, sometimes almost horizontally from cracks in the side of the ship.

Jad started running, following Lilea toward the ship. *There are steam lines near the bottom of the ship. Some of the excess heat from the fission reactor is used to generate steam for Mina's sterilizers, but that venting is too strong to be a steam line —*

"Good god!" he yelled. "That's not steam, that's liquid hydrogen! The fuel tank has ruptured! It's leaking!" *The fuel tank is just one level below the reactor and it's still more than half full. If that flammable liquid pours over onto that hot fission reactor . . .*

"Lilea!" Jad yelled as the image erupted in his mind. "Lilea! Don't go any farther! Come back! It's too dangerous!"

Jad ran faster, as fast as he could through the mud and puddles of water. In a few nanosectors he caught up with Lilea and grabbed her arm. "Don't go any farther!" he yelled. "It's too dangerous."

Lilea stopped and spun around. "What are you doing?! Let me go! Let me go!" She jerked her arm and tore at Jad's hand, struggling to get free, but his hold was tight and her feet slipped on the muddy ground. She almost fell, but Jad kept a tight grip on her arm and kept her from falling.

"It's too dangerous!" Jad yelled again, but he wasn't sure she understood him. "The liquid hydrogen tank! It's ruptured. It may —"

Jad didn't get to finish his sentence. He and Lilea were momentarily blinded by a searing flash of light and heat. In less than a tenth-nanosector, an enormous fireball engulfed *Explorer*, and a churning, fiery mushroom-shaped cloud rose into the air and hovered above the site. The force of the explosion completed the process of ripping the ship open from top to bottom that the fall had started, and a huge amount of debris from the interior of the ship was sucked into the air by the explosion and scattered to every part of the landing site. The fireball engulfed Aero One, and the small amount of liquid hydrogen in its fuel tank ignited. The shock wave hit Aero Two on the other side of the runway and flipped it into the air like a toy plane in a sudden gust. It landed on its back several hundred links away, the wings sheared and torn into pieces, the tail twisted and bent into a cockeyed angle, the landing skids ripped from the fuselage.

Jad turned around and bent over. "Look out!" He threw both arms over his head as debris from the explosion rained down around them. When he stood, the sight that greeted him was one of total destruction. The ship, that magnificent ship that so many hopes had ridden on, that so many people had expressed so many superlatives about, the ship that had brought them to this new and exciting planet and had been their home for more than two hundred T-sectors, was now nothing more than a scorched hunk of metal and scattered debris. The superstructure of the ship had been sheared apart by the force of the explosion, and an acrid black smoke spewed from the gaping wound.

Jad and Lilea stood in the mud and debris for a few nanosectors. Someone's jacket, the left sleeve on fire, burned on the ground in front of them.

"Oh, my god," Lilea said quietly, and her legs gave out and she dropped to her knees. She closed her eyes and put her hands over her face. She trembled like a leaf and had difficulty catching her breath. Then she began to cry. "Oh, no," she said several times as the tears poured down her cheeks. "Bent was in there."

Time Element 461.235.5.9.

Jad stood in the mud, staring at the destruction. He didn't move for several microsectors. His mind turned to the two dots of color. *Who were they?* Wila and Trea were outside—they might have returned to the ship when they heard the first claps of noise. But the two dots of color could have been others from the ship—Jer, Mina, or Bent. He could no longer see them. Where were they?

He began to walk toward the desolated ship, hesitantly at first, but after a few steps he started running, faster and faster, with only one thing on his mind—Wila. She could have been one of the two he'd seen from so far away. He had to find her.

Fires still burned in the blackness of the ship's interior when Jad arrived. Pieces of metal on the ground glowed red hot, some sizzled on the wet surface. The heat from the fires was so intense he couldn't approach closer than several hundred links and he raised his right arm to shield his face from the furnace-like blast. Small, misshapen blobs of metal, pieces of the outer skin of the ship and made of state-of-the-art high melting point alloy, lay scattered everywhere. He stepped carefully around a trickle of molten sodium as it sizzled and hissed along the ground, occasionally exploding into a cloud of white whenever it hit a puddle of water.

He circled the ship, moving cautiously to his left, down the rock surface toward the runway. Nothing remained he could identify. Several times he called Wila's name and surveyed larger and larger areas of the destruction. He turned to where the aerodynes had been parked.

Aero Two lay several hundred links from the remains of *Explorer*, and he ran over to it, but Wila wasn't there, and he returned to the runway. As he scanned farther down the runway, a blue-green smear, lying horizontally across the surface about a thousand links away, caught his eye. "Oh, no." His heart pounded in his chest, and he could feel it throbbing in his temples.

Trea lay facedown on the runway. He turned her over and checked the carotid pulse, but he couldn't find it. Cuts and bruises covered her face and some facial bones appeared fractured. Her jumpsuit was torn in several places.

She's dead.

He left Trea and continued down the runway, scanning the area, right and left. His heart pounded faster and a developing terror invaded his mind. With Trea's body at the landing site, Wila should be here, too. He saw them drive away together and they must have come back together. But where is she? He saw nothing until he got about three-quarters of the way down the runway when he noticed another small fragment of color beyond the runway's end, and the horror of what that color meant hammered away at his mind with every urgent heartbeat.

Wila's body lay partially hidden from view, tangled in the small grove of trees beyond the end of the runway. She too had cuts and scrapes all over her face from being dragged along the ground by the water. Jad carefully disentangled her body from the woody stems and laid her on the wet earth next to the shrub. A large gash covered her left cheek and jaw, and blood was caked around her nose. She wasn't breathing. He tried mouth-to-mouth resuscitation but he couldn't even force air into her lungs. She probably had clotted blood in her throat, maybe even her windpipe. He stood up next to the body.

The runabouts will have first-aid kits, and there should be suction equipment in them.

He looked left, looking for the runabout. It was still mired in the mud a quarter-anthan from the ship, though from where he stood at the north end of the runway, it must have been a half-anthan or more away. He looked for Runabout 1 and located it a short distance east of the landing site, but it too was heavily enmeshed in the mud. The feelings of helplessness almost made him want to scream—he couldn't do anything to revive Wila. She had no pulse, no respiration, and her pupils were fixed and dilated.

Wila and Trea must have left their runabout and run over to the ship, arriving just before the water came. He looked back up the runway past the remnants of the ship to the opening in the hills. He strained his eyes trying to see. He wondered if someone, or something, was there. His heart continued to pound as the anger swelled within.

But he saw nothing and he knelt back on the ground beside Wila.

CHAPTER 58

ACCEPTANCE

Time Element 461.235.6.2.

Lilea rose from where she knelt and, still crying, turned and ran back to the runabout. She opened the right side door and sat sideways in the seat, her head in her hands, her body shuddering and quivering. She stayed there for several millisectors, breathing heavily, sometimes gasping for breath, wondering if this was a dream, or if she might wake up in the warm, comfortable bed in her compartment with Bent sleeping soundly beside her. She looked for the red light above the bed. No, this wasn't a dream, she wasn't having a nightmare. In the span of mere microsectors, *Explorer* had been taken from them — eternally and forever.

Her hands shook and tears streamed down her face. Bent was dead. He certainly could never have survived that blast — unless by the slimmest of chances he'd been outside when the ship blew up. Yes! That's it! He was outside walking around when the ship blew up. That has to be it. That thought alone caused her to turn and look at the destruction to see if Bent was still alive. She stood from the runabout and closed the door. She began walking, but after a few steps started running and yelling. "Oh, god! Let him be alive! Let him be alive!"

By the time Lilea reached the landing site, Jad had pulled Wila's body from the trees at the end of the runway. Lilea ran past the smoldering ship down the runway toward Jad, stopping first to kneel beside Trea. She felt for a pulse at Trea's wrist and again at her neck, but found none. She continued down the runway.

When she reached Jad, he was sobbing heavily. He knelt beside Wila's body, covering her face with his. Lilea knelt beside him and tried to say something, to try to comfort him, but all she could think to say was, "Jad, I'm sorry about Wila."

She stayed with Jad for a few nanosectors, but there was something she had to do. She walked back up the runway, looking for Bent. Several times she called his name, but she received no answer.

She ran over to Runabout 1, still mired in the mud east of the landing site and entered the left side. When she pushed forward on the joystick, the runabout groaned and creaked, straining against the mud caking its wheels. The motors in the wheels hummed, trying desperately to turn, but were held fast. The amp load display for each wheel turned red on the com screen, and she backed off slightly when a double-bong alarm sounded. After a few nanosectors, one, then both front wheels freed themselves and started spinning, uselessly at first, but when the two rear wheels broke loose the runabout crawled slowly across the muddy terrain. She stopped near the remains of the ship and got out, looking for Bent in every direction. Repeatedly she called his name but no answer came. A terrible pain developed in the pit of her stomach.

"Bent! Where are you? Bent! Bent!"

Slowly the facts took shape in her mind. Bent almost certainly was dead, the logic too obvious not to notice. He wasn't out walking around or she would have seen him. With the burn on his back having become infected, he wanted to stay inside and rest and let the new antibiotics do their work, and it was unlikely he would have left the ship. He wasn't outside with Wila and Trea when the ship fell over and exploded—he must have been *inside*.

But that was too much to accept. Bent was *not* dead. He was around here somewhere. But where? The terrain around the landing site was so wide open she could see for at least an anthan in every direction except south. Did he walk up into the hills? Oh, no, of course not—that's ridiculous. But maybe, just maybe, he was outside walking around. Maybe, just maybe, he'd decided to get some fresh air and left the ship before it fell over.

But the pain medication made him sleepy, and he wouldn't go outside. Had he for some reason gone out, he should be here by now. He certainly would've seen and heard the storm as it approached the ship, and he would've seen lightning strike the ship. He would've seen the ship fall over and would've heard the explosion. No, he couldn't be outside. The storm would've driven him back inside. Oh, god, so many possibilities!

Two emotions tore at Lilea. The logic of Bent's death and the staunch refusal to accept the conclusions of that logic struggled inside her, and she could take it no longer. She sat down on a large rock just to the side of the landing site and put her head in her hands and began to cry again. Now she would accept it. She would have to accept it. Bent was dead.

"Oh, god, no," she said, several times. "Why? Why?"

She sat on that rock for more than five millisectors, gradually yielding to reality. Finally, she raised her head. With her face still streaked with tears, she raised her fists and bellowed out to the world around her, "No! No! This can't be! This isn't real!" Then she fell off the rock to the ground, continuing to sob convulsively.

It was as though she was now totally alone in this world, totally isolated from all she held dear and precious, infinitely separated from her home, her haven, her hills. Sure, Jad was still alive, down at the end of the runway consoling himself over the death of his beloved Wila. But he was the only one else left alive, and the Command Ship *Star Voyager*, that big monstrous space vehicle that could carry both of them back to their home planet where they would be welcome and safe, was so many millions of anthans away, so far it took light one full T-sector to get there and the same time for an answer to get back, and that just magnified the separation and made them feel totally alone on the surface of this eternally damned planet.

Yes, this damned planet. This planet that had taken her love, the only one she'd ever fallen in love with, the adorable guy with the dark, curly hair and the cute smile who'd been so fascinated by that gorge over there—even before they left Anthanos—but who swung back and forth between wanting to leave this planet, yet intently studying the images of the gorge T-sector after T-sector trying to find a route to the bottom. This planet that had taken her husband and seven of her best friends, first one at a time, then—my god!—*five* of them in one inconceivable blast, one unbelievable, unimaginable, indescribable blast.

What did all this mean? Was this planet really trying to tell them something, or was she right all along, that the incidents were random and haphazard, chancy and arbitrary, and we could learn to live with them?

Oh, yeah, right, live on a planet with all this? Was Bent right when he posed the question to her after the attack on Col, the consequential question they all were supposed to answer when they got back: "Are we really thinking about living on this planet? Do we really want to colonize this place?"

What, this place? This planet, with all those fascinating sunsets, with all the allure and exquisiteness that natural forces can compose, with all the class and character that Anthanos so totally lacked do we really want to colonize this place?

No! No! Certainly not! I want to go home!

Lilea lay at the side of the runway for almost a subsector when the tremendous exertion of weeping finally took its toll and she could cry no more. The realization of the death of Bent and all the others, and the thorough destruction that lay all around her had drained grief and despair completely out of her, and when she finally sat up she was emotionally empty.

She tried to think, but hundreds of unanswered questions ran through her mind. *What do we do now? Where do we go from here? Why has all this happened?*

But another more pressing thought crept through her mind—survival. The lightning strike had certainly cut off *Explorer*'s carrier signal, and *Star Voyager* will detect that cutoff in one T-sector, and if it isn't restarted within one more T-sector, Kal Mada, the commander-in-chief of this expedition, will have no choice but to send the Rescue ship. But how will they survive until then? What will they eat and drink?

How's Jad? Did he find Wila? Oh, yes, he did, I remember now.

She sat on the ground beside the large rock for another millisector and finally regained enough composure to rise and drive Runabout 1 down the runway. She passed Trea's body again and stopped. She left the runabout and knelt beside the body.

"Goodbye, Trea." She gently brushed aside the wet, matted hair from Trea's forehead. "First Col, now you. You and I were the only ones who honestly saw this planet for what it was. I enjoyed knowing you and working with you. I wish I had something to cover you with. You shouldn't have to lie here like this." But nothing was left to make even a simple shroud.

She continued to drive toward Jad at the end of the runway and parked the runabout several hundred links from the trees where Jad sat, cradling Wila's bloody head in his lap. She wanted to leave room for him to mourn in private, without invading his personal space.

"My god, I loved her so much," Jad blurted through his tears as she approached him. "Wila knew! She knew something would happen! Now she's dead! They killed her! I hate this place! I hate this goddamned planet! I just want to go home!"

Lilea returned to Runabout 1 and sat in the left-hand seat. She tried to think but her thoughts now dwelled more on survival than grief. She and Jad were the only ones left and now they had no ship, no aerodynes and only two runabouts left. They would have to make do. They'd have to contact *Star Voyager* by one of the runabout's comm systems. Kal Mada will send *Rescue* automatically based on the loss of carrier signal, but she wanted to let them know what'd happened. It was tricky but they could do it. They'd been taught before they left Anthanos how to contact *Star Voyager* with the aerodyne or runabout comm systems, but Lilea also remembered they told her the maximum power of a runabout system was just barely sufficient to send a signal that far, and *Star Voyager* might not receive all of it. They were to use a text signal only, no voice or images. But they could do it—they would have to. They would tell them what happened and wait for *Rescue* to arrive.

Sunset approached and the air temperature dropped. A cold wind whipped around the landing site. Lilea closed the door to the runabout, though she left the window open a crack to get fresh air. She moved the runabout closer to the end of the runway, about twenty links from Jad, but he remained outside, apparently oblivious to the presence of the runabout nearby. She got out and went over to him.

"Jad, why don't you come inside the runabout? I started the heat. It's warmer in there."

"No, thanks, I'm going to stay here. Wila needs me."

"Okay." The concept that Wila, now dead, needed Jad seemed overly melodramatic to her—more likely Jad needed to be with Wila—but she decided to leave him alone and she went back to the runabout. She glanced in the direction of Trea's body as she walked to the door.

She'd have to bury Trea sooner or later, but she was not up to that task right now. She excused herself because the weather was too cold. She entered the runabout to wait for the warmer weather that might or might not appear the next lightime.

But perhaps more significantly, she excused herself from burying Trea because she didn't know how to take all this death and destruction. It was all around her and it intruded on every thought. It pushed and pulled at her, threatening to engulf her and drive her running from the runabout into the looming darkness.

She tried to sort out what'd just happened and she went over the sequence of events, struggling to put some order to everything. But everything had taken place so fast, and it all added up to such a horrendous, monumental calamity that her mind couldn't process the events individually. A long time, she realized, would pass before she could step back and examine everything in a logical, dispassionate manner. Finally, she gave up, and one single thought stuck in her mind.

I guess Bent was next.

As she sat in the runabout, she became aware of the odor drifting up the runway, the odor of burning, a mixture of odors. She imagined she could smell burning flesh in the smoke, though she knew deep down that was extremely unlikely, and anyway she found it difficult to sort out only one smell. So often the odor was an acrid smell — the burning of insulation or plastic or god-knows-what. She closed the runabout's windows. A few small fires still flickered and smoked in the ship's hulk, but so much had been reduced to ashes by the explosion and fire that little was left to burn. Occasionally a pop or spark would flare up and a small flame would burn and crackle for a few microsectors, then it too would dwindle and die out.

Several other thoughts kept racing through Lilea's mind. She remembered what Case had said at the meeting the T-sector *Explorer* landed. "Nothing is going to move this ship," he said, sounding totally convinced in his rationale.

What a titanic miscalculation that was. I also remember I didn't like those hills, so close to the ship. I was right, they were dangerous.

She removed her weapon and tossed it into the back seat. When she turned back, she glanced out the front of the runabout at the western sky. The sun, about twenty degrees above the horizon, had begun to send slivers of reddish-orange light through the sky, and it reminded her of something — darkness, sleep, the little red light in their compartment above the bed. She checked the interior lights in the runabout. Plenty of lights, but all white and brilliant, placed carefully by the designers to give the operator sufficient light to see inside. No one had installed any red lights. When all the interior lights were off, the darkness was almost total. Her heart jumped, her forehead grew wet, her mouth dry. She decided to leave the com screen and one light on. For Jad, she told herself.

Jad stayed beside Wila most of the night, but when the air temperature dropped he entered the runabout. He extinguished the light and turned down the brightness control on the com screen, and reclined his seat back almost to horizontal. Though it was likely he didn't get any sleep this darktime, Lilea certainly didn't. She stayed awake in the darkness, her eyes wide open and fixed on the only light left, a pale blue LED just above the main com screen that indicated the reactor was active.

She balled her hands into fists. Her forehead perspired freely, her breathing became rapid and shallow, and her heartbeat doubled against the demons of the dark.

This damn planet will kill me yet.

CHAPTER 59

BURIAL

Time Element 461.237.0.0.

Star Voyager had already detected the termination of *Explorer*'s carrier wave signal by the time the sun rose at Site One, and a broad band of salmon-orange light crept up over the desert horizon in the east. Lilea'd spent the night in the left-hand seat of Runabout 1 with the seat back only slightly reclined, and with the sunrise behind her and enough pale pink light reflected off the hills to her left that she could make out their familiar profile, she finally began to relax. Most of the clouds left over from the storms had remained through the night, shielding the surface from a precipitous drop in temperature. Nevertheless, it was only 3 Tal when she opened the door and stepped outside.

She glanced up the runway toward the charred hulk of *Explorer*, still smoldering in places. But the sight of the remains and the knowledge that Bent's body still lay in there brought out too many memories of the explosion and she looked away. She spied Trea's body, about a thousand links from where she stood.

We'll have to do something about the two bodies this lightime.

Jad had already left the runabout and stood beside Wila. "We're going to have to bury them." His voice was flat and weary. He sounded as emotionally empty as she, and a spasm of concern for him floated briefly through her mind.

"I know. I thought about that, too. Would you like to have me bury Wila, or do you want to do that yourself?"

"Why would you think I wouldn't want to do it?" He glanced at her—an indignant glance, his eyes angry, yet at the same time blank and devoid of emotion.

"I just thought it might be easier for you if I did it."

"No, thanks, I'll do it." He opened one of the tool chests on the runabout's right side and pulled out two shovels. One he handed to Lilea. With the other he began digging about ten links east of the clump of trees.

"I'll go bury Trea." Jad did not reply.

Lilea took the other shovel and walked up the runway. The odors of the burning spacecraft had largely dissipated, and she picked a comfortable spot on the east side of the runway where Trea's body still lay, around a thousand links from the smoldering hulk.

It took her most of the lightime to dig a satisfactory grave about six links deep in the rocky soil. Midway during the digging she took a break and walked over to Runabout 2, still sitting in the desert a quarter-anthan away. Her water bottle, camera, and sampling kit were still there and she took a few gulps of water. By this time the soil caking the wheels was almost dry and the wheels moved freely, so she drove the runabout back to the runway and parked it a few links from Runabout 1. She offered Jad some water and he drank a few swallows.

"Thanks," was all he said.

She went back to digging, and when she decided the grave was deep enough, she went over to Jad, standing at the edge of Wila's grave, lost in thought.

"You'll have to help me move Trea's body."

"Why? What's the matter?" He glared at her. "All you have to do is drag it to the hole and dump it in."

"I can't do that. Trea is, well . . . she's a friend of mine. I can't just —"

"She's a friend of mine, too." His glare was even more intense.

"You're right, she is, but I can't just dump her body in the hole. We should try to lower her into the grave as gently as we can. That's how I feel. I'll help you do the same with Wila."

Jad didn't answer for a few nanosectors. He continued to stare at the hole, his face still blank, impassive. "Okay, I'll give you a hand." He dropped his shovel. They walked up the runway to Trea's body and together carried it to the gravesite, placing it as carefully as they could on the bottom. They filled the hole with dirt, and returned to Wila's grave.

"Did you know Trea tried to kill herself?" Jad asked as they walked. His voice was quieter now, not as angry. Like a mourner at a funeral.

"Yes, Bent told me. He said she tried to drown herself."

"There was more to it than that. She gave herself half a vial of painkiller. She was so stoned she wandered off and fell in the water. But the water was just a trickle and we found her in time."

"I didn't know that."

Jad said nothing more. He picked up his shovel and finished Wila's grave. They lowered her body and filled in the hole, and then stood quietly beside the site for several microsectors. They put both shovels back in the tool chest and took several more swallows of water from Lilea's bottle, now almost empty.

Using a knife he found in the runabout, Jad scratched four lines from a poem about flying—one of Wila's favorites—on a stick and placed it in the ground at the head of the grave.

For once to die,
No more to fly—
For once to fly
No more to die.

Both Jad and Lilea were streaked with dirt and dried, caked mud. "There's no way to wash your hands," Jad said as he walked back to the runabout. "We're going to have to find some water and food soon. Your water bottle is the only water we have."

"I know where some water is, and I saw a bag of edible nuts in the runabout. I guess Wila and Trea brought them back when they returned to the ship just before they . . . before the ship fell over."

Jad retrieved the bag of nuts. He pulled a few from the bag, and Lilea showed him how to crack them open with her teeth. Jad opened and ate a few. "We're going to need lots more of these before the rescue ship gets here."

"Shouldn't we try to contact them soon?"

"Why should we? They've already detected the shutdown of the carrier wave signal and they're getting the rescue ship ready. But it's going to take forty T-sectors for that ship to get here." He did a quick calculation in his head. "Forty Anthanian T-sectors is about thirty T-sectors here, which is fifteen revolutions of this planet. But they won't be able to send the ship until next lightime. That's 239. So it can't arrive until 269 at the earliest. We'll need to find some more food. Where's the water you said you knew about?"

"There's a creek to the east of here. That's where Trea and Wila went just before . . . do you remember? They talked about it before we left." Lilea pointed in a generally southeast direction. "I think we can get some water there. Maybe we can get more of the nuts."

"How did you know how to open the nuts?"

"Trea showed me. Col had found some earlier."

Jad splashed the remaining water from Lilea's bottle on his hands and dried them on his jumpsuit. "Those nuts are kind of oily."

"I'm going to try to contact *Star Voyager*."

"Be my guest, but you're wasting your time." Jad walked around to the other side of Runabout 1 and entered the left-hand seat. He closed the door, tilted the seat back to a partially reclined position and closed his eyes.

Lilea walked up the runway to Runabout 2 and opened a compartment on the right rear marked **HIGH GAIN ANTENNA**. She pulled out the slender, black parabolic antenna and flipped it open, then removed the laser-core transceiver from its storage holder and snapped it into place in the center of the parabola. She jerked the tall whip-like omnidirectional antenna from its plug-in site on the back of the runabout and jammed the new antenna in its place, adjusting the dish to face forward and upward at 41 degrees — the latitude of the landing site. She entered the left-hand seat of the runabout and backed it around to face geographic north by the digital compass in the runabout's computer.

"It should be pointed directly at *Star Voyager*. Let's hope so."

Star Voyager had taken a position one light sector above the planet's North Pole. There it could stay in constant contact with the team wherever they landed on the planet's northern hemisphere.

She typed a hurried message on the keyboard of the runabout's computer, and turned signal amplification to maximum. With her message displayed on the com screen, and with a barely perceptible high-pitched squeal coming from the transceiver, she touched 'Send.'

FROM: Surface Exploratory Team-G: Lilea K

SENDER MATRIX: Runabout 2

RECEIVER MATRIX: DSEV-1: Star Voyager

CODING TIME: Standard: 461.373.5.2.7 Surface: 461.237.8.7

ROUTING VALUE: Urgent — Deliver Immediately

Explorer destroyed Jad and I only ones alive All others dead

Send rescue ship soon as possible Have limited food and water

Will need help soon as possible Only runabouts left Both

aerodynes destroyed

"Okay. I've sent them a message, but it'll be a T-sector before they get it."

CHAPTER 60

TREA'S GROVE

Time Element 461.237.8.9.

Lilea terminated comm and replaced the high-gain antenna with the omnidirectional, and walked over to Runabout 1. She tapped on the window, jerking Jad from his rest. He rolled the window partway down.

"We should try and get some water and more of the nuts."

"Okay. I'll drive." They left in Runabout 1 toward the grove of trees that Lilea had nicknamed "Trea's Grove." They detoured north at the dry stream bed to find a crossing shallow enough for the runabout, and when they encountered the creek Jad sped south, paralleling the stream, arriving at the grove after a drive of about two millisectors.

Lilea understood immediately why Trea enjoyed this place. A quietness enveloped her as she entered the thicket, and the pungent scent she smelled the first time she stepped outside of *Explorer* filled the air. The trees that formed the greatest portion of the thicket muffled and fragmented the chilly wind, and the only sounds Lilea could identify were the songs of a few birds in the trees and the gentle trickling of the water over the rocks in the creek bed. The landing site was invisible from the grove, but even had *Explorer* been standing, it would have been obscured by the trees.

"A person could get lost here. It's so secluded and cut off from the rest of the world. It's really wonderful here." Lilea knelt beside the creek and dipped her hands into the icy water, washing off the mud and dirt of digging, and then she filled the water bottle. "I'm going to check and see if there's any food in the runabout."

"You won't find any. We never left food in a runabout or aerodyne."

"I know. But I'm going to look anyway. It can't hurt."

Lilea rummaged through the various compartments in the runabout, but found only tools, a small stove and cooking pots, two high intensity lamps, a portable radiation monitor and an empty water bottle. They filled the other water bottle and picked up as many nuts as they could find. They returned to the landing site where Lilea went through the storage compartments in Runabout 2, but found only the same articles, including another empty water bottle, but no food.

"We could try going through the ship," Jad said. "There might be some food that wasn't burned in the explosion. Most of the food was in the refrigerators and freezers, and some of it might have survived."

"Okay, but you go. I'd be afraid I'd run across Bent's body. I don't think I could take that."

"All right." Jad zipped his jacket against the evening chill and drove Runabout 1 up the runway.

Lilea slipped into Runabout 2 and turned on the heat. All the work she'd done this lightime had kept her warm against the raw, cold air, but now as the temperature dropped with the setting sun, she felt chilled. Jad returned several millisectors later, and she rolled the window part way down to talk to him.

"There's nothing left." His breath produced faint wisps of condensate in the cool air. "The ship's been completely destroyed, especially where the storage deck and reactor and fuel tank were. The refrigerators and freezers were almost vaporized."

"I was afraid of that. That means we'll have to find food around here. Like more of those nuts."

Jad looked around at the sky, his face emotionless and dreary. "It's too dark now. Did Col ever grow any Anthanian plants here? Outside where we could get to them?"

"No. He started some yanto plants on Life Sciences. That's all."

"Then we're going to have to live on what we can scavenge, before the rescue ship arrives."

"I guess so."

Jad pulled Runabout 1 closer to Wila's grave and Lilea spent the darktime in Runabout 2.

Time Element 461.239.3.9.

They collected fifty-one nuts, but when they divided them, Jad insisted Lilea take the odd last nut, so she took her twenty-six and went back to her runabout. He still parked his runabout near the clump of trees at the end of the runway. He wanted to be near Wila, and after foraging for nuts, he always returned to this position.

Lilea certainly didn't mind, she was willing to allow Jad his parking space, but she wanted a comfortable leeway between them. So after she returned from filling the water bottles at Trea's Grove, she parked her runabout farther up the runway, separating them by almost 100 links. She always parked across the runway facing west. She wanted to see the sunset.

But she would have to wait several subsectors before the sun dropped below the horizon. Now came the part of the wait for *Rescue* she'd begun to dread: the long, uninterrupted, wearisome time spent sitting in the runabout. They'd already performed this lightime's ritual, they retrieved nuts and she'd filled the three water bottles. No more tasks were left—nothing to do but sit and wait until the next lightime when they would repeat the process.

She wanted to look for that partially-completed spearhead. Other than Bent, she missed that spearhead more than anything else. She couldn't have Bent, but maybe the spearhead had been ejected by the explosion, just lying out there, waiting to be picked up. She wanted to look for other debris, too. Something useful might be lying around, perhaps a heavier jacket. But she recognized early that walking around fighting the cold would use precious energy. Better to hibernate in the runabout.

But she did make one special trip once every lightime, usually around the middle of the lightime, a short trip to pay her respects to her friends. She visited Trea's and Wila's graves, spending only about a microsector at each because of the cold, taking herself back in her mind to some incident she enjoyed with each friend. There were so many she could think of with Wila, yet she thought it strange she had so little personal interaction with Trea and Col. They kept mostly to themselves. Yet it was Trea who got out to see the animals. Several times Lilea passed Trea on Life Sciences or the Personnel Deck as she sprinted toward the interdeck ladder to descend to the Entry Deck to get outdoors. She'd run out to see and image the big, lumbering animals that occasionally passed near the ship. Often she took a runabout over to meet them. Many times she'd go out without her weapon and Case or Col would yell at her, but she got great videos of the animals, and she always showed them at the team meetings. Trea was so into everything she did.

After Lilea finished at Trea's grave, she tackled the most painful part of her obligatory trip, walking or driving up the runway toward the hulk of *Explorer*, to pay her respects to Jer and Mina. In her mind she apologized to Jer for lying about the busted PersComm, and for not bringing it to her as she asked, but Jer would be suspicious if she saw it because it'd been damaged so heavily. And she thought of Mina, her best friend and all the good times they spent together dating back to their time in college. In her mind she apologized for driving Dell out into the path of that storm, but still wondered what Mina meant about "other explanations."

Then she turned to thoughts of Bent, but she had so many memories of him she found it hard to concentrate on only one, and she stayed back from the ruins, afraid she might see his body, charred and burned in the blackened ship. That would be too much for her and she decided not to take the chance.

When she finished, she'd hurry back to the warmth of her runabout to munch on a few nuts. Then she'd recline the seat back several degrees so she could settle in for the rest of the lightime.

She turned to the animal Col shot, fixing in her mind an image of it as it was about to spring. The most prominent feature of the animal wasn't the huge knife-like teeth—and this seemed a bit odd—it was the animal's eyes, those great yellowish-green eyes that stared at her with a look that was identical to the look in the gray-green eyes of the slithering creature as it fixed on the furry animal just before it struck. The viciousness in those eyes signaled an intent to attack and kill and even devour. They scared her more than the big teeth.

Oh, god, how morbid. If I'm going to make it through thirteen more protracted lightimes sitting here waiting for Rescue, *I'm going to have to think about good stuff. I'll go mad if I don't.*

She wanted to play a movie on the com screen, but runabouts didn't have movies installed. Were *Explorer* still standing, she could download one from the ship's movie store, but with that no longer possible, she closed her eyes to help concentrate on the "good stuff."

CHAPTER 61

DESTRUCTION

Time Element 461.243.6.1.

Jad always parked his runabout north, facing the grove of trees. Wila's grave lay just to the right, marked prominently by the stick. He stared at the stick for several nanosectors, and then focused the runabout's rear-facing camera on the area of Trea's grave behind and to the runabout's right. He couldn't see the burial spot itself, but he could see the stick Lilea placed there to mark the site. Many of the plants in that area rocked silently in the cool wind, but he was warm and safe inside the runabout. The outside temperature reading on the com screen read 13 Tal.

That's chilly, but not too chilly. I'm going to get out and stretch.

He stepped out of his runabout and went through his usual routine of stretching, the same routine he always went through before running. He paid most attention to the lower body, but he did a few upper body stretches as well — that evened things out. When he'd pulled out the kinks in most of his major muscle groups, he turned around and looked up the runway toward the remnants of *Explorer*.

I should check the reactor for leaks. He pulled the radiation monitor from a storage compartment on the back of the runabout and energized it. The indicator light on top turned blue — *That's good, the background level is normal.*

He drove up the runway, past Lilea's runabout. She seemed to be asleep in the left-hand seat. The fires that burned sporadically in and around the ruins had died by now and the hulk of the ship was covered in many places with a dark gray ash, though a faint burning odor still drifted from the interior.

He stood at the edge of the ruins, scanning the lower section of the ship where the reactor and fuel reservoir had been. Oddly, he noticed, the outer skin of the ship hadn't been blown into bits by the explosion. The skin had been ripped into several large sections, and a number of pieces, bent and twisted by the explosion and heat, lay nearby, but they largely held together. The most prominent effect of the blast had been to blow the skin outward from around the reactor and fuel tank, melting some sections into odd shapes and blobs which covered the superstructure. The many vertical beams and horizontal girders which defined the general shape of the ship had been ripped and knotted and tangled together like so many strands of fine wire. The superstructure had sunk in on itself, like a balloon from which one might withdraw the air. A large hole at the exact site of the fuel tank gaped at Jad. With his eyes he traced the perimeter of the hole, almost perfectly circular, empty and black in the remnants of destruction.

Within that opening resided a real terror, and as he stared at it, a chilliness developed that reached into him and grasped at his entrails. He became frightened and intimidated—feelings he did not have the last time he approached the ship, looking only for food. At that time he attempted to squirm his way through the snarled superstructure, but couldn't get in and left.

This time he didn't leave. He stayed and fastened his jacket more tightly. As he stared at the remains, he discovered the origin of the terror. It lay in the completeness of the destruction of this part of the ship. Nothing below Deck 12, the Reactor Deck, remained except the reactor itself. Everything was not simply burned, nor burned beyond recognition, but missing—eliminated—evaporated—erased.

The ability of this planet to destroy things is monumental. Like the storm that obliterated that little island in the southern ocean—I couldn't believe it when I first saw it. And we're thinking about colonizing this place? That's crap.

He pointed the monitor toward the reactor. The light turned red. The reactor would have shut down automatically in the few microsectors between the lightning strike and the explosion when computer control was lost, and the fail-safe relays would have closed every port and jammed the control rods to home position.

There's some radiation coming from it, but it's a low level. There's not enough to matter as long as we stay away from it. But without cooling it'll eventually become unstable. We'll have to leave as soon as we can.

He turned the monitor off and returned to his runabout.

As he drove down the runway, he glanced frequently at the image from the rear-facing camera as though he expected something to come bearing down on him, something that might take him and Lilea and fling them into oblivion, completing the process of eliminating the Gold Team. What vicious, murderous method would they use this time? Another flood to sweep the runabouts away? Or would something else come hurtling out of those hills—something more malevolent? An army of Lilea's native 'humans,' perhaps?

After he arrived at the end of the runway, he kept the rear-facing camera on for several millisectors, watching and waiting,. The view gave him a fragment of comfort—it would allow him a few nanosectors lead time.

"They're not going to get me. I'm going to get out of here alive if it takes all year. I'll stay in this fuckin' runabout till that goddamn sun out there freezes over if necessary."

He settled back in his seat, reclining the seat a few degrees to get comfortable, and ordered the computer to darken all the windows except the front windshield. His mind drifted to Wila, Taeni, and Trea. These had been the women in his life, all taken from him by forces he couldn't see and couldn't control and couldn't understand. Wila, his most beloved, Taeni, his first love, Trea, the tall gorgeous woman with the cute face and magnificent thighs, the woman who shared his love of running.

Wow. She was so nice, so attractive, so sexy—perfect in almost every way. We had so much in common. I think I know now why she'd want to kill herself.

He drifted off to sleep and slept for several subsectors.

CHAPTER 62

WAITING – I

Time Element 461.245.3.7.

Ever since she woke around 245.0.0, the fifth lightime after the destruction of *Explorer*, a particular question kept passing through Lilea's mind, but during the trip to Trea's Grove to fill water bottles, and while gathering nuts, she hadn't had time to explore it fully. Later, as she sat in the warm, comfortable runabout, her mind turned to the unfinished business of that question.

What will the people of Anthanos think about us when we return?

They may honor us as heroes, or they may feel we've let them down. We did the best job we could, but they might react with anger and disappointment and tell us we should have tried harder. I can see that happening. But we certainly weren't going to stay home just because it was a dangerous mission. SpaceComm drilled the danger into us repeatedly from before training until blast off. At what point do the risks of exploration outweigh the repercussions of doing nothing?

But that wasn't everything, and a new and more serious vision formed in her mind. More than what the people of Anthanos would think about the Gold Team, she wondered what they would think about . . . the Blue Planet. That impression would certainly affect their feelings toward colonization. She and Jad could bring back many images and descriptions of places of staggering beauty, and she could deliver a powerful argument for colonizing the Blue Planet, though she doubted anymore Jad would agree. But no matter how charming would be her descriptions, the deaths and destruction would forever form a continuous veneer shielding the population of Anthanos from her positive portrayals. The deaths, the destruction of a well-known and popular spaceship, the unexpected termination of an expedition the people of Anthanos worked so hard to put together and paid trillions of monetary units for and expected positive results from — what would be their reaction? They might blame the Team. Or worse, they might blame SpaceComm.

There was more. The deaths of eight members of the Gold Team and the sudden end of exploration presaged consequences reaching much farther than merely to the end of the expedition. This was not about the death of eight explorers sent to a New World to seek a warm, accommodating place to live. This was about much more than that.

This was about the death of a civilization—an entire group of people—a planet—a race of individuals trying desperately to maintain themselves and their way of life in the face of enormous adversity. The Blue Planet, with its varied and changeable living conditions which Anthanos had so completely misjudged and misunderstood, had so violently exterminated the one enterprise that held any hope of producing an alternative to its expanding sun that the population couldn't help but be upset. The entire planet had worked on this expedition for hundreds of years just to see if another nearby planet might have conditions capable of supporting Anthanian life. Everyone came together to do all the things necessary to send it on its way. They put aside regional and racial differences to bond together to send this little group out so that it might eventually return and give them the news they wanted to hear: "Yes, there is another, better place we can live." So much was riding on this expedition, yet it failed utterly.

No, wait, that's not entirely true. Everyone on the team sent regular reports to *Star Voyager* on what they'd accomplished in their time on the surface, and that information would always be available. Lilea vowed that her camera—with its full record of all she'd done—would make it back to Anthanos. It was a special camera, made as one of eight for the members of the team, and she felt obliged to return it. She could pick up a few specimens and take them back, too. And she could say for certain that the intelligent peoples in the north—her "humans"—did not exist in the vicinity of the landing site, and they wouldn't be a threat to the establishment of a permanent colony. She fulfilled her obligation to SpaceComm. All that information might *just* be enough to allow the Assembly to make a decision to fund a return.

Everyone on the team did their job and did it well. No one could be held accountable. They may have made some honest mistakes in judgment, but no, it wasn't their fault. It was the *planet* that did this. The *planet* must bear the responsibility for the end of exploration.

Hold on—that sounds too much like Wila's rambling theory about the planet making life difficult for everyone here, as though it didn't want these visitors. But that's not what she meant.

Certainly, SpaceComm did have some poor information about the Blue Planet which may have contributed to the disaster. And perhaps they rushed into sending a landing party. Lilea always felt that the 700 T-sectors they'd spent in training as the Gold Team was barely sufficient for a mission of this magnitude. SpaceComm accelerated their training to meet a narrow launch window because a new one wouldn't occur for almost a year, and the Assembly didn't want to "waste time." Even if they'd had better information, they couldn't have foreseen every incident. Better data might have made a difference, but the Team's job was to get that data, and eight people died doing just that. They accepted the risk.

She wavered in her thoughts and glanced to her right at Jad's runabout.

And what about the Assembly? Even with all the information the Team sent back, would it have the courage to vote a return trip? In the face of enormous calamity, could they make that decision? A pessimistic doubt grew malignant within her mind.

She looked to her left up the runway. The remains of *Explorer* lay quiet in the autumnal wind, still dark and black from the explosion and fire. She activated the runabout's drive system and drove up the runway. She parked at the north end of the large rock that had been the touchdown point for *Explorer*, near the area from which the aerodynes left during take-off. A cold west wind clawed at the bare skin of her hands and face and pattered at the thin jacket she wore when she stepped out, but she paid little attention. Her frustration and pessimism were turning to anger. She hiked up the rock toward the remains, moving closer than she'd gone before, and stood on the west side of the runway.

The overcast sky had thrown a melancholy cloak over the landing site, isolating her from everything, even Jad, as she stood on the rock that once supported the ship. She stared at the shattered hulk, desolate and forlorn in the black and gray ash that covered much of it. She scanned the hills from where the flood had come. Deep inside, anger hardened. She turned left toward Jad's runabout near the other end of the runway and the clump of trees beyond. The trees rustled and stirred in the cold wind, and a few dried plants skittered by in the distance. She turned farther to her left and saw the remnants of Aero Two. She relaxed a little, and a more agreeable, even pleasant, feeling swelled up in her chest.

Those two ships took us to some lovely places.

She turned still farther to her left and looked west at the sandstone cliffs in the distance, then east toward Trea's Grove, from this distance little more than a tiny clump of green on the horizon. She looked back at the remains of *Explorer*, and outrage—real, absolute, and incontestable—

boiled over from within.

"You bastard!" she bellowed out to the world around her, her hands balled into fists, every muscle in her body rigid against the wrath that consumed her. "You bastard! You blew it! You blew it! It's gone! It's gone forever and we can't get it back! All we wanted to do was live here and now it's gone!" She collapsed onto a rock at the side of the runway and tears poured down her cheeks. She put her head in her hands. "Oh, god, it's gone."

Now she felt the cold and the isolation as never before, and she hurried back to the runabout.

The fifth lightime was the only lightime Lilea failed to visit Wila's and Trea's graves.

Time Element 461.247.1.9.

Jad munched on four of the nuts, then opened the runabout's door and stood up. He went through his usual stretching routine and returned to the warmth of the runabout.

It's a good thing we've got these machines. Science can do some good sometimes.

He reclined the seat slightly and closed his eyes. *But the trouble with science is that it so often exists in a vacuum. Science can describe how death occurs, but not how to deal with death. Science can describe how the nuts grow, but it can't tell you where to go to get them, except by random choice, and that's not very scientific. I can describe in detail how that sun out there works, or program a computer to calculate the exact time it'll appear on the horizon at the beginning of every lightime. But no physicist or physician — no matter how good or how intelligent — can tell you how to deal with the death that comes when your sun enters its terminal expansion phase and brings all life to a grinding halt like an aerodyne grinding to a halt at the end of a runway. Science can bring you to another planet, but science can't tell you how to deal with all the chaos and confusion you find on it. Science can lead you into thinking all you have to do is visit a strange and beautiful planet and look around for a while, and then go home and everything will be okay. All you have to do is report on what you saw and did, and someone back on your home planet will make the decision whether to colonize. But it doesn't always work out that way, does it? Science will dupe you into believing it will be a simple trip to do some good for your planet, and, like the sucker you are, you will fall for it. Science will lead you astray and carry you into oblivion without so much as a faint whisper of goodbye.*

I'm not even sure I'm going to make it to the landing of Rescue. *That's still nine or ten lightimes away.*

Jad tried to relax, but the vitriol and venom that erupted inside him, the intense hatred of this planet that burned within his chest, and the excruciating agony of contempt for everything that was the Blue Planet threatened to consume him in a fiery, passionate furnace.

"What the hell am I doing here?" he said, sitting up. "Why did I volunteer for this damn mission? Out of some misguided sense of duty to my planet?" He leaned back. *That's crap. All I got was a few solar and planetary studies and my wife killed like a bug smashed under a boot heel. Nothing like that flood would ever have occurred on Anthanos. Anthanos is so warm and welcoming, so easygoing, so predictable. I liked being there and I sure as hell don't like being here. With all the deaths on this expedition, I'd be willing to bet any number of monetary units the Assembly won't vote to return. Why would anyone want to come back here? It'll just kill you if you do.*

Jad's comm beeped. With the colder weather, he and Lilea had begun communicating through their runabout's comm systems, and when he glanced at the screen he saw that under the heading "Sender Matrix" at the top of the screen—which told him who was trying to contact him—was the notation "Runabout 2." Lilea was on comm.

"I'm going to fill the water bottles. I'll stop by and get your bottle on my way out. When I get back, do you want to go for nuts again?"

"No, you pick some up while you're over there."

"Jad, you've got to keep your strength up."

Jad wasn't interested in keeping his strength up. *Why don't you just go to hell?* He just wanted to be left alone, to sit in miserable company with his thoughts of Wila and the other women in his life, though he dare not say anything to Lilea. "All right," he said, trying desperately to not show his exasperation. "But let's take your runabout. You drive this time."

"Okay," Lilea said, and terminated comm.

CHAPTER 63

WAITING – II

Time Element 461.255.0.0.

The falling white stuff ended late the previous lightime. About a decilink remained on the ground, giving the terrain a mottled white and tan appearance. Lilea stepped out of her runabout and scraped the accumulation from the windshield and side windows to keep a clear view of the landing site. When she returned, she drifted in and out of sleep, but soon became aware of several unusual feelings.

By this time, now in the quiet of the long wait for *Rescue*, she'd begun to categorize several symptoms she'd noticed earlier, but dismissed in the frantic and confusing time shortly after the destruction of *Explorer*. A swelling, not only of her tummy but also around her ankles, nausea, not long after the beginning of a lightime, a recurring flush over her face and arms, headaches, and a considerable lack of energy.

Well, of course a lack of energy, that almost goes without saying. But why is my tummy so swollen? Does that have something to do with the lack of food?

She reclined the seat back about 50 degrees and lay back to wait until time to make her usual rounds.

Time Element 461.257.5.3.

The drizzle frustrated Lilea. She wanted to make her usual rounds of burial sites, but the sprinkle of cold mist kept her confined to her runabout for all but essential reasons. She munched on a few nuts, took a few gulps of water, and by shortly after the midpoint of the lightime the falling water had let up enough to allow her to make her trip. She pulled the runabout out of its west-facing position and drove up the runway to the remains of *Explorer*. She stepped out and folded her arms across her chest to keep in as much warmth as possible. She hiked up the wet rock that defined the landing site, walking on tiptoes, placing her feet on rough areas to avoid the slippery spots. Her feet hit one wet spot and she almost lost her balance, but she made her way up the rock without falling. She stood near the bottom of the ship, spending a few microsectors with Bent and good friends in silent meditation, then turned back to her runabout.

As she carefully negotiated her way down the rock, she hit more slick spots and threw her arms out to her side to balance herself until she could step onto the dirt part of the runway. But just as she reached the dirt, she raised her head and was startled to see Jad, at the other end of the runway, fling open the door of his runabout and bolt headlong into the cold and drizzle. He ran west full-speed into the desert probably a thousand links, then stopped, looked around, and walked back to his runabout.

Time Element 461.259. 5.0.

A chilly wind out of the north swept over Lilea's back as she stood near the ruins of *Explorer*, but she was so absorbed in thoughts of Bent she didn't notice. The bright sun, near midpoint in its travels across the sky, warmed her face, tempering the cool wind. But this time, instead of standing on the west side of the runway, she cautiously moved east, circling the hulk of the ship. A large amount of debris had collected here and she stepped carefully. Several remnants of the ship's interior as well as some personal effects lay scattered about, a jumpsuit, someone's pressure suit helmet, a chair from one or another food-prep area. As she edged her way around the ship, a twinkle of light caught her eye. Something shiny lay on the other side of the remains, and when she walked over to investigate, she found Mina's nanoro. Its light tan body blended with the soil, and she recognized it only because of the glint of light from one of the keys. It was dusty and wet, and one of the keys was bent, but it was in reasonably good condition. She picked it up and dusted it off.

I'll give it to Mina's parents.

But the largest portion of the debris here was plastic sheets on which were printed images from Gold Team cameras. She picked up several and recognized many of the places they'd visited. One image, though, was unfamiliar to her, a picture of Trea, wearing a skimpy swimsuit, sitting on a rock in the middle of a lake.

Oh — Col took an image of Trea. In the mountains just before he was killed. But who printed it out? Col couldn't have. Did Trea? Explorer's computer always printed on the back the information about the camera and the image. That included the camera number. She turned the image over and gasped.

The camera number, SP701, had been printed in the upper left-hand corner along with the date the image was taken, 461.181.10.6, and the date it was printed, 461.211.2.9.

But what startled her was the handwriting scrawled in the center of the back. It was the big, bold, expansive, though somewhat shaky handwriting of an outgoing, extroverted person. Written in ink, it said:

Jad
Thanks for all your help
I appreciate everything you did
I had a wonderful time
Lots of love
Trea

Jad? Trea wrote on the back and gave this image to Jad. But whose camera took the image? She looked at the camera designation again. SP701? 'SP' stood for 'Spectrographic,' but only two cameras on this expedition were spectrographic cameras, made especially for this trip. Bent had one, his was SP700—she'd seen that number several times on the plaque on the side of his camera. Jad had the only other one, so 701 must have been his. *Oh, yes, I remember. I saw that on the plaque on the side of Jad's camera when we were on the northwest coast. That means Jad took this image with his camera. But if Trea wrote this, then he must've printed it out and showed it to her. And he gave her some kind of help. But what kind of help? What did they do together? Trea never left her compartment until the meeting after the fire. When was that meeting? I can't remember exactly, but it certainly was after 211. That means Trea and Jad . . .*

When Lilea returned to the north end of the runway, she walked over to Jad's runabout and tapped on the window. He rolled the window down and she held up the image. She started to say, "Is this yours?" but he snatched the image from her hand before she could complete her sentence.

"Give me that! Where did you find it? It's mine. Leave me alone. Mind your own goddamn business." He slapped the image face down on the seat beside him and rolled the window back up, and then ordered the computer to darken the windows.

Time Element 461.265.0.0.

The lightime dawned overcast and cold, and for the first time in several lightimes, more of the white stuff had begun falling. The air temperature had dropped over the past several T sectors, and was now down to –2 Tal. Lilea and Jad stayed in their runabouts except when necessary to answer nature's call. They made no more trips to try and find nuts, though Lilea still made her rounds of the burial sites and went every lightime to

Trea's Grove to fill water bottles.

She stayed awake for several subsectors, her mind adrift —

. . . the rescue ship should be here pretty soon . . .

. . . good god, I hope so . . .

. . . this seat is like a block of cement. My butt is so sore . . .

. . . I'm so wired from not getting any exercise . . .

. . . how's Jad? Is he okay? I should check on him . . .

. . . why does the Command Ship have to stay so far away . . .

. . . this certainly is not the place to have a nervous breakdown . . .

. . . the nearest doctor millions of anthans away . . .

. . . lousy planning on their part. . .

. . . I'll have to talk to SpaceComm when we get back . . .

. . . stupid spaceship . . .

Around 265.4.3, she reclined the seat back all the way and drifted off to sleep again, and slept for about a subsector.

Time Element 461.271.5.0.

Something awakened Lilea. At first she didn't know what it was. The interior of the runabout seemed darker — no, not darker, duller — than it should have been for this, the middle of the lightime. She opened her eyes and looked at the windshield. It, and the side windows too, were caked with the white stuff, more than she could remember having been there before, enough to diffuse and diminish the light. She opened the door and stepped outside into four to five decilinks of the white. It was coming down heavily now, covering everything, and heavy white clouds blanketed the entire sky. Jad's runabout was fully covered.

She swept away the white from the windows of her runabout and placed some of it in one of the cooking pots from one of the runabout's storage bins. She'd been melting it on the little stove and filling the water bottles. With one full bottle, she trotted over to Jad's runabout. She pushed aside the white from his left side window and looked in. He'd instructed the ship's computer to darken the side window, but only partially, and inside he seemed to be asleep. She tapped on the window, and he woke and rolled the window partway down. Sleepy and slightly groggy, he first didn't seem to appreciate the amount of white caking his runabout.

"It's coming down heavy. I'm worried about *Rescue*." She handed him the bottle. "Keep drinking water. Keep hydrated."

Jad didn't reply right away. He looked at the heavy cake on the windshield, perhaps mentally processing the meaning of her words.

"Yeah. Nothing much we can do. We'll just have to wait. I bet they'll be able to land. They have to."

"I hope so."

"What T-sector is this?"

"Two seventy-one."

"When do they land?"

"Could be here any time."

Lilea returned to her runabout and reclined the seat back again. *I am getting so damn tired of this waiting. I hope* Rescue *gets here soon.* She stayed awake for more than a subsector, but eventually drifted off.

When she woke, she got out and scraped the accumulating white from the windows again. It seemed to be coming down even more heavily than before, and she could barely scrape it away faster than it accumulated. Her fingers were almost frozen when she returned inside. She lowered the window of the runabout's left-hand door one decilink to get some fresh air, but that would also allow her to hear *Rescue* when it arrived. She lay back down.

Time Element 461.273.0.0.

*Where is that damn rescue ship? It's been nineteen lightimes since Ex-*plorer *fell over. They should have detected the carrier wave signal cutoff one T-sector later. And sent Rescue one T-sector after that. They were due several lightimes ago. Where the hell are they? I'm so hungry. My stomach is so bloated. How's Jad? Is he okay? I better talk to him. See how he's doing. It's cold out. I'll use the comm system. No, I better go over there. No, it's cold out. I can't.*

"Jad? How are you? Are you okay? Do you have enough water? I can melt some more. There's plenty out there."

"I'm okay. Leave me alone. I got enough water."

"Okay. Just checking."

At 273.5.1, the runabout's computer beeped to indicate a voice communication. She didn't look at the screen right away. "Now what does Jad want?" When she sat up and glanced toward the screen to open comm, she expected to see the usual "Runabout 1" under the heading **SENDER MATRIX** to tell her who was calling. But that wasn't what she saw.

She stared at the screen for several nanosectors, not really believing what her eyes told her. At first she thought she was hallucinating. Or dreaming. She blinked several times to clear her eyes.

The entry said, "Rescue."

CHAPTER 64

RECOVERY

Time Element 461.273.5.1.

"*Rescue*! Is that you?" Lilea almost screamed into the microphone.

"Yes." The voice blared from the speaker in the runabout. She recognized Tam Kos's voice immediately. "We're in orbit above you, but the clouds are so heavy we'll have to land by coordinates only. No visual. It'll be next lightime before we can de-orbit. Do the clouds extend all the way to the ground, or will we be able to see to land below the clouds?"

"Yes, the clouds are still several thousand links above us. But they've been dropping a lot of that white stuff. You remember Wila's reports? Frozen precipitation? It's heavy now. Covers everything. I think you can blast through it, though. Maybe two links deep."

"Okay. We'll try to land at the original Prime Site. Is that still open?"

"Yes, it's ready for you."

"Will you be all right until then?"

"We'll be okay."

"Is Jad there with you?"

"He's in the other runabout."

"Is he okay?"

"He's lost some weight and he's real weak, but I think he can make it until next lightime. I'll tell him you're in orbit. That'll make him feel better."

"Okay, good. We'll see you then. Take it easy."

Without thinking, Lilea opened the door to her runabout and stood up. The cold air bit through her lightweight jacket like the teeth of a great frigid monster, and the particles of white tickled her eyelashes and felt tingly on her face, but she didn't mind. The excitement that pounded within her chest and the elation of knowing they were finally going home pushed her to get out and run over to Jad and give him the news in person. This was certainly not the kind of news to be delivered over the impersonal audio system of a runabout, even though the loss of weight and forced inactivity of the last forty T-sectors made getting up and walking around difficult. She scooted as rapidly as she could down the runway through the white — at least a link deep now — and banged on the side window of Jad's runabout. He rolled the window partway down.

"They're in orbit!" she yelled at him. "I just heard from them! The rescue ship's in orbit!"

Jad's face brightened considerably, more than it had since the explosion. He'd reclined his seat back about 30 degrees, and with difficulty he leaned forward. "Oh, god, that's great," he said in a faint whisper. "When are they going to land?"

"Not until next lightime."

Jad's smile faded somewhat, and a trace of resignation invaded his voice. "Well, at least they're here. I guess I can wait."

"That's good. I told them you could make it." She reached through the open window and patted his shoulder. Then she hurried back to her runabout and slept better than she had in many T-sectors.

Time Element 461.275.0.0.

The lightime dawned cold and overcast. The white had tapered off late the previous lightime, near sunset, but it began again before dawn. When Lilea woke, her runabout was covered with five to six decilinks, she estimated. She had difficulty scraping it from the windows, it was so thick. Since *Rescue* had contacted her around the midpoint of the last lightime, it wouldn't be able to land until nearly the same time this lightime. Jad's runabout was also thickly covered, and the original prime landing site, almost a quarter anthan away, lay below a blanket that must be two links thick by now.

I'm sure they'll be able to land. The ship's engine can blast its way through the white, but will the runabouts be able to drive over there?

She scrolled the side window down a few decilinks so the sound of the ship's landing would come through.

The time element read 275.5.5 on the runabout's com screen when she heard a faint muffled roar. At first it sounded like the lightning noise she'd so often heard around Site One and she sat up and looked around. She didn't see any of the dark menacing clouds that usually carried the lightning, and she knew immediately she was wrong — *Rescue* was on its way down. Her heart skipped a beat or two. The noise faded and returned several times, but after several microsectors it grew louder. She opened the door and stepped into the cold. She saw nothing, but the roaring continued, slowly getting louder.

In only a few microsectors she located the noise — from the north, just as she expected. It grew steadily louder, and almost without warning, directly over the Prime Landing Site, a shiny silver spaceship with a big yellow "R" inside a yellow circle emblazoned on its side — and with bright yellow landing fins — dropped out of the clouds, engine down.

Jad heard it too. He opened the door of his runabout and for the first time in several lightimes, stood up.

"Oh, my god," he said in a weak voice. "Finally, they're here."

Lilea ducked back into her runabout and grabbed her sampling kit and camera from the back seat. She stuffed a bag of nuts in a pocket of her jumpsuit and ran over to Jad's runabout. She jumped into the right-side seat while Jad stayed in the left. "I'll drive," she said as she energized the drive system. But when she pulled back on the joystick, nothing happened. She pulled farther back and eventually, with a loud crack as the wheels broke free of the ice buildup that held them in place, the runabout began to move. She could feel a definite retarding factor as the runabout inched its way backward through the white.

She had to skirt around Wila's grave and the trees at the end of the runway. The white had accumulated to nearly two links by the time they left, almost covering the wheels, and was still coming down. Though the trip was an otherwise easy drive of one-quarter anthan over reasonably flat terrain, it took them almost three millisectors to reach the ship because she had to stop several times to clean the windshield. She parked the runabout a hundred links from the ship, and they settled back in their seats, waiting for someone to open the main door.

"Who's on the Rescue missions?" she wondered aloud.

She couldn't keep quiet. In the excitement of knowing they would make it off this planet alive, she had to go verbal. She had to talk. That was how she dealt with nervous enthusiasm. The last time this happened they'd just finished ten T-sectors in orbit around the Blue Planet and were about to de-orbit. They were strapped on their acceleration couches on the Command Deck of *Explorer*, waiting for the engine burn that would take them down to the surface. But Case and Jer seemed to take *forever* to run through all those checklists and data points and navigational aids and all that stuff, and that was too much for her. She launched into a stream of consciousness ejaculation of words and phrases so fervid that Bent had to reach over and touch her arm to encourage her to calm down. So wonderful of Bent to do that.

"They told us so long ago," Lilea said. "I can't remember any more. I know Tam—I already talked to him. And one of the space surgeons on the staff. But who's the third?"

"I don't know."

"There's always at least three people, two command pilots and a physician."

"Tac, probably."

Yes, of course, Tac, Senior Space Surgeon for this mission. The medical team at *Star Voyager* had several physicians, but the landing team always saw Tac for their medical needs. Never any of the others. But she couldn't remember who the second command pilot would be.

"Lan, I bet."

That would be a good bet. Lan, *Star Voyager*'s chief navigator—yes, his navigational skills would be essential.

A couple of millisectors after they arrived, the main door at the midpoint of the ship's hull opened. From a horizontal slot just below the door, a ladder of metal chains and rungs started to flow down the side of the ship. It stopped when it reached the surface.

Lilea couldn't contain her excitement any longer. She had to get out and be ready to greet the visitors. Besides, she couldn't see very well through the accumulating white on the windshield. She stepped into the cold and fastened her thin jacket as tightly as she could. As she stood beside the runabout, two figures appeared at the door of the ship putting on jackets, silhouetted by the light in the air lock. The first figure she recognized immediately. That portly profile was certainly Tac.

A short man, only about five and a half links tall, in stature and bald head Tac reminded Lilea of her old boss, Mr. Uvos. Tac's hair, though, was a wavy brown rather than the red of Uvos, and he certainly was in far better physical condition.

The second person she didn't recognize right away. She couldn't make out faces from this distance, but there was something about the hair on the second person, and well, the hair seemed to be done up in something like an Afro . . . *my gosh, that's Jasi! What's Jasi doing on Rescue? Jasi's not a Command Pilot. She's not even a pilot—she's a scientist.* Then she heard Jasi's voice.

"That's Lilea," Jasi yelled, and she waved. Lilea waved back.

As the expedition's Resident Science Team Leader, Jasi collected, collated, and stored the mega-reams of data sent back from the surface. Morokuu like Bent, she was a member of the sienna-brown-skinned race of Anthanians who developed nearest the center of the planet's hot side. Like the other racial groups, the Morokuu retreated toward the terminator as the temperature rose on the hot side, eventually assimilating with the pale-skinned flaxen-haired Tarkuu of Lilea, and the tan-skinned Lakuu of the other members of the Gold Team. With her darker skin and bouffant hair-style, Jasi's likeness stood out so strikingly from that of the blonde Lilea.

But much more significant for Lilea, Jasi was her pak playing part-ner. Pak was a game played only in microgravity. Two players slammed a small, white silicone ball back and forth in a cylindrical chamber, scoring points if one player got it past the other to hit the chamber's end wall, and the name of the game was taken from the sound of the ball off the paddles. Lilea's favorite game, she played it often with Jasi during the long out-bound voyage because none of the other Gold Team members played. Jasi was a championship player, and Lilea a highly ranked amateur. But that time spent with Jasi just intensified their friendship and Lilea drew closer to her than to anyone outside the Gold Team. Now, seeing Jasi here, com-ing to rescue her from these desperate conditions, Lilea's heart jumped again, excitedly waiting for her to descend. She began to walk toward the ship.

Jasi was first to climb down the ladder. When she reached the sur-face, she started running as fast as she could over the cold ground. *Rescue*'s engine had blasted away much of the white and sand below it for about forty links around, and the ground was hard and compacted. Like Lilea before her, she was stiff and weak after forty T-sectors in microgravity and she ran haltingly, but when she reached Lilea they embraced in the hearty Anthanian hug of greeting.

"Jasi," Lilea blurted out, "I didn't expect to see you."

"I just had to come." Jasi was all out of breath. "We got your mes-sage just before we left. It said *Explorer* had been destroyed and you and Jad were the only ones alive so I nagged Kal long enough and Tam said okay and finally he said yes, so here I am. What happened?"

"Oh, god." Lilea's eyes welled up with tears at having to recount the destruction for Jasi. "It was a disaster. There was a big powerful storm that hit the ship with a lightning bolt, and then knocked it over with a flood of water. Then the liquid hydrogen exploded and everyone except Jad and me were killed, and . . . I'm sorry." She turned away.

"Where's Jad?" Tac asked as he joined the women and embraced Li-lea. "Tam said he was still alive."

Lilea pointed to Jad, still sitting in the runabout. "Yes, he's alive, but he's pretty weak from not having much food for the past thirty T-sectors."

Jad stood from the runabout.

"Good god," Tac said. "You are in trouble. I want you to go into the ship. Right now. I need to get you started on IV fluids."

Jad walked slowly and carefully through the white, Tac beside him, holding onto one arm. When they reached the chain ladder, Tac climbed first, and when he reached the entrance door, he turned around and shouted to Jad to stand on the bottom rung of the ladder. Too weak to climb, Jad stood there while Tac pressed a marker on a com screen inside the door and raised the ladder, bringing Jad up to the airlock. Tac pulled him into the airlock where he disappeared from Lilea and Jasi's view.

"We should be getting inside the ship, too." Lilea said, now beginning to feel the cold through her jacket. In the excitement of meeting everyone she'd ignored the frigid temps. She turned back toward the ship.

"Oh, I almost forgot," Jasi said. "Tam wants to visit the remains of *Explorer*."

"What? Visit the remains?" Lilea looked around at the white stuff, still accumulating on the ground and on the runabout. The windshield was covered. "Oh, no, that's not a good . . ."

Jasi seemed to catch Lilea's caution. She too looked at the falling white, apparently seeing it for the first time. She pulled out her PersComm and contacted Tam. "Do you still want to see the ship? Lilea says . . ."

"Hold on," Tam said. "I'll be down in a few microsectors."

The white was coming down harder now, and the air temperature had reached –4 Tal and still dropping. As they sat in the runabout, Lilea recounted to Jasi how they buried Wila and Trea, of the long, tedious lightimes waiting for *Rescue*, of filling water bottles and collecting nuts, and of Jad trying to get into the burned-out hulk of the ship, but not succeeding. She told them of her bloating, and of Jad's loss of weight.

"That's funny," Jasi said. "I didn't think bloating like that was normally an early symptom of reduced food intake. But where's Tam? We should be getting over there."

At 275.6.2, Tam joined them in the runabout. Tarkuu like Lilea, Tam's bright thalo blue eyes and light reddish-blond hair and boyish face full of freckles made him look so much younger than his forty-seven years. He embraced Lilea and took the rear seat while Jasi drove, following the tracks in the white from Lilea's trip over. She had to stop three times while she and Lilea scraped the white stuff off the windshield, but in three millisectors they arrived at the clump of trees at the end of the runway.

"Be careful. Wila is buried around here."

The stick Jad used to mark the grave stuck forlornly above the accumulating white, the grave itself hidden beneath. As they rounded the trees, the remains of *Explorer* came into view so suddenly it surprised Jasi and she relaxed her hand on the controller joystick. It flipped back to the center position, bringing the runabout to a stop. "Oh, god, look at that," she said. "I didn't expect so much destruction."

A blanket of white coated the remains of *Explorer*, but all that camouflage couldn't hide the completeness of the destruction. It was as though the planet, after having reduced the ship to a blackened hulk, was trying to cover up the remains of its handiwork.

"Hold on a nanosector," Tam said from the seat behind Jasi. He opened his door and put one foot outside to get a better view. He stood there only a few nanosectors, then reentered with a grim, intense look on his face. Sparkling flakes of white dotted his sandy hair.

"Go," he said, quietly. "Get up closer to the remains. I want to get a good look at it."

Jasi glanced briefly at Lilea, concern on her face. Lilea, her experience with the white stuff at the northern site fresh in her mind, spoke up.

"We should be getting back to the ship. I don't know how much more of this stuff will come. We don't want to get stranded here—"

"I just want to take a few microsectors. Then we can go back."

"Tam, really, I don't think—"

"It won't take long. Just a few microsectors. Then we can get back."

Jasi took the runabout up the runway and stopped about a hundred links from the ruins. Tam jumped out and struggled through the white—now more than two links deep—up the rock to the white-covered hulk. Jasi followed a few hesitant steps behind.

Jasi seemed content to stand in one place and stare at the remains, but Tam took time to circle the ship, poking into it here and there, attempting to slip into the interior of the superstructure. But like Jad, he failed repeatedly in the tangled beams and girders of the ship's collapsed frame. Several times, perhaps from a sense of overwhelming anger and frustration, he kicked white onto the burned-out hulk and threw his hands in the air, demanding, "How? How? How could this happen?" After a millisector, he calmed down enough to return with Jasi to the runabout.

Tam seemed distracted and self-absorbed. The concept of a destroyed *Explorer* must have come as an immense catastrophe to him. Tam, Case and another test pilot whose name was lost in Lilea's memory had been the first pilots of *Explorer* immediately after it was built, and Case was head of that little team. They made the first test flights from surface to orbit and back again. They landed it on several of the moons of the outer planets in the Anthanian solar system, practicing for the landing on the Blue Planet, and in the process raised it like a child from an untested, experimental spaceship to the reliable workhorse it was when it touched down at Site One. Everyone had such high hopes for *Explorer*, especially Tam and the piloting team, and the loss of that ship had undoubtedly ripped out a large portion of his life and thrown it away like so much garbage.

Was there a tear in his eye when he entered the runabout? Or was it just white flakes that dotted his eyelashes? Lilea couldn't tell, but his eyes seemed to glisten more than usual.

Jasi turned the runabout around and began the drive back north toward *Rescue*, following the tracks they'd made driving up to the ship. Lilea pointed out the stick that marked Trea's grave as they passed, and Jasi stopped the runabout and got out. She went over to the grave and stood beside it, bending down to push her bare hand through the white cover to the earth beneath. She held it there for a few nanosectors.

"Trea and I were roommates in college," she said when she returned to the runabout. "It's just so sad. And so unnecessary. Godawful planet."

Now the wind had begun. Swirling out of the north, it blew white directly onto the runabout, scattering some that had caked the windshield, but also adding to it, obscuring visibility almost completely. The runabout tried to move, but hesitantly, bucking into the wind, occasionally spinning its wheels. Tam seemed not to notice.

"I don't understand. There's no damn way that ship could fall over."

Lilea couldn't see Tam's face from where she sat unless she turned well to her left, but she sensed impatience and frustration in his voice, even skepticism bordering on disbelief. "That ship was so damn heavy. There's no damn way . . ." He seemed to be thinking out loud, yet, really, he wasn't. He was verbalizing his frustrations, giving voice to the impossibility of a spaceship being knocked over by something as inconsequential as a flood of water. "I remember reading Case's reports on the landing. It was absolutely vertical and stable. And how could lightning strike the ship? Lightning is strictly cloud-to-cloud. I never heard of lightning striking the surface. And how could a storm knock it over?"

Lilea hesitated to answer, intimidated by the force of Tam's expressions. "Jad and I did a lot of thinking about that while we were waiting for you. After it was hit by the lightning, it tipped to one side, and it stayed that way for several microsectors before the flood hit it and it went over.

The leveling system failed."

"Of course. If lightning did hit the ship, it would knock out the navigational computers, and any of the pads that were extended would automatically retract. I remember from Case's report that one leveling pad was extended more than six links. It was the upper medial, wasn't it?"

Lilea nodded. "Actually, closer to eight." She spoke almost absentmindedly, though deep inside she was impressed that Tam would remember that one obtuse fact.

"If that one retracted, it would put the ship in a strong tilt. But how did the flood knock it the rest of the way?"

"I don't know. Jad and I were too far away to see much, but Jad thinks the water hit it hard enough to force the upper medial fin into the groove in the surface, and it—"

"The groove? What groove?" Tam leaned forward. "What are you talking about?"

"There's a large groove in the rock that forms the surface where we landed. The upper medial pad overlapped that groove."

"I see," Tam said, and sat back. "Yes, you're right, I remember the image Case sent back. So, if the pad slipped into the groove, it would fall farther, and that could throw the center of mass farther toward the outside of the ship . . ."

"We saw two people near the ship. They must have been Wila and Trea. We found their bodies down the runway later. When the water hit the ship, it carried them away."

"I guess so." Tam's voice was now quiet and resigned. Perhaps he accepted, finally and completely, the reality of a destroyed *Explorer*. Jasi took the runabout off the north end of the runway and past the clump of trees and Wila's grave, still following the track they'd made on their trip over. But the track was rapidly filling with white, and visibility had declined to almost nil. The runabout stalled briefly, then began to move, slowly, as white caked its wheels and undercarriage. About a thousand links past the clump of trees it stopped altogether and would only spin its wheels under Jasi's control.

"I was afraid of this," Lilea said. "We're going to have to get out and walk the rest of the way."

Time Element 461.275.7.4.

"Walk? What are you talking about?" Tam sat forward in his seat. "What's going on? Why are we stopped?"

"This stuff is too thick," Jasi said. "The runabout won't move."

"This is impossible. You mean we're stymied by some . . . what is this . . . frozen precipitation?" Tam opened his door. It would barely swing outward, held back by the caked whiteness at the side. Wind blew more of the stuff into his face as he tried to stand up. "My god! What is this?" He ducked back inside. "How much more of this will we get?"

"I don't know," Lilea said. "We've never seen this much here at Site One. We could get a lot more. There's no way of knowing. We better get going. I don't want to get stranded here. I've got my PersComm. It's got a compass in it. The ship should be due north from here. We'll meet at the front of the runabout and hold hands. That way we won't get separated."

"How much farther is it to the ship?"

"I don't know. I can't see. Maybe a thousand links."

"A thousand links? In this?"

"Yes. The sooner we get started, the sooner we'll get there. Hand me my sampling kit and camera."

Lilea notified Lan at the ship of what they were about to do, then pulled her PersComm from its place in her left thigh pocket and activated the compass. It seemed stable. She opened the door to her right and stepped into the howling wind and blowing white, and gasped at the bitter cold. She wore the usual Anthanian hiking boots like everyone else in SpaceComm, but they were only mid-calf high, and weren't made for hiking in this frozen material. Her legs above the boot were chilled almost instantly. The wind threw more white directly into her face, and the cold penetrated her thin jacket as though it were sheer. Tam was yelling something on the other side of the runabout, but she couldn't make out what he said. Jasi screamed as she stepped out.

"The front!" Lilea bellowed back at them. "The front!" She made her way to the head of the runabout and grabbed Jasi's hand. At least Jasi had gloves.

"I've got Tam's hand," Jasi yelled. "Let's go."

Lilea yelled back at the others. "Let's go. Stay together!" She tried to look forward toward the ship, but all she could see was white. She started out, following the compass.

Walking was tiring. And cold. She wished she'd asked them to bring some gloves or a heavier jacket from *Rescue*, but at the time she didn't think they'd have to forge through heavy white stuff just to get back to the ship.

This damn planet — at first it kept trying to get rid of us, but now, when we're ready to leave, it makes it hard just to find a spaceship in a desert.

They made headway one step at a time, holding on to each other, tightly, roughly, soundly. She watched the little direction indicator on the compass, always holding it so it pointed north.

North, north, always north. The walking was tiring, trudging. For each step they had to raise their leg high and press it down into the heavy stuff, and then do that with the other leg. It took almost a nanosector for each step. *We won't make much headway this way.*

They had to fight the cold wind, too, numbing on their bare faces. *Can we make it in this? Maybe we should have stayed in the runabout. At least we wouldn't get frozen.* The runabout was so warm and inviting. *Let's turn around. We can make it back to the runabout. How far have we gone? Are we half way there by now? Have we reached the point of no return? Where is the damn ship? My feet are frozen.* Lilea pulled on Jasi's hand, still there, always there. Still alive, still walking. But she had heavier clothing on. A nice heavy jacket and pants. Made for exploring the cold side of Anthanos at home.

North — stay due north — stay the course — god, I'm so tired — hold on — what was that? A noise, over and above the whistling of the wind. A voice. Fading in and out, hazy and uncertain in the wind. Was it Tam? Is he yelling again? It called her name. It called Jasi's name. Tam's name. It couldn't have been Tam. It came from the north. She looked at the compass. Still headed north. Her name again. The others, too. Not Tam's voice. She looked up directly into a bright yellow sky. *Has the sun come out? What is this?*

"I see it." Now she recognized Tam's voice. "This is one of the landing fins of the ship. Where's the ladder?" Jasi pulled away from Lilea's hand.

"Here it is!" Jasi grabbed at the ladder chain and started up. Above, Tac and Lan were yelling their names, still a nebulous shouting in the wind and white. Tam grabbed the ladder behind Jasi and went up. Lilea returned her PersComm to its usual pocket and grabbed the ladder below Tam. But she'd climbed only one or two steps when the ladder started to rise. They pulled her into the airlock and she collapsed on the floor as warm air swelled over her. She was exhausted from fighting so hard just to get here. Her hands and feet were numb, and her chest ached from breathing all that cold air. Behind her, the airlock door closed with a soft *thump*. That was the last thing she remembered until she woke up on one of the passenger bunks on the Personnel Deck of the ship, one level above.

CHAPTER 65

STAR VOYAGER

The white tapered off by the end of the first lightime *Rescue* was on the surface, but had accumulated to more than four links. It filled in the bare area the ship's engine had blasted away, and covered *Rescue* with a thin coating. The runabout was fully covered, looking like nothing more than a simple mound in the white, frozen to the ground beneath.

Rescue stayed on the surface for six T-sectors to give Jad and Lilea a chance to build up enough strength for the trip home. Tam ordered a course that took *Rescue* directly toward the waiting *Star Voyager* without going into orbit. That was a tough flight plan. It put a heavy strain on everyone, requiring an eight-millisector period of full engine operation to reach escape velocity, but Lilea and Jad did well enough.

Shortly after engine shutdown, Lilea ascended one level from the Personnel Deck to *Rescue*'s Command Deck to watch on one of the com screens as the Blue Planet receded from the ship. So many different emotions swirled through her mind as she gazed at the blue, white, brown, and green image. She was glad to be off the planet, certainly, but at the same time she retained a definite fondness for it. She had many wonderful memories of the place: the charm and openness of the desert, the deep green of the forest, the beauty and grandeur of the gorge, the dazzling hues of the falling leaves, the vivid colors of the sunrises and sunsets. But the memory that brought the warmest pleasure to her heart was the sight of the humans in the northern regions, and she would revisit that vision many times as the flight progressed. In some respects, she'd like to come back and see them again. Even meet them.

But coming back to the Blue Planet would have been a problem for Lilea. Though she was able to put the first tragedies—the deaths of Case, Dell, and Col—behind her and get on with her work, there was much more to her experiences. The deaths of Bent and the others, the destruction of a favorite spaceship, waiting for *Rescue*—everything that swirled through her mind seemed saturated in a deep shadow, as though the planet was a darkened room into which her fear of the dark would not permit her to enter. Returning to the planet would force her to enter that room and confront the death of Bent all over again, and that would be too much.

Slowly, another image formed in her mind. If there was any sense or significance she could glean from the horror of the passing of Case, Dell, and Col, it was that their deaths helped prepare her for the shock and frustration when her own husband was killed, too.

But sometimes enough is too much. Of ten people who landed on the Blue Planet, eight were killed, and she was one of only two remaining. It was impossible for her to not feel a sense of shame, a sense of having failed somewhere. Deep within lay a dark appreciation of inadequacy, of frailty or weakness. She thought she should have been killed in the blast too, and several times throughout the trip she expressed her feelings to Jasi, asking constantly why she was one of only two survivors.

Jasi listened to Lilea talk because, she told Lilea, it would be good for her (and, not coincidentally, because Tac asked her to), and tried to persuade Lilea she didn't have to feel embarrassed or ashamed or frustrated that she was one of only two survivors. It certainly was not her fault, Jasi told her. That was just the way things worked out.

During one of these talks, Lilea mentioned briefly that she thought that the Blue Planet, in spite of everything, could be colonized. "It might take some doing to learn to live there, but maybe we could do it."

A trace of terror invaded Jasi's voice. She seemed appalled at hearing Lilea talk like that. "After all you've been through? How can you say that? After all that planet did to you and the others? My god, Lilea —"

Lilea wanted desperately to find the words to counter Jasi's questions. She spent many subsectors trying to find an explanation that would convince Jasi of the beauty and utility of the planet, but she never came up with anything that was so overwhelmingly and fundamentally positive that it forced Jasi to immediately recognize the error of her argument. Lilea simply shrugged her shoulders and stayed quiet. No matter what she said, Jasi always came back with, "But that planet killed eight people!"

Maybe I was wrong and maybe Jasi's right. Maybe that planet is not for us.

In contrast to the openness of Lilea, Jad clammed up tighter than an airlock door. He refused to talk about anything that occurred after the storm and explosion, and little before that. Tac tried to get him to open up and express his feelings about the death of Wila, but all Jad wanted to do was lie on his bunk and sleep. Tac grew frustrated at Jad's reticence and began spiking his intravenous fluids with antidepressant. It did little good,

Jad remained silent for the rest of the trip.

Time Element 461.597.8.6. (Anthanian Time).

Rescue decelerated to a stop about six anthans from *Star Voyager*. At that distance, the big Command Ship appeared on the com screens on *Rescue*'s Command Deck as little more than an elongated, silvery pin. As *Rescue* drifted in toward the docking port, Lilea could begin to make out the thirteen different modules that made up the long, cylindrical ship, from the Command and Control Module up front to the huge Propulsion Module at the rear. The bright red lettering on the side of the Command and Control Module at the front read **DSEV-1**. That stood for **Deep Space Exploratory Vessel Number 1**—*Star Voyager*—the first Anthanian spaceship built expressly to explore space beyond the confines of the Anthanian solar system. The insignia of Spaceflight Command, a bright gold and yellow seven-pointed star in bas-relief on a dark blue background, had been fixed to each module.

The anticipation of renewing old friendships pushed Lilea to float as fast as she could through the pressurized docking tunnel into the Entry Module where Expedition Commander Kal Mada waited for them. In spite of his high rank, Executive Command Pilot, the only Anthanian with 5 seven-pointed stars arranged vertically on his sleeves, he always seemed the affable, easygoing Kal, ready with a quick smile or a little joke. Lilea had grown to respect the tall expedition leader during the long outbound voyage. She found him, like Case, fair and decent in his dealings with others, but without the quick temper. As he waited in the microgravity, the lanky Kal, only a decilink shorter than Jad, always seemed so awkward and ungainly in spite of so many years in outer space. His arms and legs wriggled and twitched as though with a mind of their own. Now, as she approached him at the end of the tunnel, a suggestion of sadness had settled into his usually sparkling deep gray eyes. He gave each the traditional Anthanian bear hug of greeting, and then accompanied them through the main access air lock that led into the Personnel Module. They climbed down the ladder into the Blue Quadrant, to the inside of the module's rotating inner cylinder that produced 0.8G. The quadrant was quiet. Kal had ordered everyone else on *Star Voyager* to remain in their cabins while the two survivors boarded. He allowed no greeting party, no celebration of their return.

Lilea entered the same cabin she and Bent vacated just before leaving, and dropped her sampling kit in one corner. The cabin seemed familiar, yet it seemed strange. It had a depressing air about it, but a nostalgic feeling too. It wasn't musty or stuffy, the ship's life support system had kept fresh air flowing since they left, but it was empty, except for the standard furniture supplied by SpaceComm. The two dark blue acceleration chairs sat in one corner of the living area, facing the com screen. The screen was still dark, dark since they'd turned it off just before leaving. The food-preparation area was spotless, just like she left it, and the bathing area sparkled as though the Blue Quadrant attendant had just cleaned.

Like others on the Landing Team, Lilea and Bent took everything they'd brought with them when boarding *Explorer*, except for the pictures on the wall. *Star Voyager* crew members were allowed several pictures to enliven their cabins, but the tiny compartments of *Explorer* precluded all but a few wall decorations. So they left most of the pictures attached to the walls, pictures of each other, of their home, family, friends, and Sabean. The picture of Bent on the wall in the bedroom was so typical, the slight smirk on his face that Lilea thought cute at first but paid little attention to later. Oddly, the sight of Bent's picture didn't make her sad or bring a tear to her eye. It seemed a fitting memorial with which to grace her cabin.

Lying on the bed were jumpsuits several crewmembers had donated, all in her size, and she resolved to thank everyone for their thoughtfulness. Several were still wrapped in plastic as they had come from the factory. These jumpsuits were dark blue, though. Only the landing team wore the bright blue-green suits, everybody else in SpaceComm wore indigo blue. The jumpsuit she was wearing was slightly oversize. It was one of the standard ones carried on *Rescue* and she slipped it off and put on a new one. It fit much better, though a bit stiff.

She took it off and tossed it on the bed. She cleaned out the pockets of the old jumpsuit, throwing the few items she'd accumulated next to her camera on the chest of drawers sitting to one side of the bed: a bag of twelve nuts, four plastic bags containing soil and vegetation samples she'd collected from Trea's Grove, and tucked well down in one of the pockets of her jacket, the little twig from the northwest coast. The last item was her PersComm, the one she got from storage, and as she set it down the recollection that flashed through her mind was the time she bashed her first one against a rock because Jer had ordered her to return to where Col was standing. She smiled at the image, wondering why she was so furious at the time, but she still had that twinge of guilt for lying to Jer. She took a hot shower and climbed wearily into bed, glad to finally be alone in her own cabin. She fell asleep as soon as her head hit the pillow. In the dark.

Time Element 461.598.9.0.

The intercom roused Lilea from a sound sleep. Tac was on comm. She energized the comm terminal beside the bed.

"Lilea, can you come to the Medical Station? I need to do a complete physical exam and draw some more blood."

"Okay." She stifled a big yawn. "After I have something to eat."

"No. I need to draw blood before you eat anything."

"All right. I'll be there in a few millisectors."

Lilea walked into the Medical Station at the far end of the Yellow Quadrant of the Personnel Module around 599.1.5. She met one of the nurses. "Okay, let's get this over with." She stifled another yawn.

The nurse held up an examination gown. "You have to put this on."

Lilea looked briefly at the short gown, split completely up the back with only ties to protect her modesty. "You've got to be kidding."

"Honest. He wants to do a complete exam, head to toe."

Lilea took the gown and went into the exam room and changed. The nurse came in a few microsectors later and drew more blood, and then Tac arrived and performed his exam. He said almost nothing, leaving Lilea alone to wonder what was going on.

Tac was like Jad in at least one respect—he'd always been hard to read. His demeanor, invariably bland and unemotional, masked what he was thinking, yet to anyone who knew him, within his head the wheels were turning all the time. That just stymied Lilea even more. Why draw blood, she wondered. Sure, she'd been without much food for more than 40 T-sectors, but she ate well on the trip back to *Star Voyager*, and she felt fine, though a bit weak, and that was mostly due to the time spent in microgravity. But Tac spent more time than usual on the abdominal part of the exam, and even performed a pelvic exam. That confused her. And why did he squeeze her ankles like that?

Tac entered the room a millisector later. Now he had a slight smile on his face. "Okay, I have the results of the exam and blood work. I'll tell you why I was so concerned. I now know why your abdomen is swelling. I was suspicious when I saw you on *Rescue* before we took off. It's the same reason your breasts are swollen and your ankles are a little swollen."

"Why?"

"It's because you're pregnant."

CHAPTER 66

SOLITARY CONFINEMENT

Time Interval 461.597-626.

The depression that engulfed Jad took his mind to many places. Running seemed to be all but the end of it. In his mind he ran through the hustling, bustling streets of Sabean, he ran through the quiet streets and back alleys of the Spaceport, he ran up and down the runway at Site One, and he ran on the track at the Physical Training Complex on the Spaceport, taking the outside lane to avoid the other trainees knotted on the inside as though they were tied together by rope or cord, each trying desperately to take the shortest route to the required minimum ten laps every fourth T-sector. This was him, this was all him, he was in his element and the wind was in his hair. Every now and then he would catch sight of a tall, lean, lanky runner ahead of him, short reddish-brown hair, floating like him, fixed on the road ahead, gliding over the pavement, barely touching the ground as she flew. He would catch up and pass by and, quite unusual and surprising for him, he would say, "Hello," and she would turn her head and her face would be . . . missing.

That would startle him, and he would wake up.

But of all the sites and venues he visited in his mind, none became more fixed than the vision of running from the runabout stuck in the mud to the ship *Explorer*, desolate and wasted, burning and hot, to find Wila, and finding Wila's body lying at the end of the runway, tangled in the trees—limp, unmoving, and not being able to revive her and the first-aid kits so far away. He would sit up in bed and call out her name as though he was still searching for her. It was a terrible dream and it filled him with grief and despondency. He wouldn't go back to sleep, he would leave a light on and watch a movie on the com screen in the living room, sitting in one of the large acceleration chairs to get comfortable, trying to force his mind to dislodge the horrible image and toss it away, never to be seen again.

The time would become millisectors, and the millisectors subsectors. Finally, the odd-numbered T-sector would arrive and he would still be watching a movie, bound to that chair, unable to answer the door when Tac or Lilea or Kal or some other member of *Star Voyager*'s crew would arrive to ask how he was, if he needed anything, or to tell him he should get out more.

I want you to come over to our cabin for the second meal.

You should go to the running track in the Recreation Module.

You should — You should — Thanks, but I would rather be alone right now.

Jad tolerated Tac. He knew Tac had his best interest at heart because Tac gave him medicine to combat the dreams, but Jad hated Lilea. Lilea survived — Wila didn't. And that just brought up in Jad's mind all Lilea's faults and foibles he'd categorized for as long as he'd known her, especially her tendency to talk too much and she could be judgmental at times. But most of all, Jad thought she shouldn't have been on this expedition. She wasn't a world-renowned scientist and didn't know what she was doing, not like Jad himself. He was, after all, the one who discovered the Blue Planet in the first place during the time he spent in Planetary Visualization at SpaceComm, and she didn't have any right to be on this expedition, especially not with her husband who argued for setting the cutoff limit so low that if they'd set it higher they would've come home much earlier and Wila and Trea might still be alive.

"Listen," Lilea said on T-sector 609, her second visit since returning from the surface. "I know you want to be alone, but you have to start talking about it. I know what you went through down there, and the others around here want to help you deal with it. You can't deal with it by yourself. Why don't you talk with Tac? Or someone."

"Who says you have to talk about it? Just because something happens, you have to talk about it. I don't want to talk about it right now. I just want to be alone."

"Okay. But let me or Tac know if you decide you want to talk."

Yeah, right, I'll talk to her.

On 461.626, twenty-nine T-sectors after the arrival of *Rescue*, Kal ordered *Star Voyager* turned back toward the Anthanian solar system, and the ship began its long voyage home. During the acceleration, Jasi sat with Lilea in Lilea's compartment, and Tac insisted on staying with Jad, even going so far as asking Kal to order one of the ship's maintenance technicians to open the door Jad had locked to keep Lilea out. That didn't bother Jad, he would have opened the door had he been able to get up and go over there. Jad respected Kal too, because Kal was the only member of *Star Voyager*'s crew tall enough to donate a couple of his dark blue jumpsuits — without the five stars on the sleeve — so Jad didn't have to wear a short one which pinched in the crotch and his ankles showed.

During the 1G phase of acceleration, the last of five phases, Tac and Jad played some electronic games, and Jad revealed a little about the events on the surface. After acceleration ended, Jad opened up and started talking about his experiences and feelings just after the explosion. He described in halting detail his desperation at the loss of Wila, and how he hated Lilea because she survived and Wila didn't. He told Tac all about Taeni, and how he met Wila and how they got engaged and married and had a wonderful life together, about how their interests in astronomy merged, about how he got Wila interested in running, and about how they entered spaceflight training together because they wanted to investigate what they saw through their telescopes. He talked with Tac off and on over the next three hundred T-sectors, though he rarely left his compartment. Only after the midpoint of the return voyage did he venture out to the running track in the Recreation Module.

And, fortunately enough — Tac ascribed this more to the medication than anything else — Jad's hatred of Lilea began to moderate.

Not once in all his conversations with Tac did Jad mention Trea.

CHAPTER 67

PREGNANCY

Time Element 461.599.3.0.

"Pregnant?" The word didn't register with Lilea. She knew she couldn't be pregnant. "That's impossible. I took the vaccine. And the booster before we left. How could I be pregnant? There's no way."

"I tested the blood I took on the surface," Tac said, "and the blood I drew now. Both tests say the same thing. Based on those results the computer calculates that you were impregnated on or about T-sector 437. That works out to around T-sector 203 when you were on the surface, but it could have been anywhere from 201 to 205."

"Two-zero one to two-zero-five? I can't remember what we were doing then. I'll think about it. But how can I be pregnant if I took the vaccine and the booster? That's supposed to prevent pregnancy."

"Well, it works ninety-nine percent of the time, but there are some failures every now and then. I've seen this happen before. There's no doubt—you're pregnant."

"That means you didn't leave Bent behind." The nurse patted Lilea's swollen abdomen. "You've got a little part of him with you here."

"Oh, god, that's right. I can't believe it. It's just so fantastic." The reality of her pregnancy was now beginning to sink into Lilea's mind, and she raced ahead to see a little girl, or maybe a little boy. She could see the tyke playing in the sand out in back of her house. The kid was growing up, going to school, graduating, getting a job—*wait. let's start at the beginning here.* "Can you tell if it's a boy or a girl yet?"

"No, not yet. But we can do some more tests later to find out. But that's not the most important problem. You'll be delivering the baby before we arrive at our solar system. That means the baby will have to go though the deceleration by itself. That's a problem. A *big* problem. No one has ever taken an infant through that much deceleration."

Lilea stared at Tac. *Oh, my god, the deceleration. I hadn't thought about that.*

An image formed in Lilea's mind and a twinge of apprehension shot through her body as she tried to visualize an infant, sitting — strapped, if necessary — in an acceleration chair, obliged to go through all the heavy G-forces that came with the slowdown of *Star Voyager* into the Anthanian solar system. The G-forces ran up to 5Gs, and that was difficult enough for an adult, but for an infant it must be all but impossible. You have to be trained to go through that much acceleration. In increments. You have to learn how to breathe, to resist it, yet to accept it and deal with it. It takes time to learn that. How would an infant breathe? How can an infant learn how to take that much pressure? How would the infant's heart beat under 5Gs? Lilea didn't like this. Not at all, and that bothered her. As she pondered for a nanosector, another question jumped out at her, another possibility, but she wasn't sure she wanted to hear the answer. "Can . . . you . . . y'know . . . keep me from delivering until after deceleration is over?"

"Sure, I can, but you'll be ready to deliver about a hundred T-sectors before the deceleration starts, and that's too long to wait. Much too long. I don't think you'd want to endure it with an over-full-term fetus in your belly."

"So . . . what . . . ?"

"I don't know. I'm going to have to work something out."

Yes, of course, there's still time to work this out and come up with an answer.

"Hold on. I just remembered. My camera might have some images I made around the time I got impregnated."

Lilea dressed and scampered back to her cabin. She returned to the Medical Suite and interfaced the camera with the computer in the Suite. She instructed the computer to scan for T-sector 203, the middle of the range Tac had given. Sure enough, she'd taken some images on 203, and she recognized immediately the northwestern beach when she imaged Jad, Wila and Mina walking north along the sand just before she and Bent . . .

"I remember. It was so peaceful and lovely. I'd been feeling so euphoric and so wonderful. I was warm and flushed, and then I got horny, and when the others left we had sex right there on the sand."

"Did you say 'euphoric'?" Tac screwed up his face and scratched his chin.

Lilea nodded.

"It sounds like that's when the booster failed. That's typical for failures. The woman reports feeling euphoric or high. A fever is common too, and flushing and erotic feelings are also common. And if you have intercourse then, you almost always get pregnant."

"Well, that certainly happened to me."

Time Element 462.222.0.0.

Even as her pregnancy developed, Lilea played a few games of pak with Jasi and other members of the crew. But as her tummy swelled she found it more and more difficult to cover her end of the playing chamber, and she lost by larger and larger scores. Finally, by T-sector 887, she gave up pak to prepare for delivery, and on 462.222, she gave birth to a healthy baby boy. She named him Leos.

After the delivery, Tac did a complete exam. "He's in excellent health," he said. "I was afraid the period of reduced food intake on the surface might have stunted him in some way, but there doesn't seem to any residual effect. The brain scans I did show normal brain physiological and intellectual development. I think your body used enough stored fat to feed the baby while it was developing."

"That's good. I was worried about that, too."

With no crib or cradle on board, Leos slept on the bed beside Lilea, and with breastfeeding and dietary supplements from Tac, he gained weight at the generally accepted rate for Anthanian children. Several female crew members tore up bed linen for diapers, and others made small shirts for him from older clothing. He had the entire ship's complement fawning and flirting over him. Lilea'd never heard so many otherwise sensible adults cooing and speaking in mock baby talk. Except Jad. He acknowledged the presence of the newest member of the crew and even held the little kid once, but mostly he stayed in his cabin and ignored him.

But the time for deceleration was approaching, and the problem of how to prepare little Leos to survive the tremendous G-forces still hadn't been resolved.

"The best thing I can come up with," Tac told Lilea on 462.300, "is to anesthetize him and force oxygen into his lungs so he'll have enough oxygen to live on. Otherwise, the forces generated during deceleration will make it impossible for him to breathe. Once we get down to the 1G phase, we can wake him up. I think if we put him on a small flotation unit, he'll be okay. But we won't know until we try."

"Well," Lilea said, "if you think it'll work, go ahead." She had little choice but to agree with Tac, she couldn't think of anything better. But a grain of doubt settled in the back of her mind, a doubt that grew larger and more malignant as the time for deceleration approached. It must have been her motherly instinct. She looked at any stunt, like the deceleration, with an eye toward the danger involved. But it had to be done, and she reluctantly agreed to let Tac try his idea.

"We'll have to do it in the Medical Area. That means having some of the acceleration chairs moved down there. You and I will go through the deceleration together."

"Oh. Okay. If you say so."

CHAPTER 68

DECELERATION

Time Element 462.326.0.0.

"We're almost here!" they yelled.

Seven hundred T-sectors after the return trip started, the big ship turned hectic. In a sort of controlled chaos, *Star Voyager*'s crew scurried everywhere, babbling excitedly among themselves, making last nanosector preparations, securing loose items and whatnot. Lilea, Leos, Tac, and a nurse settled into the Surgical Suite in the Medical Station at the far end of the Yellow Quadrant in the Personnel Module, away from most of the turmoil. Three acceleration chairs had been installed, and the operating table had been moved toward the rear of the operating room. One end butted against the wall. Leos slept peacefully on a small flotation unit at the end of the table, and an anesthetic dripped slowly through a scalp vein. Oxygen under pressure flowed into his lungs, and a blood oxygen monitor was clipped to one foot. All over his body were the sensors, held in place by tiny pieces of dark blue tape that made him look as though he had a necrotic skin disease. Seeing him like that made Lilea feel her worst fears had come true.

What scared her more, though, were the computer screens.

At the other end of the table from where Leos lay stood an intimidating, almost frightening, cluster of four com screens, each with an abundance of medical terms and funny squiggly lines running across them. Some of the displays were amber, some green, some a gay multicolor. Two more screens sat to Lilea's left, and several stood against the far wall to her right. Tac, sitting in a dark yellow acceleration chair on the other side of the table, watched the screens closely, his face impassive and expressionless. Lilea tried to not look at them, but they so dominated her field of view she had to close her eyes and force herself to think of something else. She visualized the natives in the northern regions and watched them carry that animal over the two ridges to their village beyond. Taking her mind off Leos gave her a chance to relax the tight muscles of her neck and back, and her heart rate dropped slightly, but the incessant *beep-beep-beep* of the cardiac monitor intruded repeatedly on her daydreams and she eventually put those images aside and opened her eyes.

By 326.3.5.0, *Star Voyager* was ready for deceleration. The ship had been turned end-for-end so that the huge propulsion module at the rear faced forward, its big engines and anti-grav drive ready to slow the ship into the Anthanian solar system. The roll call was finished — everyone was strapped firmly in a deceleration chair — and the interior cylinder in the Personnel Module had been stopped. The operating room turned eerily quiet except for the faint *beep* from the cardiac screen and the delicate hiss of the machine that pumped oxygen into Leos's lungs.

Kal's gravelly voice came over ship's comm. The one announcement everyone had been waiting for. "Standby for engine start."

Lilea settled back in her chair. The first engine will start in less than a nanosector. She tightened the muscles of her chest and thighs as the center of the seven big engines in the Propulsion Module fired. It seemed muffled and far away, but it pushed everyone back in their chairs with a firm shove. Kal's booming voice came over comm again.

"We are engaged!"

Then the first pair of engines fired and drove everyone even further into their seats. Then the second pair, and the third pair, now all seven engines firing, starting at 20 percent power then ramping to 100 percent, rapidly building the G-forces to that incredible maximum of 5Gs that almost drove your eyeballs back into your brain.

Two nanosectors later the antigraviton drive kicked in. The antigrav field generated by the coils in the Propulsion Module surrounded the entire ship and added nothing to the heavy G-forces, but the drive, feeding off the rapidly changing momentum provided by the engines, countered the supra-light speed of the ship, decelerating it into Anthanos's solar system.

"Whoooaaa!" Lilea compressed even more strongly the muscles in her thighs, abdomen and chest as the force built. "Don't close your eyes!" she remembered her instructor telling her during practice runs in the centrifuge at SpaceComm. "Focus on the screen in front of you. Watch the elapsed time. That will tell you how long the acceleration has gone on, and how long you have to go. Keep your mind active." All she could see in the operating theatre were the medical screens, so she flipped her gaze from one screen to another, not really knowing where to concentrate.

Near the end of the first phase Leos's cardiac rate started to deteriorate. An alarm sounded, rocking the room above the vibration and roar of the engines. The line on the screen turned red at first, then yellow as the rate dropped further. The computer shot in drugs, more and stronger, but the heart rate kept dropping, and Lilea's rate skyrocketed in sympathetic compensation. She closed her eyes again and squeezed her fists so tightly her hands turned white.

Second phase — 4Gs — success — heart rate plateaus at 38.

Third phase — 3Gs — still 38 — *no, dropping again.* Now 35, *Critical Value!* Flashing screens — monitors screaming, engines roaring, and vibration rattling Lilea's nerves — *it's going down further! Tac, dammit, do something!* Now 34 — 33 — 31. *God, it can't get any lower or — oh, god, I don't know what happens if it gets much lower, but it can't be good.*

Fourth phase — 2Gs — level at 30 — *that's not good* — 28 — *got to get it up.* More drugs, stronger drugs, newer drugs, the best they've got. Still level at 28 — *may be okay. Let's hope so.*

Fifth phase — 1G — *Thank the Great God Arteamos!* Now up to 30. No, 31 — 32! *We're on our way* — 35 — 39 — 42. *Hot damn!*

"Oh my god!" The worst was over. She'd become exhausted from fighting both the acceleration and the terror of what might happen if Leos's heart stopped altogether. She swung her chair around and knelt on the bulkhead, which in the 1G phase acted as a floor, next to the little flotation unit where Leos dozed peacefully.

"I wasn't too worried," Tac said. "Maybe I should have put a cardiac monitor on you." He grinned that subtle toothy smile of his, and then removed all but the cardiac sensors from Leos's skin. He reduced the anesthetic and pulled out the tracheal tube to allow Leos to wake up, and mom got to hold him for the first time in more than three subsectors.

"You little rascal. You gave us quite a scare." All Leos did was yawn.

"It'll take some time for the anesthetic to purge from his system," Tac said.

Lilea settled back in her chair to ride out the 1.8 millisector-long 1G phase before the inner cylinder started again. Too groggy to nurse, Leos slept peacefully in her arms, his breathing quiet and regular. When the 1G phase ended and the inner cylinder started again, they were interrupted by Kal's voice.

"How'd he do?"

"He did reasonably well," Tac replied. "He had some initial bradycardia and respiratory depression, but he seems to have recovered. I'm not too concerned."

"Good. Now we've got to notify SpaceComm we're here. They're not expecting us back this early."

Lilea heard what Tac and Kal said only peripherally. She was smiling broadly as a certain idea kept swirling through her head.

CHAPTER 69

A PUBLIC DISCUSSION

Time Element 462.467.0.0.

The idea of a public discussion didn't scare Lilea anymore. Sitting on a stage in the Main Auditorium at Spaceflight Command Headquarters in front of hundreds of people and millions of viewers worldwide didn't hold the heart-pounding, breath-gasping, mind-numbing terror it did when she endured the first one. She'd been through so much now that nothing anyone on Anthanos could throw at her would terrify her any more. She knew what she wanted to say—she had a story to tell. She'd thought long and hard about it during the 700 T-sector return voyage, and she knew what she wanted to tell the people of Anthanos about the Blue Planet. That was important to Lilea. She took this upcoming discussion not simply as a requirement of her place on the team, but as an obligation to tell her world about her experience.

They'd be fascinated—even a little surprised—to hear about it.

So after she rose on the T-sector of the discussion, she pulled out of the suitcase of clothes her mom had brought from her childhood home in Kalarias her favorite dress, the *budgja*, the traditional knee-length full-skirted Anthanian dress. It was bright yellow, her favorite color, with crimson, turquoise, and fuchsia flowers splashed over the bodice and cascading down the right front of the skirt. And it wasn't the hideous blue-green color of the jumpsuits, either.

"This discussion should be a lot different from the first one we went through three years ago," she told her mom as she was getting dressed. "That time they marched us out on the stage in the auditorium at Space-Comm and presented us to the world as the newly selected Blue Planet Landing Team. But Nuri didn't tell us what was going on, or how a public discussion really worked, and I had no idea what was going to happen. I was so nervous, I almost faked an illness just to get out of it. But I thought that would look bad, so I went anyway.

"I remember the auditorium was packed. I sat at the left end of the long table that stretched almost all the way across the stage. It was as though I was the last one, you know, the least important person on the team. Maybe I was. Nobody at SpaceComm ever said anything, but it was as though I was to just sit there quietly and answer when my turn came. At first I only got a few questions. Case and Bent and Col and Trea did most of the talking. You met Trea once, remember? Trea'll talk your arm off if you give her half a chance. Bent had so many high hopes about what he was going to do and what he'd find on the Blue Planet. Later they started asking me all sorts of questions about the "intelligent" life on the planet. I think they *expected* me to find something. Like they'd made up their minds. Half the questions were about the intelligent life. Seemed like it anyway. I was so nervous I don't know what really went on. We stayed there three subsectors. It was quite an endurance test. I hated every millisector.

"I'm hoping this time'll be different. This time Jad and I'll have a chance to explain what *really* happened on the Blue Planet. Instead of talking about what were *going* to do, like last time. I'm looking forward to it. And I bet everyone will listen."

As she stood in front of the mirror to admire herself and make final adjustments—she'd lost several krill since she last wore the dress—the image which materialized in her mind was the wedding picture on the wall in *Star Voyager*'s cabin. In that picture, Bent stood beside her, dressed in the blue and red *kalgja*, the military-influenced outfit heavily in fashion when they married. She'd worn her budgja at their wedding, and the reflection in the mirror so startled her she closed her eyes for a nanosector.

"I remember I was so excited when I got to wear one of those blue-green jumpsuits for the first time as a member of the Gold Team. That was exciting. Like, I'd made it. I was on the team. Now I hate the sight of those ugly things. I hope I never have to wear one of those things again."

But the sounding of the door-announce chimes told her the limousine-runabout had arrived to take her to the auditorium. Her mom held Leos while she kissed him goodbye, and then she strode through the front door, her heart beating in anticipation of her chance to tell her story. She arrived at a side entrance to SpaceComm's main auditorium a few millisectors before the start of the discussion, just behind Jad in his limousine. Two special attendants, a young man and woman in brilliant white and gold uniforms, met them at the curb and accompanied them through the building.

Time Element 462.467.1.0.

A small table covered with a floor-length white cloth and chairs for two had been placed at the center of the auditorium stage. A lecture stand for Nuri stood to the right of the table. At a signal from Nuri for both to enter, Lilea took a couple of steps forward, then hesitated. She inhaled a deep breath, threw her head back and her chin out, squared her shoulders and back, and muttered to herself, "Okay, let's do this." Then she strode onto the stage, Jad right behind. The auditorium was a boisterous den of nearly four hundred people chatting and milling around, but when the two returning team members appeared, a hush drew over the crowd as everyone stood.

Lilea went to the seat at the right side of the table. As they started to sit down, the audience, still standing, began to applaud. At first just a few, but within a nanosector the entire room was cheering. Lilea and Jad sat down at the table, but the audience remained standing. Nuri motioned for them to stand and accept the audience's acclaim, and they stood again, but Lilea only reluctantly. She was confused; the tremendous display of warmth and affection overwhelmed her, yes—she certainly hadn't anticipated it—but it startled her too and she briefly wondered why. *What is this? What's going on here?* An inconspicuous tear trickled down her cheek.

While she dried her cheek with a handkerchief, Jad acknowledged the applause by waving to the audience. He said, "Thank you," several times. He smiled broadly, and even seemed to stand a little straighter, throwing his shoulders back, not slouching so much. Finally, after almost a millisector of sustained applause, the audience settled down.

Every seat was taken, and many people sat on the steps in the aisles or stood two or three deep around the walls. Lilea recognized many of the same people from the discussion three years ago, especially the journalists from the Information Services. Their bright eyes and almost super-attentive manner and the way they sat on the edge of their seat gave her the impression they were, like the large-fanged animal in the north, ready to pounce on anything she said.

Before he started the discussion, Nuri asked for a microsector of quiet to honor the eight who'd given their lives in the service of their planet. Then he asked for questions and hands shot up everywhere. Some stood shouting, struggling to get his attention.

The first questions were mild and wimpy, undemanding questions intended only to give the two returnees a chance to describe the Blue Planet in the broadest of terms. They asked about the water on the planet, the deserts, the mountains, and the gorge. They expressed tremendous curiosity about Lilea's 'humans' in the north and how dangerous they were, and about the animals, and even the plants, growing out in the open with no one to water them.

But the greatest number of questions concerned the sunrises and sunsets, and the variation in temperature during each light/dark cycle. "How could you work while the sun migrated across the sky like that?" several asked. "How could you work while the temperature changed that much?" others wondered.

Later questions became more substantive, dealing with death and destruction. Jad and Lilea described, as best they could, the deaths of the other eight. Then, they insisted, that was the last they would say about that difficult time.

Lilea enjoyed the interplay between the questioners and herself, and delighted in the repartee. She spoke easily of the Blue Planet, answering each question as briefly as she could, not dwelling on any one subject too long. She relaxed in her role as communicator and illustrator of the expedition, and the discussion turned loose and easygoing. But Jad seemed hesitant to answer many of the questions, and though his answers were adequate and couched frequently in scientific jargon, he seemed uncomfortable with the give and take of the discourse.

Late in the discussion one questioner stated bluntly to Lilea, "It sounds like you really enjoyed your visit."

"Yes, I did. Regardless of what anyone else thought, I liked the place. Trea liked it too, especially before Col was killed, but after she recovered from the shock of his death, she began to see the Blue Planet for what it really was. I remember talking to Trea only a few T-sectors before she died. She told me she still wanted to return with the next expedition. In fact, when she was killed, she and Wila were outside. They'd gone to see a special place about a half-anthan away from Site One. I'm sure she and Col would have wanted to colonize, and I think Bent would have too, if he'd survived."

"But your husband was killed in a violent explosion. Doesn't that color your vision of the planet?"

"Oh, yes, of course it does."

The questioner asked Jad the same question, but in spite of an angry scowl from Nuri, Jad decided to pass. "I'm sorry," he said. "I didn't find the Blue Planet that beautiful or nice or lovely or whatever. I just didn't enjoy it that much." Jad probably didn't see the look of utter astonishment that came to Lilea's face.

The questioner sat down and a veteran member of the IS rose. His voice was soft and quiet. "Lilea, Jad, we've heard a lot of detail about how the members of the exploration team were killed, and about what you two thought about the planet, but I would like to take a broader view. What, in your opinion was the major reason for the failure of the expedition? Was it lack of planning? Bad information? Incomplete intellectual development? Can you shed some light on it for us?"

Jad jumped. "It wasn't any of those. The planet didn't want us and it told us so."

"Lilea, what do you think?"

Lilea paused and collected her thoughts. She'd been waiting for a chance to describe not merely her experiences on the planet, but her impressions and feelings, and in response to this question she finally opened up. "No, I don't think the planet had anything to do with it. I've never believed that. We were set down on that planet to explore it. Or rather, a small part of it. But we were so singularly unprepared for the critical values of life there that we were doomed to failure even before we landed. Look at the humans in the north. They live in huts of sticks and skins we would consider barbaric. We lived in a warm, ultrasophisticated spaceship capable of cruising the solar system. We traveled over the surface in complex, advanced aerodynes and runabouts that kept us warm and cozy while we traveled. But they can't go anywhere except by the power of their own two legs. They probably haven't even domesticated animals to do their work for them. But we were the ones driven from the planet, and in only a short time. They still exist. They still remain. They live within the boundaries of life as it exists there. We lived on top of the planet. We only skimmed the surface of life there. We were never a part of the ecosystem, and when it reacted we paid the price. We got caught in the interplay of the various factors that make up — that are — the planet.

"The complexity of the planet is overwhelming. Nothing is as simple as it is here on Anthanos. Everything is interrelated, but it would take years to unravel that complexity so that we can understand it. I'm glad to have been a part of the first landing, and I wish things had turned out better, but I didn't have anything to say about how they turned out.

"We can go back to the planet, but we can never return to it. We can learn to live there, I know it, and I hope we do. Whether a desert planet or an ice planet or a water planet or a mountainous planet, we'll have to merge with the planet to live there. We forgot that before we left. We forgot that we were merely visitors to a strange and beautiful land."

"Wait — what — ?" the questioner spluttered. "Did I hear you correctly? Did you say we could *learn to live there?*"

"Yes."

"And did you say you *hope we do?*"

Lilea nodded. "Yes."

The questioner paused and his eyes grew large and round, the whites whiter than the powdery stuff that fell on Site One. The Hall turned quiet and Jad shifted uncomfortably in his chair. Every eye focused on Lilea. Even Nuri glared at her. "On that planet? After all that happened? Surely you must be—"

"No, I'm not."

"How did you come to that rather bizarre conclusion?"

"By the time the return voyage started, I'd almost decided to recommend that we not return. There was just too much death and destruction. But I thought a lot about it during the return voyage, and I wanted to recommend a return—I wanted to find a way to come to that conclusion, even though so many people were killed, even though the sun moved across the sky and we had to sleep during the darktimes and it was black outside, and there were so many animals and water fell from the sky. But I needed something to prove to me we really could do it, that we really could live there. Then something happened during the final deceleration. It was my son, Leos. When he was only about 100 T-sectors old, he went through the deceleration. He was still an infant and it would have killed him if he hadn't been helped by the medical staff on *Star Voyager*. I thought, my god, if an infant can survive those tremendous G-forces and come out of it alive, then surely we can learn to live on the Blue Planet and come out alive. It may be difficult, and maybe some people will be killed, but we can do it."

The questioner seemed at a loss for words. "Er . . . ah . . . well then, would . . . would you be willing to recommend to the Assembly that another landing team be sent?"

That question caught Lilea off guard. She'd tried to anticipate as many questions as she could, figuring most would be about the planet and the landing team's activities on it. Leos's experiences during the deceleration had been the final nudge she needed to change her recommendation about another landing from "No" back to "Yes," and she would definitely put that in her report to SpaceComm. Logically it was a stretch, and she understood that. The connection between Leos's survival during deceleration and survival of Anthanians on the surface of the Blue Planet was true only in the broadest of terms. A metaphor, perhaps.

She'd resolved to make her recommendation not only to Space-Comm, but also to the Anthanian Science Council. The Council regulated scientific research on Anthanos, and she knew personally several members on the Council. A "Yes" from them would carry so much more weight than from SpaceComm, and she didn't want to bypass the Council and send it directly to the Assembly. But now, so soon after returning, to be put in the position of suggesting it directly to the Assembly, that was beyond her authority and she shrank back. "Oh . . . I don't know. I'm not sure I should answer that question right now."

Her hesitation gave Jad the opportunity to jump in. "No. I would never go back there again and I would never recommend that anyone go there. That damn planet killed my wife and seven of my friends. It's a hellish place where people can be killed at a moment's notice by big animals, by freak storms, by all sorts of . . . of despicable things." His voice turned hard and strong, like a dam had burst and he poured his words out. "From the first lightime we landed it was trying to get rid of us. My wife, Wila, knew that almost from the start, and looking back, I know now she was right. I would never go back there and I would never recommend that anyone else go either." He shook his head and turned slightly away from Lilea, crossing his lanky legs away from her.

"How about you, Lilea. Do you believe the planet was trying to get rid of you?"

"No. I never believed that. I think what happened was natural, and it was just the way things are. If we want to live there, we'll have to take those things into consideration. There's a real magic on that planet, and it doesn't have anything to do with a supernatural force."

"That's all well and good," the questioner insisted. "But the Assembly's going to have to make a decision. Would you —"

"I don't think it's my job to tell the Assembly what to do."

"If the Assembly did decide to send another team, would you be willing to go back?"

That was a question she'd thought a lot about on the return trip. Her answer was quiet and unobtrusive, yet final. "No."

"Jad?"

"No."

Nuri jumped in. "That's all, everybody. We've been here three subsectors. I'm going to wrap up these proceedings. Thank you all for coming."

Jad and Lilea had barely stood at the table. The applause returned with a *whoop!* and in less than a nanosector it crescendoed to a noisy, ring-ing, rowdy pitch that startled both of them. Even Nuri applauded. For almost a millisector the audience stood and cheered and clapped and hurrahed as though this was to be their last T-sector on the planet. Lilea remained standing at the table, not sure what to do. She smiled, but only briefly, afraid that any lengthy display of open emotion might signify she was enjoying the adulation, a signal she was determined to avoid sending.

I don't know why they're applauding so much. I didn't really do anything. I just did my job. That's all.

Time Element 462.467.4.6.

When the applause finally died down, Lilea and Jad made their way off stage. Jad lingered backstage talking to several people and even auto-graphed a few electronic notebooks, but Lilea decided to leave the audito-rium. She wasn't interested in engaging in small talk—she had an infant son waiting for her. She gave Jad a brief hug goodbye, and a young female attendant—blonde hair, blue eyes, just like her—led her through the maze of hallways toward the side entrance of the building where her limousine waited. As she walked, she reflected on her answers, and she was proud of what she had to say. She told the world of her experiences, and she could hold her head high now.

Her next move was obvious. She would persuade the Science Coun-cil to recommend another landing on the Blue Planet—that was the appro-priate way to do it, not directly to the Assembly. She knew the Chair of the Science Council personally—an anthropologist like her, a former professor of hers. A second landing could be a turning point in the life of her planet. It would prove she was right, but more importantly, the Blue Planet could be a fascinating place to live, and nothing existed there that made life im-possible. Difficult, yes, but not impossible. She knew it, and she wanted her world to know it, too.

She relaxed and even smiled a little as she walked through the hall-ways.

But as she walked, her attention was diverted. Her eye was caught by her escorting attendant a few paces ahead. Something was odd about the young woman's uniform, but for a split-nanosector she couldn't place the peculiarity. It was the same military-inspired uniform she remembered from many years ago—the white blouse and skirt with the gold trim and gold accessories—when she'd been an attendant at SpaceComm during the year she took off between tertiary school group and college. She was only eighteen, the youngest attendant they'd ever had. It was the same uniform it had always been since attendants, all young men and women of college age, were first hired to give visitors a guided tour around the complex and escort VIP's through the network of hallways and corridors to their appointments. Yet something about the uniform of her attendant was different, even exceptional. What was it?

Oh, yes, she noticed, it was the boots, those knee-high boots all attendants wore. Lilea's boots had been white, but her escort's boots were gold. All attendants wore white boots, every one, except the Senior Attendant. Senior Attendants always wore gold boots to indicate their rank, but the only person the Senior Attendant ever escorted was the President of the Assembly when he or she made the required annual visit to Spaceflight Command — never anyone else. Yet here, now, Lilea was being escorted by the Senior Attendant.

That singular, almost trivial detail made all the difference in the world to Lilea.

EPILOGUE

Time Element 463.325.9.7.

Lilea arrived at the main administration building of the Sabean Hydroponics Gardening Complex several millisectors before her scheduled arrival time of 326.0.0. She was running early because the Anthanian Assembly had merged into full representative session exactly one year after the survivors of the Gold Team returned, preparing to vote on a measure to authorize and fund a return mission to the Blue Planet. An interplanetary spaceship, *Nova*, a smaller precursor to *Explorer* with facilities for six, was available. The time had come to make a decision and she wanted to get to Assembly Hall before the debate started.

At the main entrance to the Gardens she met Til, Director of the Gardens. From one of the pockets of her traveling cloak she pulled out a small plastic bag containing one of the two remaining nuts that had not already been dissected, extracted, crushed, chopped, sectioned, solublized, dried, frozen, boiled, X-rayed, CAT scanned, MRI'ed, PET'ed or otherwise examined in excruciating detail by Anthanian scientists — or as Lilea liked to put it, "bashed, smashed, and mashed." She handed the bag to Til who led her on a short trip through an imposing set of stainless steel double doors marked in big bold letters,

CULTIVATION AREA—AUTHORIZED PERSONNEL ONLY

into the main section of the Gardens. There he turned left and walked through another stainless steel door with another bold sign:

RESEARCH

Here a dedicated nursery had been created. A 25 X 25 link hydroponics box had been set into the floor, surrounded by a clear plastic enclosure that reached to the ceiling, thirty links above. Several banks of fluorescent lights ringed the enclosure, and a special heating and cooling unit hummed in the background. Til planted the nut a few decilinks below the surface of the rocky soil in the center of the box. A small amount of nutrient-rich water dribbled from a slender hose near where the nut was planted. He touched a blue marker on a com screen set into an electrical panel on the far wall, activating the lights.

"Those lights are computer controlled to simulate the cycles of light and dark on the Blue Planet," Til said. "They're variable-spectrum lights, tuned to the light from the planet's sun. We'll also control the cycles of heat and cold. It's a long shot, but it might work."

"It's worth a try. It's too bad Col isn't here to see this."

Lilea said goodbye and left the gardens. A limousine-runabout, chartered by SpaceComm, took her directly to the Legislative Chamber of the Anthanian Assembly, and as the vehicle sped along, she speculated about the impending vote. The Science Council *had* recommended a second landing, and SpaceComm backed them up. But she had doubts about the Assembly. She wondered if they were capable of looking past the death and destruction to view the real beauty and utility of the Blue Planet.

Time Element 463.326.8.1.

The vote was 19 in favor, 205 opposed. Anthanos would not return to the Blue Planet.

In the end the Assembly was persuaded far more by the venomous and vitriolic impressions of the Blue Planet of Jad and his supporters than by the positive descriptions of Lilea and a few members of the Assembly who still held to the Blue Planet as a colonizable reality. Lilea was angered and saddened by the vote, but not terribly surprised.

"I'm sorry they didn't pass the measure," Lilea told the assembled Information Services when they asked for a comment as she left the Chamber. "I don't really understand what they were afraid of, but I intend to talk about the Blue Planet for as long as I live." Then she took the limousine-runabout to the Mag-Lev Transportation Depot in the city-center of Sabean where she and Leos boarded the train to her family home in Kalarias.

And what happened to that nut?
It grew. Of course.

END

ACKNOWLEDGEMENTS

An author does not write in a vacuum. A novel may be the product of one person's vision and imagination, but ideally it flows through the minds of many others before any form of publication can take place. Most of those who helped me in the production of this novel are acknowledged below.

Warm thanks to Kirsten Holm—who graciously started me on the long road to publication—for all her advice and encouragement. And for the free copy of her book.

I also extend special thanks to Michael Banks for helpful discussions about the book, its structure, and its impact on the reader. Special thanks go also to Cassie Barnes, Lynwood Battle, and Jerry Weiper for feedback on an early phase of the manuscript.

An extra special thanks to all the members of the Bill Bray Writers Group of Winston-Salem, NC, moderated by Carrie Graves, and to the members of the Major Manuscript Critique Group of Winston-Salem Writers and its moderator Tom Seaman, for their comments and criticisms which went a long way toward making this novel readable and entertaining. Serious thanks also to all in my class at Wildacres Writers Group, particularly the leader Nancy Bartholomew, for their insightful comments.

Tremendous thanks to Marco Palmieri for his critical review of the manuscript and suggestions on how to cut it down to its present length, even though I didn't accept all his suggestions. Also to Dr. Kathy Kitts whose answers to my scientific questions about star lifetimes put me on the right track

Special thanks also to my cousin Terry England and to my good friend Sandy Bazinet for critical comments on the first two chapters. Their comments helped refine those obstinate sections. And special thanks to the members of the novel critique group led by Maria Espinoza whose ideas and suggestions led to getting the manuscript into its final form.

Extra-special thanks also goes to Kathy Schuit, the artist who designed the cover and prepared the illustration of the *Explorer* landing site.

Extra-special thanks go also to Mary McArthur whose class on formatting in Microsoft Word, presented through SouthWest Writers, gave me the knowledge — and the courage — to attempt to publish this book on my own.

But most especially, I extend super-special thanks to my editor Cara Lockwood, whose critical reading of the manuscript, and insights and ideas about the story and characters led to the final form of the manuscript. And, ultimately, the book.

And finally, I extend my sincerest thanks and grateful appreciation to all who take time to read this book, whether solid or virtual. I trust you will not be disappointed.

ABOUT THE AUTHOR

Roger Floyd is a retired PhD researcher in the field of virology, the study of viruses. He spent most of a 40+-year career working in hospitals and medical schools around the United States, examining various viruses to see how they work and how they interact with one another and how to kill them and how to isolate them from infected patients. He received his Bachelor of Arts degree from Trinity University in San Antonio, Texas, in 1963, and his PhD degree from Baylor College of Medicine in Houston, Texas, in 1971. He's been a life-long reader of books, both nonfiction and fiction, and especially including science fiction. In 1998, after so many years of reading and writing scientific papers, he decided the time had come to write his own novel. What the hell—that can't be too difficult, can it? Little did he know . . . This book, and the next two which together comprise *The Anthanian Imperative* trilogy, are the result of that decision.

Albuquerque, New Mexico, January, 2023